The
MINERAL
PALACE

The
MINERAL
PALACE

Heidi Julavits

G .P. Putnam's Sons • New York

FLIP

Copyright © 2000 by Heidi Julavits
Published simultaneously in Canada

G. P. PUTNAM'S SONS
Publishers Since 1838
a member of
Penguin Putnam Inc.
375 Hudson Street
New York, NY 10014

Library of Congress Cataloging-in-Publication Data

Julavits, Heidi.
The mineral palace / Heidi Julavits.
p. cm.
ISBN 0-399-14622-9
1. Middle West—Fiction. 2. Women—Fiction. I. Title.
PS3560.U522 M56   2000   00-024221
813'.6—dc21

Title-page image courtesy Library of Congress,
Prints and Photographs Division, FSA-OWI Collection,
LC-USF 34-028455-0, Arthur Rothstein, photographer.

Lines from "Turkey in the Straw" quoted from Struthers Burt,
The Diary of a Dude Wrangler, © 1924 Charles Scribner's Sons.

Printed in the United States of America

1   3   5   7   9   10   8   6   4   2

This book is printed on acid-free paper. ∞

The text of this book is set in Bembo.

Book design by Gretchen Achilles

In memory of my grandmother
Jean Dabelstein Troup,
and my editor, Faith Sale

I would like to thank the following kind people for their encouragement: Dan Imhoff, Ethan Canin, Richard Locke, Maureen Howard, Lois Rosenthal, Will Allison, Adrienne Miller, David Granger, Sam Schnee, Dave Eggers, Katrina Kenison, the editors at the *Voice Literary Supplement.*

Thanks to draft readers Mary Pols, Manny Howard, and Susan Julavits. Thanks to Manny Howard for so much more than reading drafts. Thanks to Amanda Davis, Jill Leviton, Kirstin Zona, and my colleagues at Alison on Dominick Street (especially Kerry O'Blaney) for vast and mundane contributions. Thanks to Red Withers for his rancher's tour of the Front Range. Thanks to the very nice people at the Pueblo Public Library. Thanks to Yaddo and The Writers Room and Bread Loaf and Ben Marcus. Big, big thanks to Henry Dunow, Faith Sale, Aimée Taub, Anna Jardine, my family.

CONTENTS

1. THE STOLEN PILLBOX

As soon as the Ford Touring Car crossed the St. Paul city limits on April 20, 1934 ("You Are Leaving St. Paul, Minn., Home of the Inlagd Sill Herring Festival, Please Visit Us Again"), and passed into the great, square-upon-square expanse of the surrounding farmland, Bena jotted down the odometer reading with the golf pencil she kept in the ashtray: 5,434.

She did this cautiously, steering with her left hand. She wrote it on the cover of *Lectures on Surgical Pathology*, the first in a stack of medical journals that rested between her and Ted. She wanted to record the mileage, because it would provide a way to appreciate the distance they were about to create between their old existence and their new one. As the city receded in the rearview mirror, so, she fervently believed, did their life up to that moment.

Ted glared at her scribblings. No doubt he wanted to scold her for defacing his reading materials. But he held his tongue. Bena knew he considered himself fortunate that his wife was an inquisitive woman, not bound by the usual female fears and preoccupations, such as ringworm, rabies, cold cream, colic. Besides, she imagined, it would be entertaining, when his interest in, say, "Synovial Cysts of the Choroid Plexus" lagged, to try to break the code of numbers jotted in the empty margins. A string of 22s, 23s, and 24s that he might attribute to the daily high temperatures one week in March could actually be a tally of the birds that visited the feeder outside their kitchen window. Bena was comforted by numbers, and found a sense of assuredness and direction through her constant accounting of them. While there existed numbers that were to her undeniably dark (8, for example, because her brother drowned on the eighth day of August), certain possessed the glow of fortune, like the number of her father's favorite golf club (9-iron), the number of unloneliness (2), any number of her birthday (7/13), the street number of her childhood house in St. Paul (45), and others simply because they appeared round and portentous (33, 64, 89) and full of a substance one might easily interpret as luck.

The odometer reading appeared a good omen to Bena, since the sum of the four digits (5 + 4 + 3 + 4) was the number of her father's college football jersey (16), a grass-stained crimson shirt that hung, still, in the basement next to his rifles and his fishing rods. The patterns of his sweat had burned his body into the fabric. The shirt was a relic to her, for it preserved the outlined shape of her father when he was a happier man. As a vital boy growing up near Council Bluffs, Iowa, Charles "Chickie" Duse had snapped the necks of chickens and even small, lame calves with his bare hands—apt and brutal preparations for his future career as president of the St. Paul Savings and Trust. Chickie was the one who discovered his outwardly high-spirited wife dead of arsenic poisoning after the birth of their second child, Bena Ingrid Duse (labor complications, the obituary read), and had endured his son's drowning at the summer lake house he had struggled to afford in order to prove, beyond a doubt, that he was no one's farmhand.

As the landscape frayed into the dizzying warp and weft of ankle-high cornstalks, their discouraged tendrils already a drab beige from the scarcity of rain, Ted began reading aloud from a large maroon medical text, *The Journal of Immunology,* alerting Bena to diseases relevant to their new home.

This was another aspect of herself she knew he appreciated: her fascination with his work. He'd told her how he'd been struck by this on their first date, sitting in a booth at Kaap's Soda Fountain in St. Paul, sipping on a malted through a pair of white paper straws.

He'd talked to her about his passion for fishing, because women, as he told her later, were frequently bored by medicine and bodies. To women in the past, he'd talked about the heart. He'd described the way the blood was pushed and pumped, he'd drawn diagrams on a paper napkin with his fountain pen. But these women always looked at him differently when they knew he'd held a dead heart in his hands; they'd gazed distastefully upon his fingers as if a bit of death were still caught under the nails.

Fishing didn't interest Bena Duse. Neither did Ted's sister's wedding, his cousin's new baby, his mother's recent commission to have a well-known landscape painter sit in a rowboat half a mile offshore in Lake Michigan to do a portrait of their summer property in Door County, Wisconsin.

Out of sheer desperation, then, he'd talked to her about the heart.

"Did you know," he'd inquired, seeming to detect the initial signs of intrigue in this private girl who was smart around the mouth, "that a normal heart beats seventy-two times a minute?"

She had raised a pale eyebrow. She was quite pretty, he later told her he'd thought that day, pretty in a way that sneaks up on you.

"At this rate," he'd continued, "the heart contracts 4,320 times in an hour, 103,680 times in a day, 37,843,200 times in a year, and 2,649,024,000 times in an average lifetime." Or consider the common shrew, he added, whose heart beats one thousand times a minute.

Bena had held out her wrist to him, and he, intuiting what she wanted, unhooked her silver charm bracelet and placed the fingers of her other hand over that bare place. He pressed his cold palm over her knuckles. She smiled at him when she located the beating of her own pulse. They held hands and stared at the second hand of the pink-lit clock over the cash register.

"Seventy-eight," she said.

"Seventy-seven."

"Well," she had replied, "you're the doctor."

" 'The causative agent of Rocky Mountain spotted fever, Derma-ceniroxenus rickettsi, is transmitted and perpetuated by the tick Der-macentorivenustus,' " Ted informed her now. " 'It is a minute intracellular organism found in cells lining the intestinal canal of the tick, in the salivary glands, the ovaries, and in the eggs, and in an infected animal.' "

"I thought Pueblo was in the plains." Bena jerked the steering wheel to avoid what was once a rabbit, now stretched to the size of a welcome mat across the asphalt. She glanced over her shoulder to make sure the baby was still sleeping soundly. He was. They had laid him in the top drawer of an old dresser, padded with a wool hunting blanket folded in eighths. The blanket was dotted with deer blood and gun oil. Bena had covered it with a clean kitchen apron, whose faint recollections of roast beef and molasses seemed homey imperfections more suitable for an infant.

Theodore Gaspar Jonssen, Jr., six pounds, two ounces, had been born six and a half weeks earlier, on March 5. His birth was a bloody, prolonged affair, and exquisitely painful, as Theodore Gaspar Jonssen, Jr., saw fit to enter the world as one might enter a forbiddingly cold body of water, toes first. At the last minute he made a wrenching somersault, pulled and prodded by the obstetrician's thick gloved fingers. For a long moment he was silent. Bena had watched the doctor's face harden as he slapped her gray baby with a flat rubber hand. Then the baby coughed and rasped and breathed with his seaweed lungs, and the blood rushed to color his skin, and the face of the doctor softened at the slender thrill of new life.

"It's called the Front Range. Not Rockies, exactly, but nothing to turn your nose up at." Ted pulled a map from the glove box and unfolded it in his lap.

"Pueblo is here, see," he said, his finger hovering over the map and punching it whenever the Ford took a bump. "And the Range is here." His finger made a crater in the paper where the mountains were supposed to be. Bena saw a small black dot and the name of a town. Rye.

Ted pulled a paper clip off the cover of *The Journal of Immunology* and unfolded it. He slid one end carefully under the white bandage that covered his head.

"Itch?"

He growled, seeking out the prickly stitches with the tip of the paper clip. As a doctor (and one who had recently been forced to leave a job at a reputable clinic), he was a predictably reluctant patient. Had he not been so reluctant, the mastoid infection that had grown, hot and irritated, behind his right ear, might not have required an operation to drain the abscess just as his wife was experiencing the first vise-grip clenches of labor. He and Bena were hospitalized at the same time, she on the fourth floor, he on the second. In the violent delirium of her delivery room, Bena predicted to the nurse who sponged her brow with a damp chamois that her husband would birth a child as well, just as Zeus's skull had cleaved to release a fearsome daughter. While Bena's labors yielded a clay-streaked and pleated baby boy, Ted produced nothing more remarkable than a beakerful of brownish puss.

A car passed them going the other direction. Bena noticed a woman's head turn back to look at them through the dust.

"Are the lights on?" Ted asked.

Bena fiddled with the dashboard. "I don't think so."

Of the next few cars that passed, two slowed and one honked its horn, flushing a family of pheasants that clattered over the Ford, assaulting the car with a quick rain of small stones and dirt. It wasn't until an empty farm truck nearly drove off the road as the driver turned to catch a glimpse of their retreating vehicle that Ted asked Bena to pull over.

He walked around the car, checking the tires, the lights, looking under the carriage to see if they were dragging a rope or the meaty remains of a small animal. Nothing.

Bena stepped out and stretched tentatively. She was still stitched and sore herself from giving birth, but Ted had been offered the job in Pueblo contingent on his arriving no later than May 1. Unfortunately, his infection had worsened after the first operation and he had, just the past week, required a second. As he was too dizzy and she was merely sore, Bena had agreed to do the driving. She'd stacked a pair of couch pillows beneath her to cushion her torn parts from the whimsies of the potted road. The trip promised to be even more excruciating and slow, given that they had to pull over every two hours to let the baby feed. But it would allow Bena to understand better the distance they were covering, and their dubious good fortune. Instead of watching the quick-passing grim and tawdry towns from the safety of the windows, she would be forced to stand in their midst, to smell the smoke of failing industry and hear the woody, uneven clopping of half-shod horses. She would be forced to appreciate, each time they stopped, the fact that her husband's only job prospect hadn't been in Sibley, Iowa, or Popejoy, or Latimer.

"Damned if I know." Ted folded his long legs back into the car.

They proceeded tentatively, Bena speeding up whenever a car approached. As they whipped past a grain truck just outside of Mandelia, they struck a crow picking at a pudding of hot innards on the road.

There was a snap of cartilage, of glass. The crow hung for a second, pressed against the windshield by the car's momentum, then tumbled over the roof and onto the road. Bena watched in the rearview mirror as it spun into the dry irrigation ditch that hugged the highway.

"That's a fine omen," she said.

Bena caught her husband rolling his eyes. According to her, it would be a bad day if there was a misprint on the front page of the *St. Paul Dispatch*, if the milk had spoiled overnight, if a robin broke its neck against their bedroom window, if she passed an amputee on the sidewalk before noon when the day was still impressionable.

Little Ted started crying from his dresser drawer. He didn't so much cry at this young age as cough, as if he were still part fish and clearing his lungs of water.

Bena stiffened. Before the baby she'd been a slow girl, the world coming to her through a watery layer of her own unsorted thinking. Now she'd turned wolfish, her nose and ears alerted by the slightest noise or scent. Her mind, no longer flabby and dreamy, was sinuous and lean and almost nervous. It made her life simpler, though she could understand how it might eat at her, if she wasn't careful to cultivate her own needs from time to time.

Ted reached over the seat and pulled Little Ted from the drawer. He thrust an arm through the baby's bowed legs and tucked his head into the crook of his elbow. Despite the fact that he was a doctor and no stranger to bodies, he had been rather awkward and stymied around the baby. Ted watched him with fierce interest and affection as he slept, but shied away from the crying, pissing, waking calamity of him.

Bena stole quick looks at her husband and son together, the one with his bottom wrapped in a white diaper, the other with his head wrapped in a white bandage. And there the similarities ended. There was no evidence of her husband's dark blue eyes that pushed out at the world, no evidence of his vivid, earnest, greedy face. Her husband appeared far younger than his own son, a prunish little wise man with a fish cough and pale, pale eyes that stared with a premature discernment at the bleary world around him.

"Keep talking about bad luck and you'll bring it upon us." Ted jounced his arm until the baby's crying stopped.

"Luck isn't something you court," Bena corrected. She reached out to touch her baby's forearm, so soft it eluded perception by her more callused digits, her thumbs, for example. She had a new favorite part of his body every few days. At first it was the arch of his foot, then the back of his knee, his walnut ears. She didn't feel capable of loving the entirety of him, so instead she loved him, manageably, in pieces. "It's something you observe."

She saw Ted struggling to contain his irritation.

"So stop being so damned observant." He smiled and pinched her forearm. He felt comfortable causing her pain if it seemed he was joking.

Ted returned to his medical texts while Bena stared ahead at the road, counting the rows of fledgling cornstalks that passed the car at the same thump-thump-thump pace of her pulse.

DODGE, IOWA, POPULATION 115. The second day.

The sign was the usual rural roadway variety—dull paint, metal post listing backward, letters punctuated by bullet holes. Here someone had applied a curt warning in hasty red slashes above the faded lettering.

LEAVE.

A spindly, more dispirited hand augmented the first command.

WE ALL DID.

Dodge was heralded further by a peaked water tower with a flapping tarpaper roof; next to that stood a windmill, a lone Indian sentinel, its wooden wind guide protruding like a feather from the back of its lazily spinning blades. White powdery soil and dead grass and empty white sky came together at the horizon to produce a disorienting vertical sweep of colorlessness that made the parched clapboard buildings appear to be the last outpost of civilization.

They'd spent the previous night at a road motel in Rumford Wells. The baby had slept in the top drawer of the dresser and Bena and Ted had fallen onto the concave mattress, too tired to move, or so she'd thought. She was asleep when he touched her hip and her new, slack belly. She was already so warm and dreamy that she forgot she was a mother with a baby asleep in a motel sock drawer, she forgot she was bone-angry with her husband for exiling them to the godforsaken plains of Colorado (it wasn't his fault, she knew). The way he touched her was unconscious and bodiless, and she touched him, half asleep, until they forgot each other and became new people for the night, without resentments and bitterness, with only a generous willingness to slip inside another person's skin in a dark, borrowed room.

Past the windmill, Main Street started to pick up—an empty beauty salon called The Chatterbox, where a woman in an apron smoked alone behind the screen door; the Dodge Mercantile, with its chapped western façade and dusty windows yielding gauzy views of canned goods; Dodge Grain and Feed, a building that sloped heavily to one side like the face of a stroke victim. Farther down were a sturdy yellow-brick bank, a Texaco station, a café with a faded round Coca-Cola sign.

Ted pointed to a bare lot next to Ewing Lumber and Hardware. Bena parked beneath a billboard of a woman in a black dress, hands on her hips, gazing with concern at her unremarkable thighs. "Don't be skinny," the billboard insisted. "Take Dr. Burt's For-A-Betta Diet Supplements and getta betta figure."

Bena considered her own figure, disguised inside the ample and forgiving shape of her traveling dress. She had never been a skinny girl, always a firm, efficient girl who filled out dresses and blouses just enough to show there was a person inside. Her hide was taut over her muscles that were big for her sex, muscles that came from summers sailing on Lake Susquetannah, hauling in sheets and anchor lines, and swimming across black, icy coves in a striped bathing costume that weighed ten pounds when wet.

She pulled the dress across her waist. Her skin was looser after the baby's birth, loose on her arms, her back, her legs. This body belonged to another woman, a woman with tight, low breasts and thighs that chafed and stretched in the heat, a woman who had been cored, the pit of her expelled between her legs, leaving a tired, cramping sag above her pubic bone. It didn't make her unhappy, but it did make her curious. She'd spent hours in front of the mirror while pregnant, watching the way her body groaned, her joints splayed, the way her breasts grew warm and heavy; they felt like a pair of small sleeping squirrels she'd chosen to smuggle, hidden inside her coat, into movie theaters, restaurants.

She reached into the backseat and awakened Little Ted in the dresser drawer. She unbuttoned her dress and freed a raw nipple from inside her brassiere, shading his face from the white, high-up sun. Her son had already distinguished himself as an insatiable creature, which made Bena immeasurably proud. Since his birth she'd done little but sit in an armchair and lift him from one breast to the other, then massage her nipples with a suet-and-ash salve as he slept. He was still too young to see or talk or even smile, but she could put an ear against Little Ted's spongy middle as he napped and listen to the raging, vital sounds his stomach emitted as he battled his way back to hungriness.

"I'll explore our lunch options," Ted announced. His face had grown pallid, perhaps from carsickness or dizziness. "Any requests?"

Bena watched in amazement as a dog galloped down the center of the street, dragging a wooden doll. "Whatever looks good," she said, doubting that anything could. The sky was oil-ringed where the sun sought to burn through. Because of the drought that had persisted since the previous summer (no rain, no snow), there were no plant roots to keep the world in place; the dirt sloughed steadily away, making the wind gauzy and visible. The weather was unseasonably warm, the April sun as glaring and tiresome as that of late June.

As the dog neared, she saw it wasn't a doll in its jaws. It was a prosthetic arm. The hand vibrated a wooden greeting to her as it passed. Bena tracked the dog's progress in the rearview mirror until it disappeared around the corner of the Grain and Feed.

"Might want to keep the doors locked," Ted suggested, his brows close and dark. He became unbearably handsome to her, gilded and ancient, when his chivalrous impulses overtook him. Bena felt safe and reckless in a far-back, animal way, as if they were badgers or bears or beavers, living uncomplicated, instinctual lives. She ran a finger along his belt, trailed up his shirt placket, throat, chin. Her finger landed on his lips and he obliged her by kissing it, then pretending to bite it. He bent over her to take Little Ted's foot in his mouth. He shook it wildly, the way the dog had shaken the prosthetic arm.

He kissed her breast, grazed his lips over her long nipple.

She swatted him on the shoulder. He squeezed her nipple between his thumb and forefinger.

"Be right back." He flashed her the sheepish smile that she had learned in their two and a half years of marriage to read as an apology in advance.

Bena watched her husband walk across the parking lot, a familiar anxiety crimping the muscles of her forehead. He took a left on Main Street and was blocked from view by a parked police car.

Ted's smile meant that, despite his promise to hurry, he would discover a café with a booth away from the kitchen and out of the sun, just vacated. He'd find a local paper left by the previous diner, its sections turned inside out and gravy-spattered, and there would be a daily special (calf's liver and onions, hot bacon-bean pie) that would sound far more appetizing than a ham sandwich wrapped in brown paper to be eaten on the car hood. He would tuck into the bacon-bean pie, accompanied by a tepid ginger beer, and skim stories about the railroad layoff, the folding of the Sharecroppers' Credit Union, a boy's disappearance. He'd hem and haw before ordering a slab of rhubarb cobbler and a cup of coffee that the waitress would take special pains to refresh again and again and again. He'd insist, "Wife's in the car, need to make this snappy," all the while continuing small talk with the poor girl, asking her where she grew up and how she got so pretty and making her so flustered that she'd forget his dessert order and put him back another ten minutes.

Ted attributed his gregariousness to an overflowing bedside manner, but Bena knew her husband was simply a flirt, a man who, while he loved her, also loved to witness how the world came to adore him so easily. It was a quality she'd found endearing, until she began to locate in his compulsive gregariousness a strain of desperation. What made her most anxious was the constant suspicion that what she gave him wasn't enough, that he had to look elsewhere to feel loved thoroughly and properly.

He did, she knew, look elsewhere.

She'd seen him one afternoon on her way to meet a former sorority sister for lunch. He was supposed to be at the hospital and she'd seen him through a jeweler's window, fastening a garnet choker around a woman's neck. The woman offered her collarbone to him with her chin high in the air, as if she were spreading her legs. He stepped back to admire the necklace, the woman's neck and breasts, waist and ankles, and then he touched the buttons on her coat in a way that made Bena know for certain she was no salesgirl.

A week later, the necklace had appeared in a leather box for Bena's birthday. She'd remained stoic and straight-necked as he lowered the necklace around her from behind, his breath catching in her hair as he worked the cold clasp. Bena stared at herself in the mirror and experienced a strange power. She could know his most distressing truths and remain unbothered. That she'd caught him buying a necklace for another woman was evidence of his weakness; to have caught him selecting a piece of jewelry meant for her by the way it looked against another woman's throat was the most pitiful form of compromise. Unlike many women who might prefer not to know the illicit directions in which their husband's affections wandered, Bena liked to know these truths about Ted, because it allowed her to participate in his deceit as an equal partner.

She'd worn the necklace only once after that, to a medical dinner, at his request. Flush against her skin, it made her look as though she'd had her throat slit. She tossed the necklace down the toilet, but even then it continued to plague her, wrapping itself like a parasite inside the pipes. When the plumber removed the vile object, knotted with toilet paper and excrement, she offered it to him in addition to paying his fee. He didn't thank her; he must have heard the begging in her voice. He spat in the toilet, as he probably wanted to spit on her, if he hadn't been so desperate for money or anything like money.

After the incident with the necklace, Bena tried to leave Ted. She drove up to her father's summer house at Coeur du Lac and watched the winter land noiselessly on the lake like the flocks of geese resting on their flight south from Ontario. But by then it was too late. By then he'd burdened her with another secret, one whose creation they shared equally, though Bena housed it. She cried and drank bourbon and took icy swims at midnight beneath a pared moon, hoping to coax it out of her. But the only secret she managed to coax from between her pelvic bones was an unexpected discovery about herself. The truth was that she'd come to see her husband's infidelities as a relief. She and Ted had created a comfortable life inside of which they could hide from themselves and each other. The distance he maintained from her in order to protect his philandering meant that she could rightly be unknowable to him, and he to her.

Little Ted pulled away from her and started to cry. Bena stretched him across the seat and unpinned him until his musty, earthy body was revealed. He appeared so world-weary to her with his creased skin and skeptical old-man face; innocence, evidently, was a state for which humans had to age in order to achieve.

She reached into her tartan day bag for a diaper. She never went anywhere without a cakey pile of white cloth and various talcs and solutions, the soft and wet and powdery accoutrements of motherhood. The combination of baby and bag made her heavy and slow-moving, and brought her to question the evolutionary rationale to so many things, things that would prevent her from escaping whatever primitive pursuer might engage her in a chase.

Bena cleaned the baby with diluted rubbing alcohol. The tiny polyp between his legs still fascinated her because it represented the trickiness of her own body, and its devious ability to create a being so different from itself. She didn't understand how she could have made a man like that. It didn't seem possible that she could make a man, when men were something she couldn't claim to know much about.

She let her head fall back on the car seat. It was hot in the Ford with the windows closed. She pressed her face into Little Ted's body. She felt her affections shift from his elbow to his tiny, bowed nose. He smelled of sour milk in his neck folds, and sweat and urine. She held him up so she could look into his face and see the people there. He resembled her brother around the eyes, and he had her father's lanky, oversized mouth. She thought she saw a bit of her mother in him as well, at least what little she knew of her mother from pictures of her as a girl growing up in Norway. In the time since Little Ted was born, she'd spent hours memorizing the distance between his features, the length of each finger, preparing herself to notice the minute her baby began to mutate into a longer, more wily toddler. She kissed him on the forehead and watched as his eyes swung wildly around their sockets, alternately humored and alarmed.

In spite of the crow that had struck the windshield, Bena had a good feeling about their move to Pueblo. It was new there even if it was nowhere. She and Ted could fix their tinny marriage in pleasant isolation and return to Minnesota in a few years' time, exhaustively adoring of one another.

SHE AWOKE to the sound of retching, and a muffled thumping against the car glass. Little Ted was as radiant as a hot-water bottle on her lap. She failed at first to notice the woman rapping on the car window. Instead, she focused on the white bandaged head crouched and vomiting, just visible in the alley between two buildings.

Poor Ted, she thought. She prepared herself for the likelihood that they would have to rent a hotel room in Dodge; he would be unable to ride in a car in this condition.

Rap rap rap.

Bena looked up and was startled to find herself under the close scrutiny of a woman in a beet-colored cloche. She signaled Bena to roll down her window. Black gloves ended just above her wrists, unbuttoned and failing to hide the scars there, burn marks and scratches.

"I wouldn't fall asleep with the windows up," the woman scolded. "Especially with a little one like that." Her bobbed blond hair ended in an upward point, leading the eyes of any observer directly to her very full, very red lips. Her dress was a dotted-swiss chiffon. The full skirt rasped against its crinoline as the wind swept by.

"My sister lost one of hers that way," the woman continued. "Not that she didn't have a few to spare. Gone no more than a half-hour, buying fabric to make her baby a summer suit." She shook her head and fumbled with her beaded clutch, and extracted a faux-horn cigarette case that she opened with some difficulty. Her mouth tightened.

"Don't have a cigarette, do you?"

Bena, half asleep, reached into the glove box and fished a cigarette out from between the maps. She'd been a smoker in college, back when she believed she would be a newspaper reporter, working for *The Minnesota Daily* at the university and smoking all night with the men to keep herself awake. She still smoked from time to time, and hid cigarettes behind books and underneath sweaters, where her disapproving husband wouldn't find them.

"It's a bit sorry," Bena apologized.

"Beggars can't be choosers." The woman put the flattened cigarette in her mouth. She smelled of a man's spice soap and bacon. Her porous skin was dusted with a thick layer of powder, and she'd drawn a beauty mark above her lip. The mark was oblong with scalloped edges, and resembled the first stages of rot rather than the ultimate testament to beauty.

"Well," the woman said, exhaling and surveying Dodge, Iowa,

population 115. "This town is one of the shabbiest I've ever laid eyes on."

"Not much in the way of tourist attractions."

"You a tourist?"

"We're on our way to Colorado, actually. To live."

"Ah. Colorado." The woman sounded as if she knew it well.

"Pueblo," Bena clarified. "My husband's going to be a doctor at a clinic there. I've never been. In fact, I've never been to Colorado."

She'd never been to Colorado because she'd never wanted to go to Colorado. And this was still true. They were driving to Colorado because they had to. The Depression, she'd told her friends. No jobs. Take what you can get. Before, this had applied to others, not to them. Since he'd started medical school, Ted had been guaranteed a job by his uncle who ran a reputable private clinic in Rochester.

The woman in the green coat came into the clinic six months after he'd graduated. Because of a medical conference in Duluth, Ted was on duty alone that day. The woman didn't have a name, the woman wasn't wearing anything under her green coat, Ted reported at the clinic inquiry. (Later, explaining to Bena with his hair brushed back from his face so that she could be assured he was being truthful, Ted said the woman looked like a parrot—green coat, blue hat, blue bruises on her legs, her breast.) She was hopped up and delirious, he said. She wanted morphine to stop the pain of her bruises, and he refused. The woman said that no one ever refused her. She was out of her head when she started shrieking in the examination room, when she grabbed her green coat and ran, naked, through the hallways with one cloth slipper and a bare foot, when she accused him of touching her and hitting her after she denied him access to her withered body. A pair of nurses restrained her and clucked as she spat on herself, clearly embarrassed that poor, new Dr. Jonssen had to witness such a loose, afflicted variety of female nature.

The next morning, Ted learned that the woman's father was the mayor of Rochester, a beefy-minded man who had been trying to close the clinic for months to accommodate his plans for a new highway to be named after him. Although the woman had been in and out of Black Wing Sanitarium for years, Ted was asked to resign his post in order to avoid unnecessary trouble. The woman with the green coat was apparently a fixture around the clinic, one the other doctors readily supplied with morphine to keep happy and quiet. That Ted had refused to abide by the unspoken rules was viewed by his colleagues as an act of extreme hubris. His uncle promised he'd help him relocate to another clinic, yet the false word had spread, and Ted couldn't get another job, not in Minnesota, or Illinois, or Wisconsin. While Bena believed her husband was not only innocent but also ethically advanced, she couldn't help thinking that he had somehow deserved this unjust banishment for all the just ways in which he could have had his roaming hands slapped. It didn't occur to her until they were boxing up their apartment that she, too, was moving to Colorado, that she, too, was being banished.

"Not much to Colorado, really," the woman told her. "Space. More space. Nothing to be done with it, being it's all mountains or desert. Sort of like a rich widow in her mansion. Thousands of rooms to rattle around in, but no use to make of them." She said this in a nostalgic way, enjoying the image of so much grandeur, no matter how vacant and dusty. *Thousands of rooms.*

"How about yourself?" Bena asked. "Are you on vacation?"

"Vacation!" The woman shot a quick, bitter laugh through her fine nose. It was the only fine feature she possessed; the rest were thick and sprawling, as if she'd been hit a few too many times. "We're on a business trip."

"You and your husband?"

She smiled. "Sure."

"What's he do, your husband?"

The woman stared off at the horizon to indicate, perhaps, that the answer to this question was too dreary to be answered in all its particulars. "Finance."

"Banking?"

"Some."

"My father's the president of the St. Paul Savings and Trust. Perhaps your husband knows of him."

"I'm sure he will, if he doesn't already," the woman replied. She tossed her half-smoked cigarette to the dirt and ground it flat with the toe of a black crocodile pump that wiggled on her foot. "So few of them left these days."

The woman watched nonplussed as the dog carrying the prosthetic arm reappeared and circled the parking lot. She pulled a tube of lipstick from her clutch and looked at the worn nub, weighing the color like a shopper at a cosmetics counter. She searched for her reflection in the Ford's window and pressed the lipstick so hard against her lips that it created a wave of flesh preceding its travels.

"Well," she said, clicking her bag shut. "I thank you for the cigarette."

"And I thank you." Bena glanced down at her sleeping son.

"Need to do one good deed a day so that I can go to bed even." The woman started to leave, but then turned back. "Say, you wouldn't have any aspirin, would you? My husband's not feeling well." She made a great show of checking her watch, which was, in fact, a gold bracelet. It was too tight and cut into the flesh of her wrist.

Bena dislodged her purse from beneath the seat. She handed the woman a mother-of-pearl pillbox. "Take however many you need."

The woman accepted the pillbox, giving it the briefest once-over.

"What's the little one's name?" She reached a hand into the car and rubbed Little Ted's cheek with a gloved finger. It was obvious babies made her uneasy. Bena figured she was grateful for the aspirin and felt she should show some forced interest.

"Ted Junior. Little Ted for now."

"Well, they're lucky boys, the both of them. Say, reach out your hand." She held her closed fist upside down. "Go on."

Bena offered her palm. The woman pressed something into it and folded Bena's fingers into a fist.

"For good luck," she said.

Bena opened her hand. In it was a silver charm, a water tower with "Dodge" stamped across its barrel middle. It was dust-caked and banged up, trampled underfoot by all 115 townspeople.

"I found it while I was looking for the bank. I noticed you had a charm bracelet, I thought you'd have better use for it than me." She swatted a fly from Little Ted's forehead.

"Thanks," Bena said.

"I never wanted kids." The woman sounded wistful. "You?"

Bena squinted at her. It was an odd question to ask a woman with a baby.

"It's just never interested me much," the woman explained off-handedly. She seemed impressed with herself and her distinctive, un-material brand of femininity, as if instead of motherhood she'd just turned down a closetful of new dresses or a house by the sea.

Without saying good-bye, she walked off across the parking lot. She raised a hand over her head and let it spiral there, waving, or maybe catching a bit of the breeze in her gloved palm. The crisp sound of her crinoline grew fainter and fainter until it was the sound of the empty wind, whisking seedpods and gravel around the vacant, unpaved streets of Dodge.

Bena fiddled with her bracelet, biting the water tower's ring closed. The charm hung crookedly, between a silver herring Ted had bought her at the Inlagd Sill festival in St. Paul and a fountain pen she'd received for winning the Lester B. Hawks Prize for Daily Journalism in college. She often thought about detaching the pen, because it seemed a fatuous memento to carry about, a quaint reminder of the path she hadn't followed.

As the woman disappeared between two brick buildings, Bena was struck with a yawning desolation above her ribs. Somewhere a church bell sounded twelve lazy gongs. She looked at the expanse of white sky and white earth that stretched away to nothing and made her dizzy. She remembered reading in the *St. Paul Dispatch* about a man piloting a plane in the Antarctic on a sparkling clear day, and how he flew directly into the side of a snowy mountain because everything looked the same down there at noon, when there were no shadows to distinguish mountain, plains, sky, water. So it was in Dodge. And probably in Pueblo.

Little Ted let out a few faint bird chirps. Bena unbuttoned her dress. His first few sucks took the breath out of her, his powerful mouth working away at her chapped skin.

She was about to surrender to a bout of tired sobs welling up from that hole above her ribs, when the dog with the prosthetic arm lumbered in front of the windshield. The arm still jiggled, but less enthusiastically this time. The dog traced a slow circle around the parking lot before a second dog hopped into view. This dog was missing one of its front legs. It chased after the dog with the prosthetic arm. Every time it came close, the first dog would deftly pick up the pace, leaving its pursuer lunging at nothing but a rising cloud of dust.

Bena started to laugh. She laughed until the crying from that desolate place came up anyway. By the time she saw Ted ambling back with two paper bags, she had forgotten her unhappiness and had even come to see this new white world as capable of unexpected occurrences that were poetic and grotesque, pitiful and funny, all at once.

Ted slid into the passenger seat, balancing a ceramic mug full of coffee. Bena was relieved to note that his color had returned. Perhaps they wouldn't be spending the night in Dodge.

"I smuggled it out," he said, handing her the mug. He noticed her red eyes and running nose. "Is something wrong?"

Ted stared at her, mystified, until she pointed out the dogs. The three-legged one had finally caught up to its tormentor, and they were playing tug-of-war with the prosthetic arm, their back haunches strained and lowered, their nails skitching through the gravel.

"Jesus," Ted said in amazement. He passed Bena a sandwich. "Ham."

She unwrapped the sandwich and checked under the wet corners of the bread for ants or flies or God knew what. She heard a police siren. It grew and grew, bloomed next to them and moved past, fading quickly.

"Sorry I was gone so long," Ted began.

Bena took a tentative bite of her sandwich. She rolled the rubbery, salty ham around in her mouth before forcing it down with a swig of lukewarm coffee.

"There was a grease fire at the diner this morning. It took forever to get some service."

Bena tossed the rest of the sandwich out the car window. It was instantly descended on by a pair of crows. They knocked the crusts around, held the flaps of ham in their beaks and shook them silly.

Ted unwrapped his sandwich and pulled a long, dark hair from between the bread. He grimaced and held it out for the wind to take. He stared through the window crossly and put a hand against his gauzy head. "Where's that aspirin?"

Bena reached for her purse. She paused. "I gave it to somebody."

Ted gazed doubtfully at the deserted streets.

"A woman. She was here with her husband. On a business trip."

"You gave her all of it?"

"She . . . Yes."

Annoyed, Ted changed the subject. He pulled a folded newspaper out of one of the diner bags and pointed to an article on the front page. "This may explain our strange reception on the roads this morning."

Bena propped the paper on the steering wheel. Her fingertips smudged the edges and came away greasy with newsprint. "Barrow Injured in Culver Shoot-out," the headline read.

CULVER, IOWA, a small town of 200 residents, missed the chance to earn a permanent place on the map yesterday when a deputy sheriff's bullet grazed the head of bank robber Clyde Barrow, injuring but not killing the infamous road gangster.

"He was bleeding over the right ear," testified Ryan McGivern, deputy sheriff and vice president of the Culver VFD. Barrow and his accomplice Bonnie Parker escaped in a stolen black Ford Touring Car belonging to Culver church warden Gladys Lipsky. "They won't get far," Mrs. Lipsky insisted. "Not with God's will, and not in that car."

Officials have advised travelers to remain on the lookout for a black Ford Touring Car, driven by either a man with a head bandage or a woman with blond hair. Last eyewitness reports indicate the couple to be headed south.

"Amazing we didn't get shot by some Johnny-do-good farmer," he said.

Bena turned to him, visions of that other white, bobbing head obscuring her actual husband from view. The sirens had ceased. She saw a patrol car pull over near the Coca-Cola sign, to expel a pair of policemen who pulled their pants up by the belt and shook their heads.

"You weren't sick over there?"

Bewildered, Ted followed her eyes to the empty alley at the end of the parking lot.

Bena turned and tucked Little Ted into his padded dresser drawer. She started the Ford and skidded out of the parking lot.

"Bena, the way out of town is . . ."

"I'm not looking for the way out of town."

She took a left into a driveway that led them around behind the

Dodge Apothecary, and pulled up beside a black Ford Touring Car just like their own. Ted regarded her, astonished that his wife's superstitious decoding of the world might on occasion yield a surprising knowledge.

Bena got out of the car and walked around the hood of the identical black Ford. Her sweat-damp dress stuck to the upholstery as she slid behind the steering wheel. She placed her hands where she imagined Bonnie had placed hers. She could smell her man's soap.

In the glove box she found a Culver Baptist Choir songlist, with a note in the margin: "Oil—Tea—Ginger—Cream." The silver lighter on the floor didn't work. A blank postcard from Lola's Lunch in Dawsonville, Iowa, was imprinted with the dirty texture of a shoe sole.

Bena looked at the odometer; it read 5,434, exactly the same as theirs when they had left the St. Paul city limits in a wake of dust and exhaust.

There were no maps.

The gas tank was empty.

Bena stepped out of the car and eased herself onto the hood. Her dress was still unbuttoned and the lace of her ivory slip was visible to anyone who cared to see it. She kicked her shoes off and rested her feet on the warm chrome bumper. She held the Lola's Lunch postcard over her eyes to shade them from the sun.

The parking lot was on the outskirts of town. From this vantage point she could see over the low roof of a sinking garage, out to the endless sweep of dry grasses and the single, unwavering strip of asphalt, a beaten gray vein of pavement that seemed antiquated, like a relic from another century.

Ted's door slammed. He walked with his hands shoved in the pockets of his khakis and rattling the change there. Rather than the horizon, he stared at the ground, at his boots pulling clipped young-afternoon shadows across the lot. He peered inside the car, then opened the trunk.

She heard him whistle.

"This the lady to whom you gave our aspirin?"

He walked toward her carrying the broken stock of a rifle and a dirty brassiere.

Bena took the brassiere from between his fingers. It made her angry that he felt he could wave a strange woman's brassiere about so cavalierly. One of the straps was torn. She lifted it high, until the wind filled the cups. She let it go, watched it tumble over the gravel.

"Aiding and abetting criminals. It's not like you, sweetheart." Ted stood in front of her and placed both hands on her thighs. His hands were hot and thick-skinned through her dress.

"You had a close call," he said, pushing up her dress and urging the straps of her slip farther down her shoulders. It appeared that her brush with death or fame made him want to see her naked. He rested his bandaged head against her breasts; his wet breath filtered through the fabric. She put a hand on his neck and found a little curl of hair peeping out from below the bandage that she could wind around her finger.

Bena played with his lock of hair. The water-tower charm on her bracelet jangled against the silver herring from the Inlagd Sill festival. She felt her heart strain against the head of her husband to rush out into the dry, white horizon. Considering the expanse of empty land, she imagined every person to be a vector moving through space. Sometimes you intersected with one particular person and he or she changed your path dramatically. Other times, you just hummed along on what you assumed to be your own happy, straight line.

As Ted ran his hands over her body she noticed a faded sign painted on the brick wall of the apothecary. "Tiny Ted's Famous Hand Cream," it read. Below was painted a child's hand emerging from a pond of water. Or sinking. A hand sinking into water.

Bena shivered, even though she was sweating where her husband's hands pressed against her. She didn't like the fact that "Tiny Ted" sounded so much like "Little Ted," and that the address, 88 Main, was the exact date (8/8) of her brother's death by drowning. She wanted to tell Ted, to show him this potential omen, because sometimes, when he was patient enough, he could point out how her interpretations were flawed. He'd point out to her that $8 + 8 = 16$, which was the number of her father's football jersey, for example, and she'd feel better for a moment. But she couldn't help suspecting that for all the ways in which she saw more than was there, for looking too closely, he added and subtracted from the basic truth of things, and missed what was most important about the predictions contained within the plain language of coincidence.

2. BUFFALO MASS SUICIDE

Union Avenue, Pueblo ("Welcome to Pueblo, Colorado, King of Iron, Population 50,096"), was a drab assemblage of block-shaped buildings—some constructed of brick, some of tawny buckled sandstone, some of paint-stripped clapboard with traditional western façades. The last were hung with warping porches that a local architect, before the drought and the Depression, must have envisioned busy with shoppers resting on rockers and musing over their purchases while watching the commotion of the street transpire at a suitable distance.

Bena walked down Union in a pinched pink suit that no longer fit, but into which she had zipped and buttoned her unruly body because she always had her way when she wore it. She enjoyed catching her unfamiliar reflection in the shop windows that, just beyond her ghostly figure, revealed rows of empty shelves and year-old wall calendars from Colorado Fuel and Iron.

Bena had been rather tired since arriving in Pueblo a month before; she'd had a difficult time getting out of bed and even missed her second Tuesday meeting of the Now-A-Day Club—resulting, she was informed by a neatly penned note from the president, Bess Duncan, in a five-cent fine due at the next week's gathering. But today she was sprightly and invincible. Probably, she reasoned, this was because after weeks of teariness, homesickness, and boredom in her new home, after washing countless diapers and milk-stained blouses and her husband's shirtsleeves dotted with iodine, she was walking to meet Cecil Belsen,

the editor of *The Pueblo Chieftain,* about a reporting job she'd heard
about through one of her husband's colleagues at the clinic.

Ted would have objected to her working, she was certain, were it
not for the fact that he felt responsible for their living in Pueblo; he
felt responsible for her unhappiness. Bena knew no one except the
women at the Now-A-Day Club, women who were new mothers but
absent ones, preferring to leave their babies all day and evening with
Mexican girls and wet nurses half their age while they drank iced tea
and discussed current events in ways more imaginative than informed.
She would become an ideal and attentive mother, she decided, instead
of socializing and courting shallow friends.

During their second week in Pueblo, Bena had discovered a feed
scale in the garage, behind a metal tractor seat and a torturous-looking
hoe attachment. She had begun to weigh the baby every morning,
placing him on the scale's rusted altar and watching as the needle made
its slow way around the circle like a clock measuring the growing
lateness of the hour. Ten pounds, three ounces. Ten pounds ten. Eleven
pounds four. She wrote her notations in a blank book she'd found, its
cover printed with the initials of the previous owner in weary goldflake.
She'd drawn a graph, x axis, y axis, to chart the upward linear shape
of his growing.

She'd also been measuring his length with a blue hair ribbon,
stretching it along his spinal curve as he lay on the kitchen table. She'd
extended the ribbon up the painted jamb of the bathroom door and
marked the place with a butter knife as if he were a real, upright child,
until the marks piled on top of one another and became a wide, unreadable chip in the wood. Ted remarked that he'd never seen anything
so ridiculous, watching her saw at the thick paint with an unsharpened
blade.

She knew he worried about her because of the fact her own mother
had died after giving birth to her. It was the sort of obvious pattern

that Ted put great stock in, and she put none at all, because the world of coincidence was far more devious than that. He thought the Now-A-Day Club might ease her concentration on the baby, shift her interests from domestic to civic, but it didn't. So he told her about the job and gave her permission to hire a laundress for the pounds of dirty clothes that stank in the warm bathroom hamper unless they were washed each afternoon. You've always wanted to, he said, pulling the Lester B. Hawks Prize for Daily Journalism charm on her bracelet.

Bena paused in front of Matheny's Family Portraits and faced the window squarely. After a mere three months of motherhood, her own reflection appeared to her scant and unnecessary without Little Ted. Her singular body wasn't enough to justify her place in the world any longer.

She'd arranged, after much worrying and consideration, to have the baby stay with the upstairs tenant, a sixty-year-old ex-vaudevillian from Texas named Florence Early. Florence survived, as far as Bena could tell, on a diet of poached eggs and tea, which lent her apartment a sulfurous, old-sock smell. Florence's apartment was more of a museum for her old costumes than a place to live. Rhinestone lassos hung by their own nooses, flayed feathered capes were pinned to the walls. Florence kept a failing rose vine in the shared backyard, which she clipped wearing a pair of stained, elbow-length evening gloves. Bena liked to prompt her into talking about all the famous men (Bena had never heard of them) she had played mistress to over the years. She showed Bena the opulent gifts they had bestowed on her as if pointing out scars and how she had gotten them.

Still, Bena became queasy as the time approached for her to leave the baby. She spent the morning in Florence's apartment, showing her where on his feet and hands little Ted liked to be rubbed and the exact manner in which his diaper should be changed. Bena stood in the hallway outside Florence's door and listened to his crying. She was about to walk back into the apartment and call Mr. Belsen to cancel her lunch, when the crying stopped. She couldn't tell which pained her more—the sound of the baby's missing her, or the sound of his not missing her.

Given the previous week's ominous headlines in the *Chieftain*—"Dust Pneumonia Diagnosed in Baca and Prower Counties"—Union Avenue was virtually unpopulated, save for the sporadic businessman hurrying from office building to bank with a newspaper shielding his nose and mouth, or the employees of Colorado Fuel and Iron who ambled along the sidewalks in packs. Their limbs, gleaming in the gray sunlight so that every muscle and tendon was revealed, possessed a lassitude somewhere between the defeat of overwork and the recoiling of a snake that might, if the proper stimulus crossed its path, strike out in vicious, unpredictable ways. Home, for most of them, Bena had learned, was the shantytown east of the intersection of Second Avenue and North Greenwood. The shantytown was full of stooped, burn-eyed men and stiff-faced women and filthy, filthy children.

Bena looked up and saw three such men approaching her. She smiled at them, but none of them returned her smile. Two went into a bar called Buck's Silo; the third slipped into the shadows of a side alley, where an unmarked door opened and received him.

Bena paused in front of the Silver State Theater, where a scarecrow hung from a gallows provided by the empty flagpole jutting out above the marquee. The sign pinned to his torn workshirt bore an angry charcoal scrawl. "Old Man Depression." But no traces of rage were evident in Old Man Depression himself. His face had the bland look of someone enjoying a stolen nap, his legs happily catching the small breezes. He appeared to be kicking up his heels, about to break into a dance down Union, across the Arkansas River, and out over the prairie until he was just a speck of dust on the horizon among a thousand other specks of dust. But then the breeze subsided, and his legs hung heavy in their soleless leather boots, and the rope tensed around his neck, cocking his head at an unnatural angle.

Bena shivered at the thought of the hopeless expanse that bordered Pueblo to the east and south. What made the town most unbearable, however, was not the barren landscape but the weather. The days were unseasonably hot for May, the afternoons scorched and blaring, while the nights remained deep and still and cold. Scarcely a day had passed without a visitation by a dust storm. She'd had to barricade herself and Little Ted inside the house countless times since they'd arrived, push sand-filled socks under the doors and hang wet bedsheets over the windows to keep out the dust. It was impossible to do laundry, and Bena had spent many an afternoon sloughing diapers over a metal washboard until her hands cramped, only to watch the tiny flags grow gray on the line as the filthy wind methodically dimmed their flickering whiteness. Since they'd been in Pueblo a young boy had suffocated, a train had derailed, a herd of cattle had been lost (when they were found, dead, the rancher cut them open, to find their stomachs filled with mud). The Ford was already partially stripped of its fine paint job. The elm in their front yard was bald, its leaves sliced off by the most recent storm. People and animals, leaves and veneers had an unnerving tendency to vanish around Pueblo, which lent the mirages Bena saw on the hotter days a spectral creepiness.

Bena fell further and further into a bleak, timid mood, until she had persuaded herself to turn around, to rush home and beg Ted to take them to a place where rosebushes could survive, where the clouds rained down useful substances, water instead of dirt. She believed the dust-ridden air was affecting Little Ted, who had been behaving listlessly since they'd arrived; he inhaled an unhealthy amount of hopelessness and decay as a matter of course.

Bena slowed her pace past the Snow White Laundry and had just begun to rotate on her heel when she caught her breath, astonished. There, between the two buildings, an unfettered view of the Rockies muscled skyward from the colorless plain, the peaks flecked with snow. The mountains were pristine and magnificent through the brown haze, and appeared to move across the flatlands like a great, ragged tidal wave promising to wash the streets and buildings clean. Bena held her arms around herself and shut her eyes, inhaling the antiseptic air from the laundry and finding, amid the dust and bleach, a trace of pine needles and damp granite. She opened her eyes and enjoyed one last sensation of vastness, then looked at her watch. Five minutes to noon. She was going to be late.

As she hurried past Savage Bros. Meats and Groceries, Bena heard a low, lazy whistle. She clutched her purse and minced along efficiently to mask her nervousness. She heard a woman's cough from the dark side alley, gentle at first, a husky wheeze, but intensifying into a wet hacking. A dollop of spit and mucus slapped against the hard-packed ground.

"Togged out now, aren't ya?"

It took a moment for her eyes to adjust to the dim light. A thin woman with a slept-on braid of red hair pressed a palm against the brick wall for balance.

"Pardon?"

The woman wiped her nose with her wrist. "Used to get togged out myself. My stepdad called me his tony little stringbean." She narrowed her eyes, as if Bena had just disagreed with her. "Nothing wrong with that, is there?"

As she became accustomed to the gloom, Bena could see the woman more plainly. Her lipstick extended beyond the borders of her mouth so that her lips hung bright and crooked.

"No," Bena said.

"Well, wish you were my mother. All my daddy's 'my little stringbean,' 'my little sassyfras,' she just couldn't have me in her house no more." The woman stamped her foot and set herself swaying. " 'No more,' she told me. 'I am putting my foot down.' Little piker."

Bena stepped into the alley to be out of the wind. She smelled the high stink of whiskey and something else she couldn't name. The woman was wearing an evening gown, of a murky green rayon. The hem and sleeves were embroidered like a Chinese coat, with swooping dragons and their fire. The gown strained at the waist and pressed her breasts flat; they protruded from the top of the bodice, gasping for air.

The woman looked at Bena's hand. "You're married," she said.

"I am."

The woman smiled. "Your husband beat you, sweetheart?"

Bena shook her head.

"I know. It's hard to remember the things that hurt so bad you could taste them. You can taste a punch, all right. I've tasted my fair share."

"Are you married?" Bena asked.

"Sure am." The woman beckoned to Bena to come closer. "To the Lord." She preened in her dragon dress. "He said He wanted us to try and look pretty for Him for a change. But it's hard to please a man. Especially one who loves so many."

"I know," Bena said. Because she did.

The woman focused a drunk eye on Bena, taking in her suit, her hat, her purse, adding her parts up in a way women do with other women.

"Poor chicken." She sounded decades older than Bena. "I don't believe you have the tiniest idea."

The woman bent down. Bena saw that the dirt was lined with soiled wrappings from Savage Bros. The paper was soaked through with the pink, watery runoff from pork chops, flank steaks, crown roasts. The alley was ripe with rotting meat, and an even more feral substance. Bena smelled the potent gaminess generated between two human bodies, that mixture of very real fluids, as well as the invisible ones like lust, love, sadness.

She watched as the woman collected the paper, ripping the cleaner parts away and stuffing the damp swatches into her bag. She straightened and leaned back over her elbow. The beginnings of her pregnant belly reared unmistakably against her dress, making the fabric seamless and shiny and wet-looking. The woman tore a piece of stained paper and pushed it into her mouth. The alley was filled with the sound of her sucking. When she was done, she spat the paper against the wall.

She turned and looked at Bena. "People always whining about how they can't survive, but I say that's windy talk. Know why?"

She stepped closer. Bena could smell the stale, putrid stink of old blood.

"Because the only thing standing between them and living"—the woman pointed at Bena with another piece of torn, stained paper— "is decency."

She pushed the paper between her dry lips, grouted with the lipstick the shade of the dragon's tongue. Bena could still hear her greedy sucking as the woman walked to the far end of the alley and disappeared.

THE CEILING FANS in Neiman's Sweet Shop were badly in need of a greasing. They creaked and groaned beneath the burden of their own senseless rotations, casting lifeless puffs of warm air back toward the dusty checkerboard linoleum and the wrought-iron chairs and tables that were, mostly, empty.

Bena adjusted her jacket and held her purse protectively in front of her chest. She counted seven other people in the restaurant, five women, a boy, and a man in a porkpie hat reading a book. $5 + 1 + 1 = 7$, the sum a traditional harbinger of luck that had always seemed like a blunt scythe to her, slight and ineffectual. But $5 - 1 + 1 = 5$ and $5 - 1 - 1 = 3$, or a 3 and a 5, March 5, Little Ted's birthday. A good sign, surely she would get the job. Or on the contrary, perhaps she should read it as a form of castigation or reproach. She should stay home with her son, not trot around a new town in a too tight suit, interviewing for a job that she and her husband didn't financially require. She thought again about Little Ted, and his odd behavior since they'd been in Pueblo. She promised, whether she got the job or not, to take him to the mountains one of these days, up to a crisper, more colorful place where the air wasn't so lugubrious.

She passed the five smartly dressed women, who hunched toward the center of their table, eating salads of lettuce and canned peaches. The boy was fat and dark. He sat alone, before a bowl of white ice cream.

Bena thought she recognized one woman as Luna Beck-Fril, president of the Zeta Study Club. The Christian club women of Pueblo were often featured in photographs in the *Chieftain*'s society pages, with captioned details of the events they'd attended ("Mrs. Beck-Fril gave a lecture on her trip to Alaska, accompanied by violin numbers played by Miss Marjorie Pierce"), as well as short quotations about their activities. The Zeta Study Club's topics, Mrs. Beck-Fril told the society reporter, ranged from "U.S. history to current topics to flowers, trees, the different nations, interesting peoples." The purpose of the Pueblo Parliamentary Club, run by Clovis Yarnell, was "to train individuals in the fundamentals of parliamentary law," while the Monday Music Club's vague and modest goal was "the promotion of things musical."

Luna Beck-Fril glanced up as Bena passed, her eyes following her while her lips continued to move in the shape of whatever story she was telling. Bena sensed her face reddening as she strode toward an empty stool at the counter. They didn't seem to harbor any animosity, these Pueblo women. It was more their lack of interest that perplexed her, as if she were far too dull a newcomer for them to even be curious about.

Bena brushed the dust off a stool. A waitress approached her and wiped a sour cloth across the square foot of counter that appeared, by virtue of her having claimed a stool, to belong to Bena. Overhead, the fans squeaked.

"Get you something, miss?" The woman gestured to the chalkboard behind her. She was dark-skinned, and wore her black hair pinned up beneath a net. Her body was thin in the taut, stark manner of a suspension bridge.

"Daly Specials (12¢)," the board read. "Foo Huey Yung Dan (Ham Omlet), Eggs a la Diablo, Salt Herring Plate, Noodles with Meat, Cream Fritters, Oyster Pattys."

The clock beside the board was broken, frozen at ten after four, the second hand on the nine. Two-four-nine. $2 \times 4 \times 9 = 72$, and $7 - 2 = 5$: again, the day in March on which Little Ted was born.

Bena smiled. "A tea with lemon will be fine."

"You eating?"

"No, thank you. I had a late breakfast."

"Sure you don't want to try the herring?" she asked.

The woman's left iris was scarred over with a dense paraffin-looking substance. Her eye seemed fixed on an object behind Bena instead of Bena herself.

"Just came in from New Orleans," the woman continued. "Before that New York. Before that, who knows. Iceland."

"Thanks," Bena declined. "I'm from Minnesota. I've had my fair share of herring."

Bena watched the woman as she cut the meagerest slice of lemon from a petrified half she had pulled from the ice chest. She clattered the tea utensils together with a carelessness Bena was certain would not have been applied to the making of the precious herring plate, had she succumbed to ordering it.

Bena looked at her watch. Ten minutes past twelve. She turned to see Luna Beck-Fril and her friends lay coins next to their plates of half-eaten food and leave.

A door opened and shut in the far reaches of the café.

"Didn't order the herring, did you?"

A plump man emerged from the water closet, still pulling up his suspenders. He approached the counter and pushed a wide hand toward the woman preparing Bena's tea.

She ignored him while she finished her task but gave one of his fingers a quick, friendly tug before walking the length of the counter toward Bena.

The man trained a flop of oiled hair back along the curve of his watermelon skull. "Miss Aurelita Trujillo tries to pawn that herring off on those who don't know better. We call it our 'Welcome to Pueblo' delicacy. Anyone who can suffer through it deserves the respect afforded the longest-standing native."

He stuck out his hand. "Cecil Belsen." His palm was slick with hair pomade.

"Sorry I'm late," Bena apologized.

"Late?" Cecil looked at his watch. "Most folks I know show up when they feel like it. Always on time, that way."

Cecil slung his dough body onto a stool that shifted precipitously at first, then grew accustomed to its burden, bearing it stoically.

"Oysters," he called out to Aurelita. "And a ginger beer."

"Unusual to get oysters out this way, isn't it?" Bena asked.

"With the exception of a booming prostitution business, I'd say it's one of the greatest benefits of living near a railway crossroads." Cecil's grin revealed a cluster of thick, boxy teeth. "This town may seem like a bag of dusty peanuts to a northerner, but we're right between New Orleans and Los Angeles. A lot of goods fall off those boxcars along the way—ladies, oysters, what have you. It was those what-have-yous that made Prohibition bearable."

Aurelita laid a paper napkin in front of Cecil, which he tucked into his yellowed shirt collar, and a fork, knife, and spoon. He pushed the tines of the fork down, over and over, causing the handle to kick up in the air and make a noise like a fly caught between a screen and a windowpane.

"So," he said to Bena, "let's take a look at those clips of yours."

She worked a manila folder out of her purse and opened it on the counter. Inside was a haphazard collection of newspaper columns, short, long, L-shaped. At the top of the inner right side she had pasted the masthead of *The Minnesota Daily*.

Cecil extracted a few columns and arranged them side by side on the counter. "Alpha Omega Sorority Gets New Porch for Summer." "Ladies' Golf Team Places in Minneapolis Intramural Tournament." "*Ulysses*: Not a Pool-side Page-Turner."

"Read *Ulysses*, eh?"

"Not entirely." She and the other girls in her sorority house had been sorely disappointed by the so-called pornographic novel. They'd read it aloud to one another after dinner in the parlor until it became too boring even to knit to. They returned to the usual literary sources of erotica, books like *The Summer of Mr. Hunter* and *A Kiss on Kilimanjaro*, stories that caused the breath to quicken and the knitting needles to clack furiously.

He smiled at her. "Good. I hate it when a lady's better-read."

Aurelita returned with a brown bottle of ginger beer and an oval plate of oyster patties. Cecil spread great, grooved flourishes of mayonnaise on each patty. He gestured to the plate, offering Bena his fork. She shook her head.

"Hot, but tasty."

"I'm not much of one for oysters."

"Not much of one for much." Aurelita returned with a glass of water neither of them had asked for. She set it between them.

"I'm trying to hire this gal, if you don't mind."

"I don't mind, long as you explain to her that there's a minimum." She examined Bena. "That'll be fun for you," she observed.

"What?" Bena asked.

Aurelita paused. "Working."

"Careful," Cecil warned.

Aurelita pointed to the sign behind her head. "There's a five-cent minimum, like it says. So far she's only spent two cents."

"I'll buy her a piece of pie. How's that?"

Aurelita looked at Bena, her milky iris fixed over Bena's shoulder. "Don't imagine you're much of one for pie, are you?" she said. "You ladies don't tend to like pie."

"I like pie just fine," Bena said. She wanted to say, "I'm not one of those ladies," but to someone like Aurelita, she guessed she was.

Aurelita stalked back to the soda fountain and began to clean the pipes with her rag.

"Don't let Aurelita Trujillo bother you," Cecil advised. "She's a gal to whom life's been less than kind." He gazed after her toiling form, then shoved another large piece of oyster patty into his mouth.

"These are some fine clips. You ever work at a real paper?"

"Just the university paper."

He cast worried glances over his shoulder toward the dark boy.

"Well, it's evident you can do the work." Cecil wiped his face with his napkin, balled it up, and threw it onto the plate, empty now except for a lettuce leaf and a drab pickle. Aurelita delivered a mug of coffee and a piece of pie, which she pushed in Bena's direction along the counter. This pie was of an indistinguishable variety, with a brilliant red center and an anemic crust.

"About the work," Cecil said, filling his mug to the brim with cream. "It's not usual for us to hire women at the *Chieftain*, but what with the Depression and our inability to pay people, we've been forced to take on quite a few women volunteers lately. Just to do some extra proofreading and to keep the office running smoothly. Are you familiar with *Silk Stockings*?"

"Not really."

"*Silk Stockings* is the name of a romance novel in weekly installments, written by our very own Lara Weems Humphrey. Unfortunately, Lara will be taking a six-month leave of absence for the purpose of childbearing."

"I'm afraid I'm not very skilled in the area of romance stories."

"Too busy reading *Ulysses*, right?" Cecil chuckled. "No, we'll leave *Silk Stockings* to Lara. I was thinking of replacing her column with a real look into the civic life of our Pueblo ladies. The women here are an active bunch. Fourteen clubs in all. What I've envisioned is a weekly profile on either a particular woman or a particular club. Advice on fine Christian living, communicated through the real-life examples of some of our more upstanding citizens."

The creaking of the fans overhead grew louder. Behind her, Bena heard a crash. She turned to see the boy writhing on the ground, his shapeless limbs quivering violently. No one rushed to help him. He emitted grunts of despair that rejected the polite artifice of words in favor of something more expressive and true. Sitting in the corner, the man wearing the porkpie hat raised his book higher to shield himself from the unpleasantness.

Cecil planted his nose in his mug and took shallow, rapid-fire gulps. Aurelita Trujillo worked away at her pipes, scraping the old syrup from the metal with a butter knife. No one, it appeared, intended to respond in any way.

Bena placed her napkin on the counter and moved off her stool to go to the boy.

Cecil put out his arm. "Don't," he said firmly.

She stared at the arm blocking her way.

"It's none of your business," Cecil said, just as firmly, with a glance toward Aurelita that implied it was her business and no one else's. He caught her attention and made a quick writing motion in the air.

Out on the street, Cecil offered Bena his hand. "You can start on Monday."

In the gritty midday light Cecil looked much older than he had in the shadows of the Sweet Shop, his cheeks traced with an elaborate circuitry of wrinkles. He turned to make his way toward the *Chieftain* offices, then stopped.

"You know," he said, "it's a difficult line to walk."

"What is?"

Cecil shaded his eyes, presumably from the sun. It occurred to Bena that he might be hiding his expression from her.

"It's wonderful to want to help people, especially nowadays. But sometimes you help people best just by letting them be."

Bena regarded him curiously. "Of course."

Cecil gave her a salute and then strode, pigeon-toed, toward the Arkansas River bridge.

Bena started home up the empty sidewalk, her purse over her head to shield her against the afternoon sun. She was alone on the street, save for the retreating figure of Cecil behind her. It was unnerving but also peaceful. The streets in Pueblo were forgiving, private places. She thought about Little Ted for the first time in nearly an hour, and the memory of him made her skin tight over her forehead. She scolded herself under her breath—she wasn't certain for what crime or failure— and walked as rapidly as her skirt would allow.

Passing the alley that ran alongside Buck's Silo, she heard hiccuping and the soothing sounds of a man's voice. She peered into the shadows and saw the woman in the green dress again, hunched beneath the arm of a tall man in a cowboy hat. He was helping her into a dark doorway, and Bena could hear the low, rhythmic roll of her sobbing.

She turned away and held her breath as she did whenever she intersected the path of something unlucky—a blind child, a bird with a broken wing, a single shoe by the roadside.

THE JONSSENS' rented blue Victorian was located on a stretch of oak-shaded road called North Grand, so named for the opulent mansions of umber sandstone erected by mining families (Baxter, Thatcher, Haas) that occupied the avenue's northwest rise.

The house, at 25 North Grand (a number with little resonance except that it was Bena's current age), was built in 1899 by Anson Sparks, an accounts executive for the Santa Fe line, and thirty years later, upon his death, divided into two furnished apartments—all this learned from Mrs. Bev Sloat at the rental properties agency. Bena, Ted, and the baby lived on the parlor floor, which featured the varying heights of the three Sparks children (Grace, Francis, Minnie) penciled on the back of the pantry door, a bricked-in dumbwaiter shaft, and a defunct intercom system between the now disassociated floors. The parlor apartment was inhabited by Louise Sparks after her husband's death, and was still decorated with the glum memorabilia that widows hoard: a single wedding photograph, outdated issues of *Collier's* sparsely arranged on a coffee table, candy dishes, porcelain shepherdess figurines, a set of etched Venetian punch glasses. Bena had attempted to box and bury the most offensive of the knickknacks, but no amount of stashing and airing could relieve the lingering, stale feeling of a dead person's house.

Bena dropped her purse in the hall and ran upstairs to Florence's apartment. Little Ted was awake in his portable bassinet, which Florence had propped on the kitchen table while she drank iced tea and organized photos.

"Slept like an angel," Florence said. She showed Bena a photo of herself at the age of twelve, astride a white pony. She had been well developed for her age but unevenly so; her large breasts strained against her beaded leotard, while her legs dangled in the pony's silver stirrups, spidery and awkward.

Bena picked the baby up and immediately her eyes began to water, as if he were a big white onion. Her chest splayed and made more room for the big heart she had for him, so much bigger now that she'd agreed to spend her afternoons away from him.

Maybe she didn't want a job. Maybe she wanted to stay home with Little Ted because her watery, needy body told her to. She wanted to be present while his bones knit themselves long and his face grew smart and lively. She had created an unfixable mess on the bathroom door jamb, and so decided to scratch his measurements on the pantry door below Grace's and Francis's and Minnie's leapfrogging climbs (between 2/4/10 and 8/15/12, Grace gained five inches over Minnie. Bena prayed they wouldn't live in Pueblo long enough for Little Ted to beat all three Sparks girls, to notch him above the highest-climbing sister (Grace, five feet, six inches, 11/4/14).

Bena shifted his bulk in her arms. He was heavy for only eleven and a half weeks old. Already he'd gained more than five pounds since birth, so that he was a little less than twice his original weight. His legs and arms were hard and sausagey. His fatness made it difficult for him to move. He was often limp when she picked him up, as if he feared that any abrupt motion might rupture his tender casing.

Bena carried him downstairs and onto the porch for some air. He gummed her suit, leaving wet mouth marks on the pink wool. She unbuttoned her blouse as she went to retrieve the paper from the side-walk. Ted hadn't bothered to pick it up that morning, and she'd left it there on her way to meet Cecil, fearing she was late. She stooped and heard her skirt rip.

Cursing, she dropped onto the front steps, and her broken skirt gaped open to reveal her loose belly, her white underthings. The baby made her careless with her body. It had been so stretched and ripped, it leaked so readily that it seemed unable to live inside clothes. Bena presented Little Ted with a nipple. Her breasts grew warm and useful as he emptied them.

She flipped the paper open over her knees.

"Bonnie and Clyde Shot Dead in Gibsland, LA."

She thought that she could recognize the crocodile shoes in the photograph of the corpse lying beneath a shade tree—head covered with a lawman's coat, the badge pinned to the breast pocket—but she couldn't be certain. A circle of sheriff's deputies gazed at Bonnie's bare ankles and riding-up dress from a respectful or fearful distance.

Bena stared at the photo. She could hear the wind in it, damp, bayou-heavy. She looked out to the plains and let the vast emptiness roll over her and buoy her with its bleak possibilities.

A breeze, bold and warm, caught the edge of the newspaper and spun through the pages. Bena's eye snagged on a curious headline: "Buffalo Mass Suicide at Crow Junction." She pressed her hand down to hold the pages still.

The article detailed the death of a herd of buffalo owned by a man named Harlan Baxter. Though Bena knew nothing of them, Harlan Baxter's buffalo had attained mythic stature around Pueblo, the article said. They had long black hair bleached a rusty tea color at the ends. They had black noses, and nostrils large enough to accommodate a lady's fist. They were fossils of another time and they lived as such, their eyes moony and lost, looking south toward the Spanish Peaks and the weather that heaped itself on those two blunt spires, menacing clouds that appeared like the slow advance of the next ice age.

Mr. Baxter had constructed a small kiosk beside the road to his ranch, and hired a Ute woman to sell Indian frybread and beaded belts and Pe-ru-na Original Spring Tonic. Next to the kiosk was a series of large wooden signs. "See the Original Inhabitants of the Plains." "Extinct Species Brought Back from the Dead." "The Old West—Only a Penny—Petting Zoo—Two Miles Ahead." Mostly the buffalo roamed free on the mesa, but Mr. Baxter always roped two or three of them at feeding time, and put them in a corral for visitors to touch if they dared.

"Buffalo Mass Suicide" proposed not one theory but many. They were the slight, contradictory premises, Bena thought, that mystification produces. It was a poacher (arrested that day a few miles from Mr. Baxter's ranch) blowing a deer whistle who spooked the buffalo. It was the backfire of a hay truck. It was the sound of the Civilian Conservation Corps dynamiting rock to make a new road between Rye and San Isabel. It was the full moon. It was the Ute woman, bitter at how Mr. Baxter underpaid her for her efforts at the kiosk, who had sent the ghosts of her ancestors to chase the buffalo over the same cliff the Ute had chased buffalo over for centuries.

The most unlikely yet evocative explanation was provided by a rancher named Henry "Red" Hart Grissom. A grainy photo showed a man in a cowboy hat. His features were blackened beneath the underside of his hat, his bearded chin the only part of him peeking out to the sun. He hung on to the corners of his pocket with his thumbs. The tops of the last two fingers on his right hand were missing. This "Red" Grissom was looking for arrowheads on his lunch break just a quarter-mile north when the incident had occurred. He claimed it was the most beautiful act of nature he'd ever witnessed, these burly, wingless animals flinging themselves into the blue, as if they aimed to fly.

3. THE WEDDING TENT

Despite the scarcity of water for necessities like bathing and dishes, Ted had decided to dig a trout pond in the backyard. He would raise steelheads, *Salmo gairdnerii*.

"I'd rather forgo a bath or two," he'd declared one night, a good night, the two of them sitting on the front porch watching the moon emerge like a jaundiced mushroom from the edge of the plains. "I'd rather eat off the same dirty dinner plate, I'd rather wear the same pair of socks day after day."

Bena ran a hand over his blond head. He had the soft-haired feel of a new chick, as long as her fingers stayed clear of the smooth and lifting-off scar behind his ear. She loved him most when he tossed his careful doctor self aside and indulged in bold, excessive thinking.

Ted had a fondness for fish. He still kept a pond full of orange koi at his family's summer cottage in Door County, their regal bodies motionless in the water. She'd seen him hold a fish in his two hands as if it were a vital organ he'd just pulled from his own abdomen, a glistening liver, a pancreas, a kidney.

He'd mapped out the perimeter of the pond with a circle of paint stirrers plunged into the ground and connected with twine. He'd return home from the clinic every evening, his tie loosened and the cold smell of antiseptic evaporating from his forearms, stir himself a gimlet, and gaze from the back porch like a farmer surveying his recently hoed fields and envisioning the rich, husky grains that would soon cast twilight shadows long enough to touch his feet. Bena expressed concern about how Florence would respond when she saw that Ted had designs on her rose garden, but Ted replied, reasonably, that the current climatic trend did not support such fragile horticultural indulgences, as Florence's failed attempts certainly illustrated. But Bena herself was unnerved by the developments in the backyard. There was something sinister about the shape created by the twine and stirrers, a wide rectangle evoking the ravenous, barren quality of a grave.

Besides, no fish could survive in this climate. Rainbow trout and brown carp floated on the Arkansas like lost hats, the water too shallow and tepid and polluted to permit much of anything save disease to flourish. But Bena suffered her husband's delusions gladly, hoping that the moment when he grasped the futility of his vision would coincide with a job offer from a clinic in Minnesota, Wisconsin, Michigan, a place where fish and people thrived in easy abundance.

IN CELEBRATION of Bena's new position at the *Chieftain*, Ted proposed a trip to Colorado Springs and a drive to the top of Pikes Peak, the popular tourist destination that jutted white-topped from the clutter of mountains due northwest of Pueblo.

Ted left the clinic early on Friday so they could arrive in Colorado Springs in time for a late dinner. He'd made reservations for them at the grand if wilting Edgemoor Hotel, a stately resort that negotiated the difference between Old World and New with its Tudor architecture and great split-log balconies. Inside, bear rugs sprawled beside Persians, and silver candelabra competed with elk antlers. The interior belied a hyocrisy that afflicted western settlers out to make their fortunes; they thirsted for new territory with new rules, while aching, in some way, to replicate the familiar trappings of wealth and success they'd been so eager to escape.

Bena and Ted arrived at the Edgemoor at seven o'clock, after a pleasant drive north along the Front Range Highway. The clerk gave them a brass key to room 331, and Ted teasingly asked Bena whether she approved. Bena said yes, she approved. She spared the clerk a tally of her reasons: because $3 \times 3 \times 1 = 9$, her father's favorite iron, and because $3 + 3 + 1 = 7$, the month of her birth. She could also, with a little manipulation and oversight, locate the number 13 (reversing the room number and dropping a 3)—a poetic allowance, which she was accustomed to when it suited her.

They dressed for dinner in their spacious, if somewhat shabby, suite of rooms, then left Little Ted in the care of the concierge's wife, a Mrs. Dubrowski, whose thin face and anxious insistence to watch the baby while they dined led them both to assume she was barren. They sat in a dark wood booth in the Club Room and ate roast beef and Yorkshire pudding, while the drunken expulsions of mineworkers could be heard from the adjoining pub whenever the portholed door swung open to admit a harried young waitress in search of lemons or quinine.

The next morning over breakfast, quite uncharacteristically, Little Ted refused to feed until Bena rubbed honey on her nipple. Ted, unconcerned, attributed his fussiness to gas. Bena stuck her index finger into the ceramic beehive and thrust her hand under her shirt when Mrs. Dubrowski, who worked in the dining hall at breakfast, wasn't watching.

"My sister-in-law had a picky one," Mrs. Dubrowski said, pouring more coffee into Bena's already full cup. "Wasted away to practically nothing before she got him to eat."

"Usually we can't get him to stop," Bena countered, licking her sweet finger. In fact, he'd been gaining weight so avidly that Ted had suggested she try to train him to a concise schedule. Besides, he pointed out, it would be impossible to leave him with Florence unless he had hungers they could effectively manage and predict. Bena had started to wean him from his own, bottomless appetites, but it was heartbreaking to listen to him cough and sob in his crib. When she held him he'd wet her shirt with his grabby mouth, smelling her milk under the layers of cloth. Most of the time she unbuttoned her shirt and let him find her, because his distress was too much for her to witness.

Mrs. Dubrowski had the gamey, stray-cat smell of fear and meanness on her. It was difficult to encounter so early in the morning and made it hard for Bena herself to eat. Not that the food was such a chore to refuse—warm cream, graying butter, bacon thinner than a wedding veil.

"I'm sure it's just the change of scenery," Bena said. "Poor little boy's moved a lot for being only twelve weeks old."

Mrs. Dubrowski returned from the kitchen with a plate of near-burnt griddle cakes. She put them in the center of the table and stared down at the baby in Bena's arms.

"You don't worry about him being blind, do you?"

Ted didn't even look up from his newspaper. "Nope," he said.

The nerve, Bena thought. What a dreadful, barren woman she was. Bena clenched her fingers to keep herself from jumping up and throttling Mrs. Dubrowski's wrinkled white neck. She'd had an unusual capacity for rage since she'd given birth. Just three days before, she'd fantasized about pulling the heart out of a man with her bare hands, after he nearly ran them down on his bicycle as they were crossing the street.

Mrs. Dubrowski sniffed, as if she felt sorry for this couple, blind themselves to their own baby's evident suffering.

"Just never seen a child so unresponsive. And those eyes. Such an unusual color."

"That'll change," Bena said. "No telling what color they'll be." Any color but the color they are now, she thought. Now they were the exact color of her brother Jonas's eyes, the color of smoke, of a translucent, suffocating substance. She turned Little Ted's face toward the sun that streamed in through the tall dining room windows. She was certain she saw his lids narrow, his pupils contract. Of course he wasn't blind.

Bena busied herself further with Little Ted, then feigned interest in a dry biscuit. Anything to make Mrs. Dubrowski go away.

"What're your plans here in Colorado Springs?" Mrs. Dubrowski asked. "Going to the mining museum?"

"We're going up to Pikes Peak," Bena said.

"You're not taking that baby up, are you?"

"Thought we might," Ted replied from behind his paper. Bena caught a headline on the page facing her.

"Dust Storm Claims Honeymooners Near Upton Gap."

"I'd think twice about that," Mrs. Dubrowski cautioned, clearing their untouched breakfast plates. "That kind of altitude's hard on such a tiny fellow. Besides. No telling what kind of weather you're likely to get up top." She rubbed a coarse thumb against Little Ted's fat cheek. Bena fought the urge to knock her hand away.

"It looks like a fine day to me," Ted said.

"It always does." Mrs. Dubrowski glanced at them sorrowfully over the stack of dishes.

Ted emitted a peeved grunt. Women and their darned superstitions. Upstairs in the room, however, Bena caught him packing a thin blanket from the bed into her tartan day bag, just in case the pleasant weather failed to hold through the afternoon.

Before they left, Ted asked Mrs. Dubrowski to take a picture of the Jonssen family in front of the Ford Touring Car, with their destination rising snow-tipped in the background.

"Let's have a smile from the little one," said Mrs. Dubrowski.

Bena tilted the baby toward the camera and looked up just as the flash popped.

In that moment of white, she sensed something different coursing through Little Ted's tiny muscles. His neck tensed and lifted from the crook of her elbow, his hands and feet reached as they had never yet reached for a loose strand of her hair or the bean-filled wooden rattle she waved above his crib. He shook in her arms. It seemed he would do anything to become a part of that brilliant moment, even tear himself limb from limb in his efforts to touch it.

"Cheers, Mrs. Dubrowski." Ted saluted. "Send the rangers if we're not back by nightfall."

"Silly cow," he whispered, so only Bena could hear, as he helped her into the Ford.

Bena stared into the baby's face, concerned about what would make him tremble so. But his eyes were glazed and unalarmed now, his legs and arms slack. Perhaps he had simply caught a chill, she reasoned, and wrapped him in the borrowed hotel blanket. She held him in her lap.

On their way out of town they passed a boarded-up bowling alley, a Conoco station empty except for an attendant observing his pumps, and a collection of wedding guests (gourd-shaped women and stringy, plantlike men) fanning themselves impatiently outside of Our Lady Dolores of the Piñons. A few of the men were glancing at their watches. The women were huddled in gossipy packs of threes and fours.

A few blocks later, Bena spotted a woman with her tresses wound into a fist of hair. The enthusiastic white of her dress sprang out from beneath a man's khaki overcoat. She stood crying under a stone archway that led to a park, or a garden, or a cemetery. A piebald cat rubbed its rib cage against the archway, disdainful, as cats are, of such sloppy displays of emotion. Just before Bena lost sight of her, the woman picked up a rock and hurled it at the cat, striking it squarely on the skull. Ted turned a corner, and nothing stood between them and the mountain. It was so beautiful, so captivating in the late-morning sunlight, that a person would do anything to find herself on top.

THEY WERE less than a mile from the summit. Bena was busy enjoying the vertiginous view from the passenger side. Small white crosses dotted the edge of the cliff like stitches flailing above a gaping wound.

"Drive nearer," she urged Ted, pointing to the crosses. He was hugging the far side, limiting her view. She saw a sign: "Alt. 12,536 feet."

12,536. $(5 \times 6) - (2 \times 1) - 3 = 25$, her age and their street address on North Grand; $(5 \times 2) + 6 - (3 \times 1) = 13$; and she found three sixes $(6, 5 + 1, 2 \times 3)$, 666 (in addition to its biblical notoriety) being the combination to the lock on the Duse family's boathouse door in Coeur du Lac. The altitude suggested the freedom of a new home, or the act of discovery in sailboats.

The sun had been muffled behind a line of clouds; now it burst forth from its fluffy barricades, brighter than before. Bena thrust her head out the window to sense the warmth on her face. Also to feel the wind. It was the first cool breeze she'd felt in Colorado, full of pine instead of dust, revivifying instead of sepulchral.

She heard Ted gasp. She assumed this was because he'd just been struck by the impressive view of the Front Range as the road wound toward the west and they could see snow drifting down the corrugated peaks. The car swerved and she heard the sharp sound of wood splintering. The Ford's fender struck the crosses, tossing broken bits up over the hood. They sucked past her ears like arrows, carrying with them an abrupt, soft darkness.

When she came to, Bena was propped against a boulder on the far side of the road, staring at a bloody shirt cuff. She shook her head violently to free her nostrils of the noxious fumes. It was Ted's shirt cuff, and it led to a similarly bloodied hand holding a glass vial of smelling salts.

She looked around wildly for Little Ted.

"He's fine," Ted told her. "You hit your head on the car window. Knocked yourself out for a second."

He smoothed her hair. Bena threw a hand to her face, searching for holes, gashes, pieces missing. He guided her finger to the hot knob on her head, then pulled down the skin below her eyes with his thumb and peered into her pupils.

"You're fine," he said. He rose efficiently from his squatting position and hurried to the car hood.

"I'm sorry," Bena called weakly, trying to decide whether or not she could stand. "I shouldn't have asked you to drive so close."

Bena stared at the wreckage of white wood next to the car. If this wasn't a bad omen, she thought. They would have to get in touch with the town hall in Colorado Springs, make arrangements to have the crosses replaced. She picked up a cross lying near her.

"In memory of Warren," the carved words read. "From his loving parents."

Bena hauled herself to a standing position. A sizable splinter of wood was lodged in her palm. She bit at the wood with her teeth as she walked unsteadily toward the car.

Ted fussed over the baby, still wrapped in the hotel blanket. In this bright daylight, so much closer to the sun, the blanket appeared pathetically shoddy, its wool rusted as if it had been tied around a spare tire in a car trunk.

Nothing held up to close inspection, Bena reflected; the whole world was in a steady state of decline. Their hotel room, dingy even at night, was desperately forlorn when exposed to the scrutiny of daylight, the carpet discolored and punctuated with cigarette burns, the wallpaper water-stained, the linens gray and transparent, incapable, even, of blotting out the mattress ticking. And here, as she looked out over the ocean of plains that used to be swelling with wheat stalks and now was nothing but desert, the landscape seemed to be responding in kind. Or predicting. Dust to dust, it said, until even the dust was washed away by the relentless winds. Rock to rock to rock. Volatile gases. And then, nothing. Not that this was a depressing thought. On the contrary. It could give one a sense of freedom.

She smiled to herself as she wove toward Ted and the baby. She held her arms out and moved along the contours of the breeze.

When she saw the baby, the air abandoned her and she pitched down into a new kind of blackness. She rushed to the car. Little Ted's face was covered with blood, some of it dry and browning on his neck, but some of it brilliant and ruby-colored and new.

"It's nothing," Ted stated. "Just a nosebleed, Bena."

"*Just* a nosebleed?"

"The altitude," he explained.

She collected Little Ted and thrust her face into his sticky neck. He smelled of milk and metal. With her hand she sought out the firm thrumming of his heart. It calmed her to count his steady punch and tick.

"The bleeding's stopped," Ted offered, "but we ought to get him down."

Bena licked a finger and tried to rub the dried blood from Little Ted's cheek. He took her finger between his lips. She offered him a nipple, but he seemed happier feeding on the blood under her fingernail.

Ted studied the narrow road ahead.

"We're not so far from the top."

"As if we'd be able to enjoy the view now!" Bena looked out over the plains, at the miniaturized town of Colorado Springs.

Ted gestured calmly to the thin curve of asphalt leading upward. "I don't think there's any way to turn the car around."

He was right. Even if they tried to maneuver the car downhill, they risked backing off the edge, or getting hit by someone coming around from above.

"I guess we'll just wait here for you." She put her nose to the baby's head, as if she might smell the broken vein under his thin skull, leaking blood until his face became bruised with it. But she smelled nothing. He was as calm and unaffected as ever. Ted was right. Ted was a doctor. The baby was fine.

Ted fanned his jacket out on the far shoulder, away from the white crosses. Just as Bena was settling herself on the jacket, they heard a car downshifting around the steep turn above. A bottle-green Baker Steam grumbled to a pause next to the Ford. Its license plate read 0912D. September 12 was the date of her mother's birth, in the Norwegian coastal town of Høne. Most of the time 9s and 12s in collaboration had been good to her, but not dependably so. More frequently she was disappointed when 9s and 12s collided, as when she took the 9:12 train from St. Paul to Chicago, only to sit next to a woman who discovered she'd lost the diamond from her engagement ring, and to become ill halfway to Chicago and spend the remainder of the trip with her face against the cold, rumbling metal floor in the WC. Bena had also been pickpocketed the next day while peering through the stationary binoculars on the shores of Lake Michigan, another misfortune she attributed to the 9:12 train to Chicago.

"Car troubles?" a man asked. He balanced a cigar on the windowsill and flicked the ash into the oncoming breeze.

"No. Thanks for asking." Ted turned back to Bena.

The man continued to stare, smoking his cigar.

"Wouldn't recommend parking there. People come speeding down this stretch here, and they're looking at the sky, the mountains, everything but the road."

"We're just moving on," Ted replied curtly. He didn't take kindly to assistance from strangers. In instances of distress, he preferred to be the one doling out the help.

The man watched while Ted walked to the car, alone.

"You're not leaving the wife there, I hope," the stranger said.

Ted failed to contain his irritation. "As a matter of fact, I am."

The man tossed his wet cigar into the middle of the road and stepped out onto the packed dirt. He was short, probably only five-foot-six, and powerfully round. He fixed Ted from beneath a pair of elegant gray eyebrows. Bena thought he must pluck them.

"I don't mean to make trouble," he said. "There's a storm moving in from the north. You can't see it from this side of the peak, but I promise you it'll be hailing here in less than ten minutes." He looked at Bena's bare legs sprawled across the jacket.

"Sorry to be curt," Ted said. "The altitude's not suiting our son so well. I was just going to turn my car around at the top so we can get him back to the flats as soon as possible."

The man pulled a cigar from his pocket. He offered it to Ted.

"No?" the man asked. "I got a whole box and no one to smoke them."

"No, thank you."

He opened a lighter and held it to the tip of his cigar. The wind fanned the flame, stretching it long and thin so that it almost reached back to lick his mustache. He walked to the mess of splintered crosses, surveying them with the detachment of a policeman looking over the dead, crooked body of yet another unfortunate stranger. A shame, but not one that touched him personally.

He picked up a broken cross, the one dedicated "in memory of Warren, from his loving parents."

"What happened here?" he inquired.

"When I saw my little boy was bleeding, I panicked. I wasn't watching the road."

"We have every intention of paying to have them replaced," Bena added.

The man took a cursory look at the cross and then hurled it off the cliff. He watched it spin out like a loose propeller caught on a lengthy updraft before it plunged down and out of sight.

"Wouldn't bother," the man said, wiping his hands on his pants. "Do people better to forget about this kind of tragedy."

He walked toward Ted and stuck out a hand. "Horace Gast."

"Ted Jonssen."

"Pleasure. Now perhaps you won't be offended if I offer to escort your family to the bottom of this hill while you turn your car around."

Ted looked at the man and the man's beautiful green car, weighing the chances that despite his evident wealth and apparent kindness he could still be a thief, murderer, kidnapper.

"We'd be much obliged," he said, then helped Bena and Little Ted into the front seat of the Baker Steam.

"How far to the summit?" he asked.

Mr. Gast took a thoughtful puff.

"Near a half-mile. Not far. You'll be right behind us."

He waited until Ted started the car. They both pulled away and disappeared quickly around opposing curves.

Mr. Gast glanced at Bena. His lively blue eyes played around her face and throat, flickered over her breasts, the swell of her belly. She felt she'd been swum around by a school of bright fish.

Little Ted started crying. Bena lifted him worriedly, searching for further traces of bleeding. To her cautious relief, he appeared fine. She offered him a nipple and he was quiet, his eyes wide and blank as he sucked. She had grown defiantly unconcerned about who saw her bare breasts, no matter if they were strangers or even her own father, because this part of her body was no more modesty-provoking to her than elbows or earlobes. Mr. Gast, however, made her recall the body-shyness of the days when her potential nudity could be only in the service of sex. She hunched her shoulder forward to protect her motherly nakedness from view.

Mr. Gast reached out the window to adjust his side mirror, and Bena noticed he was wearing a gun, strapped high around his broad middle.

"You carry a gun."

"Can't be too careful these days," he said. "My friend Claude Boettscher up in Denver had his boy kidnapped. Had to pay sixty thousand dollars to get the kid back. Paid more than the real value, ask my opinion." Mr. Gast laughed to himself. Then he became quite serious. "I didn't even ask your name."

"Bena," she replied, straightening her spine. The leather upholstery invited her to slouch, to loosen every muscle in her body. So did Mr. Gast. He was not a typically attractive man, but he possessed an air of droit de seigneur that no doubt made him attractive to some women. Bena couldn't decide whether she was one of those women or not.

"Are you Swedish?"

"Norwegian."

"A Norwegian girl, then," he replied. "I should have known. You have Norwegian hips. But not ankles, thank the Lord."

Bena was stupefied. "Pardon?"

He regarded her innocently. "You'd fault an old man for noticing your lovely hips?"

"It seems a little impertinent."

"Impertinence is a virtue at my age," Mr. Gast replied. "I thank you for the compliment." He undid his bow tie with one hand as the other coaxed the Baker Steam around the tight curves.

"So. On to more conventional veins of small talk, to avoid any more veiled charges of lechery from the young lady. You folks from Colorado Springs?"

"Pueblo."

"Ah. A hellhole if ever there was one. Folks here and Denver call it 'Pee-yew-eblo.' " Mr. Gast smiled, the cigar still gripped between his teeth. He closed his lips, too full and red for a man his age, around the thick wet tip of the cigar. "And what brought you to Pueblo?" he persisted.

"Ted"—Bena pointed upward, to indicate the man on the mountaintop far above them—"is a doctor. He was supposed to join his uncle's clinic in Green Bay, but what with the Depression—"

Mr. Gast threw a hand up. "Please. If I am not allowed to refer to your lovely hips, then you are not permitted to invoke the grim financial circumstances which strangle us at present." The lips drew back again, making a weak stab at cheerfulness. But he was visibly riled. "It's Saturday, and I'm enjoying my cigar in the company of a lovely woman. Let us not spoil the few good times that remain to us."

Little Ted made wormy wriggles in Bena's lap, as if to convey his dislike of Mr. Gast.

"And yourself?" he continued, trying to restore lightness. "Joined any of Pueblo's famous ladies' clubs?"

"I'm a journalist," Bena replied. "I begin Monday at the *Chieftain*." She touched the water-tower charm on her bracelet.

"*That* old rag," he said.

"I think it's a fine paper."

"Without a doubt it is unparalleled as a fire-starter, or a wrapper of Christmas ornaments."

Pompous, insufferable man. "And what do you do, if I might inquire?"

"I own things. Let's say, for simplicity's sake, a man of business."

"And I'm assuming, from your aversion to the term, that your manhood has been rather hard hit during this Depression of ours."

Mr. Gast slammed on the brakes. He pulled hungrily at his cigar and threw an arm over the back of the seat so that his hand rested near her neck. He might strike her or touch her cheek with a squat finger. Either was possible. Mr. Gast pulsed with an animal irregularity, his blood moving in accordance with instincts different from her own.

But neither occurred. He grunted to himself, having evidently come to some conclusion about her he felt disinclined to share, and proceeded down the mountain.

The road widened. They were near the flats now. Cows followed their progress moonily from the middle of a brown field. Their coats were dreary and dust-filled, their udders thin and slack, withered like unpicked clusters of grapes.

Mr. Gast reached into the leather bag on the seat between them and pulled out a silver flask the size of a cobblestone. He took a grand swig. He didn't offer any to Bena.

The clouds rolled over the top of Pikes Peak and snuffed out the sun. Bena squinted for traces of Ted but detected no movement along the mountain's rounded switchbacks. She shifted Little Ted from her right breast to her left. His lips made a loud, suctioning sound when she unlatched him from her skin. She blushed, fearful that the banal acts of her mothering might register as appalling with Mr. Gast. To judge from his apparent wealth and relentlessly male demeanor, he had probably never seen a woman nursing or heard the vital suck and pop of a being that was little more than an assemblage of loud, insistent bodily functions.

"I was supposed to go to a wedding this morning," Mr. Gast offered, apropos of nothing.

"Really?" She anxiously eyed the road.

"A young woman, about your age. I've known her since she was a girl."

They reached the intersection at the bottom of the mountain where the summit road met with the road back to Colorado Springs. Mr. Gast pulled over and turned off the engine. He lit the end of his half-smoked cigar, which had extinguished itself. The car filled with a sweet, charred smell, a burn upon a burn.

"About a year ago she became involved with one of her father's friends. A married man. It may sound craven to a lady such as yourself, but I don't have a problem with that. Young women and powerful men have been doing it for centuries." He paused. "But then she got herself in a way."

He took another long swig from the flask.

"Pregnant," Bena clarified.

"Now, I intervene. I find her a young man, decently handsome, clever enough. I offer him a position with my bank in exchange for being a decent husband and willing father."

"How thoroughly romantic."

"Life, my dear, is not about romance. The sooner you learn that, the less of a disappointment yours will prove to be."

Bena turned toward the window and made a face to the glass. In her experience, men were more romantic than women, if romantic meant pursuing unsuitable partners for hopeless periods of time. Her sorority sisters were never heartbroken for longer than half a week. Women didn't have time to pine away for years, what with the threat of old age and spinsterhood looming over their pale young heads. They married men for all sorts of reasons that had nothing to do with romance or love. Women could be some of the least romantic creatures she knew.

"The wedding had to happen with haste, for reasons I need not explain," Mr. Gast went on. "And the girl went along with it, all the time believing that the father of her child was going to step in at the last moment, tell her he loved her, planned to leave his wife, et cetera. She believed this would occur, even until the hour before the ceremony, whereupon she threw herself at this man—"

"He was at the wedding?"

"He's a friend of the family. She threw herself at this man, begging him to do what was in his heart."

"And?"

"And what? It was an utterly naive demand."

"What's naive about it?"

Mr. Gast raised the flask above his lips, so that Bena could watch the last few drops of yellow liquid fall into his mouth. They ricocheted between his teeth making dense, oil-drum noises.

It had begun to hail.

"Because if she'd understood anything about the world," Mr. Gast explained loudly, "she'd have known that he was doing precisely that."

The storm increased its ferocity until it became a single, uninterrupted roar. Bena pressed Little Ted's head against her stomach to protect his ears.

"It couldn't just rain," Mr. Gast said.

"What?" Bena couldn't hear him.

"All these people begging for something to fall from the sky." He pointed a new cigar at her. "Need to be careful what you wish for."

He tilted his head back and closed his eyes. Bena searched for signs of Ted, hoping he wasn't trying to navigate those switchbacks in the hail. She looked again at Mr. Gast and his oddly compelling lips, which she had to fight herself from touching.

What if Ted died.

What if the hail stopped, and the sun came out as it always did, and she and Mr. Gast were just sitting and sitting. Eventually, it would be clear that something had gone terribly wrong. They might drive back and find the guardrail sprung like a prison door. The deep tire tracks in the shoulder mud, filled with shrinking balls of ice. The glint of twisted metal and broken glass in the newly emerged sun. Maybe a head slumped in an unnatural way, indicating that something crucial had snapped. Mr. Gast, being a polite man of evident appetites, would take this advantage in lecherous and gentlemanly fashion at once, hold her close and rub his palm between her shoulder blades as she sobbed or stared numbly at the wreckage. Perhaps, in her distraught state, she might raise her face to find him offering his pillowy lips to muffle her sorrow.

Young women and powerful men have been doing it for centuries.

She examined Mr. Gast as he rested, oblivious to her minute attentions.

He was not a handsome man.

His gray hair, what remained, circling the bottom half of his skull like a dust ruffle, was heavily pomaded. His head left a permanent dark stain on the head rest. His nose was just this side of bulbous, veering toward the marbled red of a drunk's beacon. Possibly he was a drunk. And a married one, from the looks of the platinum wedding band that cinched the pouch of skin below his knuckle. She wondered where his wife was, whether she was back at the church, or not invited to the wedding, or dead.

The hail began to subside, the individual ping-ping-pings distinguishing themselves from the thunder on the roof. The cows in the pasture next to the road were carving wild circles, bucking their hind legs skyward at crazy angles.

The road, the pasture, the long-dry irrigation ditch were covered with hailstones. The sun emerged from behind a retreating fringe of black storm cloud. It went to work melting all traces of its disappearance, eroding the translucent, sky-born rocks to puddles. Dust to dust, stone to water.

Mr. Gast woke up to the new sound of nothing.

He had a startled, caged look about him as he opened the car door and stepped onto the gravel. He did a series of deep knee bends and toe touches, then raised his arms over his head and waved them, up-down, up-down.

Bena heard the sound of downshifting and the Ford's familiar high, disgruntled whine. Ted pulled up alongside them. The front windshield had cracked even further: the fracture initiated by the crow had traveled another four inches after its pelting with hailstones.

"Jesus!" Ted got out of the Ford. "Big as tennis balls up there! Never seen anything like it."

"Hailstone do that?" Mr. Gast gestured toward the crack in the windshield.

"No." Ted didn't elaborate. He walked around to the back door and wrestled with something slumped across the seat. He reappeared cradling a black bundle in his arms. "Look what I found up top," he said.

Bena wrapped the blanket around Little Ted, still tugging rapaciously on her left breast, and stepped out of the Baker Steam.

The bundle trembled furiously. It unfolded itself in a single slithery motion, metamorphosing into a recognizable shape. It was a dog.

Mr. Gast gave the animal a distasteful once-over. "A mutt. And blind. That's why they left it up there."

"Who?" Bena came closer now, intrigued. The dog stared at her dead-on, its wet ears pricked up, tracking her approach.

"Indians," Mr. Gast replied. "Utes. Those savages that aren't too drunk to remember know Pikes Peak is where they abandoned their lame young. Say it's a sacred place."

"Their children?"

"Used to be," Mr. Gast said. "Now they just leave the more inconvenient of their animals there to rot."

Bena looked toward the mountain, its peak intermittently visible between the thinning clouds. It seemed a horribly lonely place to waste away to bone.

They stood in silence. There was nothing but the low wind to be heard, and the cows moaning to one another in the parched field.

"Well," Mr. Gast said, initiating his departure, "time I got myself back." He didn't say to where. He didn't seem like a man who had anyplace to go.

"Pleasure," he said, and held out his hand.

"Likewise," Ted replied. "And I apologize for my initial rudeness."

"Not to worry, Dr. Jonssen. I understand you're the man accustomed to administering the help." His smile left it unclear whether he was merely making an observation, or offering a light bit of criticism. "And don't let those Utes catch you with that dog. They'll put a curse on you to last five lifetimes."

Ted smiled. "You speak to a man of science, sir."

"Then you should know, as a man of science, that there are some things you don't tinker with."

"We hope to see you again," Bena said. "Next time we come to Colorado Springs."

Mr. Gast kicked up the brim of a pretend hat with two stumpy fingers. He got into his car and drove away.

Bena and Ted watched him, not speaking. Bena remembered that she'd envisioned Ted's neck snapped clean inside the crumpled Ford at the bottom of a ravine, and she was convinced that he knew what she'd been thinking. She walked toward him and kissed him on the cheek. She thought to kiss his lips, but they seemed so atrophied after Mr. Gast's full, sleeping mouth.

It was already apparent how Ted's face would erode with time; his mouth was a sinkhole into which the rest of his features would slide, first the lips, then the chin, the nose, until all that remained were two cheekbones and a pair of overwide eyes slung between. His grandfather looked like this; his bloodhound eyes had followed her relentlessly at their wedding, the meaty tissue below the sockets raw and available, now that his outer hide was being pulled down into his own mouth. Ted came from a long line of men who consumed themselves. This was why he chewed his lips, his nails. She'd seen him eat scabs he'd peeled from his own body. At first she'd thought it was merely a physician's interest in the taste of healing, but then she knew it was something different, an impulse that fell between a wish to disappear and an irrepressible need to taste his own powers of regeneration.

Bena shook the vision from her head and kissed Ted flush on the lips. He responded with a few quick pecks. The sky behind them was ominous again. The sun bobbed stupidly in its diminishing patch of blue.

On the way to town they passed a field of infant sunflowers that had been cut down. The small spiked heads peeked out from beneath the thatch of furry stalks. In the backseat, the dog whined and whined. (The dog would die soon after they returned to the hotel. Ted would give the chambermaid a quarter to wrap it in a sheet and slip it into the incinerator, where no Utes would see it.)

"I thought you hated dogs," Bena said, irritably. Little Ted spat out her nipple, and she draped him over her shoulder as she buttoned her blouse with one hand.

"I don't hate dogs."

Bena looked out the window, patting the baby between his shoulder blades. They were coming into Colorado Springs now. The streets were empty, eerily so.

They passed the park outside which Bena had seen the young woman crying (Mr. Gast's doomed friend, she assumed). Through the iron fence she glimpsed a great marble statue and gravel paths circling rose trellises that were bare except for the occasional tattered bloom. To the left of a fountain she saw a white tent.

"Stop the car."

Ted pulled the Ford toward the curb and let it idle.

"Turn it off," Bena said. "I have something to show you."

She burped the baby while she led her husband beneath the stone arch toward the center of the park, its manicured perfection tousled by the storm. The cold air from the mountains had been exchanged here for a hot, invisible wind off the plains. The fountain was dry, its gray granite bottom scarred with the rusted fossils of pennies that had been retracted, put in pockets, cast back into the world without a thought toward luck.

Long before she reached the tent she could hear it. The ropes clanged against the poles, the tarp snapped like the sails of a poorly trimmed ship. She approached cautiously, in case someone should be hidden behind that petulant, abandoned white.

China plates were upside down, hiding their blank faces in the grass. Silver knives, spoons, forks lay at seemingly purposeful angles as if trying to spell out a message. (*Leave—We all did.*) The upper tablecloths had blown away, while the lower cloths, clamped to the tabletops, fluttered like women's skirts, a tentful of women cut off at the waist. If there hadn't been a storm, Bena would have thought this was the destruction wrought by the impossible bride. She imagined the girl whirling about the tent in her muddy dress, tossing plates and ripping cloths off tables. Bena looked eastward for diminishing traces of the bride in her bedraggled white, shrinking into the earth like the hailstones.

She heard Ted bump into a tent pole.

"What the hell." He rubbed his forehead.

Bena held the baby in one arm and walked to a metal basin full of champagne bottles floating in nothing but water, the ice long melted. She pulled one up, dripping and warm.

"Drink?"

Ted set a pair of overturned chairs upright at a table. Bena found two champagne flutes, intact, and wiped the dust from them on her sleeve. She handed the baby to Ted, and pulled up her skirt, grabbing the bottle between her knees.

She poured recklessly, letting the champagne explode and run over.

They clinked and sat, silent. Bena dipped the corner of a tablecloth into her glass and wiped the blood from Little Ted's nose and ears, until he was clean and wine-smelling.

It was calming in the tent, bright and the damage already done.

The second storm front of the day arrived. Bena heard the hesitant pings of rain. When she leaned out the tent flap, however, she realized she'd been fooled again. First the sky beat them with water stones, now it buried them under falling dirt.

They sat together and listened to the hiss of the dirt against the tent.

"It couldn't see me," Ted said.

He was talking about the dog.

"But it smelled me. It let up this howl like nothing I'd ever heard."

"Maybe it didn't want your help," Bena remarked. "Maybe it was warning you to stay away."

"Maybe."

He poured more champagne into their glasses, so precisely that it didn't so much as fizz.

"You know, it's not uncommon for women, while they're in labor, to beg the doctor to kill them."

"Really."

"I heard a story once about a man performing a home delivery. In the middle of her labor, the woman pulled a gun from under her pillow and aimed it at his head, claiming she planned to kill him first, then kill herself."

"What are you trying to say?" Between Mr. Gast and her husband, Bena had tired of enigmatic stories from which she was supposed to glean some truth about female nature.

Ted finished his warm champagne in one swallow. "I'm saying that pain causes backward behavior."

"I thought this was a story about why you're not an obstetrician."

Ted grinned, clearly wanting to avoid a squabble. "Maybe it is." He set his champagne flute down forcefully. He stood and offered Bena a hand. "Dance?"

The three of them—Bena, Ted, the baby—were dancing as the storm reached its peak, the wind threatening to blow the tent away. Ted removed a tablecloth and wrapped it around Bena. He sheltered the baby inside his jacket.

They left the tent, and sprinted over the gravel. Escaped napkins somersaulted over the ground.

Passing the dry fountain, Bena stopped.

"What are you doing?" Ted pulled her toward the car.

She wrestled with her skirt pocket, searching for a coin to make a wish. She thought of wishing for Ted and her to be happy, as they had been while dancing in the tent, but her thoughts were interrupted by visions of the Ford plunging through the white crosses, over the cliff, into flames.

Bena tossed the penny and ran.

4. WATER ON THE MOON

Reimer Lee Jackson's right foot was shod in a maroon velvet bag with a leather sole and noose that tied around her ankle. Before Bena left the *Chieftain* office with her reporter's pad, Cecil had warned her about Reimer's unusual affliction. Since the age of ten, when she had lost her right leg in a horse-riding accident, she'd worn a prosthesis carved from an elephant's tusk. "A most unusual appendage for a painfully usual woman," Cecil had remarked.

"I used to wear a matching shoe," Reimer explained to Bena. "But it just makes people wonder why you're limping. This way"—she gestured at the velvet bag—"there's no wondering. You don't want people wondering about you in this town."

She was driving with Bena to the Mineral Palace from the Club of American University Women, housed in the Jacksons' blocky sandstone mansion. Reimer was planning a joint venture with the WPA to restore the former tourist attraction to its original grandeur.

"No?" Bena glanced sideways at her hostess. Reimer Lee Jackson was a woman who missed being pretty by just a few eighths of an inch: her eyes were too close and high on her face, her forehead was too pinched and tall, her nose was flat and overlong. But she did have lovely black hair, silvery in places and pulled into a tight bun with a mechanical confusion of pins.

"They've got good imaginations," Reimer replied, "and they're far more interested in entertaining themselves than in giving you or anyone a fair shake."

After three weeks at the *Chieftain*, Bena had written four articles touting the tireless activities of Pueblo's fine Christian women and had effectively recovered from being assigned to work in cubicle number 8, formerly occupied by a reporter who had drowned on a recent fishing trip to the Judas River. Her column was called "Who's Who in the City Federation of Women's Clubs." She had passed a Tuesday afternoon listening to a talk on Victorian hair jewelry by Luna Beck-Fril, and had covered a book-mending party at the Bent Elementary School with Bessie Humble of the Women's Auxiliary to the Postal Workers Club. She'd attended a Wednesday luncheon at the Kappa Theta chapter of the Delphinians ("personal development through study and service"), augmented with a lecture by President Georgia Horne on the relevance of Longfellow's claim that "books are sepulchers of thought." On the previous Friday evening, Bena, Ted, and Little Ted had attended a piano recital sponsored by the MacDowell Music Club. The pianist, a Mr. Benjamin Steinhardt from New York City, drank too many Manhattans (homesick, Ted conjectured) at the pre-concert cocktail gathering and played "Chimes of St. Petersburg" thrice in succession, having introduced the piece each time with a story about how his grandmother, whom he affectionately called Ufa, used to lull him to sleep with the tune when he was a small boy living near the government horse stables in Vienna.

Bena had also covered the ceremonial ribbon-cutting at the defunct Arapaho Tractor Factory. The factory had been converted into a mattress assembly plant, employing one hundred nineteen people to make mattresses for the poor, in a project spearheaded by the Club of American University Women. The president of the association—Reimer Lee Jackson—was a perfect profile for "Who's Who" because of her grand plans to renovate the Mineral Palace, the vast, lurking, condemned structure on the outskirts of town, shielded from the street by a wrought-iron gate and surrounded by a park of bare-limbed elms. According to the articles Bena had dredged up from the *Chieftain* archives,

the Mineral Palace was designed by a local architect named Otto Bu-
low, who was instructed by the town leaders to erect a building to be
distinguished by "novelty, originality, and grandeur of design," to pro-
mote the wealth of Colorado as a mining state. An artist from New
York, a Mr. Levy (who, as a Jew, was not allowed inside the Pueblo
Men's Social Club), was summoned to the plains to paint native flora
on the walls and inside the three domes that each stretched seventy feet
in diameter overhead. Formally opened on July 4, 1891, the Palace
proved to be a tepid tourist attraction. The building fell into disrepair
during the twenties, and closed its doors indefinitely after the crash in
1929.

Reimer Lee Jackson drove a silver Chrysler Airflow specially built
for her in Detroit with both the gas and the brake pedals on the left
side. She honked as they passed the cemetery where her husband, Abbott, was buried, dead of a hard day's work, she explained, implying
that he hadn't had many such days and one had been enough to kill
him. On their way to the south side of town, she told Bena how her
father, Earl Truitt, the son of an English colonialist, grew up in Bombay
and spoke of his childhood using words like "rattan" and "Calcutta,"
capturing for her the lazy, bamboo-snap sound of his life in a distant
country. When she lost her leg in the riding accident, her father provided her with a succession of elephant tusks from a relative who still
lived in Bombay.

"Had this one since 1912," she said. She lifted her skirt and un-
clipped her stocking, pushing it down an inch. She tapped the tusk
with a fingernail. It made a hollow sound.

" 'B. Vanderloo, February 1902.' " The letters, etched into the
ivory, had mellowed to the deep, dirty yellow of infection.

"Who's B. Vanderloo?" Bena asked. She clung to the dashboard,
woozy and crackery-headed as if she'd had too much wine the evening
before, even though she hadn't had a drink in weeks. The baby had
been up all night again. He was adapting poorly to the imposition of

a feeding schedule and refusing the introduction of any solid food into his routine. Though she tried to feed him every three hours, he would typically start to wail after only two. He was inconsolable, and this, in turn, made Bena inconsolable. The night before, Ted had wandered sleep-faced into the nursery to find both of them crying, Little Ted from hunger, Bena from exhaustion and the fear that she was starving her own child. It worried her that the baby would be so slow to adjust to a schedule, but Ted, proudly, attributed it to his son's willfulness.

"You need to break him, Bena," he'd said. "Show him who's in charge." Ted had had a violent upbringing of leather straps and was even tied to a tree once for an entire day by his mother. He believed that children were horses, with wills that needed to be destroyed and recultivated. Bena didn't disagree with him, but nor did she tell him that she gave Florence an extra bottle of formula for the "emergencies" that seemed to arise daily.

Reimer failed to signal a left-hand turn and nearly struck a peddler crossing the road with his unwieldy cart of pots. She braked, but not before the man's cart overturned as he tried to avoid a collision. The man brandished a black skillet at her through the windshield, as if he'd like nothing better than to bash in her long-boned skull.

"The poacher, darling," Reimer persisted, as though nothing untoward had transpired. "Boris Vanderloo."

The pot man knocked on the driver's-side window with a balled fist. Reimer put the Airflow in reverse and drove blithely around the addled man's cart, leaving him to cope alone with his toppled livelihood.

Bena stared at Reimer. She was about to insist that her hostess stop the car so that she could help the poor man right his cart. But Bena had learned, even in the little time she'd spent with Pueblo's Christian women, that she would have to overlook a fair amount of reproachable behavior to win the trust of subjects she found, in the kindest of terms, complicated and difficult to warm to. They were a mess of contradictions, these Christian club women, dedicating their collective efforts to saving the poor, indigent, uneducated of Pueblo, while seemingly incapable of individual acts of kindness outside their sanctioned club activities. Perhaps it was a western bias, Bena conjectured, a sense that the original settlers had pulled themselves up by their bootstraps, that none of them had been given anything to start their lives save a toothless rake and a lame horse. Never mind that it was Reimer's parents and grandparents who had cajoled the reticent land with hoes and searched in vain for water, not her. The legacy of the struggle remained in the second- and third-generation westerners, even if they'd grown up in sandstone mansions filled with furniture shipped from Paris and Venice and Stuttgart. The Christian women's charitable acts, expected of ladies of their social stature, were fraught with an irrepressible sense of disdain for the weakness of those souls who pridelessly accepted their generosity.

"This tusk was one of his last," Reimer continued. "Mr. Vanderloo shot himself in the mouth a week later." She smiled at Bena. "A lovely story, all in all."

Bena imagined a poacher's bloody hands up Reimer's skirt, wielding the sharp point of a hunting knife or a nail as he gouged his name into her hard, senseless leg.

As unlikable as Bena found Reimer and her tales, she was thankful the woman had forgiven her for being late. Bena had run up North Grand from the *Chieftain* offices to find Reimer pacing in front of her big red house, jingling her car keys and fluffing the shrubs as if they were couch pillows. "You must think I have time to waste," she told Bena, then led her to the Airflow. She opened the passenger door for her, a contemptuous act of politeness.

Bena thought to tell Reimer a lie about a deadline or an editorial meeting, but decided against it. The truth was, she'd been watching the alley.

She'd watched the alley every day for the past three weeks through the window of her office. There wasn't much to see in the crevice between the buildings that the sun rarely touched—just a few cats roosting on cellar doors and garbage she could smell when the wind was blowing wrong. At least it'd seemed that way at first.

Then, the week before, she'd seen the prostitute again. She was drunk sometimes, sometimes not. When she wasn't drunk she was crying, and she would kick the cats, which, after a time, learned to clear out of her way whether she was stinking with alcohol or not. All except the one cat whose white belly, stretched low with kittens, dragged on the alley floor. The cat crouched and bared her teeth and hissed at the woman. The day before, when she'd gone to empty her wastecan outside, Bena had found the cat dead behind the office, her head stamped in. Bena had put a hand to the cat's big belly to see whether her kittens were squirming, trapped in this useless corpse of a mother, but there was no movement, no life at all, only a few maggots nesting where once there was a head.

Mostly the prostitute was alone, but twice Bena had seen her accompanied by a man in a cowboy hat. It was the same man, Bena believed, whom she'd witnessed helping her down the same alley, the day Bena first met with Cecil. The man would take the keys from the woman's hand and open the back door to the William Bent Rooming House, then step aside to let her enter first. The William Bent was on the second floor, above Buck's Silo, its windows smothered by dark curtains that were never parted except by the occasional finger, presumably to ascertain what kind of day it was, not that there was ever more than one kind.

At first Bena had thought that the cowboy was a customer of the woman. But he didn't leave the rooming house checking himself to be sure he showed no signs of having undressed and then dressed again. He didn't, like a lot of the men Bena saw, look both ways as he hurried onto the street to blend with the few other pedestrians moving from one unhappy place to another. There was a melancholy quality to this man that wasn't about shame or hate or lust. He was always heavy when he left, as if he'd accepted some of the woman's weight during his visit and agreed to take it home with him.

Since he wasn't a customer, Bena decided, the cowboy must be the father of the woman's baby. This didn't explain, though, why he was so kind to her yet hadn't married her, why he was so distraught yet did nothing to rescue her from her current predicament. She still had customers, even in her pregnant state. Bena had heard men bragging in front of Buck's about fucking the mommy slut, they fucked her so hard they popped her little bastard's skull like a grape.

The cowboy intrigued Bena. He and the woman. They were the sort of people whose lives made for the best stories, if the worst living.

Of course, this was nothing she could convey to Reimer Lee Jackson, a woman of inconsistent sympathies.

"Not for self alone," Bena recalled as the motto of the Club of American University Women, across the letterhead Reimer had sent granting her request for an interview, "But for all."

"Here we are," Reimer said as they swept through the iron gates of Mineral Park.

They came to a wide street, lined on either side with leafless elms. At the end was a muscular, Egyptian-looking structure, grand and foolish in the middle of the thinning park.

Reimer stopped the Airflow next to a defunct fountain. Broken glass gleamed on the bottom of the marble basin. Tidal rings marked where the final traces of rain water had evaporated.

"I'm not sure what you know about the history of this building," Reimer said, as she pulled a walking cane from the trunk.

Bena took out her reporter's pad. "Very little."

The Palace hid its neglect well, managing to appear majestic at first glance. It wasn't until Bena focused on the plaster of the columns, chipped off in leprous sheets to reveal the rusting skeleton beneath, on the suicidal remains of slate roof tiles, on the trash and dust the wind had heaped against the walls, that the deep decline of the place revealed itself.

"The Mineral Palace was built in 1891 to be one of the wonders of the Western Hemisphere. All the big mining families from the town got behind it. We Puebloans have a bit of an inferiority complex. Always wanting to prove to the rest of the country that we're just as rich, just as high-class, just as finely bred as the next man."

Reimer had to stop every few steps to catch her breath. Hollow or not, the elephant tusk was a ludicrous solution to a missing leg. In Reimer's case, however, it seemed more a beautiful, if impractical, accessory than a functional prosthesis. Bena concluded it was Reimer's way of transforming her affliction into an opportunity for adornment, even if it meant she effectively handicapped herself. Bena thought of the fairy tale of the red shoes—her brother's favorite story, because, as a girl, Bena was given a pair of red dress shoes that she loved so much she would wear them to bed. Surrendering to vanity, Jonas would recount, a girl not unlike yourself puts on her red shoes and is forced to dance day and night, day and night, until, exhausted, she begs the blacksmith down the road to cut her feet off at the ankles. He agrees, but only if he can cauterize the bones with his hot iron so that she may never grow feet again. She cannot be trusted, Jonas explained, she cannot be trusted, because girls will forever be weak and senseless in the face of unusual objects.

Maybe Reimer's leg had been lopped off in a similar fashion. Maybe she, too, had failed to learn the lesson that vanity maims you. Here she was with her ivory leg, unusual and maimed.

Bena and Reimer stopped before an immense copper door embossed with the giant outline of Colorado. The state's major mining towns and cities—Denver, Pueblo, Colorado Springs, Aspen, Telluride, Trinidad, Leadville, Silverton—were marked with stones of pink quartz or, where the stones were missing, what looked like bullet holes.

Reimer produced a large skeleton key from inside her pocketbook.

"My father's," she said. "When the Palace was completed, each mining family received its very own key." She held it out for Bena to inspect. The long neck was engraved with a name, "Earl Truitt."

The door swung open at a slow but steady speed. Bena was struck by the smell of wet, mold, rot. It took a moment for her eyes to adjust. There were no windows. The available light from above was diluted by its trip through the dirty glass domes overhead.

Light also crept through a gaping hole that had been punched into the northeast wall. Dust drifts from the recent storms had collected inside. There were piles of blankets and bottles and wrappers in corners and against pillars, clustered as to suggest that people lived here. Old chorus-girl magazines fanned across the floor in a dim corner, coverless and bent-spined, their bloated contents rising in a tangle of heels and legs and feathers.

Reimer did not appear at all shocked to find the place in such invaded disarray. It was curious to Bena why the door was even locked, and why Reimer pretended that this was a sealed tomb to which only a few precious families possessed the key.

"This is where the Pueblo Shakespeare Society used to perform *A Midsummer Night's Dream* each July, with candles." Reimer gestured toward a stage fringed from above with velvet curtains. The velvet was marked with wide black patches of mildew. "One year there was a tremendous wind that blew the candles out all at once. We agreed afterward that it was the closest any of us had come to feeling the presence of God." Reimer touched her cameo brooch, the white raised head of a woman.

She continued to trot Bena around the bleak interior of the Mineral Palace, pointing out the dummy lead-pipe organ and the fake stalactites, their ends snapped and deadened like old teeth.

Reimer described the opening-day ceremonies in 1891, during which the Silverton Cowboy Band played campfire tunes. She pulled a leather registry book from her bag—an heirloom rescued by her father when the Palace closed—which featured a sample admission ticket: "The Mineral Palace—Welcome to the world's finest collection of precious earthly materials." The book claimed a Miss Muzette Tracy of Salida, Colorado, her handwriting breathy, looped, and impatient, as the first visitor to step inside the marble doorway. A newspaper clipping glued inside the front cover showed an illustration of Miss Tracy, a gawky, parrot-faced girl of seventeen, about to cut the silver ribbon stretched across the doorway with a pair of jeweled scissors so heavy she had to hold them with both hands.

"A lucky girl," Bena said, handing the book back to Reimer.

"Muzette Tracy was killed in a train accident on the way back to Salida. Never made the papers in her life until that week. Then she was in them twice."

Reimer guttered along on her ivory leg, the upholstered nub striking the crushed and crumbling floor tiles. Bena looked at the empty jewel cases with their eviscerated velvet pillows and mouse droppings. Each case was affixed with an engraved brass plaque. Chalcedony. Chert. Jasper. Jade. Molybdenum from Climax. Iridium from the Transvaal. Maucherite from Thuringia.

On the floor Bena spotted a broken plaque engraved with a question meant to jar the minds of children:

"Is there water on the moon?"

She peered into the fetid darkness. She could almost hear the screams of trespassed girls, the quiet agony of poverty, of slipping low, low, lower than a person ever thought possible.

Reimer called out from the center of the Palace. She stood in front of a dry pool from which the metal statue of a water nymph, her wings slack against her back, toes pointed, must once have launched herself into the gloom with the help of the mechanical spring bolted through her ankles. Her prim little feet, soles pressed together as if in prayer, were streaked a ruddy brown, the old blood runoff of her partial crucifixion.

"She used to hold a silver nugget the size of a grapefruit." Reimer pointed her walking stick at the nymph's outstretched palms.

Bena flipped her reporter's pad to a fresh page. "So tell me why the Club of American University Women wouldn't rather just raze the Mineral Palace and begin anew, with, say, an arboretum."

Reimer's face was turned to the vast, domed ceiling. She apparently didn't smell urine, didn't hear screams or sense the palpable desperation. She saw Puck traipsing across the candlelit stage, Bena thought; she smelled her husband's eucalyptus cologne as he touched the letters on her ivory thigh, she felt as near to God as ever.

"It's always been a woman's job to provide the moral center for this town," Reimer replied, "and understanding this, I feel it is our duty to restore Pueblo's symbol of pride and affluence to its former grandeur."

She talked about the library she hoped to build, and the founders' wall, where portraits of Pueblo's mining and industrial leaders would hang. A movie theater would replace the stage, and historical mining footage would be shown on a screen framed by glowing pieces of colored glass, meant to heighten what Reimer referred to as "the grotto effect."

Soon Reimer complained that her leg was bothering her, and asked Bena whether she had everything she needed for her article.

"I think they'll probably want to send a photographer to your house, and possibly here as well," Bena said.

"Certainly. And of course, your photographer may borrow my key if he needs it."

Bena stared at the hole in the northeast wall, then at Reimer to see whether there was any more irony in her expression than in her voice. Not a bit more, as it turned out. Even if the Palace were nothing but a door leading onto a bare foundation, the walls long gone, she would probably still insist on locking it.

Reimer hobbled toward the entrance, to wait while Bena took a solitary walk around the Palace perimeter. The columns were built of native stone, according to a wall plaque. Gray granite from Silver Plume. Red granite from Platte Canyon. Sandstone from Manitou. The walls were inlaid with copper, steel, and various native rocks.

Bena used the hem of her dress to rub the dust from a stone in the wall. An alert eye of pink quartz glared at her from its filthy socket. The building seemed to shift in its sleep as she touched it.

She followed the wall until her hand stumbled over a doorknob. She looked over her shoulder, to check whether Reimer was impatient to leave. She wasn't. She was sitting on the pedestal of a marble lion, gazing out over the dead gardens.

Bena turned the knob. The latch snapped like a twig breaking. Behind the door was a narrow, dark passageway. Bena hugged the wall, using one hand for balance, the other for knocking cobwebs from her face.

She recalled how she'd felt when she and Jonas would explore coves in Lake Susquetannah so remote even the sun didn't know about them. They would find the bones of small animals lodged in the rocks and pretend they were those of girls who disappeared mysteriously from their backyards in the time it took their mothers to put a pie in the oven. They'd wrap the bones in a jacket and stow them in the bilge, talking as they sailed home about how they'd go to the police with their evidence, become famous around Coeur du Lac for their bravery in bringing to light the darkest crimes. But once they reached the dock, Jonas would laugh at her for believing their own, crazy story; he would unwrap the bones over the stern and let them sink away, because they were no more sacred than the beetle-infested remains of a squirrel. Bena believed that she and Jonas were the ones performing a killing in that moment, that she could hear the final, fading cry of the unavenged girl as her bones were swallowed by the water.

The passage curved to the left and led to a set of narrow wooden stairs. In the light from a window at the top of the stairs, she saw racks and racks of dresses, coats, tunics cluttering the walls like a line of people pressing to get into the theater.

She was in the costume room.

The walls were decorated with flimsy shields, cardboard lances, flat and misshapen ladies' hats. Bena pulled a pillbox hat off the wall, its black voile veil shot through with moth holes. She put it on and followed the hallway up another short flight of steps until she was backstage.

As she made her entrance through the mildewed curtain, the floor exploded with squeaks and the ticking of claws, as legions of mice made fast for the wings. The stage sloped toward a large hole in its center. Bena peered into the hole and thought she could see the glint of a chandelier. Overhead, a severed cord extended from the ceiling.

She walked carefully to the edge of the stage, testing each footstep to be certain she didn't hit a soft spot in the wood. Two crowned, sceptered figures flanked the stage: a king and a queen.

In the dark the queen appeared to be made of black stone, onyx perhaps, but when the light from above struck her shoulders and forehead, Bena could see that she was made of a white metal. She was seated in a boat with a curled Viking prow. Bena knelt over the edge of the stage to read the words painted across the stern of her metal boat: *The Silver Queen.*

The scepter in the queen's right hand was topped with an eight-inch replica of a silver dollar. Her hands were paddle-like slabs of cast metal; three grooves delineated her fingers. The caster had forgotten, or found it unnecessary, to provide her with thumbs; she would have had servants and footmaids to help button her into her hard silver gown inlaid with murky paste jewels. The queen's wintry beauty was protected above by a marble canopy, elevated by four pillars and guarded by a crystal eagle about to take flight.

Bena walked along the edge of the stage to examine her king. Their relationship was a chilly one, as far as Bena could tell. They didn't face each other, nor did they seem to enjoy the invisible thread that connects two people who are folded up inside each other, even when they're far apart. While the queen was cool, icy, possessed, the king was a jester of sorts, his name ("King Coal") spelled in gaudy purple bulbs, his head small atop his broad body.

She sat next to him, letting her legs drop over the edge of the stage. He was a glum yet sturdy, unpretentious fellow. Does she love you enough? Bena wanted to ask him. He evidently felt the fool, this king, captured by a beautiful woman who made it clear in the way she shunned him that it was a baldly commercial exchange, their marriage, loveless and practical. Not that this made either of them unusual. After all, Bena wanted to remind the king, young women and powerful men have been doing it for centuries.

She returned to the queen, who continued to reign senselessly over her broken-down realm as if light sources hadn't fallen from considerable heights, as if there weren't holes in her world big enough to drive a car through. The Silver Queen was beautiful in an uninhabitable way, her impeccable features enough to discourage any human expression from misaligning them.

Bena traced the line of the queen's breasts through her hard dress. She'd bet her beauty on power, on kingdoms and comfort, on a commodity that, like love, tarnished and weakened over time.

And what about her? What had she, Bena Duse, married for? What were her noble reasons? Love, could she honestly claim?

But yes, it was love. She'd married for love because Ted smelled like people she knew. It was love at the Christmas party in St. Paul thrown four years before by a widow whose name Bena had forgotten. Her house was in extravagant decline, and all the guests kept their coats on, for the rooms were thoroughly breezy and cold, the marble floors holding the chill better than any icehouse.

Bena Duse and Theodore Jonssen were destined to meet, because they were both, if not beautiful, then exceedingly appealing in ways that were impossible to locate within a single, compelling feature. Bena was quiet, with a ripe, inclusive laugh that made her appear far more welcoming of pleasure than her initial reticence led people to believe. Ted was more big than tall, his individual features failing to distinguish themselves from his impressive bulk and force. At the party, guests glided about the ballroom, decorated with fir boughs, and candles whose flames swayed to the ferocious drafts, orchestrating the encounter, drawing the two of them closer and closer until they were face to face, just drunk enough on the needle-sharp Prohibition eggnog to seem giddy and capable of immediate, far-down affection. She remembered he was larger than life and available to her as no man she'd ever met had been (certainly not her father, certainly not Jonas), and maybe, just as erroneously, he believed the same of her.

It wasn't until after they were married that Bena discovered she'd wed a member of her own quiet tribe, a man who lied to the world every day with a smile and a warm handshake and an incandescent gaze, as if his soul had been burned thin from constant examination. They took vows and exchanged rings, they promised to tell each other everything, but they never did tell each other much. She never told him about her brother, how he'd hurt people he wasn't even related to, how he died. And Ted never breathed a word about the other women he kissed, women whose perfumes he scrubbed from his cheek and neck with antiseptic from the clinic before he returned home to her at night. And it was comfortable that way; the silences were a cozy insulation from the windy, cutting truth of things.

"What fools we are," Bena said aloud, her voice fading before it could strike a wall, bounce and echo, return to her.

She'd never been much of one for acting (her experience limited to playing a scupper in a sorority production of *Drake's Drum*), but she adjusted her moth-eaten hat and scoured her brain for traces of Shakespeare. Appropriately, all she could remember were the words of a fool.

"It is ten o'clock," she began. The rest she spoke to herself, listening to the sounds of a place, not just the Mineral Palace but the whole dusty town, shifting and dying.

Thus we may see . . . how the world wags. 'Tis but an hour ago since it was nine, and after one hour more 'twill be eleven; and so, from hour to hour we ripe and ripe, and then from hour to hour, we rot and rot, and thereby hangs a tale.

Bena gazed at the morose queen. When did she know that she'd made a mistake in marrying the king with the purple lightbulbs and the too small head? She wished she could ask Her Highness and expect an honest response, but the luckiest women always lied to protect their luck. Bena remembered being struck herself with such a suspicion, as she and Ted drove away from their wedding reception (hosted at the Mohawk Men's Club, December 30, 1931) in a borrowed Lincoln with plush gray upholstery and a bottle of half-frozen champagne wedged under the passenger seat. The bottom of her former world dropped away, every familiar street in St. Paul grew foreign and mildly ominous beneath the light of this new winter. Nothing was left but the hiss of the hurled rice against the car's windows and Ted's cold hand on her elbow, and the emptiness that always follows such heady, happy moments, when you grasp that you have come out the other side of a rite of passage, alone.

Since she'd had the baby, however, Bena recalled the events leading up to their marriage differently. The baby made the manner in which she and Ted missed the truth of each other, had always missed the truth of each other, less important, because the baby had brought her to understand that the point of marriage wasn't what she'd been led to believe. The point of marriage wasn't to live forever with a man for whom her affection would grow and change and deepen. The point of marriage was to produce another creature for whom her love and generosity would become easy-flowing fluids, not stoppered by the ways that language failed her, or truth-telling failed her. It was love in the form of food and survival, an easy, watery way to offer herself.

"Mrs. Jonssen?"

Reimer's voice sounded small and slight and far away.

Bena pulled the hat off and shook the dust from her hair. She skirted the edge of the hole, peering down into it once again, and tossed the hat in. She listened for the sound of its landing, but there was no sound. She walked toward the open door, followed at her heels by the cool, breezy sensation of falling.

REIMER INVITED HER IN for a quick cup of tea, which Bena accepted grudgingly. She was always aching to get home to the baby after a few hours at work. She'd arranged her schedule so that she worked afternoons at the *Chieftain*, beginning at one. She gave Little Ted his noon feeding, and Florence gave him his three-o'clock with a bottle of breast milk that Bena pumped each morning. The breast pump was made of glass and shaped like a trumpet, with a rubber ball at one end that she was meant to squeeze. The first time Bena had used it she'd bruised the skin around her nipple. Now she'd grown more accustomed to its bland sucking. She tried not to watch as her nipple was distorted by the suction, as the milk flowed in the thinnest yellow trickle down the spine of the trumpet, dripping with painstaking slowness into the attached bottle. In these moments her body became no more sensual than a tractor engine, a mess of pipes and hoses whose fluids needed constant draining.

And today, in particular, she wanted to go home. She had measured the baby with the hair ribbon this morning and was pleased to note that he had grown a sixteenth of an inch since yesterday.

Reimer's sandstone house appeared to have been carved whole from the quarry, extracted with great forceps from the earth and then flipped right side up onto this prime patch of North Grand. There was an exterior crudeness to all the houses that, Bena theorized, drove the mistresses to overcompensate on their luxurious interiors, suffocating each room with thick drapes and overfed furniture—gluttonous davenports, ottomans, loveseats, floor pillows.

Reimer sat in an umber chair with a matching ottoman. A wan Mexican woman named Felicity brought her a special grooved pillow into which she could lay her ivory leg. "Her parents were aristocrats originally from Spain." Reimer spoke in covert tones, as though Felicity were loath to let anyone in on the truth, preferring to be a maid instead of the rightful heir to a distant throne.

Reimer lit the cigarette in her amber holder and gestured to her possessions with the lassos of smoke as if identifying members in a family portrait to a stranger. "That chandelier came from Venice. Abbott and I took our honeymoon there in 1902. If you look closely, you'll see the glass has a pinkish tinge. The glassblower's shop was in a former nunnery. The glassblower told us the color came from the wasted blood of all those virgin nuns."

"How lovely," Bena replied, smiling. How utterly grim.

"Abbott had exquisite taste. People were always complimenting me on the house, but it was really Abbott who decorated it."

"He sounds like an unusual man."

"Oh, he *was*."

Reimer rang a little porcelain bell. She instructed Felicity to fetch a photo in a silver frame. It was propped on the mantel between two ivory tapers that had never been lit, their wicks limp and pristine. Felicity handed the picture to Bena.

Abbott was standing before a fountain in a town square in Italy or Spain or Mexico. He appeared at first glance as a mandlin and reedy man, his khakis cinched to his slim waist with a wide leather belt. He held a straw hat in one hand, a white handkerchief in the other. His high-boned face was as beautiful as a woman's, and darkly tanned. The hand holding the hat was lazy on his hip, his face tired of being photographed at the same time that it expected no less. In the background, sitting on the edge of the fountain, was a youthful Reimer, her face long and houndlike beneath her straw sun bonnet. Bena could tell from her timid look that her husband didn't love her then—in the middle of this hot Spanish plaza or Italian piazza or wherever they were—and never had loved her, not for a moment.

"How did you meet?" Bena set the troubling photograph next to the tea tray. It teemed with fake fatedness and other falsehoods.

"When I was fifteen, Father bought some old silver mines in Mexico, but he had no capital to reopen them. Abbott's father owned one of the biggest mining operations in Colorado. They became partners."

And your marriage completed the business transaction, Bena couldn't help thinking. She cooed as Reimer told her the story of her and Abbott's engagement, the two of them in Mexico with their families to celebrate the opening of a mine in the Sierra Madre, and how Abbott took her down into the shaft. When they reached the bottom, he turned off his mining lamp. There, in the complete darkness, he slipped a ruby ring on her finger and asked her to be his wife. Bena thought that Abbott must have closed his eyes just the same, barricading himself twice over against the possibility that he might have to look at this woman he did not love as he asked her to marry him in the bowels of the earth.

"When is your wedding anniversary?"

"April 2, 1902. Why do you ask?"

$4 \times 2 = 8$, as did $1 + 9 + 0 - 2$. Two 8s. Reimer was a woman she'd do best to keep clear of.

Bena smiled. "I'm just trying to imagine the time of year. Winter weddings have such a different promise from spring weddings. No better, but different." Determining the date of her own wedding had been a struggle. Bena had wanted to be married on November 11, because 11/11 represented to her a parity and fatefulness fitting for a wedding anniversary. But Ted refused to be married on that day, which fell in the middle of his fall exam period. December 30 was the most convenient date, as all his relatives would be nearby for the holidays and he would be on his vacation from medical school. Bena had agreed because his schedule deemed it unavoidable. Still, the date remained foreign and offputting and inviolable. December 30, 12/30, was simply a string of unreadable numbers to her, holding no guarantees of either contentedness or catastrophe.

Reimer described her wedding in the broad, hasty terms that people do who are exterminating history as they recount it. She and Abbott were married at a mountain retreat near San Isabel, and all the best families of Pueblo were in attendance—Baxter, Thatcher, Gierhardt, Gast.

"Gast?"

"Abbott's cousins. Everyone in this town is related in some manner or another. That's why we're so good with confidences. Need to keep them in the family."

Reimer looked at her watch, indicating that it was time for Bena to leave.

"Will you be needing a lift back to town?" she said.

"No, thank you," Bena replied. "It's a short walk."

Reimer held out a hand. "I'll keep you abreast of the club's activities. Maybe you'd like to come to our Thursday meeting?"

"I'd love to." Bena grasped the extended hand. It was all bones and rings.

Felicity led her through the foyer. She opened the front door and was waiting patiently behind it for Bena to depart, when Bena remembered she'd left her reporter's pad on the couch.

She returned to the living room and found Reimer with her head tilted back, her eyes closed, her fingertips pushed against her temples as if to pinch off a most painful headache. Reimer didn't hear her. Bena took one last look at Reimer's wrinkled face, drawn tight by her own fingers. She wondered whether Reimer's relentless pretending exhausted her, made her ill. It must require an inhuman amount of energy, Bena reflected, to deliver with any credibility those perfect, crafted tales about her unusual husband and a thoughtful father who maimed her with an ivory leg.

THE SKY WAS the unsettling green color that always arrived at the latter end of the day, a sky that much more perverse and unnatural given the hopeful quality of the light usually associated with late afternoon. Not in Pueblo. Even when there hadn't been a dust storm for days, the sky was so linty with fleeing particles of earth that the sun was blotted out.

Today, however, Bena could see the sun as she descended North Grand and walked toward the center of town. It stared at her, milky and impassive, a big dead cow's eye with all the wildness gone. From this height she could see the black praying mantis of the ironworks on the far edge of town. The earth was broken there, revealing the soreness of red soil beneath.

The five-o'clock whistle sounded and the mantis ground to a stop, its body poised in a half-bow. Bena watched as the men, blackened from head to toe, emerged in a tired trickle from among the great insect's many legs. They walked alone, most of them, heading to town instead of toward their homes in the shantytown that rimmed the ironworks like a splintery suburb around a mechanical city.

By the time Bena reached Union Avenue, it was crawling with ironworkers. They brushed past her without a glance. She'd learned this about the workingmen of Pueblo: They needed a drink to feel that they were men again, to feel that they could ogle and sneer and whistle.

Bena stopped at the Snow White to pick up their laundry, wrapped in brown paper and still warm like a thick, soft dough. She was about to go to the *Chieftain* office when she saw the cowboy— the prostitute's cowboy—emerge from the alleyway. She watched him climb the wooden steps to Buck's Silo. The door opened and she could hear the sounds of music and men laughing. It snapped shut, reclaiming the raucous noise like a confession it regretted having let loose in the world.

She stood watching the door, and had the notion that she would follow him into Buck's. Instead, she went up the stairs to the office, sat at her desk, and rolled a piece of paper into her typewriter. She sat for a few minutes, staring at the walls. Just above her desk she'd pinned the photo Mrs. Dubrowski had taken of the three of them in front of the Ford. They looked so happy and bound together, Little Ted luminous as a tiny planet wrapped in his blanket and Ted holding on to her elbow, a small manner of touching that implied he couldn't live without her, not even for the instant required to take the photograph.

Her father had hung a similar picture above the mantel in St. Paul, the three of them—him, Bena, Jonas—arranged on the porch steps in a perfect pyramid. Her family never had many photographs in the house, which was why dates of births and deaths were so important to her. They functioned, better than any photograph, as the definitive, indelible image a person left behind.

In this photograph, she and Jonas were children and all knees, her father lost and encumbered beneath his hair, as though his eventual baldness were a welcome affliction that unveiled him. Her hair, like her brother's, was summer-white. She had her head on Jonas's shoulder, and Jonas had a hand on her skirt. Their father had one big hand on each of them, holding them from behind, as if they would topple headfirst onto the path if he did not protect them against the inevitable attraction that exists between children's heads and stones. They were portrayed as happy and intertwined as they never were in life, two children without a mother, and with a preoccupied father who adored them in a whispery way that made them strain their ears.

Bena heard the scrape-shut of Cecil's office door, which meant it was high time to be getting home. Her breasts, too, told her that. They were so full and sore she could feel her heart beating in both of them. She pulled the blank sheet of paper from the typewriter and crumpled it into a ball before she left.

Outside, the light had grown even greener as the sun neared the horizon. The street was empty. Standing at the bottom of the steps near Buck's Silo, she could hear the tinkle of glasses and the slamming of bottles on the thick wooden bar. And voices. Crazed and jubilant voices, embracing a hairline's width of happiness.

He wasn't even that attractive, the cowboy, she thought. He was too thin, and his face was parched and bothered. But in a town where everyone seemed downtrodden and lifeless, where nobody had caught her interest, he was the one person who had a new world to show her. She was sure of it.

Bena looked at her watch. She still had forty minutes until Little Ted's scheduled feeding time. She could go home, but then she might be tempted to feed him early if he was crying, and that concession would make the subsequent feedings more excruciating to wait for, while her husband watched as she failed to force an infant's desires to match her own.

Bena looked at the horizon, looked at the front door to Buck's Silo. Ted would compliment her on taking some time for herself, she thought. He was always encouraging her to do something other than be a mother and work. Try to make some friends, he'd said.

She burst into the bar in the way she used to dive into Lake Susquetannah in early June, when the water was still winter-cold and smelling of old snow. When she was very young she used to count to three and then make bad on her own promise to herself, her heart pounding madly with anticipation of the shock and her body teetering over the edge of the dock but refusing to cave to gravity. Later she would trick herself by refusing to build up to the event. One minute she'd be folding her towel, and the next, without warning, she'd find herself gasping for breath in the black lake water.

It was just as black inside Buck's Silo, but it was as close and damp as a hothouse. Men were spaced evenly around the horseshoe bar, while other men clustered around tables and played poker, their thick fingers snapping cards.

At first she thought she was the only woman.

Then she noticed, in a corner, a pair of women in thin dresses that pulled and bunched around their legs and stomachs. Their hair was dyed an identical shade of hay blond. One woman had her hair piled high on her head, while the other wore hers hanging down her back, the dry, grassy ends just touching her waist. Each had a wilting carnation shoved behind her ear. The woman with the long hair put her carnation between her teeth and moved her fleshy hips back and forth. The flower dye rubbed off on her perspiring cheek like a misplaced splotch of rouge. A man grabbed her around the waist and pulled her into his lap. He kissed her roughly, working the flower free from between her teeth with his tongue and then eating it whole. He smiled with his red teeth, and stuck out a tongue furred with petals. The woman hit him, pretending to be horrified, which masked a pretending to be delighted. Bena sensed she was neither delighted nor horrified but numbed by the repetitive action of these easy seductions, tired of these men who would beat their last bits of life against her pelvic bones after their shift at the ironworks.

Bena scanned the room for the cowboy but didn't see him. He who hesitates, she scolded herself, thinking of the girl forever poised at the end of the dock. A large man in a plaid shirt stood up at the bar, fixing his hat to his head. As he vacated his stool the cowboy was revealed, staring moodily at nothing, his back curved over a glass. A bare bulb dangled over his head, calling him forth from the darkness.

The stool moaned beneath her. The bartender—a blue-white man, thin as a string, with shadowy cheekbones that poked out from his face as if he'd been hit twice—stared at her hard. Bena balanced the laundry on her lap, then placed it at her feet. The paper crackled.

"Buck," a man yelled at the end of the bar. The man waggled two fingers in the air.

Buck arranged a pair of cloudy glasses on the bar and poured two long shots from an unmarked bottle. The man threw them both back. Buck filled the empty glasses a second time and then walked away, wiping his palms on his white apron.

"Excuse me," Bena called as he passed near her. Buck poured himself a shot and tossed it back into his fish-wide mouth. He lit a cigarette, relaxing against the icebox.

Bena looked at the cowboy. "What's a lady have to do to get a drink around here?" she asked him.

The cowboy glanced up. His face was rangy and crooked. His nose angled right, as if he'd been riding in the same direction for years, the constant wind eroding the skin and bone of his face like a bold upheaval of granite.

He turned from her, expressionless. "A lady has to be a man," he answered.

One of the hay blonds squealed as a man tickled her. The cowboy nodded toward the back of the bar, where the blond squirmed on the man's lap.

"Either a man," he added, "or the furthest thing from a lady." He moved his glass toward her and tapped his fingers on the bar. "Buck," he said. "Another rye."

The bartender ambled over and saw the glass in front of Bena.

The cowboy threw a quarter on the bar and Buck plunked a glass next to it. He sloshed it full of yellow liquor in a violent, disapproving way.

"Keep the change," the cowboy said.

Buck leered at him. "Buying me off, Red?"

"Just a token of my appreciation."

"Don't split hairs." Buck dropped the quarter into his apron pocket. "Makes me irritable."

He walked back to the icebox and picked up his cigarette.

"Thanks," Bena said. She took a sip of the rye. She thought she could taste the salt from his fingers on the rim of the glass.

"Want some advice?"

Bena nodded.

"Enjoy your drink, and don't make a habit of coming here."

"No?"

"Depends on what you're after."

"Trouble," Bena answered. "Most definitely."

"Glad to hear it. I hate to see people wasting their time. Makes me goddamned sad."

Bena stared at the two women. The long-haired one had a man by the hand and was leading him through a concealed door in the back wall. Bena believed there was a staircase to the William Bent hidden behind it.

Behind the card tables, a man relieved himself in a metal bucket. His piss hit the bottom with the urgent sound of a cow being milked. Bena put a discreet hand against her breasts to feel whether they were leaking. They weren't. She looked at her watch: five-thirty.

The cowboy withdrew a worn leather pouch from his vest pocket and busied himself rolling a cigarette. "Smoke?" he asked.

Bena put the pinched end in her mouth and leaned forward so he could light it.

He rolled himself a cigarette and rotated so that he was facing her. "Red," he offered.

His hand was knuckly and unbalanced as she shook it. When he pulled it away, she saw he was missing the tops of his last two fingers.

Flying buffalo, she thought. They soared against the blue on great eagle wings, their hooves curled back neatly, their nostrils flared by the force of the wind.

"I've gathered," she replied. "Bena."

"Pleasure." His eyes examined her hand as well, landing briefly on her wedding ring. She watched as his previous assumptions about her became complicated by this new information. Amazing what we know of each other, or think we know of each other, just by glancing at each other's fingers.

Red's smoking hand propped his head above the bar. His fingers knotted themselves in his crimped, dusty hair, pressed flat in places by a now absent hat. Despite his nickname, his hair was more dark blond than it was red.

"Your husband know you're hanging around with piss-drunk iron-workers?"

Bena looked around for an ashtray in which to tap her cigarette. Red, aware of her confusion, flicked his ash onto the floor. She did the same.

"He told me I needed to make some friends."

"A sweet lady like you doesn't have any friends?"

Bena rolled the sleeves of her blouse above her elbows. Her hot skin itched beneath her damp slip.

"We just moved here. From Minnesota."

"Thus"—Red waved his cigarette at their dank surroundings—"your unfamiliarity with the local customs."

"Precisely." Bena smiled and took another sip of her rye. Buck topped off her glass without looking at her.

"Bark's worse than his bite," Red confided.

"Really?" Bena raised a dubious brow.

"You'd be surprised."

Red looked older than what she thought must be his rightful thirty years—the skin under his eyes starting to darken and swell, his cheeks chapped and hoed by the long days outdoors.

"Surprise me," Bena said.

He rubbed his eyelids with his thumb and forefinger. "Key to understanding Buck," he said, speaking into his palm, "is knowing that he watched his mother get beaten to death by his stepfather."

Bena stared at the spare, white man propped against the icebox.

"Well," she said, shifting in her stool. "You're fairly careless with other people's secrets."

"It's no secret. In fact, until I told you, you were the only person in this bar who didn't know it."

A message was carved into the bar beneath his clenched hand. "Fran is a sly quiff," the letters gnarled and hasty. She looked at him, this man who kept the secrets of a prostitute and of who knew how many other people locked between his ribs.

With one long breath he inhaled his cigarette to a pinpoint of ash. He wet his fingers and suffocated the glowing end between them, then threw the damp ember to the floor. He picked up his cowboy hat from the floor and patted it onto his head. He didn't offer her his hand this time, just tapped the front tip of the brim.

"Pleasure," he said. He finished his drink and pushed the empty glass toward the edge of the bar.

Through the noise she heard the front door open, then close. She stared at the place where his hand had been.

Fran is a sly quiff.

No one noticed her as she left Buck's, wading through the sweet and salty and smoky air with her laundry in her arms.

On the street the sun was still many feet above the horizon. She thought she could smell fire somewhere, the dry, high smell of burning, but maybe it was just the day extinguishing itself like Red's cigarette, pinched dead between two fingers. She walked up North Grand, past the filling station and the Woolworth's, past the giant sandstone mansions where Reimer and her kind would be drinking burgundy and eating Welsh rarebit and pretending that all was decent and right in the universe, that as with the Silver Queen, as with her, there weren't holes in their world big enough to drive a car through.

5. A TURK'S-HEAD KNOT

A great dust storm swept along the spine of the Front Range on July 3, ruining any hope of holiday festivities. Not much had been planned, with the twin discouragements provided by the drought and the Depression. The women from the Daughters of the Revolution Club had planned a pig roast by the stump of the Lynch Pine, an ancient tree from whose branches a tribe of Utes was hung in 1850. It was rumored that the first white woman to die in Colorado was buried among its roots, her old bones woven into the soil like a virus laying siege to this newly claimed territory. Much to Bena's dismay (she was a fan of fireworks), a pyrotechnics display was deemed too risky at the Lynch Pine, or anywhere else for that matter, because of the many small brushfires that had already been started by a carelessly tossed cigarette, an accidental engine spark, a perfectly aimed bolt of lightning.

Ted and Bena had planned to spend the following weekend in Cañon City, sightseeing at the Royal Gorge and the World's Highest Suspension Bridge, until they were invited at the last minute by Clyde Ashburne, Ted's colleague at the clinic, to accompany him and his wife to their cabin in the mountains. The Ashburnes and twelve other Pueblo families had built houses together at a place they'd named Cuerna Verde, Ted explained, a summer estate just west of the small town of Rye.

"We can't decline," Ted told her as he drank his morning coffee. Apparently, the invitation was to be viewed as the highest honor the established—and notoriously closed-society—Puebloans could bestow on a pair of newcomers.

Ted stood from the table and threw his uneaten toast into the wastebasket. He'd stopped eating breakfast at home, claiming that he hadn't much of an appetite in the morning. She couldn't help suspecting that he had somewhere else he'd rather be, or someone else he'd rather eat breakfast with. Her husband had never been short on hunger.

"Nor can we risk taking Little Ted to the mountains again," Bena pointed out.

Ted ran water in his cup and set it in the sink.

"I've already discussed it with Florence. She said she'd be happy to take him for the weekend."

Bena peered down at their son, feeding blithely on her nipple.

The baby had continued to be unusually lethargic, too dispassionate, it appeared, even to cry. He slept all morning before she left for work and, according to Florence, most of the afternoon. He'd awaken every few hours and feed, then retreat into his inert, radiating body. Bena assumed his inactivity was due to the heat, which saturated the houses so thoroughly that the walls baked well into the night. Only just before the sun appeared again might a cool breeze flicker over Bena in bed, for an unfair instant, and make her reach for the cotton sheet twisted around her calves.

"I don't think it's such a wise idea." She smoothed her hand over Little Ted's bowed leg. He had grown tolerant of being fed on a schedule, once every three hours for exactly forty minutes, yet he was still gaining weight at an unusually accelerated rate. His wallowing flesh had become like scar tissue, layers and layers of protection against the outside world, to soften the blows, benumb the heat, preserve his wet and far-down bones from becoming pockmarked and desiccated. She'd begun to see his fatness as protection against her, as well. She worried that he barricaded himself against her daily departures, so that anyone's hand, Florence's for instance, on his thick skin would be as good as any woman's.

Ted picked up his doctor's bag. He gave Bena a peck that made her feel colder and lonelier than if he'd left her for the day unkissed. When he reached the kitchen door, he turned back.

"Funny." He held the door open, half home, half gone.

"What's funny?"

He drew a hand across his forehead.

"What?" Bena pressed.

"I wouldn't have thought leaving him would bother you so much."

She was stung by the thwap of the screen door. She saw him wave to the old man across the street, whose primary activity consisted of eating walnuts on his front porch and nodding at cars.

It was always hard to depart for work in the afternoon, but today, as she surrendered Little Ted to Florence, it was like ripping her arm from its socket.

"Something eating you, Mrs. Jonssen?" Florence asked. Her blouse gaped to reveal the paunchy tops of her freckled breasts.

Bena smiled, she was fine, really, thanks for asking. She was almost out the door when she stopped.

"Think it's wrong, my working like this?" she asked.

"Wrong?" Florence said, picking old varnish from her nails. "Wrong how?"

"I don't know. It's not exactly usual."

"Not exactly usual for you," Florence said.

"Maybe I'm being a bad mother."

Florence laughed. "Your husband telling you that?"

Bena looked at the floor, not wanting to speak badly of her husband.

Florence pushed up her bathrobe sleeve and rotated her arm so that the white tender underpart was exposed. She pointed to a series of round brown scars near her wrist. "When there wasn't a clean ashtray around," she explained. "But my mother stayed home with us all day."

Bena wondered what it would take for a woman to do a thing so cruel—people could be driven by rage or a misguided artistic impulse to inflict all sorts of unthinkable wounds. It was not her place to judge a woman whose frustration she could only guess at. Still, it nagged at her, a mother's capacity to burn a child like that. On the way to work Bena saw those scars each time she blinked, sunspots blooming across her vision.

WHEN SHE ARRIVED at the *Chieftain*, Ham Paxton was asleep at her desk with his feet up.

"Afternoon," she said, patting him on the knee.

She thought he might have failed to register her from his sleep, but then he lifted a groggy hand in greeting.

Ham was an unfortunately plump and pink-complexioned fellow. Upon being introduced to him on her first day of work, Bena had to bite back the inevitable desire to comment on the fact that he, appropriately, *looked* like a ham roast, flushed and sweaty. He was frequently at her desk when she arrived at the office; Cecil had warned her both to expect the invasion and to accept it good-humoredly, since Ham's wife had just divorced him. Sick of their house and the leaving it reminded him of, Ham had taken to sleeping in the office and returning home every other day to shower and change. Bena didn't know why he liked her desk in particular, except that it was in the rear, away from the dairy delivery trucks that coughed up their clanking charges below the front windows at the crack of dawn. Or maybe he just wanted to know what it felt like to be Bena Duse Jonssen, a woman who had seemingly little in life to concern her.

"What're we baby-sitting the society ladies now?" she'd heard him growl to Cecil on that first day. Cecil had the only real office at the *Chieftain*, a modest room behind a fogged glass door that didn't shut completely, so that every private conference was more or less a public affair. The last she heard Ham utter before he stormed out was, "I hope to hell that fancy doctor husband of hers is paying you well for this." He burst into the hall and, when he saw Bena standing by the water fountain, stared her down with his eyes, the two beads of gunmetal gray struggling to keep the surrounding flesh from healing up over them for good.

Bena followed him to his desk. "I heard what you said about me," she said.

"Good," he replied, threading a sheet of paper into his typewriter, the letters on the concave keys obscured by dried coffee. "I meant every word of it."

"You needn't pretend to like me for everyone else's benefit."

"I never do anything for anyone else's benefit."

"Wonderful," Bena said. "Because that would be too insulting."

"Sweetie," he said, "the last thing I want to do is insult you."

"Particularly since we've gotten off to such a fine start," she had responded.

Ham now rearranged his sleeping face with a puffy hand. He still wore his wedding ring.

Bena sat on the edge of her desk, resting her feet on the rim of the wastecan. "Ever heard of a place called Cuerna Verde?"

"Hearing's all I've done." He pointed to his fat, stale self. "I ain't exactly the type of guy they like up there."

"But what is it?"

"Some rich-people getaway in the Rockies. The mountain's named after a Ute chief who was killed there during a battle with some white settlers." He shook his head. "Leave it to rich people to name their prime piece of real estate after the Indian they killed to get it."

Bena hopped off the desk. She could see this was going to turn into one of Ham's wrathful tirades against the upper crust of Pueblo, and it was always too early, too late, too anything for one of those.

"Get you some coffee?"

"Nah," he said, stretching his arms. His shirt was sweat-stained, as if he'd been having the kind of dreams that break out all over like a fever. "Makes me anxious. Need to be on my tiptoes today."

"What's today?" Bena asked.

"Whaddaya mean, what's today? The Armadillo's coming today."

This was the residue of his nightmare, surely, but instead she inquired politely, "The Armadillo?"

"Cecil runs the place, but the Armadillo *owns* it. If you can appreciate that subtle difference. I know you ladies don't have much of a head for business."

"Funny name," Bena commented.

Ham smiled and stood up, smoothing out his hopelessly wrinkled pants. "Wait until you meet him," he said. "It won't seem so funny then." He saluted her, thanked her for her hospitality, and wandered away.

Bena wondered whether she should tell him that he needed a bath and a clean shirt, but she didn't want to press her luck. She had a feeling that people who loved Ham too attentively found themselves swiftly shut out of his life; he could maintain a steady, halfhearted intimacy only with those who left him alone.

THE ARMADILLO'S ARRIVAL was expected for two o'clock. At five minutes before two, Bena followed Ham into the back conference room and took a seat at the long wooden table. There had once been enough staff at the *Chieftain* to fill the chairs, but now there were only Bena, Ham, and Hank and Felix Best, two earnest reporters who took their name to heart, working long, energetic hours, always beaming and clear-faced. There were the two secretaries, Gladys and Maeve, who did the lion's share of the work. Most of the news printed in the paper came over the wires from Denver and New York and Washington and Los Angeles. Gladys and Maeve transcribed the ticks, their fingers blurring over the typewriter keys. Today, as every day, they were impeccably groomed, their hair expertly bobbed, and their faces livid with rouge. They flaunted the practiced vanity of beautiful women—flipping compact cases open at their desks, looking in every available reflective surface, wringing their hands with cream after they roughed them up spooling a single sheet of paper into the typewriter— as if attempting to fool people into overlooking the fact that they were relentlessly plain girls.

A fan rotated overhead and the venetian blinds were dropped clear to the sills. Ham ate a sandwich while the Best brothers were engaged in a quiet but intense disagreement. They were equally blond, but their faces were quite different. Felix had soft, starchy features and a poor complexion, Hank a prominent nose and bulging eyes that made him appear to be in a constant, unrelenting state of shock. They both wore their hair girlishly long, as if their mother were still doing the honors with the aid of a soup bowl and leaving their tresses a touch long as many a daughterless woman tends to do, hoping against all practical hope that at least one of her boys might transform into the girl she'd failed to produce.

Cecil smoked and brooded in the corner.

Bena was dreading her encounter with the *Chieftain*'s owner after the reprimand she'd received from Cecil an hour earlier.

"You wanted to see me," she had reminded him. They were alone in his office, the door half closed. She'd unfolded and folded her legs.

"Actually," he said, "I wanted to warn you."

He turned the piece of paper he'd been reading so that it faced her. It was her article on Reimer Lee Jackson. One paragraph had been circled with a red pencil, and in the margins was a notation, "C—Who is this dumb broad?" in a boxy, unfamiliar handwriting. The broad in question was clearly not Reimer but her.

Wealthy, generous, elegantly fading, Reimer Lee Jackson keeps her house on North Grand Avenue like a keepsake box, decorated with mementos of her former lives: her girlhood in San Francisco, her familial ties to colonial India, her engagement to Abbott Jackson in the bowels of a silver mine in Mexico's Sierra Madre. A thin, active woman, Mrs. Jackson not only is president of both the American Club of University Women and the Pueblo Federation of Women's Christian Organizations, but is, additionally, an immensely creative woman with a flair for storytelling. Even so, each sugared anecdote asserts an underlying bleakness that made this reporter wonder where, precisely, the truth lies beneath her fabulous confections.

She pushed the article back toward Cecil.

"Too fervent?"

"It's not that." He seemed genuinely apologetic. "There's just an unspoken rule here, that, since it's unspoken, I naturally failed to tell you."

Bena put a finger over the burning words "dumb broad," snuffing them out. "I can't be completely truthful," she ventured.

"You can't be completely truthful," Cecil elaborated, "about some people."

"Ah," Bena replied. She saw Cecil eyeing the desk drawer where, she knew, he kept a flask full of bourbon. "And shall I be issued a list of these people's names?"

Cecil laughed awkwardly. He was not a manipulative or corrupt man, but neither was he a man to battle with forces greater than himself.

"This is where the unspoken part comes in." His fingers formed a pyramid that rested on the worldly swell of his stomach. "You're a smart girl, Bena. That's why I hired you."

She left his office feeling shaky but proud. Now, however, the comment rang more as an insult than a compliment.

Behind her, the conference room door opened, then shut.

Horace Gast walked to the front of the table, his face red and perspiring. He was wearing the same black bow tie he'd worn the day they'd met, but this time a cowboy hat teetered atop his wide head. His eyes trolled the edge of the table, settling on her.

"Mrs. Jonssen," he said. "What a shock to see you here."

Ham kicked her under the table and she kicked him back. She sensed the curious stares of everyone around the table on her.

"Mr. Gast," she replied, "I might say the same of you."

She recalled his vague, elliptical behavior during their brief car ride together, how he'd asked her questions but answered none himself, only led her, without necessarily lying, to believe things to be true about him that were not. That she'd believed him made her the usual fool, rather than the exceptional one.

Mr. Gast wheeled a chalkboard closer to the table. He grabbed a thin piece of chalk in his big hand and wrote a single word.

"Bonfils."

His letters sloped and made Bena think of old pears or old women, round objects becoming rounder and losing all claim to any specific shape. She had seen them before: "Dumb broad."

Someone coughed behind her.

She turned to see a tiny, muscular man in a gray suit and a homburg, standing against the wall. He tried to appear as any stranger, a man waiting for a train, perhaps, who had ended up in the *Chieftain*'s conference room purely by accident.

"So," Mr. Gast went on, indicating the chalkboard behind him. "I'm wondering if that word means anything to anyone here."

Silence.

"Come on now, kids. Do I have to call on you like this is goddamned physics class?"

Silence.

"Skulduggery," Ham said, stifling a belch.

Mr. Gast focused his rodent gaze on Ham. His eyes made him look either fearfully alert or fearfully stupid. Gladys and Maeve let loose a series of interlocking, nervous titters and the Best brothers coughed into their hands. Bena said nothing.

"Skulduggery," Mr. Gast approved. "Very good, Mr. Paxton."

"Thank you, sir."

"Didn't know you were so well acquainted with polysyllabic diction."

"I only ask for a momentary suspension of your disbelief, sir."

"Call it suspension of disbelief, or call it charity, however you prefer."

Ham flushed an even richer shade of his usual pink and crumpled the paper from his sandwich into a tight, wrathful ball.

"How about you, Mrs. Jonssen? This word mean anything to you?"

"It means 'good son.' "

"Pardon?"

"In French. *Bon fils*. Good son."

"Interesting," Mr. Gast said. "Would somebody care to enlighten *Madame* Jonssen about the meaning of Bonfils in plain old English?"

Hank Best spoke up. His voice was quavering and monotone, his stick-out eyes bored into the wainscoting on the opposite wall. "Bonfils was the publisher of *The Denver Post*. He was a controversial figure whom many accused of encouraging the proliferation of so-named circus journalism. Rapes, executions, scandals, bank heists."

"He singlehandedly destroyed the reputation of a lot of decent, hardworking newspapermen," Ham finished.

"Perhaps," Mr. Gast conceded. He looked down at the table, a well in which he'd lost something he'd long before resigned himself to losing. "But let's not forget that newspapers are a business, as well as a service. For all his faults, while Bonfils was publisher of *The Denver Post*, the paper had a greater circulation than all the others in this state combined."

Mr. Gast walked to the window. He pried open the venetian blinds with two fingers as a man at an auction might pull apart the lips of a horse to check the teeth for rot.

Outside, the light had grown yellow, as it did when a mild dust storm was stirring up dead soil in some distant patch of barren farmland. Florence claimed she could tell where the storms had been born by the color of the cloud. Those with a reddish tint originated in Oklahoma, the yellower ones came from Kansas or Nebraska, the black ones from the Dakotas.

Mr. Gast returned to his chair. He played with the cap to his lighter, open and shut, open and shut. "Tell me, Gladys."

Gladys's cheeks blanched beneath their indelicate rouge. A hand fussed with a bobby pin at her temple.

"Yes, Mr. Gast?"

"How often does your mother listen to the radio?"

"My mother?"

"Indeed."

"Oh, I'd say every day."

Mr. Gast traced his mustache like the spine of a thin, exotic animal, a ferret or a mongoose. "And what does she listen to?"

"What does everyone listen to? George and Gracie. Ma Perkins. *The Romance of Helen Trent*. The news program."

"And your brother?"

"Which one, Mr. Gast?"

"It makes no difference, Gladys."

"Do they listen to the radio, you mean? Sometimes, yes. But mostly they read."

"The *Chieftain*?"

"Well, naturally, yes," she lied, "but what they really like are the comics."

"*Dick Tracy*?"

"Yes, oh, they love *Dick Tracy*. And the Perry Mason books. They adored those. They're always pretending to be detectives now, looking for dead bodies in the river."

"And have they had any luck?"

"Fortunately, no."

"And how about movies, Gladys? Do your brothers go to movies?"

"Yes, every week. I mean, when we can afford to let them."

"And yourself, Gladys? Do you go to the movies?"

Gladys's color returned. Bena could see her becoming the glamorous girl of her own screen-fed imagination. She almost looked beautiful.

"Yes," Gladys whispered. "I adore the movies."

Mr. Gast seemed to regard her rapture as irrevocable evidence that she was an unforgivably simple creature. "So Gladys, I want you to vow to be absolutely honest with me."

She nodded.

"Let's say it's a Saturday and you have the day off from work."

Gladys interrupted. "I watch my brothers on Saturdays and do the laundry."

Mr. Gast smiled at her patronizingly. "Let's pretend, can we do that?"

Gladys looked puzzled. "Can I pretend and be honest at the same time?"

Ham snickered. Mr. Gast appeared to have ruptured something in his oddly shaped head, a hose or a piston.

"We're playing a game, Gladys. For instance, I might ask you, If you were the richest lady in the world, would you decide to build a castle in Rome or Paris?"

"If I'm the richest lady in the world, I should have both."

Mr. Gast's face reddened.

"But I understand, now," she said hurriedly.

"It's Saturday, and you haven't anything to do. I'll give you two choices as to how you can spend this rare, free Saturday afternoon. You could go to the movies . . ."

Ham, anticipating where this interrogation was headed, slid low in his chair.

"Or Gladys," Mr. Gast continued, "you could stay home and read *The Pueblo Chieftain*."

Gladys looked at Mr. Gast as if she'd been made a fool of countless times before but still couldn't believe a man would be so mean.

"Horace," Cecil chimed in, "I think you've made your point."

"Have I, Cecil?" Mr. Gast asked. "I'm not sure that I have. Why don't you tell me, Mr. Paxton, what exactly the point is that I'm making."

Ham held up a palm, declining the honor. "You're too subtle for me, sir."

Mr. Gast walked around to Ham's side of the table, stood behind him, and put his hands on his shoulders. He bent down so that his lips were next to Ham's ear. "Take a stab at it," he demanded.

Ham rubbed his face vigorously with both hands, shaking Mr. Gast off his shoulders in the process. "You're trying to tell us that the *Chieftain* is now competing with movies, books, and radio, and if we want to keep our readers we have to make the paper an experience that is less about truth and news and more about sideshow perversions."

Mr. Gast circled the table. It seemed they were playing a malicious variant of duck-duck-goose. "Aptly summarized, Mr. Paxton. As always, I appreciate your cynicism and your candor."

"Why don't you tell us exactly what is it you expect from us, Horace," Cecil said. His eyes were dark with the sort of exhaustion that comes from the continual confrontation of deeper and deeper degrees of resignation.

"I *expect*," Horace said, banging a fist on the table and sending an explosion of dust aloft, "you all to be reporters. I *expect*"—bang—

"you to do the jobs I hired you to do, which is to say, I want you to *find me stories*. I don't want you to just look out the damned window and tell me what you see happening on Union Avenue. I want you to start turning over rocks. God knows there are enough maggots in this town. They must be festering somewhere."

He started to perspire, tiny dots welling up on his temple. The man in the gray suit approached to dab Mr. Gast's brow with a handkerchief.

"Thanks, Billy," Mr. Gast said. "Get the car ready, will you please?"

Mr. Gast balanced his cowboy hat once again on his head. "And pay careful attention to how you interpret the word 'maggots,' " he warned. "I'm speaking to you in particular, Mrs. Jonssen. I don't want to be wasting precious column space reviling the few honorable folks who still live in this town." He tipped his hat and gave her a hungry assessment that made her feel she'd been either licked or spat upon.

The room deflated in relief. The tears that Gladys had held successfully at bay surged beyond their dikes. They eroded a line through the powdered finish on her cheeks. Bena could see the raw, adolescent skin beneath.

They returned to their desks and the office was filled with the sound of typewriters. The keys hit new paper with a vacuous sound, as if the words pressed into the blank surface were lacking in content and conviction. A few minutes passed, and Ham appeared in the doorway of her cubicle.

"What'd I tell you?"

Bena looked up. "You could have told me a bit more, frankly."

"There ain't no replacement for the real, bona fide encounter," he said, smirking. "Besides, seems to me you and Mr. Armadillo have previously acquainted yourselves."

"Already looking under rocks, huh?" Bena asked, brushing past him to the wooden filing cabinet.

"He's the maggotiest of them all. But I'm not that stupid. I know which side my bread's buttered on."

"Then forget about it."

He swung a big arm across the open file drawer, impeding her pretend search for a pretend document.

"Look." Bena lost her temper. "You want to ask me a question, why don't you come out and ask it?"

"Because you know what the question is."

She flopped into her chair. She practiced folding her hands the way Cecil did, balancing fingers against fingers and thumbs against thumbs to form a pyramid. She raised the pyramid to her face and looked at Ham through it.

"Yes, I've met him before," she said.

"And?"

"And nothing. He helped me and my husband when we were in a tight spot. That's all."

"Mmmm," Ham said, still doubtful.

"And as to why he looked at me the way that he did," Bena continued, anticipating his next question, "I haven't the foggiest idea. Because he can, I guess."

Ham walked to Cecil's office, apparently to report what he'd been sent out to learn. Bena supposed her feelings should be hurt, that Cecil and Ham, two men she considered friends, would so quickly abandon their good opinions of her and cast her as a woman capable of falling under the sway of a man like Horace Gast. Then again, had she not imagined such a falling herself? She couldn't very well blame them for letting their minds wander down a similarly seedy alley.

Speaking of alleys . . .

Bena walked to the window to see if there were any signs of the woman or Red. Looking out the window for stories, yet in this case she was certain she'd found a story. But she hadn't laid eyes on either of them for two weeks, and she was eager to apologize for her inappropriate candor at Buck's Silo. She thought about Red every night when the sun was beginning to set, when the whole world—even a world this godforsaken—seemed as if some benevolent soul above was dreaming it.

BENA LEFT the *Chieftain* at three so that she'd have time to pick up the laundry, straighten the house, prepare the formula, and pack their belongings for a prompt five-o'clock departure.

Little Ted lay on their bed as she packed and listened to a concert on the radio. She picked him up and danced with him, but he began to whimper, his head lolling back and his mouth making guttural noises she read as displeasure. He seemed more content among the piles of clothes. She believed he liked music, but didn't like to be touched while it was playing. His eyes wandered over the ceiling, catching on nothing, and his legs and arms vibrated to the scratchy sounds emanating from the radio.

Bena lay next to him and placed him on his side; she'd read in a book that mothers should encourage their babies to use their stomach muscles and learn to roll over. Most babies, the book said, wouldn't require much encouragement; but Little Ted lacked physical initiative of any sort. She couldn't feel any muscles under all that skin and fat. She massaged his stomach, pushed and prodded and kneaded his middle, but even his bones were difficult to discern beneath the obstinate, fleshy mounds. Of course, it was impossible to articulate her concerns and find a sympathetic ear when her baby made women cry on the street, the very sight of him enough to make them drop to their knees and thrust their pointy faces into his warm, yeasty body. Even she could find her own worries absurd from time to time; here she was, the mother of an infant whose sweetness caused her nothing but concern.

Before shutting the suitcase, Bena remembered to pack the breast pump. She was terrified that her milk would dry up over the weekend.

She'd heard of that happening—one day without a baby, and a body forgets.

At ten to five she walked reluctantly upstairs to Florence's apartment. Little Ted continued to sleep, unaware, as she passed him to Florence, his eyes rippling like tiny minnows under the blue of his lids.

There was breast milk in the icebox in their apartment, she explained to Florence, to be used immediately. After that, Ted said, the baby would be fine for two days on the fortified sugar water he brought home from the clinic. It was the same formula used to nurse ailing calves on a nearby ranch. Clyde Ashburne swore it was better than human milk, sweeter and more consistent, its taste and texture less affected by the mother's diet.

Bena watched as Florence's body adapted to the shape of her baby. She seemed to take to mothering naturally, even though she'd never had children herself. She'd been plagued by miscarriages. Ten in all, she'd told Bena. But Ted said he'd place bets that Florence was taking a bit of license with the term. He said any fetus would have the good sense to miscarry if it was skewered enough times with a sharp length of plumber's wire.

"We'll be fine," Florence responded to Bena's worried, jealous look. "Besides, it's not as if a person gets asked to Cuerna Verde every day."

"You've been there?"

Florence looked off into the air just above Bena's left shoulder. "Oh, years ago. I went up there with a nice man, a very famous grain distributor I was involved with for a few months. In fact . . ." She disappeared into her bedroom, and Bena could hear the crunch of Florence's digging in one of her many jewelry boxes. She emerged with a blue paste choker stretched across her fingers. A lone earring dangled from the clasp.

"Said he'd picked it out especially for me." She held the choker to her neck. It made her skin look bruised and sallow.

Later, as she and Ted packed the car, Bena related the story of the necklace and how it worried her to leave their listless baby with such a misguided dreamer. Ted told her she was being silly. Nothing wrong with Florence Early, he insisted, just a woman who loved too much for the little bit she'd received in return. Who could blame her for imagining herself to be a woman on whom men bestowed scrupulously chosen necklaces?

Yes, Bena thought to herself, remembering her own necklace, chosen for another woman's neck. Who could blame her, indeed?

But it was too beautiful an evening to be bitter, the sky a brilliant orange-gold, the air crystalline and precise, allowing the mountains in the distance the unusual luxury of maintaining their sharp edges. It was too beautiful and she was too lonely and wrong-skinned to permit that quick happiness to go to waste. She let it cheer her, because the alternative was to cry and sulkily resent this man who pulled her away from her son for the weekend. She shook her bitterness and anger out through her feet, stamping her shoes against the ground. Bena reached up to kiss Ted on the cheek before running upstairs to say a final goodbye to the baby, as if to convince them both that the air between them was as clear as that between Pueblo and the facet-cut mountains.

BENA WAS in charge of the map, little more than a poor rendering of equally poor roads sketched by Dr. Ashburne on the back of a prescription slip. On their way out of town they took Santa Fe Avenue past the railroad tracks and the Baker Steam factory, driving through a sheepish neighborhood of one-room miners' shacks that, out of proportion with their station, enjoyed a most spectacular view of the Rockies through their tiny back windows.

"Odd that they wouldn't put bigger windows there to take advantage of the view," Bena remarked. She poured Ted a thimbleful of martini from a Thermos she'd prepared. Normally he didn't condone drinking on the road—he'd resewn the organs into a few too many drunk drivers—but this qualified as a brief vacation. They were lighter and giddier with each other than they'd been in a long while, with the road and the sun and the mountains moving past their car windows. She blamed it on the cheerful burning quality of the light, and the fact that they were headed skyward, soon to be suspended thousands of feet above this life that wasn't what either of them had envisioned.

"Remember the Montoosik penitentiary?" Ted asked. He had spent a summer as the fix-it man at a prison in Minnesota, putting convicts back together after they'd effectively taken one another apart. "I'd been there all day and used up all my anesthetic when I got to the last guy, who had done time at Alcatraz. A good friend of his had pushed a saucer shard through the palm of his hand. I told him it was going to hurt like hell. Know what he said?"

Bena shook her head.

"He said, 'Doc, nothing on earth could hurt as bad as being stuck in the middle of San Francisco Bay, staring at all that sky and water and having none of it.' "

Overtaken by a surge of affection, Bena knelt on the car seat and kissed him. He kissed her back, just long enough to lose sight of the road, to swerve and make them both laugh at the idea that they would risk death for the taste of each other.

Bena stared at her husband, the plains spooling past his head in the distance, trying to recall the quivery, split-open sensation she'd had when she'd first met him, a pleasant sort of seasickness that had been cured by familiarity and small irritations.

"What are you looking at?" Ted feigned embarrassment. He stared at her the way he used to, when he thought he might come to know her every old scar, her every pleasure, her every undoing.

We should lay ourselves bare, Bena thought. He would tell her about the women he'd undressed and the woman in the green coat whom he presumably hadn't. She'd tell him about her brother, how she'd seen him tear the underwear and bruise the mouth of Myrna

Voskamp, and about the look on Jonas's face before the lake erased it. She'd never told Ted about her brother because it didn't fit with how she'd allowed her husband to understand her. To him she was an acceptably flawless woman if he didn't look at her private chaos; she was pretty enough and full of the right kind of blood and life. She looked wonderful in skirts and anything blue, she was a decent shot with a rifle, she was witty and saucy and the periodic victor at cards. She was not the sister to a man who forced himself on a poor girl named Myrna in graying underwear. She was not the sister who watched as her brother sank away in a storm and who never cried about it, not once. She was Bena Ingrid Duse, who looked like a ravishing confection in her mousseline de soie wedding gown, whose veil was made of Italian lace that had belonged to her dead mother, whose bridesmaids were like exotic plants in their green silk damask.

And why not? Why not tell him everything? Look around, she thought, gazing over the burnt plains, the falling-down fences. What is not bare and destroyed, what is not eroded, what is not unrecognizable and infertile? Yet these softnesses between them were so rare that she was disinclined to complicate them with unwanted confessions, with long-hidden, unflattering stories about themselves that wouldn't make much of a difference now anyway.

Instead, she pointed to two narrow tracks pressed into the dry grasses leading away from the main road. He drove her to a deserted homesteader's house behind a wall of ash trees, the only species that required so little out of life it could survive months without rain. Inside, the table was set as if a family was very late for dinner, the china sloped with dirt like a withering roast. Bena brushed off a plate to reveal an ugly pattern, a windmill and a Dutch girl in her blue stick-out skirt. She pulled Ted by the hand to a metal frame bed. He peeled back the onion-colored quilt and pushed her down into the dusty webbing where a stranger had once slept. He unbuttoned her shirt with fingers that weren't cold and didn't remind her at all of sleek surgical instruments, scalpels, and such.

TED PULLED into the feed store parking lot and stepped out to stretch. Bena, parched from the martinis (of which, as passenger and mother without a baby to breast-feed for the weekend, she'd drunk more than her fair share), walked into the store to find a glass of water.

A bell tinkled rustily as the door shut behind her, catching the slow attention of two men—one old, one neither old nor young, both with mouths so withered they appeared not to have let loose a word in decades—seated on stools behind a high wooden counter. A board over their heads listed various grains (wheat, millet, corn, barley) and the prices per pound. The bins lining the walls were almost all empty, the gritty floor and the stale, powdery smell of corn the only evidence that the men carried any merchandise except their truculent selves. Large metal scoops dangled on chains from the ceiling, swinging with the wind Bena brought in with her.

The old man was doing figures on a sheet of paper with the flat nub of a pencil. The other man (his son, she assumed, by the similar way their hair came to an off-center peak low on their foreheads) was chewing on the stem of an unlit pipe. He had a rubbery manner about his head and neck like a dead man underwater.

A radio played in a back room. It echoed through the empty store, as there was nothing, no barley or grain or millet, to keep it from doing otherwise. She recalled a conversation she'd had recently with Ham about the drought, the lack of crops and lack of feed, and thus the farmers' inability to keep their cattle from starving. As a mercy measure, many farmers around Pueblo decided to shoot their livestock, ending their lives with a quick pull of the rifle trigger instead of listening to the accusatory lowing day in, day out. They'd drive the sick and knobby cattle in sideboard trucks to the rendering plant outside the city limits (by now, nothing more than a giant hole in the ground), line them up at the edge of the pit, shoot them, and watch their depleted bodies fall into the abyss. Ham said it sounded like wet mailbags full of candlesticks when cattle landed on those that had died before them. On days when the wind was blowing right or wrong, Bena could hear the rifle shots through her office window.

The old man looked up from his scribbling.

"Lost?" he asked. He appeared hopeful; the thought of her misfortune might amuse him.

"I was wondering if I could get a drink of water."

The man eyed her warily. He prodded his son in the shoulder with a crooked finger that looked as if it had been broken a hundred times, from years of seeking his son's attention in precisely this curt manner. "Go on," he scolded. "Get the lady her water."

The son shuffled into the back room. His dungarees hung low, and he balanced heavily on the outside of his soles so that the front and arch of his shoes were forced up, misshapen. Bena heard the squeak of a tap turning, and then the whole building shook and moaned with the effort of coughing up a glassful of water.

The son returned carrying the glass at the same angle as his tilted head. Bena grimaced at its pitiful contents—two fingers of water, reddish and nearly opaque. She could see marks on the glass where the last drinker's mouth had been.

"Thank you," she said.

He was probably fifty years old, but the son looked at her longer than a person that age should, with a bleak hunger focusing his otherwise swimming vision. She stepped back and he stepped with her, his shoes crushing down on her toes. His breath was warm and grassy, as if he'd been nipping at a horse's feed trough.

Bena glanced to the father for assistance, but he pretended to be busy, flipping through a ledger and picking the wood from his pencil's dull point with a long black thumbnail.

Bena backed away another step. The son put a hand on her shoulder. Bena gave his hand a kind but firm push. She looked again to his father for help, but now the old man was watching with interest.

Undeterred by Bena's rejection, the son raised the flat of his palm until it was even with Bena's breast. The old man smiled, exposing his colorless gums.

They were all startled by the sound of boots on the stair outside.

Ted appeared momentarily confused by the odd configuration of old man, half-wit son, wife. "Evening," he said.

The son dropped his head and loped back behind the safety of the counter. The old man didn't return the greeting. "Lost?" he asked.

"I'm with her."

The old man leered at them both. "And who says she knows where she's going?"

Ted turned to Bena. "Let's keep on," he said. "It's getting dark."

"Course it got dark," the old man chimed in. "Bluster headed our way."

"Bluster?" Bena asked.

"Dust storm." He jabbed his bent finger toward the back room. "Heard it on the radio. Pueblo got hit pretty bad."

Bena and Ted looked at each other. In her mind she saw dirt. It was blowy and deceptively pretty, it covered the house at 25 North Grand until it was nothing more than a pitched dune with a poking-up chimney.

"How much farther to Cuerna Verde?" Ted asked.

The old man snickered. "Should have figured you was headed to Cuerna Verde." He pronounced it "Kee-yoo-nah Vur-dee." "About fifteen minutes, if you know where you're going."

"Thanks." Ted grabbed Bena by the elbow, steered her toward the door.

"Watch out you don't end up on La Punta Road. Man rode his horse right off the cliff there in the middle of a snowstorm once. One second the ground was right beneath him, next it was a mile away."

"Thanks," Ted repeated. He hadn't heard a word of the old man's warning.

Ted was right. It had grown dark, but only in the direction they'd come from. Pueblo had disappeared inside a black tidal wave of dust, sweeping south along the spine of the Rockies. Dirt rasped against every hard surface like the finest rain.

Ted waved Bena inside the car. It was unnaturally quiet with the doors and windows closed.

"I'll never forgive you if anything happens to him," she said. It was his fault that the baby was alone with a woman who'd pricked her insides with wire and couldn't be trusted in a storm.

"He's better off where he is. Fact is, we're lucky we don't have him with us."

Bena watched the darkness approaching their little automobile, already squeaking and swaying on its axles in the half-wind. Ahead, the sky burned. You'd hardly suspect what destruction licked at your heels, Bena thought, unless you knew how to read the warning in the brilliance before you. Only a great amount of dust could create that kind of fire in the sky, refracting the fading day and sounding an alarm.

Ted drove them swiftly through what little remained of Crow Junction. The road dipped into a canyon with walls of smooth limestone. The world took on a wilder air—the aridity of rock, the blunt-topped beginnings of mesas, the periodic veinings of red iron ore revealed in the earth the road cut through.

Holes in the road the size of horses' skulls forced Ted to swerve abruptly from left to right and back. The road continued along the floor of the shallow canyon. Ted took a fast curve and had to slam on the brakes to avoid hitting a pair of emaciated cows. The animals stared from the middle of the road, mooing miserably as if they had planned to die this way and Ted, in an act of misguided humanity, had foiled their careful scheme. He honked a few times and was about to step out of the car when they ambled into the brush, their hipbones working like jaws at a gristly piece of meat.

The storm was making better time than they were, the cloud undoubtedly closer to them than they were to the base of Cuerna Verde. Bena guessed the soft, billowy wall to be a hundred feet high, maybe even two hundred. She watched it ink up the sky.

"We're never going to make it," she said. She tried not to think about all the people who had died in dust storms, asphyxiating in their own cars, which became, after a while, metal coffins onto which the sky threw its giant, final fistfuls of dirt.

They drove into Rye, the last spatter of civilization before they started up into the Rockies. Rye, population seventy-one ($7 \times 1 =$ the month of her birth, but $7 + 1$ produced a dreaded 8, which, given the storm behind them, wielded considerably more power), comprised a glum little church and a supply store with a tilting porch. There was not a soul to be seen, not a single light in a single window, not a single car parked by the edge of the road.

"Maybe we should stop here," Bena suggested. "Wait it out in the church."

Ted flattened the prescription slip across the steering wheel. "According to Ashburne, we have only two miles left."

"This storm's going to be on us in a matter of minutes," Bena argued, craning to see above the roof of the car.

Ted turned on the headlights and asked her to pound down on the window handles in the back, to be sure the glass was wedged as tight against the frames as possible.

Bena knew from his tone of voice that there was no space in the car for her fears or dissensions. She looked at the map to see what lay ahead. She was discouraged to note that the two remaining miles required them to make turns onto roads that according to Ashburne had no proper signs but were designated by a dead tree, a large gourd-shaped rock, and a barn with a rotted roof, none of which would be visible when the fanned ire of the storm had descended upon them.

They made one turn (Dead Tree, 0.7 miles), and even a second (Large Gourd-Shaped Rock, 0.3 miles), before the storm hit full force, with one turn and less than a mile remaining.

The birds came first, a tangled dark flock of them. They were silent as they tumbled through the air. Bena wondered whether they were already dead, their necks snapped, their bodies nothing but feathered tumbleweeds turning in the sky.

The wind followed. The car was smacked broadside by a big, meaty hand, and swayed on its wheels, threatening to roll over. Ted perched on top of the steering wheel, trying to see through the windshield. He switched on the wipers, which made a reluctant screech as they dragged dirt over the glass.

"God damn," he muttered, "I can't see a goddamned thing."

The visibility had diminished to less than two feet, and Ted drove more by feel than sight. As the wheels on one side or the other sloped downhill, he knew he was nearing the shoulder, was about to fall into the irrigation ditches along the road.

Ted stopped the car. "Did you see that?" He pointed out Bena's window.

"What?"

"I thought I saw the barn off to the right."

Everything and nothing burst out of the agitated dark, faces and cars and barns and animals. The dirt swirled and suggested a thousand shapes, but only for an instant. Then the vision was torn apart by the wind.

"I'm going outside to look." Ted rummaged under the seat for a cloth to put over his nose. He found the old shirt he used to wipe bugs from the windshield, and tore it in half. He tied this around his face so that his mouth and nose were obscured. Bena was thinking about the dust storm warnings that appeared regularly in the *Chieftain* since their arrival. "Ten Facts for Survival." Number 6 recommended that "a potential victim on the roads should never abandon his vehicle, as it is easy to become quickly disoriented in visibilities of less than ten feet."

While Ted pulled on a hat, Bena searched under the seat for the laundry line she'd purchased and failed to hang in the backyard.

Ted allowed her to knot one end of the twine to his wrist. The other end she instructed him to secure to her door handle once he was outside. They agreed that should she start to panic, she could tug on the rope and he would return to the car. He gave her a quick kiss, pulling away when she sought something more meaningful.

He motioned to her to put her head down. She covered her face with her hands to keep the dust out of her eyes and mouth.

Bena heard him scrabbling outside as he tied the twine to the door handle. He knocked twice on her window. Two raggedy steps away from the car and he was invisible, dissolved into the world of gray, indistinct particles.

She looked at her watch: seven-forty.

She started to fashion her own face rag out of the ripped shirt. It was growing darker outside. Perhaps the sun was setting somewhere behind the storm.

Seven forty-five.

Seven fifty.

Seven fifty-four.

She tied the rag over her mouth and nose, then turned the window handle. The storm pushed itself through the crack, and the wind's screaming dropped a few octaves as she rolled the vibrating window wider. With both hands, she tugged on the twine.

It was seven fifty-six by the time the end of the rope flipped up over the window. She looked at it with dismay. She rolled up the window.

Calm down, she urged herself. *Calm down.*

Perhaps he'd tripped over a barbed-wire fence and severed the twine. But it appeared that no accident had transpired at the end of the rope, save for the accident of his untying himself. The cut was razor-clean, as it had been when she'd purchased the twine.

Seven fifty-eight.

Fact Number 2. A dust storm can suffocate a man in under seventeen minutes.

Bena looked for ways to lengthen the laundry line. From her bag in the backseat she pulled out the laces from a pair of boots and two wool knee socks. She knotted everything end to end with the careful Turk's-heads that Jonas had taught her. All told, she'd added about six feet. She opened the door and hurled herself into the maw of the storm.

Standing was difficult, until she learned to fall into the wind with the same force with which it pushed against her, to keep from losing her balance. With one hand over her eyes, she started along the trajectory Ted had initiated. She watched the ground for stones and holes and tangles of dead roots. She tripped once on the blunt stump of an old fencepost, jamming her wrist when she landed and embedding a rock in her palm.

Every ten steps she had to stop and hunch over her knees, then pull her skirt above her head to create an air pocket. Sight became so useless that she didn't look anywhere but down, and prayed that she would trip over the body of her husband, curled up on the ground to protect himself.

She was at the end of her newly lengthened tether when the storm intensified, its voice dropping to a baritone and growing more desperate, like the lowing of hungry cattle. Shading her eyes, she tried to make out where the sound was coming from. There was something in front of her. A lake. She could see the water, black and spitting.

Bena lay on her stomach and turned sideways so that, stretching, she could dangle her head over the water. The upward current struck her in the face, air so cold and stale and full of shadows she knew no sun had touched that far-down place for eons.

Watch out you don't end up on La Punta Road, she heard in her head. *One second the ground was right beneath him, next it was a mile away.*

Sweet Jesus, she thought.

"Ted," she yelled down into the dark, but the wind lifted her voice away.

Bena yanked herself back from the edge of the cliff, afraid her heart might leap out of her mouth and tumble over the side. She would have to pick through the carnage after the storm, rolling aside the boned cages of horses and broken travelers with a walking stick, looking for her lost heart and her lost husband.

She covered her eyes so that she wouldn't see the mouth of the earth opening to receive her body; but she could not shake the sound from her ears, the sound of livestock and people calling from a mass grave. Never had life felt so incidental to her, the crush of every falling body striking ancient surges of granite and schist a mile below like a sigh of relief.

Bena moved her hands to her ears and watched the storm convulse without sound. She didn't remember when the mountains had shrunk away and the mouth of the earth had filled with water. She was drowning, her body wrapped to a slick, waving rudder as a squall raged around her, angry, arctic resentments swept down from Hudson Bay. Her brother's head pitched and struggled to hold on to the webby surface of water tearing under his weight.

The wind caught her brother in its scissory arms and snipped him limb from limb. It brought its prey to her and lay it on her seething threshold between air and water. But she didn't want its conciliatory gifts. They were unlucky trinkets, these manageable pieces of an unmanageable boy. She threw her brother's body piece by piece into the lake, watching as a wrist, an ankle, a shinbone sank with the cleanness of marble beneath the waves.

She was disbelieving, at first, when Jonas rose from the lake re-assembled under cover of water. He was furious that she'd tossed his body like dice or daisy petals, furious that she'd entrusted it with chance truths that no bone, no finger or ankle could responsibly claim to know. Bena screamed and tried to flee, half running, half crawling over the dirt, falling over her tether. She tripped over barbed wire that snagged the thin skin of her ankle. She ripped away, leaving a tiny flag of herself to wave in the wind. She thought about how bears bite off their own paws to free themselves from traps; she understood it now, how seemingly dear parts of a person are expendable.

He was upon her in seconds with his hands, covering her mouth. "Mrs. Jonssen!" he said.

Bena struggled until he pinned her arms and pushed her head close against his chest, shielding her from the dust.

Fact Number 12. Lack of oxygen can cause hallucinations about a potential victim's dead brother.

"Where's your husband?" the man asked.

Bena shook her head, confused.

The man noticed the rope tied to her wrist. "Follow this back to the car. You can do that, can't you?"

Bena nodded mutely.

"I'll find your husband," the man said, or maybe he said, "Don't buy her muslin." It was impossible to hear over the wind.

He was gone. It was dark now, completely dark, above and below the madness. There would be no light when this storm had finished its raging. The best Bena might hope for was a star or two, a few mocking punctures in the thick shroud of night that tempted her with the glory beyond: You could have had this, you could have had it all.

SHE'D FALLEN ASLEEP in the backseat, she didn't know for how long. She heard voices: *You should be dead you stupid bastard we should all be dead because of you.* The engine started beneath her tired body. She raised her head just enough to get a glimpse of Ted slumped in the passenger seat, hacking up muddy bits into a handkerchief. The final image that followed her into darkness was of the man stripping off a glove to grab hold of the wheel. His right hand, she was comforted to see, was missing the tops of its last two fingers.

6. THE PLAIN OF MARS

At breakfast no one talked about what had almost happened.

Even though the dishes were so gritty with dust no amount of rinsing could clean them, even though Bena tasted dirt in the coffee, dirt in the eggs, the conversation with Clyde and Gerta Ashburne revolved mostly around the day's planned activities in the newfound sun.

Fishing for the men. Tennis for the ladies, or possibly a game of bridge in the lodge if the afternoon grew too hot.

Gerta sneezed perpetually and blamed it on a pollen allergy rather than the ever-present dust in the air. Was this the western way, Bena wondered, to remain stoic in the face of near-death and possibly even death itself? Or were the Ashburnes merely expressing silent disdain for their midwestern guests, for proving to be so mortal, easily overcome by wind and dirt and vertigo?

There was no mention of Red Grissom, of how the Ashburnes knew him or how he'd come to find himself halfway between Rye and Cuerna Verde at the apex of the Jonssens' lostness. He had, it seemed, deposited his weather-weary charges on the Ashburnes' front porch, declined Clyde's kind offer of a martini, and disappeared back into the storm.

After breakfast, Bena walked to the lodge to telephone Florence. Gerta had phoned her the night before to make sure she and Little Ted had survived the storm unscathed (they had), but Bena wanted to speak to Florence herself.

Outside, the world was like a summer cottage after a long winter, every object shapeless and hiding beneath a covering of sheets and dust.

The cars and cottages sheltered giant drifts on their north sides. Every new surge of wind brought a sifting of dust from the trees, and the air was thick with it as people swept their porches and the caretaker cleared the tennis court with a giant horsehair push broom.

Bena held her painful breasts as she walked up the lodge steps. She'd used the pump at the crack of dawn with moderate success, though its mechanical snore had made her weep. The glass trumpet was cold around her skin. She squeezed the rubber ball until her hand cramped, then poured the milk down the bathroom sink. It was hot in the bottle, like urine. The woods were quiet as the sun stirred the edges of the plains. Then Bena had heard an animal screaming from farther up the mountain as the sun brightened. It made her skin prickle, and sleep impossible.

Florence picked up on the fifth ring, murky-throated, as if she'd been asleep. Bena made her put the phone to Little Ted's ear so that he could hear her voice. She strained to hear him gurgling and breathing, loud and milky.

When she rang off, Bena was exhausted by purposelessness. For the first time in four months she had no second body to dictate her activities: no empty stomach to fill, no hot diaper to unpin, no red skin to whiten with talc or milky head to wash in the big kitchen sink. She had no body to weigh and measure, no numerical assessment to situate her firmly in the day.

She searched for numbers so she could parse out the morning. There was nothing available other than the numbers carved on a wooden sign—"The 1921 Room"—above the entrance to the grand hall. She wandered inside and stared into the cobwebbed branches of an antler chandelier, and a painting over the fireplace, of an Indian wearing a green headdress made of feathers and horn. He stood with one moccasined foot perched on a featureless outcropping of rock. His face seemed incongruously small and meek and confused, as if the artist had dressed his aging father in a black wig and a headdress and directed him to stare out into the cramped living room while imagining it was his own vast mountain kingdom.

She walked down a hallway lined with photos of people playing tennis and aiming shotguns into the sky, and peered into rooms busy with billiard and card tables, backgammon boards, books. She was in no hurry to return to the Ashburnes' cottage and the promise of a day with no one's company but Gerta's. She grew angry again with Ted for making them come to the mountains. And for what? Although Ted was fond of Clyde, he complained constantly about Gerta, how she rambled on nervously and how her skin was bad.

Bena didn't dislike Gerta, whom she'd met a number of times at clinic functions. She had a pretty face, if you appreciated it feature by feature. Taken together, however, her individually pleasant features crowded her face like a narrow mouthful of too-big teeth, overlapping and cramped. Gerta's pale skin was sometimes sallow and blotchy, other times luminous and confident. She wore a lot of makeup, so that her beautiful days were the result of great effort on her part, and her not so beautiful days the result of great neglect.

Gerta's most condemning feature was her mouth. It was more on the right of her face than the left, the muscular asymmetry perhaps the consequence of the disapproving smirk that was her trademark on the days when the world scared her. Bena wondered whether her mouth might not continue to work its way to the back of her head, or whether it might become discouraged at the hairline and hide beneath the droop of an earlobe like a terrible wound.

Bena pulled an old book, *The Official History of Cuerna Verde*, off a shelf in the hall, and flipped through it absently; it was filled with poor-perspectived charcoal renderings of thin trees, precipitous rock faces, important sky. Cuerna Verde, she learned, translated as Green Horn, the name of the Ute chief Ham had told her about. He'd been killed on a battleground that was approximately where the tennis court now stood, where battles were still waged, between women with white skirts and wooden racquets.

She walked back to the Ashburnes' cottage with the book under her arm, looking at the other cottages on the semicircular drive. They were all the same—single-storied with split-rail porches, stone chimneys, blanched cattle skulls or browning sage wreaths above the front door.

At the Ashburnes', Gerta sat at the kitchen table, sneezing and muttering over a crossword, while the men sorted through a tackle box.

Bena dropped onto a couch in the living room. She rubbed the rope burn on her wrist, put a tender finger to the three stitches in her calf. Clyde had sewn up the half-inch rip the night before, as Ted vomited dirt into the kitchen sink. Bena had drunk a fair bit of whiskey to ignore the fact that Clyde was repairing her with needle and thread: that might explain her headache, and her inability to forget as well as the others the events of the previous night.

She was having the hardest time forgetting the screams she'd heard through the window at dawn. Clyde laughed when she mentioned it to him, saying it was nothing but the peacocks the caretaker kept in a pen up-mountain.

Bena held her hurting body and watched as Clyde and her husband packed their lunches in a wicker basket, grabbed their fishing rods, and headed off to a nearby creek. The peacock screams echoed in the depths of her ear canal whenever there weren't voices to drown them out.

"I THOUGHT we might play tennis later," Gerta called through the screen door. Bena was on the front porch reading the book she'd found and drinking tea from a chipped cup. She liked that it was chipped, and that even the chip was smoothed out by years of tea and mouths.

She wasn't thrilled with the prospect of spending a hot afternoon knocking balls around a pitted clay court. But of course she said, "Of course, that sounds like *great* fun," and returned to her book, sensing that Gerta was well intentioned but distractable. She seemed the sort of woman who preferred to have grand plans and not follow them, rather than admit from the day's outset that she would accomplish little more than dressing herself.

Gerta, for now, was off to the caretaker's cottage. The caretaker's wife had done hair down in Pueblo for years, Gerta explained, and she wanted to have her curls set before the party at the lodge that evening. This didn't promise a very vigorous tennis match, yet Gerta insisted she could play in rollers.

Soon after Gerta was obscured by a thick knitting of cottonwoods, the peacocks screamed from their pen up-mountain. Bena put down her book and waited for Gerta to return or a neighbor to appear, but this must have been a false alarm, the shrieks nothing but the peacocks' own nightmares shriveling in the oppressive heat of the day.

Bena heard the clap and ring of metal and a man cursing.

"Christ almighty, goddamn Gerta."

She walked to the corner of the porch.

Red Grissom was standing on the lawn on one foot and trying to free the toe of his boot from a steel-mouth trap. After a while he stopped struggling. He put his hands on his waist and glanced up, irritated. He didn't seem unnerved to find her there, watching from the porch rail.

"What's she catching?" Bena asked.

"What's she catching? Or what's she looking to catch?"

"It's fairly obvious what she's caught."

"Rattlers. There's a nest around back here she wanted me to take a look at. Of course, she didn't warn me about the measures she's already taken."

Bena scuffed her bare feet into a pair of men's leather sandals kept by the door. She grabbed the metal wand that hung from the mess-hall triangle the Ashburnes used for calling the neighbors to cocktails.

The grass was sharp. It needled her wound.

"Wouldn't go wandering around out here without boots."

Red held up his right hand. Bena liked that he treated his maimed hand as if it were full-fingered, so unlike people who hid their deformities in pockets and behind backs, people who would rather shake with the wrong hand than offer a stranger one that was less than perfect.

Bena searched the grass for a movement heavier and stealthier than just the wind blowing through. "Isn't that the joy of rattlers? One can hear them coming?"

Red laughed curtly. "How many dust storms you need to be lost in before you're respectful of things bigger than yourself?"

Bena thought about it. "Five or so."

"Slow to learn, huh?"

"I'm slow to admit my limitations." She wedged the metal wand under the jaws of the trap.

"Some people might call that stupid," he observed.

"Are you one of those people?"

"I don't know you well enough. Could be you're stupid. Hard to tell. I know you're quick to think you got people all figured out."

Red wriggled his boot free. The trap closed, quick and vicious.

"Appears we're even." He extended a hand.

"Are you keeping score?"

"On matters of lifesaving," he said, "someone's always keeping score."

Bena slapped back across the lawn to the front porch. She hung the wand and the trap next to the triangle. They swung in the breeze, threatening to touch and call the neighbors to an impromptu late-morning round of gin fizzes and rusty nails.

"Pretty," Red approved.

She stood back to survey her work. "I think it captures something about this place."

"Captures the sense of being captured."

She sat on the top step. "Perhaps."

Red pulled out his tobacco pouch and sat on the step below her. He rolled a cigarette on his knee. "You feeling captured?" he asked.

There was a levity to his tone that she found suspicious. "Do you mean this weekend or generally?"

"You choose." He stared out over the plains. It was an easy enough distraction to engage in when you were thinking or avoiding someone's eyes, a whole lot of empty to lose yourself in.

"How about I choose to ask you a question?"

He smiled as if he'd seen something out there in the plains that clarified it all, the drought, the Depression, the foolish desire to grow crops where crops could never grow. He knew her now, or he thought he did, in the same hasty way she'd decided she knew him at Buck's Silo.

"Be my guest."

"What are you doing here?" She swept her hand outward, indicating the front porch, the mountain, the plains, the world. She wanted the question to be as big or as small as he wanted it to be.

He offered her a cigarette. Bena bent forward to meet the flame of the match he had struck. She tucked her skirt between her legs and rested her elbows on her knees.

"I live here," he said.

She didn't respond.

"You find that astonishing?"

Bena stared down at the sandals. "As my friend Ham Paxton would say, you aren't exactly the kind of guy they like up here."

Red laughed. "I don't like them much, either. But I've been coming here since I was a kid. There's no more beautiful place on earth, if loneliness is what you're looking for."

"It doesn't seem so lonely to me," Bena remarked, looking at the cottages, the cars, the tennis court, the lodge. "It seems to be the opposite of lonely."

He pointed through the cottonwoods to a house with a steeply pitched roof and Alpine eave carvings. The house was gnarled and fanciful around the rain gutters.

"That's my family's old house. My mother had just returned from a trip through Bavaria when they built it. There's an avalanche hatch next to the chimney. She was easily inspired, and just as easily bored."

Bena looked toward the curious house in the woods and reviewed the elaborate and erroneous history she'd fabricated for this man, Red Grissom, as she'd spied on him from her office window. She'd imagined he was raised by first-generation homesteaders, people who had been beaten down enough times to know how to survive droughts and locust plagues and any of the other biblically proportioned atrocities heaped on them as a matter of course. Their boy had the plains in his blood, he was cursed with the love of emptiness and the daily thankless struggle of driving cattle from one bare patch of earth to another. He'd seen everything of this world and nothing at all, he was smart but not educated, as wise in some ways as he was ignorant in others. So much for her reporter's nose for truths that live under the lying surface of things. His family probably owned mines or banks or the whole damned town of Pueblo.

"Come on," he said abruptly, standing up. "I'll show you lonely."

"What?"

"My house."

"But I'm supposed to play tennis . . ." she protested.

"With Gerta? You'll sweat harder steeping tea. Come on. I'll show you the sights."

Bena hesitated, then went inside to get her own shoes and pack a small bag with the breast pump and a shirt, just in case. "Had to get some air," she wrote on a piece of paper for Gerta. "Maybe we can play later?" She knew that it was rude and that Ted would be angry with her. Still, it was preferable to sitting around on a breathless day, worrying about the baby as a way of missing him.

Red pointed out landmarks as someone would who loves a place not only for itself but for the stories contained in every wheel rut and fencepost: There was the pond where the ice was cut each winter in great foggy slabs, and where, one winter, a man's foot was so frozen he sawed right through his toes without noticing. There was the house where ice was preserved for summer on beds of hay, and where a man and his housemaid were discovered clinging to each other naked (they'd left their clothes outside to keep them warm) and nearly frozen dead, having sneaked away for an amorous rendezvous and mistakenly shut the door until it latched. There was the empty corral where the residents used to keep a team of horses, until Win Thatcher's son was impaled on his saddle horn when a rattler spooked his horse on the way down to Rye. The boy died. The horse was shot because she was lame, but mostly because she was the agent of an otherwise untouchable boy's death. Now the corral was home to a single chestnut mare. Red called her Betty and gave a rough, affectionate rub to her busybody nose as they passed.

Small bridges hopped over streams and split-rail fences cordoned off the Meadow from the Croquet Lawn, Picnic Rock Field from the peacock pen. Bena could see the birds moving colorfully behind a cross-hatch of pine needles, their broad tails flaring at the sound of intruders.

Eventually they walked between two boulders and the woods dropped away. Bena felt the breath yanked out of her.

A granite cliff, sheared off in a swift moment of geological violence, jagged its way down, out of sight. The wind lifted her and made her feel weightless in the face of such gravity. A small house on stilts had been built on the absolute farthest tip of an outcropping. Its porch was cantilevered off the front, hanging a hundred feet above the plain.

"Good Lord," Bena said.

"Don't want to take a wrong turn on the way to the outhouse," Red cautioned.

He led her by the hand along a thin, weedy path hugging the edge of the cliff, then up the side stairs, directly onto the porch. She thought she might faint if she looked down, so she stayed back from the railing, which had spaces big enough for a small child to crawl through. He offered her a crude stool fashioned out of pine and printed burlap.

He picked a rock from his boot heel and tossed it over the side of the railing as if to demonstrate the force of gravity, so much hungrier at this height.

Dizzy, Bena turned away to examine the house. It was neat, unadorned but solid, with two big rectangular windows laid sideways staring wide-eyed at nothing but sky and the occasional rainless cloud. The wood around the window was different from that of the rest of the house. She could see the name "Steinway" running the length of one of the boards.

"What's the story here?" she asked.

Red was rolling another cigarette. She watched as two vultures rode the invisible swells of air in front of them. If she squinted and let the black of their bodies draw the line, she could almost see the currents.

"My grandfather loved my grandmother more than his horse," he said.

Bena laughed.

"My grandmother wanted a piano, because she believed all decent ladies should play the piano. So my grandfather ordered her a baby grand all the way from New York. In the meantime, my grandmother started to take lessons from a woman who was too scared of her to teach her much of anything."

"Scared?"

"Could scare the rattle off a rattler, my grandmother. The teacher insisted she was a prodigy the likes of which the world hadn't seen since the untimely passing of Mozart. She'd never been good at much except being mean, so you can imagine how excited she was. She planned a party for the day the baby grand arrived on the eastern express, during which she intended to play a brief selection of the pieces she'd mastered. The piano teacher sent a note at the last moment saying that she'd taken ill and would be unable to attend the festivities."

"Smart lady," Bena remarked.

"After many, many champagne cocktails, my grandmother announced she was ready to play. The butler wore a pair of white gloves and turned the music sheets. It was all such a show that when the guests heard how god-awful she was, they assumed it was a joke. They laughed, and hard, because, like everyone, they wanted to please my grandmother."

"What was her name?"

"Bettina. Betty."

"Like your horse."

"Whom I love more than my grandmother." He winked. "Of course, the guests were stunned when she rushed out of the room in tears. After a few awkward moments, my grandfather sat down at the piano and started to play glee club tunes from his college days."

"Your grandfather could play."

"Quite well, as it turned out. Everyone was standing around, drinks freshened and singing along, when my grandmother returned with a wood ax. My grandfather kept playing while she chopped the piano to bits. Played it until she threatened to hack his hands off at the wrist if he didn't stop. At which point he went and fixed himself another drink."

"I like this Betty," Bena said.

"Not a lot to like, but it's a good story. My grandfather kept the wood in the attic because he claimed that when the time came, he was going to build her coffin out of it. He died before she did. I found the pieces in the attic."

"Incredible," Bena said.

"There's something even more incredible." Red walked to the window and put his ear against the wood. He beckoned to her.

"What?"

He put a finger to her lips. "Listen."

She listened, but couldn't find anything to hear except the wind. "What am I listening to?"

"Music." Under his breath.

She started to laugh, but Red was serious. Bena closed her eyes and pushed her ear against the old piano wood. The glossy finish had long since dried, whitened, molted away, leaving only bare black grain to battle the elements.

At first she heard nothing. Then she thought she heard a single note, a lingering, strong note, just one. She feared it was alone, a figment of her imagination, part of nothing but its own slow fading. As it was about to vanish altogether, she heard another note tilting in through the piñon pines. It was the music of air and distance and falling, the music of a loss of altitude, the music of a glorious tumble to oblivion.

Can you hear it? A question for her, like the angry voice she had heard in the dust storm: *You should be dead you stupid bastard we should all be . . .* She pulled away from the wood, and the music was nowhere. *Yes,* she thought to herself. *Yes.* I can hear it.

SHE SAW where Red slept—an iron bed full of pillows, firmly girdled by an Indian blanket—where he hung his clothes, the small mirror and washbasin he used when he shaved. Perhaps it was inappropriate for her to bear witness to these privacies of his, married as she was, and knowing him so little. But she felt far above such judgments up here in the mountains; she was lightheaded and unconcerned and freshly vehement about embracing new opportunities, now that she'd so recently faced death.

As Red occupied himself in the bedroom, Bena explored the kitchen. Cast-iron pans hung from nails on one wall. On another was tacked a postcard from Havana, a stretch of concrete seawall and the ocean beyond. She peeled it back and read the message in dark blue ink.

"R—Holsteins thriving on Cuban seagrass. Rancho Ernesto could use your poking expertise. So could Cuban women. Tempted?"

She walked back toward a pair of bentwood chairs, each padded by a folded dun-colored blanket.

Red sat down next to her, lining up objects on the coffee table— a blue glass bottle, a tin of tobacco, a pint of whiskey, a vial of saffron powder. He pushed aside a pile of *Chieftains* to make room.

The top issue of the papers was folded to an article Bena had written about the Women's Temperance Club bashing slot machines ("Beating the One-Armed Bandits") that had been discovered in a derelict railway car. The club women had worn their finest dresses, shoes, and hats, and each had had her photo snapped by the club recorder as she took her turn with a three-foot spike driver. The battered machines with their bent arms and cracked windows were left in the middle of the train tracks. Bena would never forget the sight of twenty women with fans and gloves clapping politely as the 2:40 to Las Vegas rolled over the glittering vessels of temptation, grinding all that hard luck into the tracks and strewing it across the desert.

"You knew I was a reporter."

"Didn't win you any more friends at Buck's, either. A lady and a reporter. Two strikes against you."

"You have a lot of spare time on your hands to be wondering so much about every sweet new face that wanders down Union."

"Don't worry. Even the ugly ones don't go unnoticed."

He opened his canvas rucksack and started to load it—the whiskey wrapped in a clean rag, a bottle of water, the tobacco.

"I suppose that's the closest thing to a compliment a lady can expect from a man like you."

"It's only because ladies are always expecting compliments that I can't stand giving them."

Bena drew back. "I don't believe I'm one of those ladies."

"Neither do I. That's why I told you you were quite nice-looking."

"I didn't hear anything of the kind."

"That's because you don't listen so well."

He ignored her after that, maybe because he didn't want her to think that her beauty affected him any more than as a temporary feature to remark on in the landscape, like an unusual bird or rock. Bena continued to roam his house. His bookshelf was filled with books about animals and weather and poems about the West by writers she'd never heard of. For all the clutter, Red didn't have any photographs of his family on display. A loneliness pervaded his house, an end-of-the-world weariness that made photographs, even people themselves, obsolete and unnecessary.

"Going on a trip?" Bena asked.

"An errand I have to run." He pointed through the windows. "Over by Table Mountain."

"What kind of errand?"

"Payment for services received."

"Cryptic," she said.

"Care to join me?"

Bena looked at her watch. He pulled his rucksack closed.

"I ought to get back."

He grabbed a shirt off a hook and slung the rucksack over one shoulder.

"I'll have you back by dinnertime."

Bena considered this, and thought grimly about the alternative.

"Cocktail hour," she bargained.

Red scratched his chin, looked at the clock above the table.

He stuck out his half-fingered hand. "Deal," he said.

He lent her a deerskin jacket small enough to make her think he might have a wife swirling in the photo-less backwater of his past, or a lot of women to whom he played the gallant host. I'll show you lonely, indeed.

He gave her a pair of boots with dirt-black, rounded heels. He pondered the insides of three cowboy hats, checking the headband widths stamped into the felt.

"Here," he said, putting one on her head. He stood back and looked at her as if she were a horse he might saddle up to ride to Mexico, or haul off to the glue factory for a little quick cash. She'd never been looked at by a man this way, a man who obviously found her attractive but at the same time had no palpable interest in her. It grated against how she thought she understood men and the way they grabbed a piece of whatever caught their fancy.

"You take to it well," was all he said, and then they were back along the cliff, the sun beating down mercilessly on their heads from its high-noon perch.

WHAT SHE REMEMBERED about that afternoon was the wide quiet. She rode behind him, the saddle curling up around her hips, her fingers knotted about his waist to keep herself from tipping this way and that. Sometimes she bumped her hand on his belt buckle when Betty lurched on the steeper parts of the trail. They didn't talk. At most Red would hand her a sinuous piece of salted beef to chew on, or point at some-thing—a falcon overhead or a small prairie dog poised on its haunches, tracking their approach with cheery suspicion.

They reached the blunt-topped shadow of Table Mountain, and followed the weak trickle of a creek that had cut through stone. The water ran red with iron ore in stretches, a small amount of wounding still taking place.

Once in the shadow, Red began to talk. He told her how Table Mountain was the center of bootlegging operations south of Colorado Springs, and how on clear nights he could see the bootleggers communicating with people far down on the plains, flashing a special code they had jury-rigged out of Morse.

"See all those snake holes?" he asked, pointing to a limestone wall. "That's where they hid the moonshine, after they'd transferred it to bottles." It was the perfect hiding place, he explained, because no fool would go sticking his hand down a snake hole. The bootleggers wore long leather gloves, but even those didn't ensure that a rattler wouldn't sink its teeth into the inviting apple of their biceps. You could buy a specially marked variant of liquor called Snake Bite, which guaranteed a man had died fetching the bottle from its hiding place in the limestone cliff. The moonshine wasn't any better quality; it was just the taste of a stranger's extreme misfortune that some people took a liking to.

They crossed a bridge over a narrow gulch that brought them higher than they'd been, out of the canyon and into the pounding sun. The heat made a sound like a heart through the white sky. Red flipped off his hat and poured water over his face and hair.

He urged her to do the same. "Use it all," he said. "We can get more at Mary's."

The water was hot and didn't do much to cool her down. She assumed Mary was the woman for whom the gifts in the rucksack were intended.

It was just shy of two o'clock when they rounded a rock outcropping and Betty demonstrated the enthusiasm that indicated a familiar journey was almost over.

Bena didn't see the house at first, it was so well hidden in the shadow of the granite overhang. The only signs of life were a patch of sickly-looking wheat stalks and a well built of limestone bricks and capped with a clumsy, confusing hatch of cast-off lumber. Near it on the dirt sat an upside-down metal bucket, its rope neatly coiled on top. A pair of chickens, their wings clipped, skittered about frantically and flapped their stumps, as if their desperate longing to fly was all they required to become airborne.

Betty refused to walk farther than the well.

Red groaned and kicked a foot over her mane, and landed crouched, in the dirt. He pulled the top off the well—cursing loudly when he skewered his palm with a splinter—wiped the mouth of the bucket with his sleeve, and tossed it into the well.

He pulled up the bucket, heavy with water, and dropped it, sloshing, onto the dirt. With water cupped in his hand, he let Betty drink, then did the same himself, tipping his hands until the water ran over his jaw, soaking his collar. He dipped his hand in the bucket one last time and raised it high to Bena. She crouched as low as she could without falling out of the saddle, and pressed her mouth against the ends of his fingers, catching the water as he lifted his hands. It tasted of metal.

Under the outcropping, a door opened. "Thought maybe you'd forgotten about me." It was a woman's voice, viscous and full of lumps. Bena could make out her pale face and hands inside the shadows. She was wearing a long black dress that allowed her to hide beneath the imposing wing of rock.

"Not like you to get nervous, Mary." Red handed Bena the rucksack and took Betty's reins.

"You're the one should be nervous, double-crossing me," Mary called back. Her words bounced inside the jaws of granite, which threatened to snap shut on her and her shack wedged far back into the crevice of the overhang. As they approached, Bena could see the shack was actually an old railway car with a teetery porch tacked onto the front and a crude pair of windows cut in the sides. Despite these homey touches, the car was not very different from the ones put to pasture in the oily lots outside Pueblo. "Colorado Fuel and Iron" was still legible in fading white paint across the grooved metal siding.

Bena watched Red tie Betty's reins to a post. The air was cool under the great rock, providing relief Bena felt someone might have to pay for in this world of balances and imbalances. It smelled of rot and wet and old cooking.

Red extended his hand to help her dismount, taking the rucksack from her. She walked up a path eroded into the granite floor, dodging chicken droppings with her big boots. She noticed a few tumbleweeds pressed against either side of the porch stairs, forlorn shrubbery marking the entrance to an equally forlorn estate.

"Is this your notion of payment?" Mary asked.

She squinted at Bena, until even her wrinkles seemed to take on the power of sight. The seeing bled out through those tributaries and turned her pupils into two dark suns. Mary still had her teeth, though her face had sunk toward her spine the way toothless people's faces do.

"No, ma'am," Red said. "She's just along for the ride."

Mary wore a necklace of clumsy coral beads that brought out the fine nest of veins in her cheeks. Her hair was dark and straight and pulled back from her face in a low plait; her right iris had split like an overripe fig with the underlying pink-gold flesh visible beneath the skin. Her feet were knotted and ugly and bare, testimonies to the fact that she'd crossed many deserts on hardened soles and broken each toe separately, her souvenirs of the Mojave, the Malpaís, the Black Hills.

"Pretty." Mary talked to Red as if Bena weren't there, or were deaf or too young to be addressed directly.

"It's the blush of life." Red walked up the steps and squeezed Mary with his ropy arms. "She came this close to dying yesterday." He pinched his fingers to show that there was no room between that state and its opposite, that they could easily collapse and become one.

The interior of Mary's house was as cluttered and random as a curious but uncareful mind—books, papers, irregularly shaped swatches of fabric on the walls, rusted rakes and spades, odd pieces of metal such as a bicycle frame and a big, smooth ship's cleat. There was a table with three chairs, and against the back wall an army cot that looked as though it hadn't been slept in for years. An old photograph hung above it, encased in a gilt frame. The photo showed a woman and a lean man with Mary's withered jaw, their faces gray with the exhaustion of immigrants whose new lives failed to match even their most modest expectations.

Bena and Red sat at the table. To the far right was a black cookstove, the wall behind it strung with dried herbs. Mary poured hot water into a teapot and cut the leaves of one of the herb bundles into it with a pair of tiny scissors.

She pressed a cup into Bena's hands. "Elder-blow tea," she said.

When she turned to give Red a cup as well, she saw him picking at the splinter in his palm. She pulled his hand to her face and extended it with one gentle, practiced motion.

"It's that damned well of yours," he said. "What happened to the cover I made for you?"

"Stole." Mary reached into a toolbox and pulled out a glass jar, its top closed with a piece of cloth and some string. There was a balm inside. She also withdrew a rusted needle, whose tip she stuck in the flame of the kerosene lamp. It blackened and smoked.

Bena took a cautious sip from the cup. She couldn't tell if it was the elder-blow leaves or the water, but the tea was more skunky and foul than any she'd ever tasted. Mary worked on Red's hand. She caught the splinter with the tip of the needle and drew it out.

"Hold still," she admonished. "A splinter breaks in two, it's the worst kind of bad luck."

When the wet sliver of wood was free of the wound, Mary laid it in a crockery dish and held a match to it. She dumped the particles of ash into Red's tea.

"Drink it."

He looked at her, bemused, then drank the mixture and slammed the cup on the table when he was finished.

Mary untied the string around the jar and scooped out a fingertip of balm. She massaged it quickly into his palm with two strong thumbs. The only sounds were the chickens scraping their nails in the rocky yard and a clock's irregular tick. Mary played with the piece of string, rolling it into knots between her thumb and forefinger.

Bena was transfixed by Mary's hands. Her palms were so wrinkled they were like a face, smiling, frowning, seeing. It was as though another being lived in there. Bena thought of when Jonas had had a tumor removed from his abdomen; he'd told her it was his twin sister. He had smothered her while he was sprouting limbs in that shared watery place; he'd pressed his fledgling organs around her and captured her beneath his new skin. Don't think you're special, he'd said to Bena. I would have done that to you, too. When she was a girl, Bena would wake up in the middle of the night hot and breathless, as if she'd been struggling for air through the porous tissue of a lung, a liver, a kidney.

"How's your lady friend?" Mary asked.

Red glanced at Bena. "Maude," Red corrected. "Not so good."

From the way his body took on an invisible weight, Bena could tell they were referring to the prostitute.

"The powder didn't work?"

"Made her sick as hell, that's about all."

"Used to kill locusts with that powder. Bran and arsenic."

"Turns out locusts and babies are two different problems."

Mary peered into the gloom as though seeing a whirring cloud of insects. "My brother used to say when one died, a thousand came to its funeral."

"I guess it's good we didn't kill it, then," he said.

Mary sealed the jar and placed it in the toolbox. "Well, don't say I didn't warn you."

"I'm not blaming you, Mary. You asked, so I told you."

"A Saturnian rising so late on the Plain of Mars it practically wasn't there at all."

"You're an astrologer?" Bena asked.

Mary looked at Bena as if she'd never seen a woman so stupid.

"She's new to these parts," Red told Mary. He turned to Bena. "Mary's worried that Sally Crawford down at Crow Junction is going to steal her business."

"I'm not worried about anyone, especially no make-believe witch." Mary returned to the kitchen with the empty teapot.

"There are witches in Crow Junction?" Bena asked. I think I've met their menfolk, she wanted to add, thinking of the father and son at the feed store.

"Sally Crawford made her husband disappear pretty darned quick, didn't she?" Red called out. "But that's about it for her magic tricks."

Mary guffawed. She set a plate of molasses cookies in front of Bena.

"If you're dumb enough, Sally will try to change your future by scarring up your palm with a piece of glass." Using the edge of a cookie, Mary drew a line across her own hand. "Virginia Webb had to have her hand cut off at the forearm, it got so infected. Changed that woman's future all right."

Bena pressed her palms together to suffocate the thought of a woman carving a ravine through her hand with a dirty shard of bottle.

"It was because of Mary that Virginia went to visit Sally Crawford in the first place," Red explained. "Mary told her she was a woman who lost things, that she would lose something dear to her once each year."

"So what does she do?"

"I didn't say you were wrong. I'm explaining to our guest in case she wants to have her palm read. I don't want her to think you're going to mince words."

"I mince them now. And who says I'm going to read her palm? You still owe me for the last one."

Mary held out her fleshy hand for payment. Red pulled the rucksack from under his chair. He dropped it on the table, sending the hanging kerosene lamps swinging.

"Greedy woman," Red muttered.

"A woman asks for what's owed her and she's greedy." Mary grinned.

As soon as he pulled one item from his pack, Mary was onto it, pressing it close to her face for inspection. The vial of orange powder was quickly unplugged, the glass stopper allowed to roll away, off the table, powder pinched between her fingers, held to her nose, touched with the tip of her gray tongue.

Red set the two bottles on the table.

Mary opened the whiskey, took a swig. The blue glass bottle she held up to the scant light coming through the windows.

"Pretty. Used to be rosewater in here." She gave it to Bena to smell. Bena could smell only dirt.

"You going to read her palm?"

"Nobody's asked me if I even want my palm read," Bena pointed out.

"It's a gift. You don't get asked if you want a gift." Red was playing with a nickel he'd found at the bottom of the rucksack, twirling it on its side so that it spun on the tabletop, a transparent sphere. Bena felt he was playing with her, too, spinning her so that he could see her transparent fullness.

Mary unhooked a kerosene lamp from its swinging perch and

placed it on the table. The light it threw was low and brought the ceiling close.

"What hand are you?" Mary asked.

Bena waved her right, and Mary made it into a fist and pressed it between her breasts. Bena sensed Mary's lungs fill and empty, her heart thump distantly. Mary hummed a single, low note that vibrated in the well of her rib cage, a train approaching but never coming closer than far away.

Bena was relieved to see Red putting his hat on. She heard his boots on the steps, his boots on the rock and gravel, the scrape and titter of the wingless chickens parting to let him pass.

"Ever been read before?" Mary opened Bena's palm as if freeing an orange from its rind.

Bena shook her head. "I went to a fortune-teller once at a county fair. She stared into something that looked like a bowling ball."

"I don't doubt it was." Mary traced the lines and rises in Bena's palm with her thumb. Bena had to struggle against the impulse to clamp her hand shut. It was an eerie sensation, tickly and uneasy, as if someone were drawing the veins from her arms, one by one, out through the creases between her fingers.

"She told me that I had to nurture my creative spirit, that patience, time, and nature were the physicians of life, that I would marry once and hard."

"You have married hard," Mary replied. She pushed a finger into the center of Bena's palm.

A curious statement. Mary didn't elaborate.

"A large thumb. This means you prefer history to romance." She pressed Bena's fingers together and held her flattened hand close to the lamp. Light showed through the chinks between her fingers.

"See the light? Your fingers are differently shaped, so you are curious. They are also flat, spatulate. Your needlework is useful rather than showy."

"I don't do needlework."

"This here," Mary continued, poking a pad of skin on the edge of her hand, "is the Mount of Mars. It spreads into the Plain of Mars. This means you are prone to fury, violence, bloodthirstiness of the slow-burning kind."

Bena dragged her free palm across her wet forehead. The sun had fallen low enough in the sky to peek beneath the lip of rock, and it shone directly on the metal siding of the railway car.

Mary reeled through the lines on Bena's hand as though she were at the doctor's office having her vital signs read. Life line, long and without irregularities or cross bars, but with a slight break at the fifth period, indicating an illness or event that threatens the life; the line of the heart, neat and well colored, extending to the Mount of Jupiter and indicating an affectionate disposition and strong health; a long line of the head, giving great coolness in danger and difficulty and excessive cleverness, but a tendency toward *brusquerie* and overambition; the line of Apollo, or brilliance, pale and suggesting an inclination toward art and a love of beautiful objects, if not an actively artistic temperament. Mary was sweating an herbal-smelling sweat that made the graying hair around her temples coil and gleam. She was almost feverish, her body swelling and warm with the urgency of illness.

She located something that interested her at the bottom of Bena's palm. She turned it close to the kerosene lamp, so close that Bena's skin burned. She jerked her hand away. Mary looked at Bena as if seeing her for the first time, a stranger in her metal house, which once sped across deserts and through mountains with goods to be bought, sold, traded, stolen. She gave Bena back her palm, resting it gently on her kneecap.

"Sometimes I wonder why a person would ever want to know about herself like this," she said, staring at Bena's dress. "Don't make any difference, right? Oedipus still lay with his mother."

"People are curious," Bena said. She glanced down and saw that her chest was stained with milk. Mary got her a rough cloth from the kitchen. Bena pulled the breast pump out of her bag and struggled to fix it around her nipple. She winced as she squeezed the rubber ball and the glass mouth breathed her in. Mary watched with the impoliteness of a person who spends too much time alone.

"Sometimes I look in a girl's eyes and I know she doesn't need to hear what I have to tell her. Not going to make a difference one way or the other, so I keep my mouth shut, or I tell her the sky is sunny and blue even if I can see the thunderheads pitching over the rise."

Mary cleared the teacups and continued. "Once I told a woman she would kill the man with whom she shared a bed, and sure enough, she did. Shot her husband through the chest with a deer rifle not a week later. Claimed she mistook him for an intruder, even though she shot him in broad daylight and she'd wished him dead from the night she'd married him."

"You think you gave her the idea?"

Mary dried the cups with an apron. "Maybe I gave her permission to do what she'd always wanted to do. It makes a person wonder sometimes." She fixed Bena with her overripe gaze. "You understand what I'm saying."

Bena nodded. But she didn't understand.

"You're a nice girl. I'm sure I have you all wrong. I want to give you the chance to be had all wrong." She patted Bena on the hand and picked up a flat basket of feed. Letting the screen door clap behind her, she called to her wingless chickens with a high, windy whistle.

Bena sat alone in the railway car for half an hour, pumping one breast, then the other. She put on the deerskin jacket and buttoned it so Red wouldn't see the stains on her dress. On her way out to the well, she ducked behind the railroad car, where it was darkest. She unhooked the canvas bag from the metal mouth and poured her milk onto the ground. It disappeared quickly amid the weeds.

. . .

RED HAD HER BACK by the cocktail hour, just as he'd promised. Ted, Gerta, and Clyde were on the porch in their dinner clothes, drinking red and green cocktails. Gerta's hair was as big and red as the sun. Ted was tracking through a rifle sight. Bena watched him sweep the barrel downhill until his crosshairs caught on them, ambling past the tennis courts.

Ted continued to hold them in the gun's gaze as they approached the Ashburnes' cottage.

"You can put that down anytime," Red said, circling Betty to the porch steps. Although they'd met only the previous evening, it was clear to Bena that Red had developed a dislike of her husband.

Red tipped his hat to Gerta. "Mrs. Ashburne."

"Mr. Grissom."

Gerta smiled and cupped her cheek with her hand as though it were threatening to break into a million pieces from the effort of being pleasant.

"Get you a drink, Red?" Clyde waved a highball in the air.

"Thanks. Have some work to do yet."

"You're a busy fellow," Ted said. Sun did wonders for him, bringing up the color in his cheeks and blanching his hair. He was like a photo negative, dark where he should be light, light where he should be dark. His eyes were bluer, too. There was a time when Bena would be ruined by the mere color of him.

"You people keep me busy," Red replied.

Ted laughed. "We're bringing a compass with us to the lodge tonight. Just in case we get lost between the dance floor and the bar."

Red helped Bena dismount.

"Mrs. Jonssen," he said. "Thanks for the company."

"What about your clothes?" Bena asked, taking off the hat he'd given her.

"Just leave them here. I'll come by and get them sometime."

Sometime, Bena thought. She glanced at Ted, staring at her, the gun resting against his leg. No doubt he was angry that she was late, angry that she'd so rudely skipped her tennis date with Gerta, angry that she was wearing boots too big for her, and another man's soft jacket.

She sensed a new anger poking up under her dress like a wrong rib. How dare you be disappointed with me, she thought. *You should be dead you stupid bastard we should all be dead because of you.* In her mind she saw the woman extending her neck so that the sun through the jeweler's window caught the small garnets, setting them ablaze. Bena imagined Ted and the woman erupting in flames, their clothes and hair and faces shriveled and blackened by fire, while she watched, brazenly, through the plate glass.

You are prone to fury, violence, bloodthirstiness.

Yes, well. Maybe so.

Bena watched Red and Betty walk among the cottonwoods until they were hidden behind the silver bark. She climbed the porch steps, accepted the bright drink that was thrust into her fingers.

Ted kissed her roughly, the way he did when it appeared she might be falling away from him. He could sense it on her like the strong smell of burning.

"It's not a costume party tonight," he said, surveying her clothes.

She smiled weakly. She was tired. She didn't want to put on a dress and go to a dance.

"We were wondering what happened to you," Ted ventured. She thought he was irritated about annoyances other than just her disappearance. Probably Gerta was driving him crazy. He disliked women like Gerta who talked too much and were vehement about simple ideas.

"Yes," Gerta chimed in, her mouth pinched and sideways. "We thought maybe we'd lost you again."

Bena looked at the sun nipping the edge of the prairie, every bald, ugly acre aflower with purples and oranges, the fleeting harvest of a dying day.

Maybe you have, she answered to herself, watching the light bloom brilliant, then drain below the horizon, taking all the colors with it.

7. TURKEY IN THE STRAW

Bena suspected something was truly wrong with Little Ted the moment they returned from Cuerna Verde.

Florence had found it impossible to persuade the baby to take a bottle after Bena's phone call Saturday morning; she logically attributed the fussiness to his mother's departure, the previous night's dust storm and the green light that preceded it, the oceany shushing of the dirt against the windows. Whole buildings were swallowed up; cars, signs, statues disappeared beneath the gauzy, shifting earth. The streets were vacant, Florence said, save for a young boy, a towel wrapped around his face, calling for his missing dog. By Saturday evening, she'd begun to worry in earnest. She took Little Ted to a friend who was a wet nurse, thinking it might be a nipple he needed.

Hearing this, Bena felt herself wanting to strike someone; the thought of her baby suckling another woman's breast while she rode horses and danced halfheartedly and drank to distraction cups of bad, sweet punch made her furious and guilt-stricken.

But even the nipple failed to interest him, Florence recounted. He slept through Saturday as if he had a fever. That night, she'd found him lying awake in his crib, staring at the ceiling. "His eyes moved quick like he was having a fit," Florence told her.

Bena lifted the baby from the bassinet. He was asleep, but he awoke immediately when she rubbed her nose over his face.

He looked wild at first. He didn't remember who she was, she thought. His fierceness receded and he stared at her in the blank way she'd chosen to read as recognition. He lay in her arms, limp and warm. *So well behaved,* Reimer Jackson had said to her when they'd met on the street the week before. *Such a good little boy. So well behaved.* Now his good behavior seemed suspicious. Nobody she knew had a child so still and so quiet. When she tried to speak of the baby's condition to Ted, however, he became quiet and angry. She kept her worrying to herself.

The weekend wounds healed gradually. Ted's limp declined to the rare wince when the bones in his ankle rolled wrong, and the stitches on Bena's calf turned black and loosened. Little Ted's eating remained sporadic Sunday evening and Monday, but then he took the nipple, the bottle, whatever was offered, without problem or complaint. Ted convinced her that he merely had a touch of colic, which explained his fussiness and his lack of energy. They spent a pleasant Tuesday evening listening to a Dixieland band play beside the Lynch Pine and watching the first fireflies compete with the twilight.

On Wednesday night, Bena woke up needing a glass of water. She heard rustling from the baby's crib, which made her body cold. She'd heard tales of babies being eaten by rats in the shantytown, mothers waking to find nothing but a reckless pile of bones picked clean. But there was no rat. The baby was alone, staring into the featureless black above his crib. His eyes jumped as if still following the movements of fireflies. She thought he was dreaming with his eyes open, but when she tried to pick him up, his sweaty body was rigid. Bena called out to Ted. By the time he appeared, the baby's body was slack and cool. He broke into a wail that built and built, lasting for nearly an hour, until he'd exhausted himself.

Bena hovered as Ted, half asleep, checked his pulse and his temperature (100 degrees) and concluded that he might have a touch of a cold. Bena tried to concoct her own diagnosis with the digits, but felt stymied by the irrefutable doctors' numbers. The two of them slept in the baby's room, Bena on the floor next to the crib, Ted cramped in a narrow upholstered chair meant for small-boned nursemaids. He didn't speak to her the next morning, because he was exhausted, she knew, by her constant worrying.

On Thursday morning, Little Ted refused, again, to eat. Bena stayed home from work that afternoon. She worried he'd contracted dust pneumonia during the storm, but when she put her ear to his mouth, his breathing was fine, whistling and sweet and decidedly un-labored. His head wasn't hot or cold, his complexion wasn't translucent with chills or sallow with infection. When she stretched the ribbon along his spine she found he'd grown another eighth of an inch. He was merely irritable and unhungry; she tried to convince herself that his symptoms were not necessarily anything to become frantic about; they were not strictly harbingers of death or even illness.

Bena waited until Ted was halfway through his evening martini, balanced on the overturned wheelbarrow in the backyard, before she approached him.

"Still digging?" She bounced Little Ted on her hip and watched as her husband hacked at a new part of the yard with the hoe he'd bought at the hardware store. He'd had to buy the back-breaking short hoe because all the shovels had gone to the CCC camps to be used for building roads and reservoirs and dams. It was the hoe the Mexicans used, the hardware man had explained to him. He called it a *mata cristiano*. Christian-killer. Ted said the man had relayed this information proudly, as if he felt noble about doing his own part to discourage the copper-hides from coming north.

Ted was digging a new pond. His first had failed, the steelheads floating to the top, stomachs ballooned and gassy, before the end of two days. Ted drained the water and threw old dirt on top of the dead fish, so that the former pond appeared to be a giant grave for a few ill-fated pets. Now he was digging in a shadier area, where the sun wouldn't strike during the hottest hours of the day.

He finished his drink and sat, sweaty and tired, on top of the wheelbarrow.

Bena sat next to him on the grass. "Something's wrong with the baby."

Ted couldn't look at her. The sun was in his eyes. "He's not eating again?"

"Well, yes . . ." Bena didn't know how to tell him that her suspicions went deeper than physical symptoms.

"Yes he's eating, or yes he's not eating?"

"He's not eating."

Ted took the baby from her. He lay Little Ted along his thigh, and propped his head up with a palm that was bigger than the baby's skull.

Little Ted squirmed until Ted blocked the sun with his body. The baby was sensitive to bright light, an early sign Bena took to mean that he wasn't blind, that his responses to external stimuli were normal. But he was four months old now, and she'd noticed little change or development in his behavior. She'd tickle him, and he'd fail to laugh or resent her for it. She'd dangle bright spoons and earrings in his crib, and he was never mesmerized. He'd kicked more in her belly than he'd kicked outside, as if his excitement for living had waned, once he saw how the world failed to live up to the expectations he'd developed while bobbing about inside her.

"That's not so unusual. He's taking more bottles, he's being breast-fed less. During any time of transition there's a possibility of irregular behavior."

"I think we should take him to a doctor."

She could see Ted struggling against his natural response. *I'm a doctor, Bena.* He stood up from the wheelbarrow. "If it makes you feel better I can take him to see Clyde tomorrow. He's our best pediatrician."

"That would make me feel better."

"Fine, then. What's for dinner?"

"Fish," Bena said distractedly, staring at the new hole in the earth, the Christian-killer protruding like a tiny, meaningless harpoon from the welling flesh of a whale.

"What?"

"Pork chops," she corrected herself. "We're having pork chops."

She found a penny in her dress pocket. Her brain was so busy that she couldn't think of anything manageable to wish for. But she tossed the penny into the shallow pond anyway, when Ted wasn't looking.

BENA WAS STARING out the window of her office when she felt the air around her shift and harden. She heard feet on the gravel outside, saw the quick scattering of cats.

She was trying (and failing) to keep her mind off Little Ted. She had dropped him off with Ted at a coffee shop adjacent to the clinic. Ted forbade her to come to the clinic herself, not even to deliver the baby, and had agreed to the examination only when she agreed to stay away for its duration. He was tired of her hysteria and her superstition, two things that would not be tolerated or appreciated, he said, in the precise, scientific confines of a clinic. "Clyde's doing us a favor," he reminded her. "I don't want you around, pestering him or influencing his diagnosis."

Ted told her that Glory, the receptionist, would give the baby his three-o'clock bottle and watch him until Ted brought him home at the end of the day. The visit was nothing more than a routine checkup, and he didn't want her to turn it into something conveniently vast and tragic that she could fret about all afternoon because she didn't have friends or lunch dates and hadn't made much effort to that end. He made Bena promise again not to phone or stop by. He hadn't told Clyde about her excessive worrying and measuring and imagining, and didn't want him to experience it firsthand.

Bena realized, then, that her mothering embarrassed Ted. It made her hope, for a terrible moment, that Clyde would find something wrong with the baby, so that her disparaged ways of loving could be vindicated. When she said good-bye to Little Ted at the coffee shop, she was inconsolable for having wished him, monstrously, to be sick just so she could win a fight.

Bena walked alone to the *Chieftain*. She knew Little Ted would be measured with a cotton tape measure, he would be weighed and his mouth probed with a gloved finger, a wooden tongue depressor, a glass thermometer. His heartbeat would be magnified through the cold foot of a stethoscope, his ear canals lit red and glowing. She suspected, however, despite her despicable hope, that he would be returned to her this evening with the clinic's stamp of health across his forehead, because doctors, even the most empathetic ones, were trained to look in the obvious places. Malignancy was a disorder more stealthy than those bland and stupid sicknesses that could be located with a stretch of scored cotton ribbon or a metal heart-listener.

"Keeping busy, I see, Mrs. Jonssen."

Horace Gast stood in the entrance to her cubicle. He played with his watch chain.

"I was just getting some air." She hurried back to her desk and flipped through her notepad, searching for some activity to hide in.

"Not *in a way*, I hope," he said, entering without an invitation. "Women who need air are always in a way."

"No, sir, I don't believe I'm in any sort of way."

"Just looking out for the good of the paper, Mrs. Jonssen. I wouldn't want to see us lose one of our most promising reporters."

He reached into his coat pocket and withdrew a handkerchief, which he wiped across his damp face. It was one hundred one degrees outside. "Yes, that would be very unlucky," he continued, bemused. "Don't you think it's odd that what women refer to as 'the curse' is actually the undeniable absence of pregnancy? Seems it might more rightly be the other way around."

"I would imagine it depends on what a person's hoping for. I've personally never thought of pregnancy as a curse." This was a lie. Bena saw herself wrapped in a blanket on the porch of the Coeur du Lac cabin, blue-cold from another long lake swim, and still, her fingers, after she pushed them into her bathing suit, came up white and unbloodied.

Mr. Gast laughed. "Talk to the more *adventurous* girls around town, and you might find they have a different perspective on what constitutes a curse in this world." He made a motion with his head toward the William Bent Rooming House across the alley.

Bena walked to the window and peered down into the shadows. The cats had returned, roosting on the flaps of cardboard boxes. Whoever it was she'd heard had come and gone, enclosed by the recesses of the William Bent.

She hadn't seen Red since he'd left her at the Ashburnes'. She'd rarely been as lonely as she had that night of the party at the Cuerna Verde lodge, wearing sandals that wiggled uncertainly over the gravel walks and hooked in the big knots in the pine floor. She was sore from riding, and unable to make conversation with the loud, pastel-colored people whose ties loosened and lipstick wandered as the evening grew cool. Clyde was playing records, and Ted and Gerta were having a fine old time tripping drunkenly over each other's feet to Bobby Burlap's instrumental version of "Indefinitely Yours." At one point Ted dipped Gerta so low over the punch bowl that her stiff curls were partially submerged, displacing floating slices of oranges and limes to the farthest shores. Bena thought that would put a definite, tearful end to their frolicking, but Gerta was either drunk or smitten enough to find the flirtatious debacle thoroughly hilarious. She squealed and shook her wet hair at Ted, covering his pale linen suit coat with a fine spattering of punch. Bena watched as he stalked off in search of seltzer.

She, meanwhile, went to find some quiet in a study off the big hall. The shelves were stacked with unimportant-looking books and decks of cards bound with twine. Photos in birch frames staggered up the north wall, documenting the construction of each of the Cuerna Verde cabins. In one photo, a heavyset woman in a raccoon coat stood outside the skeletal beginnings of the cottage Red had pointed out to Bena through the trees, the roof just beginning its fanciful curl skyward. The woman had Red's burdened demeanor that compacted her body, making her spine curve toward the earth. Her chin dropped into the collar of her coat as if she were hoping the puzzled-together pelts of ten raccoons might provide convincing camouflage in the woods.

Bena discovered matches and a tin of tobacco in a desk drawer. She rolled herself a cigarette using a page from a coverless book someone had tossed into the wastecan, *Lassoes and Horseshoes: The Life and Times of Burlton Dodge*. She felt less lonely now that she was truly alone, listening to the drunken rubbings of an anonymous couple on the porch outside the study window.

"What do you know about the William Bent?" Bena asked Mr. Gast.

"I'm more curious to know what *you* know. Handy little perch you have here."

"I assumed from the looks that it was more than a rooming house."

"Or less than one. Maybe you ought to go exploring one of these days."

She sensed he was criticizing her. "But there's been a great deal happening with the Christian club women."

"A great deal of the same old boring crap," he said, hopping off the sill. "Another goddamned benefit tea. Another flute performance by tone-deaf Mexican kids. Another gripping lecture on popular wild flowers of Gaul." He sat in her desk chair and swiveled around.

"I thought those were the subjects you wanted me to cover. Barring a University Woman impaling Reimer Lee Jackson with the sugar tongs, I don't know what else you expected."

"We should only be so lucky."

"I thought you *liked* Reimer."

"Reimer Lee Jackson is one of the least Christian ladies I've ever had the displeasure to encounter. That doesn't mean she doesn't have a lot of money she'd be happy to donate to the paper, especially if she reads favorable assessments of her pallid character with reliable frequency in the *Chieftain* society pages."

"You have such a laudable journalistic ethic," Bena observed.

"Business ethic. Thank you."

Bena recalled his haughty car navigating the narrow curves at Pikes Peak, and how she'd imagined herself beneath the lips of this repugnant man. She'd even sent her poor husband over a cliff, broken his neck amid a heavenly shimmer of metal and glass and sunlight.

"Aren't you even the tiniest bit repentant about tricking me?" She thought back to how he'd let her run on at the mouth while never revealing his identity. "You let me talk on and on without saying a word about yourself."

"That would be called chivalry, Mrs. Jonssen. Lest you headstrong women have forgotten. Chivalry."

Mr. Gast walked back to the window and gazed out at the William Bent. "Leave the Christian women alone for a while," he suggested. "I'd prefer if you'd find me some heathens."

TO JUDGE from its façade, the William Bent Rooming House committed no greater sin than to be drab and uninviting. The staircase, nearly invisible in its faded coat of sand gray, lost most hours in the shadow cast by the porch of Buck's Silo. A plain wooden sign was nailed to the wall halfway up the staircase, impossible to see if one was not already purposefully ascending: "William Bent Rooming House. Rooms for Let— Daily, Weekly, Monthly. Cheap, Decent. No Pets, No Trouble."

Cheap and decent. Nowadays this sparse promise passed as the finest guarantee a person could hope for. In smaller lettering was the word

"Proprietor," and next to that, on a piece of wood evidently covering some former owner's name, a clumsily scrawled "B. McGee." There had been a change of hands, though not recently. The patch looked as old as the original sign, suggesting that B. McGee had enjoyed a long and uninterrupted reign as the William Bent's proprietor, staunchly living up to the establishment's modest aspirations.

Bena climbed the rest of the stairs. They creaked as she ascended, conveniently sounding an alarm to anyone above that a stranger was approaching. She knew that only strangers used this entrance. The girls came and went by the side alley, the real customers through the back staircase in the bar. She reached the door at the top, with its peephole, and rang the bell.

"Help you?" It was a woman's voice.

"I'm curious about letting a room," Bena announced.

"Don't do no night-to-night here," the voice said. "Best bet is the Hyde House. Around the corner on South Gunnicker."

"I'm looking to rent long-term. Could you please let me in?"

The door yanked open, but only as far as a chain allowed it. Bena stared at half a face, a half so hideous she was relieved not to be confronted by the whole. The woman appeared to be stitched together with fishing twine and parchment paper. A burn victim. Bena couldn't see much of the interior behind her face, which consumed most of the view afforded by the small crack. There seemed to be a foyer, empty of furnishings save a bare desk and a chair. A framed certificate hanging over the desk attested to the official clean decency of the establishment.

"No rooms here. Short term, long term, don't matter."

A glint of recognition—then suspicion—crossed her face.

"You live around here. What're you wanting to let a room for?"

"My brother," Bena explained. "He's coming to town and needs a place to stay."

"Why don't he stay with you?"

"I don't see how that's any of your business."

The woman attempted a smile, the dead corner of her mouth tacked firmly down, the rest of her smooth lips straining upward. "I got something you want, honey. Seems to me anything I ask you is my business."

"He and my husband don't get along so well." It would be true if Jonas were alive.

"Ain't it always the way," the woman said. "Men are dogs, sooner tear each other's throats out than share a bone." The voice seemed to find pleasure in this image, either impressed with the animal quality of men, or thrilled at the notion that, if cooped up together long enough, they might naturally extinguish themselves.

"Are you B. McGee?"

"Who?"

"The proprietor." Bena pointed down the stairs toward the sign.

"I've been her," she replied. "Most times I just go by 'Helen.' "

The door closed in Bena's face—a slow, apologetic shutting.

She made her way down the creaky staircase. She rested on the bottom step, in the shade. It was as hot a day as there'd been in a summer, so far, of nothing but hot days.

A young nanny passed by, wheeling a bamboo stroller, the opening shielded from the sun with a layer of thick lace. Bena couldn't see the baby, but she heard its cries. They made the undersides of her wrists—that place where her veins were closest to the surface—hurt, in a stringy, unthreaded way. This baby's cries were far more urgent and willful than Little Ted's. His were ranging and inchoate; they didn't have the shape of a need that a wordless creature struggled to communicate. They didn't have thought or feeling behind them.

Bena pictured him at the clinic lying next to a long wooden ruler, doctors standing over him with clipboards and pencils, faithful that their numbers would collect at the bottoms of columns in the formation of a healthy prognosis, because there was no way to measure desire or its absence. It was a mistake she'd made as well. There was no scored tool for measuring that.

She put a hand over her nose. The ever-present stench from the sewers had become so effectively integrated with the normal air that it shocked her when she noticed its pungency. Pueblo's sewers were medieval, the waste flushed, untreated, into the Arkansas River. The pollution had become bad enough lately—typhoid rates soaring to alarming heights, infant deaths from diarrhea and enteritis doubling, then tripling—that a group of doctors from Ted's clinic insisted that the city introduce a filtering system to treat the contaminated water with chlorine, lime, and alum. With the drought and dropping water levels in the river, it was a losing battle. The riverbed was little more than a sewage pipe, hauling Pueblo's waste south to Trinidad. And the flies. Instead of the sound of water, Bena had come to associate the river with the low, heavy hum of insect wings.

She put her head on her knees, and smelled the soapy clean of her skirt. Soon she was dreaming of a spotless tiled laundry room, with women in white aprons folding fat sheets that turned into warm loaves of bread she could split with her hands and press her face into. The loaves of bread became a man's damp, yeasty-smelling chest that closed around her face and prevented her from seeing who it was that buried her. She could only reach up with a hand and feel the contours of his nose and cheekbones, his raspy beard. She sensed in the depths of his chest that he was trying to speak. She put her fingers to his lips as if to quiet him.

Hello, he said into her fingertips. *Hello there.*

She reached out to touch his face, to feel whether he was the man in her dream.

"Getting a little shut-eye, I see."

Bena started.

Red crouched in front of her, with a smile that said, You're a funny one, you are. He passed a palm over his knee as if to shoo some ache away.

"Here," she offered. "Have a seat."

They squeezed onto the step, their hips rubbing. Bena looked around to see whether anyone was watching them, but she saw no one.

"Man grows old quick out here," he said. "Sand in my joints."

"I thought maybe I'd broken something after a day on that horse of yours."

"She's tough as granite, that Betty. Make mighty poor eating someday."

"Are you planning on eating her?"

He thought about it briefly. "Nah," he said. "But no doubt somebody will. People been pulling cattle carcasses out of the hole over by the rendering plant and eating them. Animals couldn't have much more meat on them than a workboot."

He didn't appear to have any intention of mentioning their trip to Mary's. Each time she'd met him after their first encounter, it seemed he came to her fresh, without any history of her.

"How was the party?" he asked.

"Fine. Everybody got righteously drunk. Including Gerta Ashburne. My husband dipped her head in the punch bowl."

"She's got a wild streak in her, that one. Little Miss Hay Bale, 1922."

"Really."

"Harvest queen that year, too."

"Pueblo's own fertility goddess."

"Not exactly. She's barren. As a man careless with other people's secrets, I thought you ought to know. Scarlet fever. Caught it the year after she was married to Clyde. He's a good man. Or a weak one. A different man might have left her."

They sat in silence while Bena burned on the narrow step.

"I saw a picture of your house at Cuerna Verde," she offered. "In the library. Your mother has your face."

"I think maybe I have hers. She left it to me when she passed on."

"She's dead?"

"She is indeed."

"How old were you?"

"Eighteen. She wasn't much for living, frankly. But she had her lighter moments. She liked rainstorms, and bicycling."

"And Bavarian architecture." Bena saw the woman in the raccoon coat, the fur blown flat as she whisked down a mountain on a small blue bicycle. "Was she from Pueblo?"

"Born and bred."

"So she didn't use that as her excuse."

"What?"

"Maladjustment." Bena was thinking of her own mother, a woman who died when Bena was an infant, because, as her father explained it to her later, she missed Norway. It was presented to her as sound reason: Missing Norway was a natural cause of death, as natural as attacks by bees, or a heart. Her mother had grown up outside the town of Høne, on a horse farm. Bena had seen pictures of her in dark coats and big hats, holding the lank reins to furry ponies. These photos were kept around the St. Paul house to prove the undeniable pull of this place on her missing mother, a mother who missed so hard she went missing. Who wouldn't want to go back to a land with furry ponies? Who could ever fault a woman for wanting that?

The two-fifteen break whistle at the ironworks blew. The noise rolled toward them, over them, beyond them, having nothing to stop or disperse its sharp cable of sound—no crops, no trees, no significant relics of civilization willing to absorb it. Bena imagined it continuing to circle the globe, traveling the earth and arriving in Pueblo precisely at two-fifteen like an audible sun.

"My mother was maladjusted," Bena said. "She died from missing Norway."

Red regarded her quizzically and put a hand on her knee. Maybe he was worried about her, she thought, making such nonsensical comments. Maybe he was taking her pulse, feeling for traces of a functioning heart through her kneecap. His hands were confusing to her: he had eight intact fingers if she counted both hands together, or three and five if she didn't. March 5 was Little Ted's birthday, which made her feel safe and right in Red's presence. It was crazy for him to touch her like that, or for her to allow herself to be touched; yet the gesture fell within the perimeters of their relationship, whatever their relationship was, and the pleasantly suggestive, nonbinding intimacy it seemed to sanction.

"How about you accompany me on another cryptic errand?" he asked. He picked her hat up off the ground where it had fallen during her nap, and brushed it on his dungarees. When he held out his hand she took it, lifting herself off the step and following him wherever he planned to take her.

BENA SAT on the bowed porch of Savage Bros. while Red bought sausage and cheese and pickled tomatoes and bottles of ginger beer for a late lunch. She could hear cattle being shot at the rendering plant.

They walked up Santa Fe Avenue to Mineral Palace Park, where, Red claimed, he had to meet somebody just past three o'clock. The mansions bucked upward on either side of them like the walls of a canyon. A Mexican man in a straw hat tossed water around the front lawn of Reimer's house. Her silver car was in the driveway and the shades to the living room were drawn against the day.

The Mineral Palace was looking no less forlorn than when Bena and Reimer had visited in June. If there were any improvements under way, Bena couldn't see evidence of them. The decay resembled a con-

struction process, new, tumorous shapes appearing as stones upended
and plaster buckled.

Red carved sausage with his pocketknife. His large, peculiar hands
bent in unexpected ways, the stretch of his existing fingers above the
top knuckles splaying backward. She stared at his right hand with its
missing joints, trying to understand better how they were destroyed,
how they were healed. The scar tissue was thin over the new tips. She
could see the bumbly contours of his foreshortened knuckles underneath.

"Forgot forks," he said, handing her a ginger beer and a gray,
pickled tomato. Vinegar ran down her wrist, and she lifted her arm to
her mouth to stop it with her tongue.

"Forgot napkins, too." He grinned at her to suggest this was on
purpose.

They ate beneath the shade of a Chinese elm, one of the few trees
within the park that still clung, tenaciously, to its leaves.

"What happened to your hand?" Bena asked.

A dog patrolled the perimeter of their picnic with a hobbled gait.
Red threw a rock to encourage it to keep a distance, but the possibility
of food overrode the risk of being stoned to death. The dog continued
to circle them, each time winding closer. When she stopped chewing,
Bena could hear the animal breathing through its matted muzzle, desperate on the inhale, patient on the exhale. Desperate, patient, desperate, patient. The rhythm made her tense in the neck. She stared at the
dog and it scurried away, to enter the hole in the Palace's northeast
wall.

Red held his right hand in front of his face, as if he could barely
remember how he'd mislaid the tops of two fingers.

"Before they built the house at Cuerna Verde, my parents used to
take me up to the Red Feather lakes for summer holidays. Ever been
there?"

Bena shook her head.

"It's a sweet enough spot. Not the fanciest shore you've ever stretched your towel on, but that's why my father liked it. Unlike my mother, he wasn't one for fancy. Just a door, roof, couple of windows was all he needed to feel he was living in a kingly fashion."

"I imagine she wasn't very happy up there."

"She said it was cold and common. To which my father would say, 'But at least it's uncommonly cold.' "

From the echoing depths of the Palace came a shriek. Bena and Red both turned, expecting to see a panicked bird lifting from the roof. But the animal became quiet again, whatever it was.

"We were having a race one day, me and the boys who lived there year-round. See who could touch the other side of the lake first. Naturally, my mother was reluctant. The lake was a good half-mile across, and cold as all get-out. She decided she'd permit me as long as I could promise not only that I wouldn't drown but that I'd win. They were common boys. She didn't want them thinking they had anything on us."

"And did you think you could win?"

"Sure, I told her, I'll win for you. She came down to the shore to see me win. She gave me a penknife to put into the pocket of my swim trunks. For good luck, she said. To use if I absolutely had to."

Bena sensed the story turning dark. The breeze picked up and rattled the leaves overhead.

"Until we reached the middle of the lake I was winning. The two boys and I were neck-and-neck for almost the last half of the lake. I heard my mother yelling from across the water. So I pulled the knife out of my pocket and cut off the tops of two of my fingers. I threw them to the shore, just before the bigger of the boys reached it. But I won." He held his hand up to her. "I was the first to touch the other side."

"That's not true," Bena guessed in a low voice.

Red pushed back against the elm's shabby trunk. "No, it's not. But it could be." He rolled a cigarette, trying hard to keep the silty tobacco from blowing away.

"I don't suppose I could ever coax you to tell me the real story," Bena said.

He made a shelter out of his shirt and hid his head inside. She saw the flame blaze through the fabric, thought that maybe, in the midst of this strange storytelling, he would even set himself on fire to prove a point.

Instead he emerged with a cigarette, which he passed to her, but she refused it. She'd been careful about what she ate, drank, breathed since Little Ted's eating patterns had become disrupted—no alcohol, no bitter herbs, no aspirin, no cigarettes.

"I was home from college one winter holiday. Nineteen or so at the time. I told my dad I wasn't going back, because I didn't want to be a lawyer, I didn't want to be a doctor or a businessman. I wanted to be a rancher. So he said, Fine, fine, son, I'll find you some work with Sandy McCullough for the holiday. But I'll make you a deal. If you prove able, you can be a rancher. If not, you take the train back east come January and resume your studies."

"Seems reasonable enough," Bena said.

"Precisely why I should have been suspicious. I went to work for Sandy McCullough, who put me through the paces, western style— driving cattle from midnight to dawn through the coldest stretch of prairie this side of the Rockies. Had to keep the cattle moving so they didn't freeze to death. Back and forth, back and forth over five miles of frostbitten scrub. I found out later that Sandy had a barn for his animals, but he was doing my dad a favor by letting them out in the cold all night. My dad promised to reimburse him for any losses to the herd that happened on my watch."

"How did you find this out?"

"People talk. And my dad liked for me to know he'd stop at nothing to get his way. My third night out, a blizzard came down from Pikes Peak. Had myself good and lost because we'd been traveling well over three hours and we hadn't reached the fence at the end of the property where I would start back for home."

"Couldn't you just turn around?"

"Could have. Problem was, I didn't know which way the barn was. If I could find the fence I could get my bearings. Then we found it. The stakes had been pulled up by the wind and two cows got tangled in the barbed wire. It was an awful mess, around their necks and legs."

"And you couldn't go back without them."

"Could have," Red admitted, "but then I wouldn't have proved myself adequately 'able' at ranching. I cut the first cow out no problem. The second one had the barbs wrapped tight around her neck. One wrong jerk and she'd have crushed her carotid artery. So I wedged my fingers inside the wire to protect her from herself. I'd almost snipped her free when she knocked the wirecutters out of my hand, pulled the barbs tight around my fingers. Like a damned tourniquet. I couldn't find the cutters in the snow. I had two options—cut my fingers off with my knife, or freeze to death. Wasn't much of a choice."

"Good Lord."

"Didn't hurt much." Red wiggled his fingers playfully, proving to her they'd never known suffering. "Wasn't much left of them after those barbs, and they were frozen pretty much clear through. Probably would have lost them to frostbite anyway."

"Did you save the cow?"

"Not a chance. Couple of minutes later and there were a few gallons of blood in the snow, frozen solid. Mine, hers. Jesus. Beautiful, too, if you could forget what it was."

Bena shuddered. But she could see how it probably was beautiful, especially in the sunlight of the next day, everything crystalline and then this red shadow of a life fanned out across the whiteness.

Red looked at his watch and began to fold up the remnants of their picnic. "You need to get back?" he asked.

She couldn't tell whether he was trying to be rid of her, in the politest way he knew how. "I have some time," Bena said. She was desperate not to return to the office, where she'd do little more than worry about the baby. She'd be tempted to call the clinic secretary and bribe her for information, then threaten to have her fired for stealing needles or chloroform if she told Ted. Bena felt herself becoming manipulative and mean, particularly when left alone. And besides, she was hoping she might find a perfect chance to ask Red about the William Bent, and maybe even ask him for help getting inside.

Red didn't seem disappointed to have her company for a while longer. He stood and pulled her to her feet, so they were very close for an instant.

"Where are we going now?" she asked.

He nodded toward the Mineral Palace. "Ever been here before?"

"With Reimer Lee Jackson," Bena said. "She showed me around and talked about her renovation plans."

Red snorted. "They've been talking about renovation since I was a kid. I swear they built this palace and let it fall down just so those church ladies could feel they had something to save." He snorted again. "Hate to say it, but there's no saving this place."

"That's a shame."

"Depends on what you like. I think this place gets more beautiful the more it falls apart."

They approached the Palace from the front, which made Bena wonder if Red, too, had a key and would insist, absurdly, on using it. But he veered around to the side, following a faint path that had been pounded into the dirt.

He stepped through the hole in the northeast wall and stuck his hand out to help her. She was assaulted again with the smell of urine and mildewed air that hadn't known the cleansing power of sunshine for a good long while.

They passed the empty mineral cases and the nymph cast out from her dried-up pool. Bena thought she heard voices from a far corner, and the sound of whimpering. She could discern no knowable shapes, and concluded that it was nothing but wind and dust conspiring to pass as human.

When they reached the stage, Red approached the Silver Queen and felt under the folds of her metal robes. He withdrew a brown package, which he slipped into his pocket.

"I don't imagine she appreciates you putting your hand there."

"Don't worry." He pulled a small cloth bag from his other pocket and wedged it in the hiding place. "I pay her amply for the privilege."

Red hurried Bena back through the chilly rubble.

"What's in the package?" Bena asked. "If you don't mind my prying."

"I do mind," he said. "Laudanum."

"For you?"

Red didn't reply.

"For you?" she repeated.

"For a friend."

A friend, Bena thought. "Your lady friend? For—what's her name—Maude?"

Again he didn't answer. Bena recalled seeing Maude weaving home through the alley. Whiskey, she'd assumed, while it was actually something altogether sleepier blurring her steps.

"She's *pregnant*," Bena said indignantly. "How could you possibly imagine you're helping her?"

Red's face was placid and tired. "And how could you possibly presume to know how she needs to be helped?"

They would have had an argument, Bena was sure of that, had not the still air around them sharpened into an icepick of sound, the same shriek they'd heard while they were eating lunch beneath the Chinese elm. This time the scream was more urgent. They saw a shadow near the nymph fountain that belonged unmistakably to a human body.

"What's going on?" Red called out, stepping over piles of clothes and glass and cans.

"He was stealing my food," came the phlegmy reply.

My Lord, Bena thought. Someone's been murdered.

Red walked closer and bent to inspect a bundle on the floor. "Not anymore he won't. Made a fine mess here, old man."

"Can't have none of that," the figure garbled, "no, sir. Can't have nobody stealin' my food." The figure wandered off to a darker part of the Palace, swaying and cursing to himself.

Red picked up the bundle from the floor. As he approached, Bena saw he was holding the dog that had been circling their picnic. She followed Red out to the weak sunlight. The dog whimpered. Blood blossomed in the gray caverns of his ears.

"What did he do to him?" Bena asked, scared to go too near. The dog smelled fearfully bad, and she could see fleas swarming in its thin fur. It broke her heart the way the creature was so quick to trust one stranger, when another had just caused him irreparable harm.

"Crushed his spine with his foot." Red picked up the dog's muzzle and turned it this way and that.

"Let's take him to the clinic," Bena suggested. "Ted'll be able to do something." Failing dogs are somewhat of a specialty.

"Maybe we ought to ask him what he wants. What do you think, boy?" Red asked, stroking the dog's grizzled face. "You had enough?"

He straddled the animal's body and lifted its head on one forearm, his other forearm pressing against the top of its neck. He lowered his face to the dog's muzzle and jerked his arms together like a pair of wirecutters.

The sound of the dog's neck breaking was clean, sharp, woody, distant. Bena's stomach surged.

Red lay the dog's head down. He straddled the limp body, and stared at his hands. "Fleas," he said. "Jesus." He wiped his hands on his pants and looked at Bena.

Perhaps he was challenging her to think less of him, challenging her to think him a brute. She stared back, meeting his defiant gaze with one she hoped just as defiant. "I've met her before, you know," she said.

Red didn't respond.

"In the alley behind Savage Brothers. She was sucking on old butcher paper."

Red laughed, but she could tell this news pained him. "She's a resourceful girl."

"I want to help her." And it was true, she did want to help her. They could help each other.

Red sniffed. "Don't know if she's a woman who wants to be helped."

"You evidently think she's worth helping."

"I said I didn't know if she wants help. Take it from one who's near dead from trying."

He entered the Palace and returned with a shredded wool blanket that he let the wind shake out. He lay it next to the dog and hauled the body into the center.

Who is she to you? Bena watched him fold the dog in the blanket, then turn the bundle over to keep the corners secure.

"I want to meet her," she said.

Bena thought she saw a flicker of admiration, but he seemed to fight it back just as she had fought back her nausea. They were careful to appear precisely as they knew they should appear. She wondered whether that would ever change between them, and what it would mean if it did.

·   ·   ·

HE TOOK HER through the alley. A black and then a brown cat scampered past. Bena saw a pile of kittens behind a hill of bricks, soft little balls squirming and mangy. She paused to look, but Red pulled her onward.

"They're dead."

"But I saw them move." She looked again. The kittens swarmed with rats, their tails tangling and writhing like a bucketful of bait worms.

She held her hand over her mouth. Something was wrong in a world where rats dined blithely on their predators. It was an apocalyptic inversion of the natural order of things and made Bena feel that she might expect anything. A sun at midnight. New rain.

The hallway was dark, the dirt floor stale-smelling and sour.

"Afternoon, Henry." Bena heard a familiar voice from behind a curtain that functioned as a door to a side room.

"Helen." Red parted the curtain with his fingers, hung his head inside. There was a single cot with a graying quilt and a lame rocker. Enamel washpans hung from the wall, and the tiny fireplace was bricked up with cobblestones. Bena was careful to keep out of Helen's view, knowing she'd be suspicious at the sight of her twice in one afternoon.

"Miss Maude here?" he asked.

Helen coughed and spat it into a bedpan. "She's here and she's mad. Said she was expecting you just after three."

"I got a little busy."

"You better of lost another finger or something. Said if you hadn't she'd hack one off for you." Helen laughed, low and gravelly, relishing the notion of such an outlandish form of revenge.

They ascended a lopsided staircase that turned to the right. Bena could hear the muffled striking of piano keys, one at a time.

The second floor was the William Bent's main area of business. Though lacking in the predictable bordello overgrowth of dark red drapes and davenports, the makeshift salon possessed a lusty clutter—

standing marble ashtrays filled with cigarette butts, a coffee table awash with used train tickets and playing cards, a silk-papered wall stuttered with lurid paintings of Indian squaws spread-legged in the bows of canoes. A leather couch was shaded by the protruding head of a bison mounted on a length of fence planking. Its stiff ears served handily as a post for a silk curtain tie, the tassel hanging by its jaw like an earring.

The landing smelled of antique cigarette smoke and rosewater that stank like old piss.

A balding Persian runner led them down a narrow hall with doors on either side. The rooms were named after tourist attractions—Niagara Falls, The Pyramids, The Great Wall of China—promising not only a sexual thrill beyond the peephole but a bit of a voyage as well. None of the expected sounds attended their walk, not the depressing moans of faked pleasure or the frantic bouncing of mattress springs. Vampires might have lived here, and they were all, within the confines of daylight, asleep.

Red stopped outside the room at the end of the hall, The Eiffel Tower. Someone had tacked a postcard on the door: an artist's rendering of a woman in high heels, red bathing suit, and beret, holding firmly to the tower with both hands, either pulling it toward her or holding it at a provocative distance from her crotch. *"Venez ici,"* read the caption.

Red opened the door and let it swing wide to reveal a corner bedroom. The walls were unfinished, bare slats that couldn't have kept a winter wind at bay for even a moment. A modest vanity was scattered with glass perfume bottles, a tortoiseshell comb-and-mirror set, a teacup full of ashes. Wedged into a corner of the mirror, curling out, was a photograph of a woman in a maid's uniform. In another corner was a newspaper clipping whose headline made Bena smile: "Bonnie and Clyde Shot Dead in Gibsland, La."

A Victorian glass lamp painted with rhododendrons glowed from atop a scarred leather trunk. The hourglass next to the lamp was used,

Bena assumed, to mark time with clients, each slipping grain of sand another fraction of a cent earned. She saw a plate of old biscuits, a mother-of-pearl pocketknife, a few half-empty bottles of sandalwood oil. There was little else in the room but a rag rug and a white enameled bed, low like an infirmary cot, covered with a quilted spread and sunken pillows.

"What a pleasant room," Bena said, not meaning it.

"It gets hot back here," Red replied, "but she can see the sunset from her bed."

He pulled back a sheet that hung before a shallow closet, and shielded from view her few possessions: three colorful dresses on wire hangers, a blue silk robe, a pair of embroidered bedroom slippers, a man's moth-eaten chesterfield, a cowboy hat. The room had an odd smell to it, sharp and medicinal. It reminded Bena of Ted's odor when he came home from the clinic, his shirtsleeves stinking of disease prevention. Maybe it was the scent of a brothel she'd been smelling on him all along. She would ask him when she returned home. Maybe she'd even ask Maude, once she came to know her better. Have you seen this man? she'd ask. Has he cowered in the thick shadow of Mount Rushmore, burned his lips at the base of the Pyramids, peered between the spidery haunches of the Eiffel Tower?

"She's gone," Bena said.

They climbed to the third floor, with its pitched ceiling and dry, dizzying stench of mothballs. The landing was cluttered with unwanted furniture, chairs piled on tables, headboards, shadeless, bulbless lamps. As they walked down the hall, the notes grew louder and lower, giving Bena the sense of being led toward an unknown and forbidding conclusion.

They came to a closed door. Red turned the knob and pushed, but the door was locked. He knocked.

They waited, listening to their own breathing. There was no answer, just the continual dropping of single notes.

He knocked again. The hands came down violently on the piano, two discordant bunches of sound erupting from it. A key could be heard turning inside, then dropping to the floor. The door drifted open a few inches, just enough for a white cat to slither through and disappear behind a bookcase.

Maude sat on top of a swivel stool in front of a listing upright piano. Without her gaudy patina of old makeup, she scarcely resembled the woman Bena had encountered in the butcher's alley. Her face was chalky, her eyes sunk in a smooth hollow of bluish-purple skin like two perfect, seeing bruises. She wore a white cotton dressing gown that was little more than a gauzy slip. Bena could see the heavy swell of her belly, the dark of her nipples. Maude swung back and forth, back and forth on the stool, with her legs splayed.

"What took you so long?" she asked.

"Doesn't matter, does it? I'm here now."

"And you've brought company." She waved her quick-bitten fingers at Bena. "Get you some tea, darling? A biscuit? How good of you to visit your Auntie Maude, she hardly gets any visitors these days."

"This is Bena Jonssen. Mrs. Jonssen claims you've met before."

Maude smoothed her dirty hair with her palm. "If I'd known you were bringing guests, Henry, I'd of had my hair bobbed. Now Mrs. Jonssen is sure to think I'm nothing but a two-bit whore." She grinned cunningly.

"You were pawing through the butcher's trash at the time," Red reminded her.

Maude feigned withering. "Forgive me if I don't remember. One is always quick to forget one's proudest moments." She held out her hand to Red. It trembled as if she were cold or feverish.

Red reached into his pocket and pulled out the package he'd dug from under the skirts of the Silver Queen. He handed it to Maude.

"Want me to do that?" he asked, as she unwrapped a small glass bottle and tried with shaking hands to dissolve a few drops of its tincture into a glass of water on top of the piano.

"I'm not that pathetic, my gracious. He takes me for an invalid," she confided to Bena. She raised the glass and drank. Water spilled down her chin onto her dressing gown. She threw the empty glass against the wall, shattering it.

"Well, then," she said, plopping herself heavily on the swivel stool. She pulled the hem of her gown up and tucked it under her legs so that her feet could reach the pedals unhindered by the thin cloth. "Shall we have a singalong?"

Red held his chin. "I think maybe it's time to rest."

"Are any of you familiar with 'My Spanish Cavalier'?" Maude continued, ignoring him. "How about 'Eva the Girl Vaquero'? Nothing striking your fancy? How about 'Turkey in the Straw'? Everybody knows that one."

She rubbed her hands together and poised her fingers over the keys.

> *"Oh, old Ben Bolt was a fine ol' boss,*
> *Rode to see th' girls on a sore-backed hoss;*
> *Old Ben Bolt was fond of his liquor,*
> *Had a little bottle in th' pocket of his slicker."*

Red slouched against the pitched attic wall, apparently wishing for a drink of something.

Maude followed with a light tinkling of "Chopsticks."

"You had enough yet?" he asked, lighting up a cigarette.

"Don't be a sad old piker, Henry. The show's just getting under way." Maude stared hard at Bena. Her eyes went everywhere, around Bena's nose and mouth, over her breasts, waist, feet.

"Fetching little number you found yourself, Henry."

Bena stood straighter. Maude's eyes narrowed. "What's wrong with her?"

Red frowned. "What do you mean?"

Maude brought her hands down on the keys again, to produce a punishing burst of music. "Intermission," she announced, and walked to the dormer window. She propped one palm against the glass, the other on the back of her hip. Bena could see the outline of her thin legs, hardly wide enough to hold her up.

"At least a girl might be allowed to have a cigarette," Maude said to the glass.

Red obliged, rolling her a cigarette and lighting it between his own lips. Maude did not look at him, did not thank him as he handed it to her.

"So how'd you two meet?" she asked.

Red cleared his throat. "Mrs. Jonssen and her husband were lost in the dust storm last weekend."

Maude laughed meanly, as if a suspicion of hers had been confirmed.

"That's not true, actually," Bena broke in. "We met at Buck's."

Maude turned. She stood with her arms down, crossed over her large abdomen, shielding her breasts from view. Her face was drawn and heavy now, the laudanum beginning to take effect.

"Doesn't that husband of yours provide for you well enough? Keep you fussied up in cashmere and crinoline?"

"He does just fine, thank you."

"Well, darling, not a single other reason to be at Buck's unless you're looking for a little extra jack." Her lids closed and then sprang open.

Red put a hand on her elbow. "I think it's time we took you downstairs."

Maude wobbled toward the stool. She gave Bena a big smile. "Henry's got a good enough heart. He thinks he loves *real hard*, but really his old ticker's only wired for pitying. I'm sure he pities you, sweetheart. Don't doubt it for a second."

"He certainly pities my navigational skills," Bena said.

"What is it, Henry?" Maude insisted. "What is it that you pity about Mrs. Jonssen? Best you tell her now, before she starts believing that you like her for her glamour and her wit, her wise old soul. Go on, Henry. Tell her it's the weakness in her you most adore. Go on," she urged.

Red didn't say a word. This enraged her more.

"What a peach," Maude said. "Woman insults him and he doesn't raise a hand against her." She turned to the piano and attacked it with newfound fervor, lurching against the keys.

> *"Foot in the stirrup and a hand on th' horn,*
> *Best damned cowboy ever was born;*
> *Foot in th' stirrup and a seat in th' sky,*
> *Best damned cowboy ever rode by."*

Bena considered the possibility that Red was planning to hit Maude. He was already moving toward her when she grabbed her abdomen and began to slip off the stool to the buckled floor. He caught her before she landed, a clumsy catch, her arms sticking out at painful angles, her head jerking back on a loose neck.

"She's fine." Red spoke as much to Maude as to Bena. "Just a little tired from being so mean. Wipes a person out, don't it, Maude?"

She tried to spit at him but only dribbled down her chin.

"Should try being a little nicer to the people who care about you. Save your energy to fight those who don't."

"Is she going into labor?" Bena asked.

"Nah. Happens when she doesn't lie down."

"Happens when you listen to goddamned witch doctors," Maude mumbled. She allowed Red to lift her. Bena could see the veins in her arms, all glassy skin and wicker bones. She shuddered to think of the child locked inside that dwindling shelter, a structure that would implode like a waterlogged lean-to, reduced to a mush of rotted sticks.

"Did you know," Maude said as Red walked her over the threshold of the room, "a man who beats his horse is almost certainly a man who beats his wife?" She stared at Bena. "Your husband beat you, sweetheart? Does he?"

"No," Bena said. "He's never lifted a hand against me."

Maude smiled, as at a sweet story. "That's nice, honey, that's nice. Of course you know what they say."

Bena shook her head.

"What they say is"—her voice dropped to just above breathing—"there's more than one way to beat a wife."

Maude's head fell back, fitting itself into the perfect hollow that awaited her in Red's collarbone. He carried her to her room. They were two long-drifting pieces of a continent finally notched back together, their jagged coastlines catching crooked hold.

BENA WATCHED from her office window as the sun hit the side of the William Bent and crawled its way free, up the wall, over the rotting gutters and between the missing roof tiles, then flinging off to join the big grieving orange of the sky. The five-o'clock whistle blew. Empty lunchpails banged against the lean retreating thighs of the ironworkers.

She sat at her desk for five full minutes before she phoned the clinic. She twisted the phone cord around her fingers until the tops became red, then purple, then blue. The secretary, who identified herself as Miss Lang, told Bena that the baby (such a sweet little beechnut) hadn't been examined yet, because Clyde had been busy with a boy who'd jumped from a moving train and splintered his femur. She'd been watching the baby all afternoon, though, and he'd done nothing but sleep.

Bena hung up after extracting a vow of silence from Miss Lang (no threats required), and contemplated going home. But of course she couldn't go home; home would be stifling and full of the unhappinesses of two families, hers and the former inhabitants'.

"Still here?" Ham Paxton stood outside her cubicle.

"Not for long."

"Good," he said, and settled himself in her chair. "I need a change of scenery." He pushed her papers out of the way so he could put his feet on her desk. As always, he was wearing his lizardy ankle boots. "Where you been all day?" he asked.

"Out."

"You were with Red Grissom."

"Possibly."

"He's a real sad man."

Says the real sad man, Bena wanted to say. "He strikes me as a rather unusual man," she said.

"Because he's in love with that lowlife jane? Maybe. To me that's just dull."

"What do you know about her?"

"They were raised together. Her mother, Nonie, was the Grissoms' maid."

"So they're like brother and sister."

"Sure." Ham grinned. "Like some brothers and sisters. Maude and her mother moved here from Trinidad when Maude was six or so. Never knew who her father was, but everyone assumed it was one of the patients at the Trinidad Hospital for the Blind, where Nonie worked before she worked for the Grissoms."

"Is she still alive, Nonie?"

"Nope. That's why Maude became a whore. Before she died, she told Maude her father lived in Pueblo. Said he wasn't some blind guy, that he was actually a very prominent, very married man, who couldn't claim her, for the obvious reasons. Maude figured her father'd be the one man in town she couldn't coax into her bed. Of course, there was no telling where the truth stopped and Nonie's imagination picked up. Ask me, Maude's father was probably some sorry sightless coalworker back in Trinidad. Maude's screwed every rich man, poor man, Indian, Mexican, hoodlum this crappy town has to offer. Didn't find her father. Only thing she's found is herself, a little bit knocked up."

"Lord." Bena returned to the window to search for Red. "There should be a less degrading way to go about determining one's paternity."

Ham put his hands behind his head, revealing the black sweat stains at his armpits. "Not in this town," he said. "Truth and degradation are easy mates. People have proud mouths."

"Unlike you," Bena said.

"That's why you're fond of me."

"Why's that?" Bena pretended to be trying hard to remember.

"Because I strike you as such an unusual man."

Bena heard footsteps in the alley, saw the pale of Red's hat. She grabbed her purse and rushed from the office. Just outside the door, she found her face buried in the soft, boyish chest of Felix Best.

"Hell," he gasped, the breath punched out of him.

She patted him apologetically, then retrieved her purse from where she'd dropped it.

Red was waiting for her on the steps of Buck's Silo, smoking and looking at the street full of ironworkers. The dust grew around them and the sun picked out rainbows at their knees.

"Walk you home?" he said.

They wandered up Union Avenue, past an elderly man and a gawky, bespectacled boy on a bench. The man peeled an orange with a knife, creating a single golden coil, and the boy, a bit too old to be entertained with such an example of painstaking, useless craft, sneaked looks at the sight that really interested him, a pair of crows picking messily at a rat's carcass.

"How is she?" Bena asked.

"Better. Helen took a look at her. Said she was a couple of weeks away yet."

"And Helen's is considered a reliable medical opinion?"

"Oldest of twelve. Helped her ma deliver the last six. I guess she knows something about it."

"What's Maude's objection to a good old-fashioned physician?"

Red smiled. "God knows. Feel free to ask her next time you see her. You'll get a story you can take or leave."

"And what about the laudanum? Is that part of Helen's treatment?"

This seemed to make Red uncomfortable. "She needs it for her stomach. She's never been right since I took her to Mary's."

"Did Mary read her palm?"

"In a manner of speaking. You saw how Mary is, talking circles."

I'm sure I have you all wrong. I want to give you the chance to be had all wrong.

Bena wondered whether Mary had told Maude a disturbing fact about her palm, whether she'd intimated that she'd seen a bad event lurking there, a bad act, bad thought, bad outcome. Maybe she'd told Maude what she'd seen spelled out in her mottled hand, and Maude had believed her enough to swallow Mary's magic powder of bran and arsenic.

"Can I ask you a prying question?" Bena said.

"Is this for your benefit or the *Chieftain*'s?"

"Mine." It was partly true.

When he didn't say anything, she took it as a sign that her question would be tolerated. "Who's the father?" she asked.

They walked half a block before he answered. "I suppose you think it's me."

Bena laughed. She could laugh because the sun was behind her and the world was pink and gold and so resplendent that the tips of the Rockies were prouder than she'd ever seen them. "I used to," she admitted.

"Had some time to think about this, huh?"

"I've been watching you. From the window."

"You came into Buck's looking for me."

"Yes. Yes, I did."

"And I suppose you're going to tell me those antics in the dust storm were just a way of getting to know me better?"

She smiled. "Absolutely."

He shook his head. "The lengths you'll go to for a story."

"It's not for a story."

"Isn't it?" She thought she'd never seen a more glorious man in her life, the sun in his beard, his eyes hurt and wise and the color of bleached wood.

"No," Bena insisted. "No." It wasn't a lie, not exactly.

"What, then?"

She looked at his hands, the ghosts of fingers that had once been pinned against the frantic veins of a cow's neck, the hands that had led her back to his picture in the paper and the story of Harlan Baxter's buffalo, *it was the most beautiful act of nature he'd ever witnessed, these burly, wingless animals flinging themselves into the blue, as if they aimed to fly*, and she believed her heart might split open at the thought of touching him, or never touching him.

She shrugged the feeling into the sky, where it turned in the sun, unclaimed. "I was curious."

"Curious?"

Bena was about to ask him what was wrong with being curious, but then he said, "I was curious about you, too."

"Me?"

"I saw you with your son one day along the river. You took off your shoes and walked barefoot. You lay down next to him and took a nap under a live oak."

Bena remembered that day, when she couldn't bear the house a moment longer, the idle sounds of Florence's doddering above her, the same view of the same house across the street where the old man lived, cracking walnuts with a wrench. She'd never felt so displaced. She knew no one except her husband. So she walked. Down North Grand to Union, amazed how people hurried past her without a glance. The sky was uneasy and the sun sightless by the time she reached the river. It was foul-smelling but alive; a balding tree was the only shelter she could find.

"You saw us?"

"You looked like you belonged there, asleep in a place where no one would ever think of sleeping."

She'd opened her eyes to discover Little Ted covered with fire ants—swarming in his eyes and ears, collecting in the hammocks between his fingers. He remained still while she picked the ants off, hoping not to irritate them or encourage them to bite. When she reported this to Ted later that night, he said, "He's a Jonssen, all right," which she took to mean that her husband was proud to have fathered a child who would suffer foolish amounts of pain in silence. At the time she agreed with him, and they toasted their hardy midwestern stock.

"It wasn't such a good place to sleep," she told Red. "Fire ants."

Soon they were in front of her house. The door was closed behind the screen: Ted had yet to return from the clinic with the baby. Bena became enraged. She envisioned another potential ending to the day. Ted would come home and Clyde Ashburne wouldn't even have seen the baby that afternoon. Ted would offer an excuse and ridicule her concern, then take great pleasure in dragging out the conclusion of the visit until she became a mad, sobbing wreck of a woman whom no doctor would believe.

From this vantage point, at the crest of the North Grand hill, she and Red had an ideal view of the ironworks machinery poised above its own foulness, the thick Arkansas wallowing in its poisoned bed, the low, prickly skyline of the shantytown, the eastbound train tracks like stitches sewing up a long, skinny wound.

"I don't know the answer to your question," Red told her. "The father. I think maybe she thinks I might do something foolish if I knew."

"Is it someone from around town?"

"Chances are," he said.

"Maybe I'll try to find out the answer myself."

"I wouldn't advise it."

"When I find out, I'll be sure not to tell you."

He balanced on a raised brick in the sidewalk with his heel, rocking back and forth over it. "As long as I don't read about it in that paper of yours, I don't care what I don't know."

She held out her right hand. "Deal." Behind her back she crossed the fingers of her left. "Are you seeing her tomorrow?"

He nodded.

"Can I come?"

Red started down the hill without even shaking her hand. Bena watched him go, waiting for him to turn around or wave. He did not.

She walked up the steps of the house, collecting the evening paper and letters from the mailbox. She was at the door when she heard him call out to her.

"Meet me at the Idle Hour at one o'clock."

Bena turned. She couldn't see him against the angry horizon. "I don't know where that is," she called back, but he didn't hear. His dark carbon body had been burned up by the sun.

TED CAME HOME, as Bena had predicted, with glowing reports from the clinic. The baby was big for his age, true, but Clyde had found nothing outlandish or worrisome in his round body. He agreed with

Ted that the baby might have a touch of colic, which would explain his erratic feeding.

The real problem, Ted informed Bena as she gave Little Ted his six-o'clock feeding, was her. Her behavior was common among young mothers, a form of depression that manifested itself in extreme anxiety over the baby's well-being. They imagine illnesses. They dream of the baby's dying because they want it to die and don't want it to die.

"I'm not depressed," Bena said, even though she teared up when she heard the good news, when Ted had delivered the baby into her arms and kissed her proudly as if she'd just given birth a second time.

Ted fixed himself a drink. He stewed over the counter as he stirred his gimlet with his finger.

"Sometimes I think you prefer to be unhappy," he said, then walked out to the back porch in his unbuttoned shirt and loosened tie, to watch the sun set over his trout pond.

"I don't prefer to be unhappy," Bena clarified after dinner, passing Ted a plate to dry.

The baby slept soundly in his bassinet, which was set on the kitchen table. He hadn't seemed bothered by the experience at the clinic, nor had he missed her terribly. He had fed without complaint this evening; Dr. Ashburne had prescribed a rust-colored tincture for his appetite, which she was to drop into his mouth half an hour before feeding.

Ted tossed the dishrag onto the counter and moved behind her. His hand encircled her waist and rubbed her belly beneath the fabric, up and down, so she could feel the warp and weft of the cloth against her skin.

She turned to face him, suds scooting toward her elbows.

His hand moved over her ribs, one at a time, counting to make sure they were all there. When he reached her breast, he pinched her nipple, softly at first, then increasing pressure.

He pushed her dress down her arms and kissed her bare shoulders, lifting the apron over her head and letting it fall to the floor, where it soaked up the water that had dripped from the sink. He pressed against her, and she could feel water from the counter creeping into the small of her back. Her body sagged and drooped. She thought of the Eiffel Tower. Bena saw Ted beneath the spreading iron legs, his face cross-hatched by the shadows.

She stared at the clock on the wall as his lips moved along her collarbone. Eight-thirty. She remembered the clock at Kaap's, when Ted had shown her how to find her pulse. She couldn't breathe, couldn't catch her breath in the heat. She pushed Ted away.

"What's wrong?"

Bena didn't know why he would ask, except that she was crying. She slid down until she was sitting in the center of her wet apron.

It confused her, the way she'd meticulously tracked Little Ted's ever-growing numbers, his height, his weight, and yet the more of him that existed, the less of him there seemed to be. She thought about leaving people, about people who left.

At least Jonas had had the decency to leave without a blood trail, to sink beneath the waves of the lake and never reappear, not even for his funeral. The lake was a glacial puncture in the landscape that dug hard toward the middle of the earth. People who died in that water were rarely found, unless their bodies had the misfortune of getting caught in the pipes that pulled drinking water for Coeur du Lac. Whenever there was a sickness in town, that was the rumor children passed around. A corpse was caught in the filter. Billy McGulligan's corpse. Sadie Jungfren's corpse. After Jonas drowned, Bena never again drank from the tap at the summer house.

"Bena." Ted's hand was on her wrist: One, two, three, four . . .

"Yes."

"Let's get you to bed."

What was it about men, she wondered, always trying to get you into bed, as if bed were an answer, as if bed were a cure, a solution, a place where any amount of healing transpires.

"I'd like to ask you a question." She shook off the hand that sought to help her up from the wet floor.

"I'll answer if you promise to come to bed."

"Truthfully."

"Truthfully."

Bena touched her hand to her forehead. Her skin was cool, not at all feverish.

"Have you ever been with a prostitute?" she asked.

Ted turned crimson, but she could sense that he was relieved. She had not asked him the question he did not want to be asked.

You're a smart girl, Bena. That's why I hired you.

He put an affectionate hand on her hair, as one might do with a child who has posed a question too wise and vast for her age. *Is there water on the moon?*

"What ever made you ask such a question?"

Bena was stunned at her own lack of daring. She looked at her hands, objects that had failed her. "It doesn't matter," she said.

Ted brushed the hair from her face, tucked it behind her ear. "Your hair's getting long," he said wistfully. "You could almost tie it back." He had liked her with long hair. She'd cut it just before she'd had the baby, and he had looked at her ever since with an expression that said, *It's shame, what a shame, you have such beautiful hair, women would kill for hair like yours*—as if she were obligated to other women to keep her hair long just because they could not.

She let him lead her to the bedroom, unbutton her shoes and unhook her dress. He helped her into a silk dressing gown. He let her kiss the baby good night and then took him away, because she was not to be trusted, she was a crazy mother who thrilled herself by imagining the worst about her baby until she made it true. Soon she was asleep, vaguely aware that he wasn't beside her, that he was sleeping instead in the spare bedroom on an unmade bed, wrapped in one of the Sparkses' sheets from the linen closet. She assumed he was wary of lying next to her because she was rummaging around too close to his secrets. She might try to steal them from him under the cover of sleep.

That night Bena dreamed of the trout pond.

She arrived home from work and found the clocks blank-faced. She called out for Ted; his jacket, his tie, his pants were strewn through the house. She followed the trail of clothes to a back window. She could see him by the pond, naked. He was bent over a woman, kissing her. He kissed her intently, urgently, trying to save her life or snuff it out with his lips. Bena moved outside to yell at him, to show him she'd caught him in the act, but as she stepped onto the lawn the woman transformed herself into a thick, heaving fish.

Ted looked up at her. It's dying, he said. They're all dying.

The fish were all around him, belly up and shining in the sun. He was breathing into their mouths and casting them aside as their lungs failed to fill with the air he tried to force into them.

Stop, she said. Maybe you should ask them. Maybe you should ask them if they've had enough.

He paused. Have you? he asked the fish in his arms. Have you had enough?

He held the fish out to her and she saw that it was Little Ted, and that all around them were babies, not fish, their bellies sunken in the sunlight, their eyes closed, hearts quiet.

8. THE GREEN DRESS

The last half of July 1934 was unusually marked by broken heat records and the unfortunate death of a pair of newlyweds, lost in a dust storm near Keota. It was marked also, more usually, by Reimer Lee Jackson's annually rescheduled Christmas party.

Reimer invited Ted and Bena when she spotted them in the lobby of the Silver State Theater, waiting for a Saturday matinee of *The Black Cat* with Bela Lugosi. Reimer was alone and seemingly nervous about it; she tore her ticket stub into tiny pieces as she chatted with the Jonssens and fawned over the baby. She had held her annual Christmas party in July for years, she explained, ever since Abbott had decided that the actual holiday was more wisely spent in the Mexican town of Saltillo, where he could keep an eye on his silver mines. Abbott claimed the native blood ran hotter around the holidays: the filthy kids were always sobbing in the streets for oranges, the mothers were off with the farmhands teaching them a lesson or two about the world, the fathers were busy softening their sorrows in the *cervecería*.

The story sounded far-fetched, Bena commented to Ted when they returned home. Bena measured the baby for the third time that day; she'd measured him before the movie, when, she found, he hadn't grown since she'd measured him after breakfast. She thought the heat might make him expand, the way it made her fingers swell so much that she had to take her wedding rings off with cooking oil.

Since the clinic visit, Bena had been more scrupulous in her measuring than ever. She'd purchased a journal at the stationer's and made careful note of the length of Little Ted's arms and legs, the diameter of his palms. She was more precise and organized, yet far less satisfied; her recordings only accentuated to her the ways in which numbers were powerless to communicate her suspicions about the baby to her husband. If anything, the numbers served to prove her the hysteric he believed she was, a desperately myopic hysteric who was distrustful of the most convincing evidence of her baby's flourishing.

Despite her excessive attentions, Ted no longer teased her about these fixations on the baby. Possibly this was because she'd seen him herself the morning after the visit to the clinic, stretching a tape measure along Little Ted's spine and making a mark in a pocket notebook. She'd also seen him dangle keys over the baby's face and tickle his legs with a look suggesting his intent was far from playful.

The baby in her arms, Bena walked outside to watch Ted feed his fish. He was trying out a new species—*Lepomis macrochirus*, or bluegill—after his failure with the steelheads. During the mating season, Ted told her, the male bluegill acquires a bright red breast. The bluegill had faltered at first, refusing to eat the dried locusts Ted threw them each morning. Now, however, they would snap up the dead insects before they could float to the bottom, catching the knotted, leggy bodies in their jaws.

Bena told Ted she thought the story about the unruly holiday spirits of Mexicans was an excuse concocted by Abbott so he could run around Saltillo with Mexican prostitutes instead of trotting among claustrophobic Pueblo Christmas parties with Reimer, tense and rustling in her taffeta skirts, her winter face the color of eggnog.

Bena held Little Ted away from the pond as Ted dropped a handful of locusts into the water. He wore leather gloves, for even the deadest creatures carried disease. The locusts made hissing noises as they hit the water.

Annoyed, Ted argued that Reimer was a pleasantly garrulous dowager. He suggested that Bena might check herself before casting aspersions on such a lovely old lady and her dead husband.

Bena maintained that she wasn't interested in attending, and she continued to do so, until the actual day of the party. Then she found out Red would be there.

Bena and Red were eating lunch at the Idle Hour, a spare café with sagging pine tables and coffee that looked and tasted like rusty water. She'd met him there two afternoons the previous week, after which they'd gone to deliver food to Maude at the rooming house. He rolled cigarettes for her and gave her more laudanum when her stomach cramped up, and Bena helped with the chores only a woman could help with. Red went for a smoke beneath the bison's head in the hallway while Maude wound her thin arm around Bena's neck and squatted over the enamel bedpan, letting loose a stream of dark urine.

"Reimer's Christmas party? Wouldn't miss it." He'd been going to Reimer's Christmas parties since he was a kid, he told Bena. He and Maude used to go with his parents and sit on St. Nicholas's lap, St. Nick who was actually Abbott Jackson, his gaunt frame disguised beneath red knickers and a red coat lined with the sort of sheep's wool that was fine for winter but stank in the summer heat. Despite his best efforts to appear corpulent and jolly, Abbott was all bone edges and gin-smelling when he rocked them on his knee. The licorice he gave out from his warm pocket molded to the shape of your palm when you held it.

Red folded up his ham steak inside a piece of white bread and drove his fork through a mound of fried potatoes; he finished everything off in a few bites, as Bena sipped her coffee. When they were ready to leave, Red stacked his coins neatly on top of the metal napkin dispenser. He knocked on the counter twice before leaving, and said, "Heck of a meal, Martin," to the cook, who raised his free hand in reply over the griddle, flipping meat and bread with the other.

Maude was lively and belligerent when they arrived with their offerings—bologna, tepid cheese, bread, a canteen of coffee from the Idle Hour. Her hair was freshly washed, the damp coils blood-dark in the light. She'd put on a clean dressing gown, a large, satiny, wide-collared man's robe. She was smoking, knocking the ashes into an empty teacup on the bedstand. She'd powdered her face, Bena noticed, perhaps attempting to blot out the heat rash that flared on her cheeks.

Red found the bed tray in the corner and propped it by her elbow. He poured coffee into a water glass, lay a few wan slices of bread on a napkin. Maude regarded the coffee with disdain.

"You know, Martin thickens this crap with flour."

"Martin's a loyal fellow," Red replied. "He does the best he can."

"Martin's loyal to his own good time and not much else."

"Well, I know he's loyal to me."

"That's why he's always asking for me when he's looking for a fuck, is that right? Loyalty?"

Red busied himself with the meat, taking great care to unwrap it without tearing the paper.

Bena held the hourglass up to the window. What did it feel like to be underneath the body of a strange man who called you by a name that didn't belong to you, a name you swapped with your girlfriends when your own became uninteresting to you? Delia. Doris. Carmen. It probably made the act easier, having a stranger breathe a name that wasn't yours, breathe, *Good, Carmen, good, that's the way, sweetheart, that's the way, Carmen.*

"Pains him, I'm sure," Maude continued, "but perhaps he feels he owes it to you to keep me off the street."

Red peeled free a slice of bologna and held it up to the window so that the sun shone through it. To Bena it looked like a soul, a raw, shuddering soul, hung out to dry.

When Red spoke, his voice was as flat and measured as the wind that rattled through acres of dead prairieland. But the words were mean, whetted and gleaming and wishing to sink themselves in a vulnerable place.

"You need to keep throwing it in my face, don't you? Just in case I don't go to bed every night with the image of you being fucked silly by any man I might dare to call a friend."

Maude took large, clumsy bites of bread. She seemed driven by the need to destroy something more than by actual hunger. "I just hate to see you laboring under any illusions," she said.

"Illusions of what?"

"That I need saving. That I'm yours to save. That I really give a good goddamn one way or the other. That kind of illusion."

Red folded up the slice of bologna, in halves, then fourths, then eighths, until it was nothing but a fleshy stone. He pushed it through his lips, not wanting to eat it, his body knowing it didn't want to ingest a soul, but he pushed anyway, pushed until his lips parted and the soul disappeared inside him.

"You know what tonight is?" Red inquired.

Maude took a sip of coffee.

"Reimer's Christmas party." He answered his own question.

She wiped her mouth with the back of her wrist, smearing her lipstick so that it looked as if she were running very fast, fast enough to leave her mouth behind. "Are you going?"

"As is Mrs. Jonssen."

Maude glanced at Bena. "Don't you two dance together. You might raise the hackles of Reimer and a hundred other ashy busybodies."

"There's nothing to be suspicious of," Red told her.

"No?" Maude seemed forcibly amused.

"You know there's not."

"Oh, I know?"

Red didn't answer.

"I know, because I'm standing in your way of happiness, isn't that right?" Maude turned to Bena as if to the only sympathetic, rational witness within earshot. "I'm not a real obstacle, despite what he'd have you believe. I'm just another one of his sad habits."

"Maybe I ought to go." Bena stood up.

"No," Red protested. "No, I need to go. I need to pick up my suit at the presser's."

He tossed the package of meat on the vanity. It landed with a wet slap.

"You coming back?" Maude asked.

"I don't imagine."

"I didn't know you even had a suit," she said.

"Yeah. I have a suit. A blue suit."

"It sounds nice," she said, her lips side-stretched and wrong. "A blue suit."

He didn't say good-bye, he didn't bend down and kiss her in the way that usually made her grimace afterward, as though he were her filthy uncle looking to touch any innocent part of her.

Red nodded formally in Bena's direction. "See you this evening?"

Bena answered just as formally. "Ted and I are looking forward to it."

The door shut behind him, and she and Maude were alone.

Maude pushed her food away and lit another cigarette. Elsewhere in the rooming house, someone played the piano, stopped and started, stopped and started, always the same refrain of the same song.

"Drive you crazy," Maude said.

Bena agreed. "Like some kind of torture."

"You don't even know."

"Do they practice every day?"

Maude regarded her queerly. "I mean Henry."

Bena walked to the vanity table. She touched the greasy bottles of rosewater and sandalwood oil, the beaded evening bag with the fake pearl clasp, the empty inkwell, the curled photograph of a woman in a maid's uniform.

She glanced in the mirror and rubbed an errant swoop of lipstick from her top lip with her ring finger. Her diamond flashed in the low light.

"Pretty ring," Maude said.

"Hmmm?"

"I said pretty ring."

Bena smiled, neither agreeing nor disagreeing.

When Ted first gave her the engagement ring, she would hold her newly bejeweled hand next to her face in a mirror. She'd always considered herself odd-looking (verging on plain in winter), a girl made of pretty pieces but on the whole undistinguished unless the sun was in her hair. The diamond, however, made her eyes flash, made her teeth clean and white like the bones of a long-dead animal. She had the mark of desirability on her hand. She sat in restaurants, pondering the chalkboard menu with her hand under her chin, or resting on her collarbone as if she were dizzy or shocked or coyly appalled. But really she just wanted to flaunt this new self, to have others admire it whenever she was unable to admire it herself, because it was a fleeting beauty, she knew, a novelty that burned hot and ended quick.

Bena caught Maude looking at her in the mirror. She pointed to the newspaper clipping wedged in the frame. "Bonnie and Clyde Shot Dead in Gibsland, La." "Are you a fan of Bonnie Parker?" she asked.

Maude first denied it, but then said, "Of course."

"Why 'of course'?"

"Because she dared to."

"You admire her for killing people?"

Maude gestured toward the first drawer of the vanity. "Fetch me the nail paint, will you?"

Bena handed her a bottle of red varnish. The piano had ceased to traverse the same tired territory. Instead, somebody had cranked up a gramophone. It played a record that skipped and repeated the same first few notes until someone nudged the arm, sending the needle skipping into the smooth center of a song.

Bena sat on the trunk. "I admire your daring," she said. She watched as Maude spread a palm flat over her stomach and pulled the brush along her thumbnail, bitten so close that the surrounding skin was inflamed.

Maude assessed her work. She'd painted her thumbnail and her pinkie. She rotated her hand for Bena to see. The color looked terrible against her skin.

"You admire an old slut like me? Funny. I'd think Reimer Lee Jackson'd be more to your taste. Not that she isn't an old slut in her way."

Bena bristled. "There isn't a woman I'd less want to be like."

Maude dabbed at her middle fingernail. "So you're saying you didn't come from a perfect pretending life, and you don't pretend your life is perfect?"

"I don't complain, which isn't the same thing."

"And neither does Reimer, sweetheart. She just takes it and takes it and keeps that stringy little mouth of hers shut."

Bena picked up the photograph of the woman in the maid's uniform. "That seems a rather mean thing to say."

"Mean," Maude repeated, as if to imply, What's not mean? The world is mean. Shouldn't come as any great amazement to anyone.

Bena went to the window to get a better look at the photograph. The woman held herself soldier-straight before the great oak double doors, hands at her sides. She didn't resemble Maude except around the lips; her moth-shaped mouth was parted and loose, while the rest of her remained unbending.

Bena put her hand against the wall to steady herself. The heat pounded through the thin clapboards that were their only protection against the punishing day. It was all about lines, survival was, the very finest of lines.

"What would she say, if she could?" Bena asked.

Maude blew on her nails and waved them in the air. "Who? What would who say?"

"Reimer Lee Jackson."

Maude laughed. "Reimer? I'd imagine she'd say something like, 'I married a man who loved me for my fortune if he loved me at all, I married a man who brought young girls, only young girls, up to his room far, far away in the western wing and taught them how to make something of themselves.' "

Bena went to the closet and reached in. Her hand found the hilly crown of a cowboy hat. She pulled it out and put it on her head. "What did he teach them?" she asked.

"He'd say, 'You haven't got a dime to your name, sweet girl, but you've got two legs and half a brain. You'd best know how to do a few things well.' "

Bena fiddled with the hat's leather strap and its sliding amber bead. She moved it up tight against her neck until the blood couldn't flow to her mouth. Her lips would grow white, silvery; a glacier would extend down her throat, encase her vocal cords. There would be no words, no feeling, only a preserved fossil of sadness for a future people to discover and put in a museum and shake their heads over: *What a shame, such a pretty girl, you have such beautiful hair, that's why I hired you.*

"Learned all I needed to know from Abbott Jackson, silver miner. Gold digger. Santa Claus." Maude screwed the top back on the bottle, her fingertips held out carefully. "Know what it's like to have an old man between your legs, Mrs. Jonssen? After you get over feeling proud and different, it feels a lot like riding a horse with a chapped saddle. And then after that it feels like sacrilege to let a young man love you back. Seems like the wrongest act imaginable." She laughed, even though there was nothing remotely funny about what she'd said. Her hair hung around her face.

Bena stood near the edge of Maude's bed. "You're not a sad habit," she said. She pushed the hat off her head so it hung down her back.

Maude was dismissive. "His heart bleeds like a damned sieve."

"He talks about you," Bena said. It was true. No one could get near Red; he was closed off to all other bodies.

Maude formed a puppet with her hand, made it jabber noiselessly. She fell back onto her stack of gaunt pillows, the dome of her stomach rising level with her head.

"It doesn't matter anyway. Mary says it doesn't matter."

Bena started. "What did Mary tell you?"

"A love story. This is the story of how a woman gets pregnant, and the baby is like that hourglass you're so fond of, ticking down the moments until the man won't love her anymore. When the baby is born, the man will come to know the most unattractive parts of her. And as much as he hates himself for it, he'll come to despise the very sight of her."

So the woman eats bran and arsenic, Bena thought, so the baby won't be born.

"Mary's predictions don't mean anything," she said. She wanted to claim that it wasn't safe to look for comfort in random fault lines, in the way a hand is creased because it has held a shovel or a pickax or a child's elbow. It wasn't right, she knew, even if she believed otherwise; it would leave you lonely, lost, bereft.

"No," Maude agreed hollowly. "No. Of course not. It doesn't mean anything." She reopened the varnish bottle and painted hasty, thick lines on her open palm, lines that cut through her own natural pleats. The varnish ran down over the pad of flesh below her thumb, trailing over the blue tributaries of her wrist and thickening into hard enamel beads.

Maude closed her eyes. "Draw the shades when you leave," she instructed, lying with her palms held upward.

Bena pulled the curtains over the windows. An applause of dust issued forth. She returned to the bed to say good-bye. This time she dared to touch Maude's arm, the white soft underpart.

"I've met her."

Maude didn't answer immediately. Bena thought she was asleep.

"Mary?" Maude asked.

"Bonnie Parker."

"Oh."

"It's true," Bena said. "She gave me this." Bena removed the silver water tower from her charm bracelet and placed it in Maude's hand. "It'll bring you luck, I think. Make you dare to."

Bena turned Maude's palms over so that her painted welts would not be visible to whoever woke her. She closed Maude's left hand around the water tower.

SHE WORE the green dress.

She wore the green dress because then she could wear her red ribbon heels, the ones that made her calves look sinuous and full of danger. The dress didn't fit her, but she wore it anyway.

Of course the green dress had a spot near the hem, a rust stain from the time she and Ted went rowing at his cousin's wedding in the fall of 1931, a lake affair in Wisconsin held at the height of hunting season.

The ceremony was punctuated by erratic gunfire, some shots muffled in the spasming haunches of deer, others moving forward into the skeletal remains of the fall foliage. She and Ted were drunk and bored. The music was provided by a single, quavering flute played by a fat woman. The cake looked impenetrable, a caustic pile of sugar requiring a hatchet to break its skin, and the bride was too drunk to be trusted with sharp objects.

Ted suggested they walk down to the dock. They didn't need coats, after all, because they were drunk and the night was cold. They found a rowboat and Ted strummed them out over the sleek black water to the place where, had it not been late October, there would have been a swimming float. He tied them to the rotting log that bobbed there, holding until spring the chain attached to an anchor at the bottom of the lake.

The oarlocks were rusty. If the oarlocks hadn't been rusty, she wouldn't have acquired the stain on the hem of her green dress. Even if the oarlocks hadn't been rusty, however, she still would have let this man to whom she would be married in a matter of months slide her dress up and put her hand on his tuxedo trousers to feel his unusual warmth despite the cold. She still would have let him lay her out across the thwart and rock gently against her so that the boat didn't swamp with the autumn water. She still would have married him, even though she knew then that their bodies moved together badly (she blamed it on the smallness of the boat, the oarlock in her back). She still would have had the stinging patch of rubbed-off skin along the middle of her spine that she hid from her friends, because you weren't supposed to give yourself away to your fiancé before you'd earned that second, plainer ring, even if they all secretly did.

THERE WAS a brass band. A brass band and a choir of Mexican boys in red waistcoats and torn huaraches, the leather strips so stretched that Bena could see the toes peeking through.

She was two glasses of rum punch into the evening, imprisoned in a tedious conversation with Gerta Ashburne. Gerta was fresh down from the mountains. She'd had too much sun at Cuerna Verde, she complained, playing tennis and killing rattlesnakes.

"Clyde's bought me a shotgun. You should see the yard," she said, wide-eyed at her own powers of destruction. "I've shot it bald." The snake infestation was so bad, in fact, that she'd moved back to Pueblo for the rest of the summer.

Gerta searched the room, her pupils afloat. Her attention momentarily locked on Ted, flirting with the Now-A-Day president, Bess Duncan.

Bess had hardly acknowledged Bena's existence since her formal split from the Now-A-Day Club. Bess appeared to have been assembled with the halves of two mismatched women. Her neck and torso were thin, her fingers were willowy, perfect for piling rings, sapphires atop rubies, emeralds atop diamonds, gold atop gold. Her hands were so light, despite the jeweled stacks, that the vaguest crosswind made them lift and flutter by her temples. Good-bye, she always seemed to be saying. Good-bye.

From the waist down, however, Bess Duncan was thick and shapeless. Her legs were short, her waist as wide as her hips, her calves driven directly into the tops of her feet like stovepipe chimneys into shanty roofs. While her top half swooped and dove and angled, her bottom was limited to blunt movements and awkward, brief strides, her thighs clunky beneath the loose twirl of her skirts.

Ted was mesmerized by her, or at least by her top half. He followed her hand with its many rings, wielding a silver punch cup, the other flitting in the space between them.

"So," Gerta chirped woodenly. "How's your little one?"

"He's fine," Bena said. In fact he'd been crying that afternoon since she'd gotten home, and had spit up sour mouthfuls of whatever small amounts of milk he'd managed to ingest. Just before they left for the party, he attacked her breast greedily, nursing until his stomach swelled and he cried from the pain. He had no sense of boundaries, no way of gauging the depth and frequency of his own appetites. But as Ted had decided that Little Ted definitely suffered from colic, the baby's crying, his erratic feeding, his general unhappiness were to be expected rather than responded to with undue alarm.

"You're part of the problem," Ted had reminded her earlier. "Your worrying isn't helping him."

"At this age, you know," Bena told Gerta, "they're sponges." In truth, Little Ted was a stone to her, impervious to sound or light or touch. He didn't absorb the world at all; he refuted it.

Gerta began to fix her hair, agitating her fingers over the immaculate curls in search of some imperfection that was obvious to all the world but her. "Actually," she said. "I don't know."

Bena pretended to be unaware that Gerta was sterile, her tubes the sad trellis on which a vine has thirsted and died. "Children are quite a commitment, of course," she said.

Gerta wrinkled her mouth. "After a while, you run out of things to wish for. We have a house, a cottage, a new Buick. Friends."

"Is that why people have children?" Bena was amused.

"Boredom is the driving force behind childbearing," Gerta remarked.

Bena could see Gerta was the furthest thing from bored. She was despairing; her body spoke of such fertile riches but was like a pod lengthening on its stalk, empty of beans.

"Well," Gerta said, "soon enough I'll know for myself." She smiled and reached out a hand to welcome a new party to the conversation.

Bena met the wide, sweating face of Horace Gast. He wore a seersucker suit and white shoes that seemed to belong rightfully to a far taller man.

"You know Mrs. Jonssen, Horace?" Gerta inquired.

Bena noticed the man in the homburg, Gast's bodyguard, standing by the grand Christmas tree in the foyer. He had an absent air, an air of not looking, which meant he didn't miss a handshake, a passing canapé, a spilled drink, a party trick.

"Horace is such a dear old friend," Gerta said. "In fact, he's arranged for us to adopt a baby."

"Any day, now. Should be any day."

"I didn't know your business dealings extended to babies," Bena said.

"I'm simply helping out a girl I know who found herself in an unlucky spot."

"In a way, as it were."

He laughed. "In a way, yes."

"You seem to know a lot of those women."

"A blessing and a curse, Mrs. Jonssen, a blessing and a curse."

He turned and smiled as a photographer took their picture.

"And how is the young woman you were trying to marry off in Colorado Springs?" Bena's hand, holding an empty punch cup, pointed through the drawing room, toward a park where a white tent had decomposed to threads and champagne glasses ground to sand had been whisked off to join the red, black, yellow particles of a storm.

"She reconsidered, married the boy after all. She's in Venice on her honeymoon as we speak, no doubt being fed a pomegranate by her newly beloved in the back of a gondola and wondering what she made such a fuss about."

"What's this?" Gerta asked.

"Nothing to bother your pretty self over, Gerta. Just a woman much sillier than you, making her life harder than it has to be."

Gerta bowed her head, thinking she'd just been paid a great compliment. Bena was losing patience with both of them—Gerta and her nervous primping and little-girl giggles; Horace Gast and his smugness and arrogant, arresting mouth. She still couldn't take her eyes off his mouth. It was so fascinatingly wrong on his face, those cherubic lips you'd expect to find on a boy a quarter his age.

"I hear you've planned a surprise performance this evening," Gerta said.

"It won't be much of one if you persist in spoiling it," he chided her, then changed the subject. "And how are things unfolding for you, Mrs. Jonssen?"

"Fine," she replied. "We should talk in a few days."

"I can hardly wait." He held his glass up as if to toast her, then drained its contents in one quick swallow.

Gerta was recounting to Mr. Gast her adventures with her new shotgun when a hand grabbed Bena's arm.

He was soapy-clean and unhatted and free of dirt and tiredness. There were still the shadowed cheeks, where the weather had raked his face. But he was sparkling and visible to her, his features that much more familiar now that she'd discovered them looming out of a stranger's polished face.

She knew, in that instant, that she would kiss him. Maybe not that evening, maybe not for months. But she knew: She would kiss this man who was not her husband.

He shook Gerta's hand, and then Mr. Gast's.

"Good to see you, Henry," Mr. Gast said. He'd extended a guarded hand.

"Likewise."

"Your father well?"

"California suits him, apparently."

"We sure do miss him up Cuerna Verde way."

Red smiled, implying that his father didn't miss Cuerna Verde much.

"Give him my best when you talk to him."

"I'll do that." Red offered Bena his arm. "Dance?"

"I'd love to." Her expression suggested it was less the dance she wanted than the excuse to leave. "Where's the dancing?" she asked. She didn't see Ted anywhere.

"There isn't any."

She laughed and let him pull her through the crowd, past the buffet table with its cookie pyres and angel ice sculpture, its planet-wide punch bowl, down a quieter hallway adorned with wintry pine boughs that smelled out of place in the heat.

He opened a door and urged her inside. It was a study, with a single leather lounge chair and a fireplace guarded by a pair of greyhound andirons. With the door shut, only the higher pitches of the party were audible—women's laughter, the clinking of a ladle against punch cups, the screech of chair legs over the parquet floor.

Red gestured to the armchair. He crouched on an ottoman, pulling up the trouser legs of his blue suit.

"You looked as if you needed rescuing."

"I understand you're somewhat of an expert," Bena said.

"I blame it on my uncanny sense of intuition."

"I thought women were the sole possessors of that."

"I'm unusual that way."

"In lots of ways, I'd imagine."

"Yep," he agreed. "In lots of ways."

They stared into the cold fireplace, where no flames jumped, no sap crackled. But they acted as if there were a fire roiling there, the splendid sight that could mesmerize two people, strike them mute, alleviate the awkwardness of a quiet moment.

"Horace Gast has a house up at Cuerna Verde," she said.

"My family's old house. His house burned about a year ago, right about the time my father wanted to sell ours. Worked out pretty tidy, all told."

"What an unfortunate accident."

"Unfortunate perhaps. Definitely not an accident."

"I suppose that's why he's got a bodyguard."

"Little Billy McSweeney can't be much of a bodyguard. Used to get beat up fairly regular since he was a kid."

"They're the fearsome ones." Bena thought of Jonas and how his weakness made him mean. "Nothing like a man who's got a score to settle with the world."

Red reached into his suit coat pocket and pulled out his leather pouch. She enjoyed knowing these small things about him—the insides of his pockets, the insides of his house—even if she didn't know the first thought that went on inside him.

"My feet hurt." She removed her red shoes and let them drop. She looked at them, tilted and menacing on the carpet. *She cannot be trusted, she cannot be trusted, because girls will forever be weak and senseless in the face of unusual objects.*

He inched the ottoman closer until he was directly between her knees. "Give me your foot."

She thought of the cauterizing iron in her brother's story, the way the bone and skin would melt and harden into a black stone where her feet used to be. She'd have to hide them inside embroidered drawstring bags like precious relics, great polished knobs of onyx she could massage with a casual thumb to see the future.

She extended a thrilled and cautious foot.

He thumbed her angry feet until her rage came to her in a leisurely, manageable stream. It used to be she'd think of Little Ted and fill up with the bigness of the world; she'd see in her mind a white-headed boy somersaulting over a painfully green lawn, she'd see a handsome, earnest adolescent she had to struggle not to touch. Now she couldn't imagine that he'd ever love the feel of grass on his back or the world spinning, that he'd ever know the pitfalls of earnestness.

Her rage, however, was not toward Little Ted but toward her husband. He wouldn't hear her, he discounted her gut feelings as if she were no more reliable than a tea-leaf reader. Her instincts represented nothing in the face of a doctor's tape measure and thermometer; the nine months she'd housed the baby under her own skin counted for nothing.

At the sight of the man in front of her, Bena felt the wild urge, not to kiss him, but to talk about parts of her she'd never talked about with a man. Was it because she wanted to punish her husband, or was she so compelled by Red Grissom that revealing truths would be just the beginning of her betrayal?

"My brother killed a girl," she said.

He pressed the heel of his hand into her arch. This confession did not appear to unnerve him.

"Her name was Myrna. She worked at the gas station near my family's summer cottage. She drowned herself, but it was his fault. He was a weak boy. He had a score to settle with the world."

Red's hand moved up over her ankle. He ran a finger the length of her Achilles tendon. He wasn't interested in her story, or maybe he didn't believe her.

"Myrna always said she wanted a hat that would float," Bena continued. "If she ever drowned herself, she said, there would be a hat marking the place she'd disappeared."

He kneaded her calves, her dangerous calves, and all the danger drained from them. "It sounds like she knew she wanted to drown herself long before she did it." His hand was beneath her knee, squeezing the tendon hinges between his thumb and forefinger.

"No. She didn't want the man who wanted her most. A girl like her should consider herself lucky to be wanted at all."

"Who says that's true?" His hand was on her knee, under her dress and on her knee, his fingers straying up and down. She enjoyed the sensation of the injured hand. It was like being caressed by a different part of the body, an appendage more unusual and intimate than a hand. The bundled branches of his lungs, perhaps. He breathed her in through those blunted joints.

"My brother," she said. "Jonas says."

Red stood and kneeled in front of her. He smoothed her dress over her legs, running his nails against the grain of the fabric. It sounded like a zipper unzipping, like clothing parting at the seams and dropping away.

"I looked for the hat," Bena said. "I walked up and down the shore for days. I thought perhaps the wind had blown it from the place she'd gone under."

"And did you find it?"

She shook her head. "I think maybe she forgot to wear it. But it was a cold day. Anyone would have thought to wear a hat."

"Maybe not a woman setting out to drown herself."

"Maybe not," Bena conceded. "Maybe not a woman setting out to drown herself."

His hands were on the chair arms to brace himself. He was lifting himself over a wall to see, finally to see, and his mouth was on her mouth, and then she was the drowning woman, she was the drowning woman without her hat, no sturdy milliner's vessel to mark the spot of her disappearance.

What amazed Bena most was that this was not so different from how they'd encountered each other before. Maybe it was because his mouth on hers was just another kind of talking; the words were pillowy and passed from tongue to tongue, clumsily, the way children might pass oranges under their chins.

It had not been like this when Ted kissed her for the first time, outside Kaap's, his cold fingers running their marbly tips across her cheek before he drew her into his chest and pressed his lips over hers. His mouth was too wide and tall and obliquely bowed, the cartilage curve of a fish's mouth. His mouth would make a popping sound if a hook embedded itself in him, if she landed him like the prized catch that he was. But she had landed him. She had landed herself a fine fish, a fine husband fish who could do nothing to save her from drowning beneath the mouth of this man that was rimmed with hair that was soft one way, needly if pushed against the grain.

She was stung about the mouth.

They heard footsteps, a woman's footsteps, outside the door, and bucked apart, knocking teeth and noses.

"So did you get your wish, honey?"

They turned, stuporous, to observe Maude push into the room. She wore a plain housedress underneath a man's stained coat. A belt struggled to reach around her impressive belly.

"I don't suppose he told you what went on in that chair. Then again, maybe he doesn't know himself. Do you know, Henry? Do you know what happened in that chair?"

She stood behind the chair, trailing her painted fingers over the leather. "What *used* to happen," Maude continued, her hands now on Bena's neck, "is that we children would sit on St. Nicholas's lap right here in this very chair and wish for ponies and bicycles and trips to the sea, isn't that right, Henry?"

Red tried to stand, but Maude pointed a finger at him, warning him to stay seated.

"But things and people don't stay the same, do they, now? Things and people change their usefulness. Take this chair, for instance. This chair used to be where the children sat on St. Nick's lap, wishing for a pony or a trip to the sea. Then it was the place where St. Nick sat with his pants around his ankles and said, 'Make a wish, darling, go on, wish you weren't such a whore why don't you, wish that a man won't taste your spoiled self and know you're rotted to the core.' "

Red tried again to come toward Maude, but she reprimanded him. "Don't." She put a hand to her head, steadying herself.

"I don't know why you've come here," he told her. He refused to look at Bena, as if the failure of their gazes to meet might erase the fact that other parts of their faces had pressed together.

"He'd let his belt loose, Henry—remember that big silver belt? King of the silver mines, remember? He'd let his belt loose and that two-pound buckle would strike the floor."

She stamped the floor with her heel, simulating the sound. Once. Once. Once, twice, three times. She stamped faster, then faster.

"That two-pound buckle would strike, over and over and over again," she announced, still pounding with her heel. "Recognize the tune? That is the music of whoredom, Henry. That is the music of no going back."

Maude moved from behind the chair to face them. Bena had never seen a woman so exquisite—her color high, her hair loose and furious.

"And this one," Maude spat at Bena. "This one thinks I'm something to admire." She fumbled at her throat, trying to disentangle an object that hung from a piece of twine around her neck. "Here."

Bena looked at Maude's palm, still streaked with nail varnish.

She held out the water-tower charm. "You need this more than I do, sweetheart," Maude said. "I already dare to."

Bena took the charm out of Maude's open hand and felt its luck slip away. It was no luckier than a bottle cap, than any odd piece of discarded metal one might find and rescue and imbue with powers to do more than break the skin, pass along a weak strain of tetanus.

Bena heard the door slam. Maude was gone.

Red still refused to look at Bena. He sat within touching distance, his hand dangling uselessly over the precipice of his knee, not knowing whether to reach out or hide its pruned, ugly self in a pocket.

"You should go to her," Bena said, meaning it and not meaning it at all.

He braced himself on his knee, preparing to rise for an unpleasant task. His look said, I know you understand, I know you won't think less of me for this. He stood and left the room, closing the door behind him.

Bena stared at the greyhound andirons. Her feet burned from the rubbing. She unhooked the stockings from her girdle and rolled them down her calves. She peeled them off the tips of her toes, then hurled them into the cold fireplace and watched them settle over the grate.

I know you won't think less of me.

But she did think less of him, considerably less. She thought less of him and less of her husband, too, wherever he might be, with whichever giddy wife in whatever place, well lit so that his flirtation would be deemed benign by all who witnessed it.

Bena lay back in the leather chair. She thought again about Myrna

Voskamp—the alive, the wisecracking Myrna, the Myrna with the tattered nail varnish and the big calves. Myrna was a merciless flirt who made old men's bodies weep as she pumped gas at her father's garage every June, July, every August. She'd lunge over the car windshields and press her breasts against the glass, she'd stand with the dripping cloth, suds running down her arms and soaking her dress. A saucy girl, Myrna Voskamp, a girl who would most likely get her big, bold heart into trouble if she didn't meet a good man early on, a man who could keep her busy with a breed of children and laugh at her outrageousness, which would never dim.

Bold-hearted though Myrna was, she wasn't bold enough to love Jonas. Bena knew because she'd heard her say it to him, over and over, Honey, she'd say, you're a sweet boy but I don't imagine I'm in love, I'm too young for that kind of silliness. She talked like the rich women for whom she'd been pumping gas since she was a stick of a ten-year-old girl—low-voiced, with round, awestruck words. She was forever pushing her shabby nails through her hair, pushing the curls from her face and trying, unsuccessfully, to wedge them in a hairpin. Sometimes she painted a beauty mark to the left of her mouth, but she always wore unflattering orangey lipstick and blouses that were too small in the bust, the buttons pulling apart to reveal figure eights of flesh as she wrestled with the gas hose.

Still, Jonas was a boy, and a city boy at that. Myrna waited for the time when the summer families came with their sons, who were that much more attractive because you could remember them from the summer before, gangly and thin-faced and stammery. Now their arms had filled out, their torsos had lengthened and spread, their faces were wide and hungry. Jonas was eighteen that summer, newly beautiful but unsure of it. He didn't know, yet, how to assume the birthrights of attractive people. He asked Myrna the silly, begging questions that an ugly boy would ask. At first she thought she'd found the handsome boy with the banker father, the boy who was going to college in Connecticut come fall, the boy who would rescue her from a life of gas headaches and nine-month winters in the shadow of Canada. But it turned out he was young and worshipful and weak. He was not the man for her, yet she agreed to be his girlfriend because there were no more eligible candidates at the lake in early summer that year; the Elliot boys had gone to Europe, the Walkers were hiking in the Rockies, Jibby Hatchet had been struck by a car over the winter and maimed.

She and Jonas would take walks, sail to the bluffs, sit at the end of the dock and draw in the water with their big toes, bundled in sweaters and pants against the cold, new summer. Sometimes they'd encourage Bena to sit with them, and Myrna would pull her into her lap and pretend they were a family. She'd say that anyone who passed them in a boat who didn't know them would think they were a family. But no one ever passed them who didn't know precisely who they were. Once, during a full moon, while she was sitting on the dock with Bena, Myrna announced that she knew an old Indian trick, so they took off their clothes and looked at their long white reflections in the lake. If the night was cooperative, Myrna claimed, you'd find the face of your future husband instead of your own body in the black water.

Other times she pretended that she and Bena had never spoken. She'd refuse to look at Bena when she lurked near them, and Jonas would throw rocks to make her go away. Leave us alone, he'd say, and Myrna would stare at the lake as if she'd never once pretended to be her mother. Bena would hide in the bushes and watch them hold hands, or watch Myrna lie with her head in Jonas's lap and look up at the gray sky. Once Bena saw them kiss, but their noses and chins and teeth bumped together. They stopped and didn't speak for a very long time. "Where were you? Were you spying on us?" Jonas asked her later that day, and Bena said, "No, no," and she'd never seen him so wild, wild with the notion that she'd witnessed how his mouth didn't fit with another person's.

In late June, one of the Elliot boys came to the lake for a week.

He'd been to Lucerne, he'd been to Berlin, he'd been to Madrid and Naples and Dijon. He arrived on a bus with a trunk covered in bright stickers and a loden hat that made him look like somebody's mountain grandfather. The bus left him at the Voskamps' gas station, where he waited for his mother to retrieve him.

By the end of that week, Myrna was no longer interested in Jonas, even though the Elliot boy (Thomas or Larry, Bena could never remember which) had returned to Chicago, with little more than a promise to write when he wasn't too busy. He was studying to be an architect, a notoriously rigorous course of study, according to Myrna, who knew a lot about it now and would tell Bena about Thomas or Larry whenever Bena walked past the gas station on the way to the post office. Myrna would make a fuss about asking her how Jonas was, really, how was he, as though he hadn't spoken to her in years instead of days and might be married by now, live in Philadelphia, be a lawyer, own a dalmatian. Give him my best, she'd say, and then appear to be remembering him and their time together fondly: life and circumstances had conspired against their love, but she had struggled to reach a certain peace and had, after many teary evenings, reached it.

I have a message for you, Bena told her one afternoon. It was early July, the day before Jonas was leaving to take an accountant's job in St. Paul. Later in the summer he'd take the train to Connecticut.

Jonas needs to talk to you. He wants you to meet him at the boathouse at six.

Myrna smiled and pushed her hair back and said she'd be late, six-thirty, if she came at all.

It was raining. Bena spied on her brother through the boathouse window. She saw Myrna walking down the path to the boathouse in her slicker, her hair tied beneath an orange scarf. She carried an umbrella but didn't use it, because that was the sort of girl she thought she was, prepared for, but never deterred by, the usual inconveniences.

The lights were on. Jonas had been inside for some time, pacing and then sitting still, pacing and sitting, and the window was partially fogged.

At first Myrna was distant but coy. She took off her slicker and folded it over the stern of the *Ingrid Duse*. The boat named after Bena and Jonas's mother became the *In se*, which Bena repeated to herself, *In sea In sea In sea*. She knew in her heart that they were all about to be swallowed by something salty and foul.

Myrna sat on the *In se* gunwales and raised her head, taking a foolishly long time to undo the knot under her chin. She twisted her arms around to fix her hair, pushing the wet curls behind her ears. She looked nicer wet, as grass and flowers do, her colors intensified, her surfaces succulent and holding their own against the rain, water against water.

Jonas hunched against the long carpenter's table, where every spring weekend, before the edges of the lake had thawed, he and Bena and their father varnished the spars.

Their voices were quieted by the windowpanes but Bena could still hear them.

You're looking fine, Jonas.

Same to you.

I hear from Bena you're doing well.

Well as could be expected. Myrna examined the amber welts of varnish on the boathouse floor.

I hear you're doing fairly well, Jonas said.

You think I'm heartless.

Heartless would be just the beginning of what I think.

He walked around her, circling as if one of them were dangerous.

And you're so perfect? she asked.

Seems to me a girl like you is hardly in a place to demand perfection.

You may think I'm nothing but a desperate girl who'll take the first ticket out of here, but I can pick and choose, too, you know. I can wait around for the best thing.

And I'm not the best?

You're scarcely the best, she sneered. You're a boy. You're just a scared little boy.

He grabbed her by the back of the head and kissed her, forcing their bad-fitting faces together in a way that must have hurt, hard bone and teeth clacking.

Myrna pulled away. She smiled.

So you're a man now? That's right. Now you're a man.

She turned and shook out her scarf, apparently preparing to leave. She didn't notice the paint scraper until the point of it was against the side of her neck.

She paused but didn't turn around.

Jonas began to unbuckle his pants. As I said. Seems to me a girl like you is hardly in a place to demand perfection.

Bena thought perhaps he was going to bind Myrna's wrists and leave her in the bottom of the boat, to shiver in the dark and wonder how many hours or days it would take for someone to find her there, her ribs imprinted with the ribs of the boat named after his mother, a distant, useless woman. That was why he'd insisted Bena watch, she assumed; she would then be available to rescue Myrna after he'd given her the appropriate scare. Let her whimper in the twilight, listen to the rain off the lake, the loons, hoping for footsteps but frightened of them, too, not knowing who owned them or what their intentions would be once they wrestled the boathouse door open and found her, crying with her ripped-up mouth against the hull of a boat.

Jonas pushed up Myrna's dress, and Bena could see her splotchy thighs, her poor-girl's gray-white underwear, stodgy, without a hint of lace or embroidery. He pulled at this, too, even as she rolled her pelvis, kicked her legs with their gleaming black rainboots, spat at him. He reached beneath the tiller and withdrew a winch handle, then struck her across the cheekbone. Bena heard her face cracking, then the nothing sound of her submission.

Myrna let him rip her gray-white underwear, and turned her head as he pushed his trousers down around his knees, revealing himself to be the man he believed he was, as if a boy couldn't stand as tall, as if a boy couldn't use his own body against another's as well as any man could.

Jonas left the next morning for St. Paul. Bena no longer walked past the gas station on her way to the post office, but Myrna found her anyway, at the end of August, when the trees closest to the water were starting to blaze.

Bena phoned Jonas, but he sneered at her, his voice busy with summer numbers and the promise of a new college life. No telling whose it is, he said. Tell her to call Elliot, since she likes him so well.

A week after Labor Day, Myrna sank into the lake without her hat.

Bena and her father went to the funeral. Together they looked at Myrna in her coffin, basking in the stained-glass glow of Our Lady of the Lake, her body smooth and pale and perfect. Bena stared at Myrna's stomach, wondering whether Jonas's baby was still inside—or whether it had swum out of her, like a tadpole into the lake, in search of less despairing surroundings in which to grow.

The shock of Myrna's death was only heightened by the knowledge that she'd been in a way, that she'd killed not only herself but the budding life inside her. A collective disapproval haunted the funeral. Like it hasn't ever happened before, the old ladies whispered by the sandwich trays. No need to go and drown yourself. Myrna became a murderer rather than a trespassed girl with a secret so heavy it pulled her to the bottom of the lake. Selfish. Weak. The old ladies clucked around the coffee urns, each of them feeling she would have happily drowned herself at one time or another over the course of her bad life, but she hadn't, and for that reason she was superior to the dead girl, superior and halfway resentful. This made Bena angry. She'd said something to her father about the injustice of it, but he dismissed her reaction, belittling the hypocrisy. Nothing but small-town nonsense, he'd said. Of course she'd forgotten that small-town nonsense had kept their own family secrets for them, better than any bank vault. No one fought to know who the father of Myrna's baby was, because everybody already knew. *Sleeping dogs*, Mr. Voskamp said, willing to let the whole tragic business be buried like his daughter. His gas pumps were closed for a year after Myrna's death.

Bena looked at the charm in her hand. Dodge, Iowa, population 115. She caught a glimpse of Bonnie Parker kicking off her shoes and running into the bright-wide desert; of Maude, a younger, beaming Maude, submitting to the brittle advances of Abbott Jackson in a leather chair.

Bena's was the watching life. She thought of her son, the still, numb bundle of him, and thought, No wonder, no wonder at all.

THE QUIET STARTLED HER. No young boys chortled in the hot dark of the garden, no glasses clinked, no drunken hoots spun out to the carved sandstone rafters.

She slipped into her shoes and opened the door a crack.

Nothing.

Once in the hall, however, she knew she was not alone. The air was torpid with the weight of people holding their breath.

She heard Horace Gast's voice, disdainful and booming.

"Don't be a fool," he said.

She walked to the end of the hall and found the entire party, motionless. The only movement to be heard was the trickle of water as the ice angel's wings retracted in the heat.

In the center of the ballroom, facing each other as if contemplating a dance, were Mr. Gast and Maude. Mr. Gast drank freely from his punch cup. Maude, her arms outstretched, held a derringer, a lady's pretty, pearl-handled weapon.

Was this the surprise performance Gerta had referred to? The guests were silent and awkward enough, Bena felt, to imply that the couple on display had more than mere party entertainment as the object of their drama.

"Best not to insult the sweetheart with the gun, Horace," Maude said.

"Insults can work like magic for having your way."

"Not with me they don't. I need a good, warm coddling. Not that I ought to be giving away my secrets." She grinned. "You wouldn't want me to give away my secrets, would you?"

She waved at Reimer, bread-faced by the bar. "Lovely house you have, Mrs. Jackson," she offered. "It hasn't changed a bit since I was here last."

Reimer summoned an armored hostess smile. "Get out," she said. "Get out of my house."

Bena searched the room for Red. He was nowhere to be seen. Next she searched for her husband, whom she located with his arm around Bess Duncan. Bess's head was buried in his chest. He rubbed her arm soothingly, up-down, up-down.

"Of course you've failed to invite me to your party for quite a few years now—an oversight, I'm sure—so you'll understand if I'm not quite ready to leave yet. Such memories I have of childhood, or rather the end of childhood. Probably why I'm so fond of this place. I would say my childhood ended in this very house."

"You've always been a hideous fibber," Reimer said, her words starched and unconvincing, as if she were complimenting a friend on her very ugly hat. "One would have hoped you'd outgrow it."

"Like that fibber husband of yours?"

"You came here willingly, if I recall correctly, you little whore.

You have no one to blame but yourself if you didn't find what you were looking for."

"Neither do you, Mrs. Jackson." Maude smiled at her pityingly.

Reimer caned through her guests, out the French doors toward the gazebo. Not a single person offered to help or comfort her, because to acknowledge her trouble would mean eventually having to own up to it. The couples would talk between themselves later, in the privacy of their drunken retreats home and late-night undressing. When they encountered Reimer at the Silver State in a week's time, they would simply acknowledge: Fabulous as always, outdid yourself, just the most fun we've had really, really.

Reimer's retreating tusk leg beat against the floor, reminding Bena of the silver belt buckle, the music of whoredom.

Horace Gast lit a cigarette, then offered one to Maude. As she waited for him to light hers, she laid the tip of the gun against his temple in a most affectionate manner. She backed up a few paces and blew a funnel of smoke into the air. She took aim again at Mr. Gast's head.

"So," she said, moving the gun up and down his body. "Shall you tell them, Horace, or shall I?"

Mr. Gast wiped his wet hands on his trousers. He pulled a pen from his trouser pocket to bang his silver punch cup. Once. Once. Once, twice, three times.

He tapped his thin, ferrety mustache. "It's a pleasure and a shame to stand in front of you and confess to a devastating something, or to nothing at all. And what would you imagine, all of you? A wealthy man, a pregnant whore, demanding her pound of flesh at gunpoint. I forgive you all for your assumptions, because, of course, given the circumstances, you could not be blamed for considering the basest possibilities when your only clues are wealthy man, gun, whore, unclaimed child. As a newspaperman, I only ask that you consider the fact that a story, that any good story, should play with perception and with truth.

And that this is a truly good story. One in which the obvious contours have been offered to you irrefutably as fact."

There was not a sound in the ballroom, not even the sound of breathing.

Mr. Gast smiled lovingly at Maude. "Naturally, nothing you see before you could be further from fact." He threw his cigarette to the floor and ground it to ash with a single, merciless turn of his shoe. "But perhaps if we all applaud Miss Maude Hewitt for her clever manipulation of character, setting, and audience expectation, she will put down her little gun and let us get back to our lovely party. But I urge you to remember this: that degradation is the result not only of crass bodily desire, but also of the equally crass desire for financial gain." He looked at Maude. "Toss your stones, but know why you toss them."

Bena sensed something sticky between Mr. Gast and Maude, a shifting, adhesive quality of their hate. It wasn't hard to imagine the two of them in a bed, tearing at each other desperately, trying to work free of their mutual yet compelling disgust.

Ted was the one who initiated the applause. He raised his hands above Bess's head and clapped in his resolute way, the same way that convinced him he could fool his patients out of dying.

He clapped alone for a moment; then others joined him, until the ballroom was scratchy with sound.

Maude looked around the room and took a modest bow, the most politeness her swollen stomach would allow. She raised the derringer and took aim at Mr. Gast's head.

To his credit, Bena thought afterward, he never appeared frightened, not even with a pistol pointed straight at him, seeking to chip away his skull and bring his lying brain to light.

"All this good story deserves is a worthy ending." Maude blew him a kiss as she released the safety.

A few of the women screamed when the gun went off. Sparks

scattered and hissed, a fine-edged dusting of sand, or so Bena thought, rasped and tinkled as it hit the floor.

The noise and bright settled, and everything was dark.

Maude had yanked her aim at the last second, pulled the gun skyward and pointed at the chandelier that Reimer and Abbott had procured on their honeymoon in Venice, the assembly of pink glass blown into lightable shapes in an old nunnery. She'd sprinkled the wasted blood of a hundred virgin nuns over the heads of selected citizens of Pueblo. They were filthy with it, this hard rain, it was in their hair, it pricked their scalps, it nestled deep in their suit coats and dresses.

And it was quiet. It was quiet as the guests, wrapped in the dark, could still see the white wings of the explosion when they blinked.

With the grinding of a lighter, the dark was broken. Mr. Gast held the flame under his chin. In the glow, Bena could see he was alone in the center of the ballroom.

People were talking, and one woman was crying. Servants rushed about lighting candles. Bena looked to the front of the ballroom and saw Mr. Gast signaling for quiet. He thanked the guests for their attention, and said he hoped they had enjoyed the first surprise performance of the evening. If they would find their coats now, there were cars out front waiting to escort them to the second.

People shook their heads to dislodge bits of glass, and tiptoed over the ballroom floor, every step accompanied by a breaking crunch, as of an iced-over pond threatening to give way to killingly cold water. Some women's arms were dotted with tiny marks of blood where they'd been cut by the falling glass. She watched partners find each other and walk obediently to the waiting autos. There was no sweet hiss of gossip, nothing of that low, vaporous whisper that normally swirled about skirts and pant legs at parties—*Can you believe She's such a Really who would have imagined, her, him?* It was as though nothing bawdy had transpired, as though a pregnant prostitute waving a gun was a tired party trick they'd seen a thousand times before.

Guests walked in pairs out the front door. Bena thought of the wives settling into the car seats and finding blood on their arms. They would say to their husbands, *How strange, how strange, how ever could this have happened*, and the husbands would give them handkerchiefs wetted with bourbon from their hip flasks. They would look away as their wives scrubbed their forearms, preferring not to witness this private act of women's washing.

"I CAN'T BELIEVE YOU."

Bena had discovered Ted comforting Reimer in the gazebo as the Mexican choirboys chased one another through the garden, their huaraches making meaty, slapping noises on the flagstones. Everyone else had left by the time Bena and Ted found each other, so Reimer, too distraught to follow her guests, had her chauffeur drive them to the site of the performance.

Bena was sitting as far away from Ted as she could. In Reimer's car, this was quite a distance.

"Can't believe what?"

"I can't believe you applauded."

Ted was carrying a silver punch cup from Reimer's house. He radiated with an unhearing power, warm and senseless and quite drunk.

"The woman's looking for some way to make money off whatever sorry creature she manages to produce. And it will be sorry, from the looks of her."

"And that's her fault?" Bena didn't know what to think of Maude's claim in the ballroom.

"Yes," Ted replied defiantly, staring straight at her. "It's her fault."

Bena's stomach was queasy. The punch, perhaps. Or the way she'd been kissed and then been torn away.

"It's fortunate you're a doctor, being so bighearted."

Ted reined up, indignant and hiccuping. "I have a big heart."

"You certainly do. For just about any woman but me."

She thought he might hit her. His hitting arm fidgeted in his lap not knowing what to do with itself except strike out at her, blacken her eye or crush her lip against her bottom teeth.

"Watch yourself," he warned.

"Take your own advice." Bena wouldn't have minded tasting blood, even if it was her own. "You think I don't know you well enough by now? I know you've got somebody. You've always got somebody."

Ted turned his head back out to watch the mansions spin by. They were near the cemetery where Abbott Jackson was buried, dead of a hard day's work. The tombstones looked like groundhogs rearing up beneath a full moon, still and straight and watchful.

"You're so pleasant when you're drunk," he said distantly. "You're so pleasant when you're with your rancher friend. You think I don't know about that?"

"I've done nothing I haven't been forced into," she said. She hoped he suspected much worse than a simple kiss, hoped he saw her naked beneath a strange man's white, swooping hips.

"Oh, *really*? And who might have forced you into that?"

Bena didn't answer. She wondered what had happened to Red, to Maude. Ghosts, the two of them.

"I suppose you've been forced into everything by me. Marriage, the move to Pueblo. I suppose that should also explain how motherhood is such an unusual burden for you."

It was as if he'd struck her. "It's not an unusual burden," Bena said.

"All your unceasing nonsense about how sick he is, how listless. Why do you think that is? Why do you think?"

She knew what he was implying. That it was her fault, she was too frosty and removed, that no seedling could be expected to flourish in the tundra of her. That was why their child was dim and colicky, that was why her husband had to seek out warm handfuls of affection from other women.

They entered the gates of the Mineral Palace, its drive marked with Japanese lanterns stuck into the dead soil.

"I have no idea," Bena said. The driver parked alongside the other cars and turned off the engine. "I've thought and I've thought, I've blamed myself a million times over, and I still have no idea why."

In all the ways she had changed since giving birth to him, Little Ted had not. He was bigger, yes. His arms and legs and torso were thicker, his head was heavier, and his skull had closed over his soft brain. His body grew, but his person remained invisible to her, dwarfed and muffled because she had failed to make him feel safe enough to reach out and inhabit his own arms and fingers. It was her fault, she could admit she'd done something wrong. She'd prefer to know it was her fault; that would mean he was hidden inside himself, he simply required the right person to coax him to the surface.

She sobbed once and then stopped. This was not the place; there was not enough room or time to let her despair loose.

The driver opened her door. The night, she noticed, was hotter in the park than at Reimer's. The driver waited, his gloved hand held out to assist her.

Bena glanced at Ted to see whether he was willing to stay with her and pound their useless anger into something resembling a clumsy tool for building, despite the fact that there was a party, despite the gloved hand, waiting. But he refused to look at her. He rolled down the window to shout something at Clyde Ashburne, walking none too steadily with his arm around Gerta. They'd found an inner tube and Gerta wore it around her waist like a life preserver.

"Ahoy!" Ted called out, as if she and their argument had never existed. Their arrival here marked the end of an unraveling they could have only between social functions, between one party and the next.

Clyde bumbled over with a flask, which he put to Ted's lips through the open window. The liquor spilled and ran down the window like rain nobody had seen in months.

"Coming, ma'am?" The driver sounded impatient. She stared at the white hand. It caught the flickering of the lanterns in its creaseless palm. She looked at Ted one last time, as his upturned face drank the rum that poured in the window.

"Of course," she said, accepting the white hand, stepping into the uncertain light of the Japanese lanterns.

SHE WOULDN'T EXACTLY have called it transformed, but the interior of the Palace had certainly been tended to since she'd visited—the garbage cleared, the hoboes relocated, the stale air baked crisp and lively by oil lamps. A young woman, whom Bena recognized as one of Reimer's club ladies, handed her a long white candle and a blanket and pointed her toward the stage, which sported new gold curtains. The chandelier had been retrieved and rehung, and the hole in the stage floor planked over with new wood.

Ted held her elbow and steered her toward the Ashburnes, already sprawled on their blanket. "What's this all about?" he asked.

"Mr. Gast is doing a tribute to Reimer," Clyde said. "She's donated a very generous sum to the *Chieftain*."

"I used to perform ballet recitals here." Gerta straightened her spine. "I was a swan, once." She laughed messily and nudged Ted. He was drunk enough not to mind her, with her bad skin and loud ways.

On the stage, Bena noticed, the statue of the Silver Queen was covered by a cloth, the contours of her boat, her eagle, and her scepter vaguely hinting at the presence of royalty below. King Coal, meanwhile, had had his purple lightbulbs replaced, and his name blinked enthusiastically like an out-of-favor monarch giddy with his restored popularity.

"I wonder what these are for," Clyde slurred, and looked with amazement at his candle.

Bena spoke as if she were reading lines from a play. "We will blow out the lights until we are in complete darkness. We will pass along a

flame until all the candles are lit. There will be a performance of
A Midsummer Night's Dream. We will all agree afterward that it was the
closest any of us had come to feeling the presence of God."

"My," Gerta said.

For the second time that evening, the lights were extinguished. A
woman giggled uncontrollably, as if she were being tickled in the dark
by her husband or lover and anything could happen, fingers could bur-
row anywhere, stumble over buttons and zippers if they liked.

A flame passed through the crowd, slow and spotty, a blaze refusing
to take hold except in tiny moving places. Gradually pinpricks of light
fought the blackness, and Bena could see people's faces, the reflection
of hair and teeth. Reimer was right, she thought. This was like being
in the presence of God at the beginning of time, a scratch of dust and
flint and fire, and then the sight of humans, newly formed from the
rubble.

Something moved on the stage. The curtain folded aside and a
figure stepped forward shielding a candle with his hands. When he
reached center stage, standing bravely beneath the newly rehung chandelier, he spread his fingers, lifted one hand, and began to speak: "Now,
fair Hippolyta, our nuptial hour draws on apace: four happy days bring
in another moon; but O, methinks how slow this old moon wanes!
She lingers my desires, like to a step-dame or a dowager, long withering
out a young man's revenue."

Bena searched for Red. She searched for his hair in the glow of
the candles, his blond-brown, not-at-all redness, she looked for the
nose-chin-lips that had become so familiar to her in the course of many
sideways-stolen looks.

Nowhere.

*Four days will quickly steep themselves into night; four nights will quickly
dream away the time; and then the moon, like to a silver bow new-bent in
heaven, shall behold the night of our solemnities. . . .*

Maybe he was with Maude. No, definitely he was with Maude.

. . . with bracelets of thy hair, rings, gawds, conceits, knacks, trifles, nose-gays, sweetmeats, messengers of strong prevailment in unharden'd youth . . .

"Ted." She whispered and tugged on his sleeve. "I'm feeling kind of shabby."

He appeared skeptical. "Want me to help you home?" It was a most insincere offer, one she was expected to decline.

"No," she said. "No, I'll just ask Reimer's driver to take me."

She reached into his pants pocket for a handful of change, then kissed a finger and pressed it to his damp forehead. She navigated the blankets and people in the half-dark. Once she cleared the blankets, she pulled off her shoes and walked barefoot across the chalky tiles so that her heels wouldn't click. The large hole in the northeast wall had been covered by curtains. She parted them and stepped through.

She found the driver staring at the reflection of the Japanese lanterns in the stagnant fountain water.

He peered at her from under the pert brim of his cap. "Need a ride, ma'am?"

Bena nodded.

"Look at these moths. Drowning themselves when they think they've found a flame." He walked toward the car. Bena followed, barefoot, her shoes swinging from her hand. "Not that I think that burning's any better," he clarified. "My sister died in a fire, in fact. Caught in a sweatshop in Denver. My ma was on the sidewalk begging her to jump."

"There was a fireman's net?"

He shook his head. "My ma thought it was better than waiting for the fire to get her. She yelled to her to pretend she was diving into a pool of water.

"She was crying and screaming down to my ma, 'I can't swim, you know that! Damn you for never teaching me to swim!' Fought like cats and dogs, those two."

"So she burned to death."

"Better than drowning, way she saw it."

The driver opened the door for Bena, then got in the front and began the lumbering business of turning the car around. "Where we going, by the way?"

"Buck's Silo."

He smiled at her knowingly in the rearview mirror. "Husband know you're going there?"

"No. And I'd appreciate your keeping quiet about it."

"Money says I might."

They drove in silence down Union Avenue. The windows of the buildings were black and lifeless, the streets empty except for intermittent shadows thrown long across the alley side of a building. The shadows moved when she looked closely enough, the violent jerks of a man and a woman pressing their quick desire into each other.

Buck's glowed like an ember. The driver pulled the Airflow over across the street, left it running. He made no move to open Bena's door.

"Here," she said, fumbling with her purse.

He held his white palm up to the light from a streetlamp, let it catch the coins so he could count them, put the coins in his shirt pocket, and waited for her to leave.

She opened the door. "You know," she said, pausing, "my brother drowned."

He tapped his fingers on the edge of the rolled-down window. "All gotta go sometime," he said.

She must have misheard him.

He continued to stare out the windshield.

Bena shut the door and crossed the street woozily. She heard the driver put the Airflow into gear and rumble off slowly up Union, back to the Mineral Palace to await the end of the play, to witness the deaths of misguided insects in the stagnant fountain.

She grabbed the porch railing of Buck's Silo. The breath choked out of her, her limbs were shaking and sweating and cold. The sickness came on so abruptly she didn't have time to hide. Her body jackknifed, her stomach clenched, and she vomited the evening's share of rum punch onto the ground, already violated with spilled whiskey and piss and cigarette butts. She vomited between her own bare feet, the fire of her insides sparking against her ankles.

When she lifted her head she saw a man watching. He reached for her, and she flinched, cowering behind the porch.

"*Tómalo,*" he said. He held out a handkerchief.

She hesitated and he waved it, impatiently.

"Thank you." Bena wiped her mouth and face, not caring that the cloth stank of a stranger's pocket.

She handed it back to him, and he passed her a flask. He made a drinking-and-spitting motion. She took a drink of what seemed the dregs of moonshine from the rusted bottom of a bootlegger's still. She swished it around her mouth and then spat it on her toes, washing them clean. She'd forgotten her shoes on the backseat of the Airflow. She could only hope that Ted would see them and think to take them home. That is, unless he had somebody in the backseat with him, some-one for whom he would push the shoes onto the floor so that he could extend himself over her body, whoever she was; maybe he'd even pay the driver—"Money says I might"—to leave them in a copse of oaks at the edge of the park and take a long walk with his new coins.

The man tucked his flask into his vest pocket and walked up the stairs into Buck's. She was alone again, and burning. Her mouth and feet burned, from the moonshine, the brown plaid, the white mule, the white lightning; her throat and ribs burned with the effort it had taken to expel her despair with suddenness and force. She dropped onto the bottom step to catch her breath, and listened to the men drunk and rowdy behind the thin curtains.

Her head was tangled with pictures of herself, true and imagined. Herself letting Ted pull her nightgown off the evening of their wedding and watching him as he bit her nipples with his teeth. Herself screaming as her body split wide and the hot curve of her baby's skull emerged into the blue-white light of the hospital room. Herself in a dream, wandering between the bodies of the withering-up baby fish. Herself in a leather chair, her dress bunched around her waist, pushing against the creaking pelvis of Abbott Jackson. Herself in a boat, the hem of her dress rubbing on a rusty oarlock. Herself in a boat, watching the waves sharpen and the noon sky turn nightish as Jonas steered them farther from shore. Herself on a step, her feet burning with vomit and strike-me-dead, wondering who her husband was with, where Red was, what was wrong with her baby, where Maude was, if she'd ever see her ribbon shoes again. *Girls will forever be weak and senseless, she cannot be trusted, in the face of unusual objects.*

She heard voices.

Bena turned and saw a blond woman, the same hay-blond woman who'd sat on the man's lap the one time she'd been inside Buck's. The woman's long arm was wrapped around the neck of a fat man, as though she might choke him if she felt like it. He walked with a limp and nuzzled her hair, saying, "You tough little quiff, I'll beat you tender," and the woman laughed without smiling and tossed her head.

The woman saw Bena sitting on the stoop and ceased her laughing.

The man shook the woman free. He pulled up his pant leg and reached for a knife strapped above his sock. "Better shove in your clutch, doll, or this here shiv's going straight up you."

The woman knocked the knife to the ground. "You're too hopped up to be flicking one of those around," she scolded him. "Jesus. Go wait for me around the side."

The man picked up his knife. "Don't have all night," he growled.

"Good, sweetie," the woman replied. "Neither do I."

Bena saw him pinch her behind with his whole thick hand, saw the woman smile at him as if she'd never been so exquisitely adored.

She didn't come much closer to Bena. "He's right, you know. Better shove off."

"I was just catching my breath."

"I've seen you around. What's your name?" she asked.

"Bena."

"You're friends with Red. He's a nice man. Nice as they make them around here." She scrutinized Bena's disheveled party clothes, her bare feet. "You looking for him?"

"Yes," Bena said. "Have you seen him?"

The woman shook her head. "Nope. But Helen came down a while ago and told the bartender to turn the phonograph up real loud. Someone's going to be screaming bloody murder upstairs. And not because she's getting murdered."

Bena hadn't the faintest idea what she was talking about.

"Screaming bloody murder." The woman smiled pityingly at Bena, as if she understood too well the rigors of caring about a man like Red who preferred his girls and horses lame. "Only one place he'd be," she said. No one, she made it clear, had ever bothered so much about her.

THERE WERE no cats in the alley. Someone—Helen, she assumed—had sprinkled rat poison along the seams where the buildings met the dirt, and everything that called the alley home had been killed, rats and cats alike. The white powder glowed in the dark, leading her to the William Bent's back door.

The dirt floor was cold under her bare feet. She could hear Helen behind the curtain, singing to herself. Bena edged toward the curtain until she could peek through the narrow parting.

Helen knelt on the floor before one of the many washbasins, dipping a sheet. Her motions were practiced and quick; it was as if her hands had re-formed themselves into blunt hooks to facilitate the activity. Dip-flip-scrub, dip-flip-scrub. The water had turned pink and splashed out of the basin onto the dirt floor, creating a large dark ring. Behind Helen was a pile of unwashed sheets, knotted and bloody.

"Hell." She looked resignedly at the bloody sheet in the washbasin, now thoroughly pink. "Gripes my soul, this does."

Helen raised her big body and disappeared from Bena's view, and returned with an old suitcase. She wrung out the sheet and folded it, placing it in the bottom of the suitcase. She folded the unwashed, bloodied sheets behind her and placed them in the suitcase as well, one atop the other. She forced the latch shut, then lashed the suitcase with a yard of twine.

An animal ran over Bena's foot, its claws digging into her skin. She was about to shriek, but caught herself, making what amounted to an alarmed hiccuping.

Helen grabbed a fire poker and jabbed it through the parting in the curtains. "Who's there?"

Bena jumped aside. "Red," she stammered, "I'm looking for Red Grissom."

Helen pushed the curtain aside with the poker. The light from the room streamed into the hall, causing a surge of roaches to scurry for the remaining dark. Bena's stomach surged again, sore and unstable after its recent emptying.

"I know you," Helen said. "Brother needs a place to stay. Or some such bull." She spat on the floor.

"I'm looking for Red," Bena repeated.

"He went somewhere, didn't say."

Her gaze roamed the length of Bena, taking in her dirtied dress, her falling-down party hair, her bare feet. "What happened to you?" she asked.

Bena looked down, thinking she was referring to her lost shoes. Blood burbled up between the fourth and fifth toes of her right foot.

Helen held back the curtain. "Come in, let me look at it."

Bena hobbled to the one-runnered rocking chair. Helen took her foot in her hand, much as Red had done earlier in the evening. Had it really been earlier that evening that he had pressed his thumb into her arch, pressed his hands under her dress? It seemed a lifetime, a galaxy, a desert ocean moon ago. It was a span of time not measurable by clocks.

Helen poured the contents of a brown glass bottle—rubbing alcohol, Bena hoped—over her bleeding foot.

"You stepped on a piece of glass."

Bena tensed as Helen grabbed hold of the glass with a pair of rusted tweezers. Blood filled the hole, ran down the sole of her foot, fell from her heel onto the dirt floor.

Helen dressed the wound with gauze from a frayed roll.

"Taking a trip?" Bena asked, gazing at the suitcase.

Helen laughed. "I've never been out of Pueblo. Not me, or my mother before me, or her mother before her. We're natives here, the hard way. Trip." She laughed again, talking to herself more than to Bena. "Wouldn't I like to take a trip."

"Somebody else is taking a trip," Bena ventured.

"Only thing taking a trip is this valise. Leave it alone on the train platform for two minutes, some hobo'll pinch it and off it'll go to Grand Junction or God cares where. It's the surest way of making something disappear you don't want coming back to you. Run a cathouse long as I have, you know the rules. Sell sex, babies, don't matter. Long as they can't trace it back to you, don't matter. Take your pile of jack and keep quiet."

Bena thought of Horace Gast's elliptical speech in the ballroom. Her tired, once drunk head pulled the riddle apart. Gerta Ashburne. Horace Gast. Maude Hewitt. Gast, as an esteemed man of business, found women in a way and offered them compensation for the babies they couldn't afford to keep themselves. That's why Maude had come to the party flinging her pretty gun about. Gast was just another form of pimp.

Helen went to search in a closet and emerged with a pair of men's brown bluchers. Bena thrust her feet into the shoes. They were dry and scaly.

Helen escorted her to the curtain, the suitcase in her hand. "Walk you out." She made it clear she had no intention of leaving Bena in the William Bent alone.

Bena waited until Helen was a fair ways down Union, shuffling toward Victoria Station with her battered valise. She ran back through the alley, in the door, down the dirt hall.

Now, at night, she heard the brothel at work, a factory with its machines creaking and rubbing and gasping. She made her way to Maude's room. She pressed her ear to the door, just above the postcard. *Venez ici.*

Come here. Come here.

Quiet.

Bena had slept for ten hours after her labor; her father had stopped by with a vase of tulips, he'd read the paper front to back, and she hadn't stirred. No doubt Maude was just as impervious to the mechanics of lust and commerce that ground noisily around her. Maybe Red had gone out for food or to find a real doctor, someone to neaten up the job, to stitch and sew and swab.

She knocked lightly. No answer. Not even, to the best of her hearing, the regulated up-down of sleep breathing.

She slid the door open until she could see the naked mattress and enough of the room to ascertain that it was empty. She swung the door wide and was hit with the corpulent, tired smell of a room after two people's lust has been expelled over and over and over again in it.

The mattress was bare, and stained dark in places. The window was open, the curtains winging up on a weak breeze. She saw a half-empty bottle of whiskey on the bedside table and Maude's housecoat, thrown inside out over the traveling trunk.

Nobody.

Bena dropped, exhausted, on the cleanest edge of the mattress. She looked around the tiny, ruined room. It's wrong to be here. Wrong. The light weakened as a shadow crossed it. A large moth, the hairs on its body distinct and gray and visible, rested on the glass globe. A fleet of tinier moths flew around the lamp by the table.

Ugh, she thought, having had quite her share of bugs and vermin for the evening. She walked to the table and extinguished the lamp.

The wan light of the moon dropped through the window. She hoped the moths would fly toward it, though she didn't know quite how moths thought about planets. Maybe they flew until their dust-sized hearts expired, burning themselves into oblivion and falling back to earth. Maybe that's what the moths were hurling themselves toward in the fountain outside the Mineral Palace. It wasn't the reflection of the Japanese lanterns at all, it was the moon, the moon that was suddenly below them, this distant, pearly creature miraculously within reach. All you had to do was drop from the sky to touch it.

She went to the window to get a better look at the moon. Maude's window was in the back of the building. If she strained she could see over the roof of the *Chieftain* building, out and over the razed and scarred industrial plain that led to the train yard. It was quiet and almost beautiful in its stark homeliness, nothing but the sag and bow of cables tethering phone-pole crucifixes one to the next.

Amid those spindly crosses, Bena saw her walking. Maude threaded her way between the capsized oil drums and truck axles kicking skyward. She was alone. She stumbled, stopped, rested, continued.

Bena crept down the stairs, past Helen's room (quiet, no Helen), and out to the alley in a matter of seconds. She walked quickly through the parking lot behind the *Chieftain* offices. A hole in the fence separated the lot from the wide stretch of nothingness.

It was colder on the other side of the fence, the night oilier and more concentrated away from the lights of town. The air stank of coal smoke and fumes from the iron smelters. The fires burned all through until morning, a tear and flicker in the night landscape beyond the sagging roofs of the shantytown. She was happy now to have the shoes: the ground was littered with glass shards, the sprouting coils of old mattresses, rusted nails, forlorn auto parts.

She hurried along, gaining ground.

Maude, oblivious, tramped purposefully through the night—through the train yard, skirting the jagged hem of the shantytown, past the still mantis of the ironworks caught in a reverent half-bow until Monday morning. Bena drew close enough to hear Maude's heavy breathing, so labored it might have been sobbing if it hadn't been so regular, without the acceleration or arrhythmias common to despair. She wore a thin chemise that the moon shone through, blackening the sticks of her legs against the fabric, and a man's wool hunting shirt. In her arms she carried a bundle of blankets. Bena assumed it was the baby, but couldn't be sure because of the awkwardness with which she held it—far from her body, like a smoldering log that would burn her if she pressed it to her chest.

The bundle was still and silent.

It's dead, Bena thought. Oh my Lord, it's dead.

Maybe Red had gone to find a priest, or a simple box for a burial, and Maude, as usual, had taken matters into her own hands. She would perform the burial herself, she would put this stillborn baby into the ground under this moon, and that would be the end of it.

Bena followed Maude past the town dump and the vultures that slept wrap-winged on the garbage peaks, kings of their own hideous domain.

Without a breeze to dispense and dilute it, the stench of the rendering plant hit Bena like a wall of thick, hot urine. Not even the sewage in the Arkansas could have prepared her for the stink of people's rotting livelihoods, a hole the size of a large pond filled with the bodies of cattle, horses, sheep, pigs, goats. She pulled the bottom of her dress up to her face and breathed through the fabric. It smelled of spilled rum punch and cigarettes, a fine alternative to the liver-kidney stink of the rendering plant.

Maude marched forward until she was at the edge of the hole, then dropped to her knees. The long sleeves of the hunting shirt hid her hands. She held the dead child up for the moon to see and bless with its cold white heart. Then—with one hurling motion, the sort that might accompany the release of a bird back to the sky—she let the child go free.

The baby was at the top of its arc when Bena heard it cry. Its cry was the only sound, strong and outraged and clear in the midst of such ugliness and apathy. The baby cried louder as its body turned downward and started to fall, somehow knowing, though it had only a few hours' worth of experience by which to judge the sensation of gravity and injustice, that its little life was fast descending to meet a wrongful end.

Bena heard the faintest thump as the falling bundle struck a cow skull, a hull of rib bone, a thick, crotched femur.

9. THE STONE TOWER

Bena didn't go to work for five days.

When Cecil called, she told him Little Ted was sick and she needed to stay home. When Ham called, she told him she was feeling under the weather. Flu, she said. Too much fun, she explained to Reimer. Problems at home, she offered to Gerta. She read the *Chieftain* every morning to find out if anyone else knew what she knew. She sat at the kitchen table with the baby in her lap and scanned the pages for mention of an unpleasant discovery at the rendering plant. She found little of interest in the paper, save for a photograph of her talking to Horace Gast at Reimer's party. "*Chieftain* owner Horace Gast enjoys a rum punch with one of his lady volunteers," the caption read.

Henry "Red" Hart Grissom didn't call.

When Mr. Gast phoned before breakfast on Saturday morning, she asked Ted to tell him she was asleep. Ted spoke to Horace Gast as he'd spoken to everyone since the night of Reimer's party, boldly announcing that he didn't remember the play, he didn't even remember how he'd arrived, thankfully, at his own home. This was for her benefit, she knew, a way to have the discussion they'd never had the morning after the party, when he'd woken up and found the contents of his pockets arranged in a neat, condemning line across the bedside table.

"Out like a light . . . hasn't been up to her usual ginger since Sunday . . . No, well, luckily for her she has a husband who's a doctor. . . . Oh, without a doubt . . . A first-class soirée . . . Absolutely, Horace . . . the moment she's conscious . . ."

Consciousness had not been hers for days, not since the previous Saturday, when she'd remained hidden in the shadow of a listing oil tank, her face against the bolts, until she could no longer hear Maude's footsteps shuffling back to the William Bent.

She'd stood at the edge of the hole, her face assaulted with the piss-and-leather stew of cattle carcasses. She could see the bundle ten feet below her. It was moving. She looked down into the hole and started sobbing because she couldn't go down there, she wasn't strong or brave enough to do that. She took a deep breath and descended the ladder anchored to the side of the hole. A haze of flies attacked her face and ears, tried to wiggle their little thread feet into her mouth. She climbed down until she could see the baby's crimped and folded, floury face, the awkward set of its head, the way it wasn't breathing. She recalled the kittens in the alley, how she'd mistaken their teeming death for life, and she would have been sick a second time that evening if she hadn't been the emptiest woman imaginable. When she climbed out, she almost lost her balance, hanging, for a moment, over the seething sea of flies. They followed her and she ran, she ran and ran until the flies forgot about her and she forgot about herself, running in the darkness until she reached home.

It was one-fifteen, and the house was dark. Ted wasn't home yet. Florence and the baby were upstairs, asleep. Bena filled the bath and washed herself without once looking in the mirror. She was scared her face would appear as it always had, despite what she had witnessed.

She let herself into Florence's apartment. The baby was awake and calm. She nursed him on the davenport while Florence snored in the bedroom like a man. Little Ted was eager and hungry, but she pulled him away from her nipple when she believed he'd had enough; she no longer trusted that he knew when to stop. He cried in his ragged, shapeless way, then drifted into a distressed slumber. At four in the morning, Bena wandered groggily downstairs and put the baby, full and sleeping, in his crib.

She found her husband dreaming on their bed. He was drunk enough to have forgotten to wash his face, and he still smelled like the woman whose skin he'd rubbed his lips over. The room stank of alcohol worked through the stomach and liver and then released through the pores of a wrist, an ankle, the back of a knee.

He'd flung himself wide across the bed, the left leg of his linen trousers yanked up around his knee. There was a bug bite on his calf that he'd worried to a raw sore in his sleep, streaking the blood across the sheets. The wound had drawn something like the number 3 in the bed, as if he were a dying man trying to provide a clue to his murderer with his own blood. *There were three men. No, one man, with three fingers. He had three moles on his cheek, three scars, he had had only three original thoughts in his life.*

Bena pulled the vanity stool next to the bed. She put a hand on his chest and felt his breathing, his drunk-beating heart. She moved her hand down the gully of his rib cage, where she would dig in, her fingers and hands pressed together hard, and then she would pull in opposite directions to expose the sleepy, rhythmic meat of him. From there to the soft shallow bowl of his stomach, sparsely haired with blond, then around his waist, one finger under the waistband, teasingly. She slid a hand into the front pocket of his pants and palmed the ham of his leg.

She found nothing but a few coins, the empty silver money clip with his initials, and a crumpled cigarette leaking small, hard bits of tobacco.

She put these on the bedside table and lined them up as evidence. She investigated the other pocket. This one was more fruitful: A wrapped dinner mint, softened by his body. A white ball of candle wax. A lipstick tube, like a single silver bullet.

Did it fall out of her dress pocket? Did Ted find it on the car seat after she'd been let out at home, after a slow-pull-away kiss?

Bena raised the nub with a half-turn. Plum. A shade she'd been advised never to wear, with her coloring. *Washed out,* they'd say. *What a shame. Such a beautiful girl. She was so washed out.*

The woman's lips had worn the oily point away.

Bena applied the lipstick. In the dark, she drew a wide plum mouth. Her thinking: In the dark, we are all of us washed out, all of us or none of us. She put the metal tube, upright, open, along with the other plunder from Ted's pockets, between the dinner mint and the ball of wax, which finished the oblique line of accusation like a big, white period.

The streetlamp cast her shadow over him. In the middle of her shadow she planted a dark plum kiss, smack between his nipples. She kissed him down, down, leaving a trail of wet fruit to the loosened buckle of his belt.

She stopped there.

But she did unveil him, peeling back the two halves of his unzipped trousers because she wanted to smell the woman on him, the sour bakery smell of woman on him.

"Horace needs to talk to you," Ted told her when he returned to the living room. She sat in a rocking chair with Little Ted in her lap, one of Florence's cast-off *True Confessions* magazines in her hand. The stories were all the same tale of unrequited love, about women with doomed, homely names like Lorna or Gail and men with gold pocket-watches or gold teeth.

"Mmm hmmm." She tried to approximate distraction. In truth, she was terrified to know what Horace Gast wanted from her.

"He said it's urgent."

She looked up from her reading. "And did you tell him I was sick?"

Ted appeared stymied, perhaps at the possibility that she hadn't heard the conversation he'd meant her to overhear. "Yes. Yes I did."

"Good," she replied, returning to *True Confessions* and her slow rocking.

"He said he'd call back in an hour."

Bena stretched her neck from side to side. "I imagine I'll still be asleep in an hour."

Ted regarded her from beneath an eave of pale, unwaxed hair. He knew she was hiding something, but as a man who was hiding something, he was unable to pry, for fear of the reciprocal querying. "I imagine I'll be out fussing with the trout pond," he said.

Bena watched as he grabbed a peach from the fruit bowl and walked into the bedroom. She'd experienced an alarming lack of emotion toward him since the night of Reimer's party, not rage or adoration or annoyance. She observed him from what seemed to her a vast distance, a space filled with glass that was transparent but distorting, so that he was less imposing than usual, his voice smaller, his presence smaller.

In part, she'd attributed this to the week she'd spent at home with Little Ted, a span of time that only served to convince her, even further, that he was not a normal baby, that he would not lengthen and expand into a normal child and a normal adult. His face was perpetually moony, drawling, never sharpened to alertness by sound or light. She'd become so distraught one day that she'd captured a handful of fire ants in a glass and let them file out onto his fat arm. The ants nestled themselves in the hottest places—between his fingers, in the crook of his elbow— and she allowed them to bite him as she watched.

When he didn't respond, she picked the ants off and pinched them between her fingers, then wiped the wet grainy death on her calves. She watched as the bites rose into welts, which she dabbed with calamine lotion. The irregular rounds of pink looked like the scars of cigarette burns, and she spent the rest of the afternoon rocking and crying in a windowseat with Little Ted in her lap. When she was finished crying, she took a kitchen knife and cut the pages out of her measurement journal, because the numbers she'd recorded so diligently were the most cheery and foul sort of delusion. She tossed the pages and the book into the trash. Her own system had failed her. She spent the rest of the day in a deadened, weightless haze that might have been a form of happiness. She made a pie with some cherries that were about to turn. When Ted came home she didn't tell him about what she'd done or what she'd discovered, and how it was almost a relief; she was released, directionless, unprotected, godless. Anything was possible now. They ate the pie and bemoaned the fact that they didn't have ice cream, that they hadn't eaten ice cream in months. This reminder of the lack of cold sweetness in their lives may have been what made Ted unbutton her blouse and pull her down, undress her on the dining room rug, where they were hot instead of cold, where there wasn't a lot of sweetness to be found.

That night she awoke before the baby's three-o'clock feeding to discover herself alone in bed. She found her husband leaning over the baby's crib with a match, holding the flame in front of his eyes. When Ted saw her in the doorway, he explained that he'd heard a noise and believed there was a snake in the crib; but his behavior spoke of a different fear. He behaved guiltily, as though she'd caught him in the act of setting fire to the baby's cotton blankets or the spiky tufts of his hair.

Ted entered the living room in his straw hay-skimmer and a pair of old khaki work trousers. His chest was bare and unsunned, the blond hair darker than usual from being kept under a doctor's coat for summer days on end.

"Careful about the sun," she said, not looking up from the magazine.

He grunted an acknowledgment of her concern. She heard the back door slam, heard him rummaging in the porch corner among the rusted snow shovels for his *mata cristiano.*

He was digging a new pond because his fish were failing once again. After an initial period of thriving, the bluegills had developed a fungus on their scales, white and fuzzy. Their eyes were gummy and blank and they'd stopped eating the locusts Ted dropped into the water. The insects' clenched bodies had bloated and loosened and sunk. Now the fish were in an aquarium in the dining room while their new home was being built. It was true that their scales had cleared up, but the goal of departure was still there, she could see it in the lifeless way they hung in the water, lamely spiraling their fins. "They look better," he'd say to her. He said the same thing about Little Ted, checking his heart, his lungs, his face for clarity and purpose.

He's fine.

For once, Bena sensed that Ted's ruthless optimism wasn't put out into the world to convince his patients of their sure survival. This time, it seemed, he was trying equally hard to convince himself.

She carried the baby to the kitchen window and let the sunlight fall on his face. She rubbed his palms with her thumb, his incomprehensibly soft palms.

Outside, Ted sat on the overturned wheelbarrow, spinning the wheel idly, trying his luck at luck. He stared at the pond, which resisted growing and deepening, no matter how diligently he chipped away at the dirt with his bent-handled Christian-killer.

Bena thought of the story she was reading in *True Confessions*, about a woman named Lola, a migrant worker who was in love with her tomato-farmer employer. Lola had a baby, and she left it in a tomato basket one day while the farmer kissed her between rows of his plants. They were interrupted by an alarm bell—his barn had caught fire. The barn burned down, the baby was bitten by a snake and died, and after his tomato plants were picked clean, the fruit pulped and canned, the farmer never again kissed Lola.

Bena saw herself walking out a back door, followed by the screen clap that announces a young mother in a housedress with a baby. The mother's hand is always over her face to shade herself from the shocking brightness of the outside world. Her hand is red and bitten from picking garden tomatoes. Bena saw herself walking toward her farmer husband on the overturned wheelbarrow, a husband who spins the wheel and spins the wheel and doesn't notice her sultry, fresh-baked-mother approach. She stops in front of him, baby propped on a prominent hip. She puts out a single, long finger and stops the wheel from spinning.

The husband looks up.

What's eating you? she asks.

She watches as the sunlight catches on his chest, tangles in the hair, loops and ducks over his man's nipples.

Nothing, he says. Beginning to think this was all just a big waste of time.

She knows he's talking about something bigger than his little fish pond, but she agrees to keep the conversation lying and small.

Aw now, I hate to hear you talk like that.

Normally, the husband's brows thicken and cluster. So don't listen, he normally says. Normally she would walk back into the house, her bounteous chest and hopes deflated. She'd fix a pitcher of gimlets and the two of them would sit on the davenport and eat white salted nuts and watch the house grow dark.

She sways nearer so he can smell the scent of baking and motherhood on her. She curls the baby in her lap and pushes next to her husband on the rusted bottom of the wheelbarrow.

Come on now, she says, running a finger along the crease where his neck and shoulders join. Tell me what's bugging you.

I dig and I dig and I just don't get anywhere, he says.

She laughs. Where you digging to, sweetheart? China?

He crunches his head and shoulder together so that her finger is pinched inside.

She wiggles it, digging, digging, digging to China. Where are you trying to dig to? she teases. Where are you trying to dig?

He wiggles a thumb through the gaping buttonholes of her dress and pushes between her breasts where the ribs come close to touching and disappear.

I'm fairly squirreled up, he says, his voice thick and low. You?

They put the baby under the wheelbarrow, where it's dark and cool. He steps down into the fish pond and offers her a hand.

It's going to be fine, one of them says, she's not sure who. Everything's going to be fine.

They lie in the bottom of the pond still and straight as though it were a grave. There's a rock under the small of her back. She hears the baby crying. Maybe he's hot under the wheelbarrow, she worries. Maybe there's a nest of fire ants or tiny rattlers feasting on his soft little hands.

Stop, she says to the kissing husband, Stop, she mouths against his pillowy, prickling mouth. But she doesn't mean it. Stop. With her tongue she licks his hot gold tooth.

She hears a bell. In her head she hears a bell, a whistle blown, an alarm sounded. Her pulse speeds. She tries to say something to her husband like, Quick, quick, let's hide, sensing they're in trouble for some reason. The baby's dead, perhaps, under the wheelbarrow. We've let him starve to death under there.

But when she opens her eyes, it's not her husband with one hand pressing against her pelvic bone, the other whittling away at the last few buttons that are the difference between clothing and her simple self. It's not her husband she's imagined herself with.

"Bena!"

She glanced through the corroded mesh of the screen door.

In the middle of the pond, Ted rested on the *mata cristiano*, an expectant look on his face. "Are you going to answer that?" he asked impatiently.

The doorbell rang again, longer and more urgent.

Red.

It had been hard to think of him or not think of him. Over the course of the week she'd conflated the two most shocking events of that evening—his kiss, the baby's descending howl—so that the second provided a strident accompaniment to the first. In her mind she saw Red's face fall dark and warm over hers. She heard the high-pitched yelp, then the thump as his lips touched hers, two quick, hideous collisions of flesh and bone.

She opened the door and he thrust a handful of daisies at her.

"I'm not disturbing you, I hope?" It was Horace Gast.

Her heart dropped on her toes, her hard, ten-pound heart. She took the flowers and forced a smile.

"You do look pale," he offered, following her into the living room and taking a chair. "Flu? Or is it your little one who's got it?"

"We both do." Bena arranged herself on the couch. "You know how it is. Things get passed back and forth."

"I do know, alas. Dreadful house here. Ever meet Louise Sparks?"

"No."

Mr. Gast picked up a candy dish and turned it over like a piggy bank, hopeful that if he shook it, it might disgorge a coin. "If you're looking to know Louise, you need look no further than that object over there."

He pointed to a lamp on top of the dining room highboy. The base of pink granite was carved in the shape of a cherubic girl riding a swan. The girl, more the likeness of a doll than a human, had a twice-removed relationship to the world. Bena and Ted had stored most of the other Sparks belongings in the basement, but they kept the lamp to prove to themselves that they had a sense of humor about how their life had disappointed them. They saved the Swan Girl, as Ted called her, to serve as a reminder that this life of theirs in Pueblo was temporary, not to be taken seriously in the least.

From outside, Bena could hear the dry, violent thunks as Ted impaled the yard with his hoe.

"So," Bena said, "you have children?" Mr. Gast's lips were even more pronounced in the morning, as if still full of sleep. He licked them frequently and rested his hand on them, his index finger wedged lengthwise in the crease of his mouth.

"Child. Warren."

"He lives in Colorado?"

"He used to live in Los Angeles. Persuaded me to invest in a few of his irrigation schemes, until I figured out he was a damned hophead, spent every penny I gave him to irrigate his own bad habits. Hardest decision I ever had to make, cutting that boy off."

"I'm sorry to hear that. I had no idea."

"He'd call, he'd write, he'd send telegrams fifteen days in a row, and then we wouldn't hear from him for months. Just like his mother. A weak, wholly inconsistent creature."

"It must have been a terribly hard decision." Bena was curious about what sort of woman would marry Horace Gast, or what sort Horace Gast would agree to marry.

"The appalling truth is that it was quite easy."

"You're no longer in touch with him?"

"In a manner of speaking. He died about two years ago. At least, we assume he did. We received telegrams periodically from different women claiming Warren had died, and would we mind forwarding some money to cover the costs of the burial. We paid for five funerals before he died for real. At that point, it was somewhat of a relief." He appeared unperturbed by the act of dredging up this tragic episode of his life for her.

"Mind?" he inquired, holding up a tobacco pouch.

Bena shook her head.

Mr. Gast rolled and lit his cigarette, and reached for the candy dish to use as an ashtray. He gestured at the baby in her arms with the burning end. "How old is he?"

She waved the smoke away from Little Ted's face and had the urge to lie. "Nearly five months," she replied, opting for the truth.

"Five months." Mr. Gast peered at the sleeping bundle in her arms. "Could I hold him?"

Bena balked, and he caught her hesitation. He looked at her with interest but did not ask. And why had she hesitated? Distrust, in part. A desire to withhold. And protectiveness. The baby was too larval to be in the world at all, he was unusually susceptible to damage, or more damage.

"You have to be careful with him," Bena said, putting Mr. Gast's paw behind the baby's head. "He's been slow to grow up."

Mr. Gast rubbed the baby's nose. "And who could blame him? It only gets worse from here." He stared at Little Ted's face. "I think he looks a bit like his mother."

"You think he does?" Bena slid closer to Mr. Gast, to see the baby from his perspective.

"Here," he said. He moved a finger along the bridge of the baby's nose down to his mouth. "And here." Little Ted moved his lips soundlessly, his words and meanings lost in the tight, elliptical swirls of Mr. Gast's thumbprint. He accepted the thumb, sucking earnestly as if there were milk to be pulled from the skin, the nail.

Mr. Gast turned to Bena and touched the bridge of her nose with his thumb. It was wet with the baby's saliva. Despite her instinct to slap his hand away, she didn't, fascinated instead by the ease with which he could offer a woman not his wife such minuscule and vast intimacies. His thumb fell over her lips, then nicked her chin before withdrawing into his lap.

"So," he said, handing her the baby, "I imagine you're already well aware that Maude Hewitt has disappeared."

What a clever bastard, Bena thought, momentarily startled. Yet she couldn't keep from smiling in admiration for how he'd knocked her off her guard, preparing her for a compliment instead of an interrogation.

"According to that creature Helen who keeps the gate over at the

William Bent," Mr. Gast continued, "she hasn't been seen since last Saturday evening."

"Not that Helen can be trusted to tell the truth."

"True," Gast conceded. "But in this case I feel that she was. You can tell when someone's relieved not to be forced into lying."

"Perhaps," Bena said.

"She left Reimer's, as we all know, around nine. I found her wet coat draped over the front stoop at the house."

Bena looked at him as if to say, So?

"She went into labor."

"Ah."

"What I'm getting at, Mrs. Jonssen, is this." He pushed his face into hers. "Where is she?"

"I beg your pardon, Mr. Gast," she said, pushing her face even farther into his, so far that her talking might be mistaken for an attempted kiss, "but I haven't the vaguest idea."

"And I suppose you'll also claim not to know where that cowboy has galloped off to."

Bena didn't answer.

"A bit of advice," Mr. Gast said. "The only people Red Grissom is interested in are those he can pull from the gutter so he can feel splendid about himself afterward."

Bena sniffed. "It seems to me you're never above the desire to feel splendid yourself."

Mr. Gast stood and circled the living room. He picked up a silver cricket cage, a candlestick, a photo of Bena and Ted on their wedding day, embracing coatless in the snow in front of a church. An unlit cigarette hung from Mr. Gast's lips. He retrieved a single wooden match from his coat and ran it fast and hard along the face of the Swan Girl, pulling a flame from her pink cheek.

"I prefer to look at the work I do as charity. By definition, an act performed so that others can feel splendid."

"Which is why your charity is so suspect, given you're not a man known for his charitable inclinations. It must make more than a few people start to wonder, Mr. Gast."

He smiled at her patronizingly. "People know what to wonder and what not to wonder about, Mrs. Jonssen. I thought you had grasped the social necessity of that."

"And what about those of us who don't care a whit for social necessity? Surely we are free to wonder all we like."

Mr. Gast walked behind the couch until he was directly behind her. He put his hands on either side of her and bent close, until she could smell the cigarettes on his shirt cuffs. He seemed about to whisper some wisdom or advice or warning, when they heard Ted in the kitchen.

"Hello?" Ted walked, hot-bodied, into the living room. His chest was wet. He was wiping his hands and face with a kitchen towel meant for drying dishes.

"Horace," he said, extending a hand, then thinking better of it. "Sorry, I'm quite unpresentable."

"Not at all," Mr. Gast replied, grasping his sweaty hand and shaking it with enthusiasm. "Your wife and I were just attending to business."

"If you're still attending . . ."

Mr. Gast held up a hand. "I think we've settled all we're going to today."

He bent down to give Little Ted a kiss on the cheek. Bena jerked the baby away so that Mr. Gast's lips fell on dead air.

"You'll call me if you hear anything." It was a demand.

"Naturally."

"Perhaps I'll see you in the office on Monday?"

"Perhaps."

Ted led Mr. Gast to the foyer. On the way, Mr. Gast walked close to the highboy. Bena saw him reach out an arm and swipe the Swan Girl to the floor.

Ted turned, hearing the dense knocking of granite and breaking of glass.

Mr. Gast looked at the lamp.

Ted patted him on the shoulder. "It wasn't a favorite of ours."

"Surely you'll have to pay to replace it. You must let me know so I can reimburse you."

"Really," Ted assured him. "Not a worry."

Mr. Gast began picking up the larger pieces, but Bena abruptly told him, "Don't." She smiled to soften her outburst. "I'd hate for you to cut yourself."

She heard the two men talking in the foyer—Trout pond . . . Yes, well . . . Always been an avid fisherman . . . Really? A cabin? Well, of course I'd love to . . . Yes, yes, call me at the clinic . . . Thanks for stopping by . . . I'm sure it's nothing but heatstroke, or a little woman's melancholia—then the door shut and it was quiet.

Ted reappeared. "What did he want?"

He flopped into the chair. She was sure his sweaty back would leave a stain on the upholstery, but she no longer cared if this temporary shelter of theirs collapsed around them.

"Nothing," she said. "Work bric-a-brac."

Bena handed the baby to Ted and went to the kitchen for a broom.

She swept the shards of bulb into a dustpan. The big pieces of granite she carried to the kitchen and dropped into the wastebasket. When it came to the head, however, she couldn't throw it out. She looked for a place to hide it, feeling furtive: keeping the head of an object they'd mocked and hated could expose her in a way she didn't care to be exposed.

She lifted the lid of the flour tin and pushed the Swan Girl's head down until the white powder closed over it. She returned to the living room, streaking the white residue of a burial across her dress.

· · ·

NORTH GRAND SEEMED wider and more empty than she remembered it after not having left the house in a week. It was Sunday, of course, which meant that people had even less of an occasion to be outside. It was hot enough that just the act of breathing made her mouth papery, and the air was filled with the bone-marrow-and-celery smell of cooking.

Ted had gone for a day of fishing with Clyde on their way up to Colorado Springs, where they would spend the night and on Monday attend an early-morning lecture entitled "Infant Typhoid Rates and the Uses of Alum in Town Sewage Systems." Clyde had picked Ted up after breakfast. Clyde appeared cautiously sad when he greeted her, as if he felt sorry for her about something in advance. After they left, Bena went upstairs to Florence's to ask whether she would mind watching Little Ted for an hour or so. She needed some air, she explained.

Before leaving, Bena resurrected the breast pump from the back of the silverware drawer and affixed it to one breast, then the other. She put the glass bottle of milk in the icebox for Florence to use at feeding time. It had been a welcome break not to feel the pump's indifferent mouth clamp around her breasts for the past week. And yet—it was a horrible admission—she'd begun to see very little distinction between feeding the baby and watching the milk trickle through the laboratory glass of the breast pump. She'd run out of excuses to explain his distant behavior now that she hadn't gone to work for a week. She could no longer calm herself with the excuse that he was angry with her, punishing her by refusing to lock his gaze on hers, smile or laugh or otherwise allow her into the puzzle of his wordless brain. He had never laughed or uttered a stream of sound that had the purpose or force or intention of words. He seemed to have no clear-cut desires that she could discern. He didn't cry when his diaper was dirty. He didn't cry when his arm was stung by ants. He merely gorged himself on milk, not knowing enough even to sense his own fullness.

By the end of the week she had broken three coffee cups and hadn't bathed once; she watched as her hair grew dirtier, and considered dyeing it a chestnut color come autumn. She'd forgotten to do laundry, she'd forgotten to order food from Savage Bros., so that the pantry was empty by Thursday. She'd lost the hair ribbon she used to measure him, and the grain scale was broken, its needle stuck at seventeen pounds. Sixteen pounds, sixteen ounces. Twice a father's football shirt, though the luckiness of that gave her no pause or comfort.

Maybe Ted was right, she thought, as she saw him fold his lean body into the passenger seat of Clyde's car that morning. He laughed at something Clyde said and looked out fondly at the day. Maybe she was disproportionately worried and sad. Maybe there was nothing wrong with the baby. Maybe there was something wrong with her.

Bena tied a scarf under her chin and walked up North Grand, to the top of the hill, until she could see the domes of the Mineral Palace and, beyond them, the boxy townscape. From this height, the town still had the raw, crude appearance of a frontier settlement, all angles and function. It was odd to her that no architect had turned his face west and found craggy, vertical inspiration in the mountains that lurched up from the horizon thirty miles away. Even the town's church spires were cropped and flat, as though someone feared the sky might prick itself on a needly tip and fall into an infinite slumber.

Bena followed North Grand as it wound to the west and became Larch Avenue. The Gast residence was a mile out of town at the end of Larch, Florence had told her. There was little chance she'd miss it.

In fact, Bena discovered, Larch was less an avenue and more the elm-lined driveway to the Gasts' gargantuan house, a Victorian constructed of a bloody sandstone. Its humorless turrets recalled the starkness of grain silos sooner than the lush, protected heights of wealth. The windows enjoyed an uninterrupted view of the Front Range: there was nothing between the Gasts' property and the mountains except a few ragged remnants of fencing.

Bena looked for a bell at the iron gate and, finding none, strolled up the long walk. The door knocker was a woman's curved hand, extending from the door so that the gentle points of her nails rapped against the thick glossy black of the wood.

She lifted the little hand and let it drop.

"Yes?" a hostile voice asked moments later.

Bena stood face to face with Aurelita Trujillo, her bad eye covered with a neat black patch.

"Yes." Bena was bewildered by the coincidence. "I'm here to see Mr. Gast."

Aurelita's uniform still had the box creases. Her shoulders folded inward, creating two wing-shaped concavities above her collarbone.

"You don't have an appointment."

"No."

"Might recommend you make an appointment before you go calling on people."

"If I could just have a moment with him . . ."

Aurelita wore shiny new maid's shoes. "He's not here." She smiled and closed the door.

Bena started down the steps. The house made lowing sounds in the wind. All of the drapes were drawn. She almost didn't believe Mr. Gast lived there. She suspected he'd hired Aurelita Trujillo to answer the door and pretend the house was functioning with real people and real lives. If Bena had managed to peer beyond Aurelita's body, she would have seen an empty house, void of furniture. Or maybe she would have witnessed nothing but the motionless flanks of the mountains. There was no house at all; the door was but a hole back onto the world, leading from unsheltered place to unsheltered place.

She picked her way down the stone path, making it more dangerous than it was, inventing mines beneath some stones, investing others with the power to sink under her weight. She had to make the right choice; each footstep required careful thought. The truth was, she didn't have anywhere to go. She didn't want to go home, because it would make her think too much, it would make her tired and achy-boned and blue. It would make her conduct more unmotherly experiments on her son because she was tired of ignorance and hunches, she wanted answers, she wanted a son who would read books and spin tops and reflect a kind of knowing back at her.

She'd decided to resign from the *Chieftain* the day before, when she'd found a tiny fragment of pink granite wedged in her hand; she'd teased it out with a pair of tweezers. She'd teased it out whole. She'd even put the sliver of stone in her mouth and washed it down with a glass of water.

"Mrs. Jonssen!"

Bena turned. It was Aurelita, running in her stiff maid's shoes. The patch had slipped down over her cheek, revealing her murky iris.

"The lady wants to talk to you, ma'am."

Bena followed Aurelita up the steps. The lady? Bena looked at the windows; for a change, she was the one being spied on.

Aurelita led her inside and up a wide staircase. The windows on the first floor were covered by drapes that kept out light and sound. The only source of light was a stained-glass window on the second-floor landing, which made the house seem judgmental and prismatic like a church.

"Have you worked here long?" Bena asked Aurelita.

Aurelita didn't answer her.

"Someone gave you an opportunity you couldn't refuse?" she pressed.

Aurelita stopped in front of a closed door. "Good or crummy, I ain't never refused an opportunity." Smiling, she turned the knob and let the heavy door swing open. "Mrs. Jonssen here to see you, ma'am."

The room was dark except for a blue-glass hurricane lamp. Bena heard the clanging of a radiator and smelled the wet burn of steam heat. Heat! In addition to being hot, the air was thickened with the nauseating sweetness of flowers past their prime. She could make out the ghostly, wilting petals of a lily leering at her from atop a dark bureau.

A woman was propped in a high-backed chair, half hidden beneath a careful piling of afghans. "Leticia Gast," she introduced herself, gesturing to an ottoman. "Have a seat." She had a man's voice, low and shredded by cigarettes or a general weakness in the lungs. The few words chafed in her throat and made her cough aridly, as though she were hacking up sand.

"Bena Jonssen." The woman didn't appear to want to be touched, so Bena sat down without offering her hand. She'd never seen a face so desiccated. The shadowy olive jowls and the ship's-prow nose indicated that Mrs. Gast had been a striking woman in her youth, the sort of beauty known for her forthrightness and precision. No doubt her black eyes and black hair and piercing features caused the pudding-faced prairie girls to be unsure about their own purported beauty, even as the boys flocked in adoring droves to their pale heads.

"I apologize for the heat, Mrs. Jonssen. A medical necessity."

"I suppose I'm used to it by now. Pueblo's no stranger to heat."

"You hail from a gentler clime?"

"Minnesota."

"Ah," said Mrs. Gast. "Not gentler. Just differently unpleasant. Your husband's the doctor. The charming one."

Bena shifted on the ottoman. "I don't suppose you've had the pleasure of being charmed by him?"

"From what I understand, I'm one of the few yet to have that pleasure."

Bena sat straight and alert despite the lulling heat. "I didn't know his reputation so preceded him."

Mrs. Gast laughed. "One can be a conventional bore and still be known by everyone in this town."

"Is that so?"

"Please help yourself to the water. My infrequent guests frequently become thirsty." She said this as if thirst were a mark of weakness, and one to which she rarely succumbed.

Bena poured herself a glass from the decanter. The water was warm and metallic. In the dark she could have mistaken it for blood.

Mrs. Gast's hands fiddled with the loose threads on the afghan over her lap. "Take yourself, for example," she said.

"Because I am a conventional bore?"

She looked at Bena approvingly. "I know you work at the *Chieftain*, that you have a child who suffers from a persistent case of colic. I know that you've found a friend in Trudy Grissom's son."

She reached into an ivory box and withdrew a brown-papered cigarette, a bone lighter. The flame cracked the gloom for an instant. "Mind if I smoke?" she asked, already inhaling. Her face contorted, and Bena feared she'd stopped breathing. She began coughing violently.

"My objections aside, Mrs. Gast, it doesn't appear as if you ought to smoke."

"To hell with ought to," she said, the smoke leaking out between her thin lips. "I ought to have shot my husband dead the first time I found him with another woman. Not that I have any right to complain. The first time I caught him was before the wedding. He was with the maid. An intruder, I naturally assumed. I had one of my father's deer rifles pressed into his neck before I knew it was he."

Bena unbuttoned her blouse and lifted her skirt, so that her perspiring knees were uncovered. "Why didn't you shoot him?"

"Who can remember? It was so long ago. Years and years. I'm sure I had a good reason at the time."

"And what about the other times?"

"If someone sees you weak once, Mrs. Jonssen, you're forever weak. That's what marriage is about—witnessing the weaknesses of your husband as though they were the very qualities you'd dreamed of in a man, dreamed of when you still wore pinafores and pretended to smoke with birch twigs." Mrs. Gast indicated the bed with her ash-heavy cigarette. "Be a dear and fetch me my pill."

Bena made her way to the bed. She found a pill on the side table, below the framed portrait of a boy in knickers and tweed cap. He was dark and round, with a wise gaze unsettling in a boy so young.

"Is that your son? He looks very knowing," she remarked as she gave Mrs. Gast the pill. She took the pill dry, then struggled to swallow it, her neck in spasm until she got it down.

"He does, doesn't he?" Mrs. Gast said finally. "I've often wondered if he knew what was to become of him. I've always looked at that portrait and thought that he knew quite clearly."

Bena envisioned a much older boy, his wise look turned cynical and wild, driving through the desert east of Los Angeles, dreaming that money and orange groves in equal abundance might take root in the transient dirt. "You lost him young," she said, hoping Mrs. Gast might provide her side of the story. Just like his father, she'd say. A weak and wholly inconsistent creature.

"Mere days after, in fact."

"Days after what?"

"After the portrait was finished."

Bena stared at the boy on the wall, bewildered.

"He was six," Mrs. Gast said. "One day shy of seven. We were taking him to Pikes Peak for his birthday."

"This is Warren you're speaking of."

"I nearly died giving birth to him. After Warren, there could be no other." She gestured down at her piles of blankets, at the emptiness at the core of her, her uterus years since pulled out and discarded.

She stubbed out her half-smoked cigarette. "We were headed to Pikes Peak, because Warren wanted to see the Cave of the Winds. Halfway to the top, he started to feel ill. We sat by the roadside and waited for Horace to turn the car around. It was a beautiful, clear day, the sort of day you can't imagine anything bad could happen. We walked up the road to wait in a less sunny spot. We didn't have time to jump out of the way."

"A stranger hit you."

"No," she said. "Horace struck us dead-on."

Bena put a hand to her head. She pushed her hairpins deep into her scalp.

"We were lucky, really, that we didn't all three die, that we didn't lose more than a son and my legs." She pulled the blankets back to reveal two withered sticks protruding from beneath her robe. They were thinner than arms.

"And that's why," Bena said. That's why he'd stopped to pick them up that day on the road to Pikes Peak. Making good on some past bad luck.

"That's not why," Mrs. Gast scolded. She threw off the layers of blankets. "The truth of it all, Mrs. Jonssen? My husband was relieved. Poor man, people think. He killed his only son, his wife is lame and barren. Who can blame him for behaving the way he does? Who could ever find fault with a man so unfairly cursed?"

Bena thought back to Mary, her fear that to predict people's futures would only give them license to misbehave in the ways they'd always dreamed of misbehaving, of fulfilling their darkest yearnings and comforting themselves with the thought that they were simply complying with the designs of forces bigger than they.

Mrs. Gast began coughing in earnest. Bena poured her a glass of water, which she declined. Outside, the wind rattled the windows as it moved across the front of the house, like a woman being chased.

"You must receive the brunt of the dust storms out here," Bena remarked.

"That's why I insist on keeping the curtains drawn. I can't bear to watch them bearing down on us for hours. On a clear day you can see forty miles." Mrs. Gast seemed to shudder at the thought of so much land and sky.

Mrs. Gast fumbled with the lighter and lit another cigarette.

"It really doesn't matter, you see," she said, to Bena's palpable disapproval, the flame on her lighter dangerously high and threatening to set ablaze her old woman's peppery thatch. "I have tumors on my lungs. I'll be lucky if I see the first snow on Pikes Peak."

You'd be lucky at any rate, Bena thought, living sealed up tight like this. "I'm sorry to hear that," she said.

"Why should you be? We don't mean a thing to each other."

Bena watched the glow of the cigarette bloom and fade, bloom and fade as Mrs. Gast breathed the blue smoke. "I can't help but wonder, Mrs. Gast, why you invited me in today."

"Must there be a reason?"

"You strike me as too deliberate—and too inhospitable—to have merely invited me into your house on a whim."

Mrs. Gast laughed, seemingly pleased with this description. "I aspired to be a grand hostess, you know. Perhaps it's lucky I was confined to a wheelchair at such a young age. I don't know that it's in my constitution to care so much about other people's pleasure." She dropped her cigarette into her lap. It rolled, sparking, onto the carpet.

Bena stamped out the sparks and patted Mrs. Gast's lap. Up close, her hostess had the scared, hopeful smell of the dog at the Mineral Palace.

Mrs. Gast coughed and smoothed her lap with her long hands. "The reason I asked you is that I saw your picture in the society pages talking to my husband at Reimer's party, and I recognized a bit of myself in you. This happens when you're older, Mrs. Jonssen. You see yourself everywhere. At first I thought this urge was nothing more complicated than an old woman's desire for immortality. But then I understood the ways in which I saw myself in others as a far less noble impulse. I wasn't seeing remnants of me, I was seeing the potential that I had as a girl realized in others as it had never been realized in myself."

"And what potential did you see in me?"

"I saw a woman who thought she was strong enough to break people who aren't worth breaking. I saw a woman who would soon come to realize the futility of this."

It was like having her palm read all over again, Bena thought. "I can't imagine what you're talking about."

"I could have married any man in Pueblo. For a woman, it was a heady sort of power. And so I married the most unbroken of men. Yet Horace is so broken, he is actually the most broken man—he was broken long before he killed his own son and maimed his wife. Do you see?"

Bena shook her head.

"I've had a deer gun in his neck, Mrs. Jonssen, but it's a trigger I've never been able to pull. I can't break a broken man, no matter how much he breaks me day after day after day. We are both of us cowards in the guise of impossible creatures."

Behind Bena, the radiator resumed its hissing.

Mrs. Gast reached out a skeletal hand. Her wedding rings looked like jeweled nubs of arthritis, the petrified joints pushing through the skin.

"You want me to live my life better, so you can feel that yours wasn't a waste."

Mrs. Gast smiled. "That would be nice, wouldn't it? That would be noble, at least, or graceful. No, my dear, I want to break the broken man, and I want your help."

"And why do you think I'll help you?"

"Because," Mrs. Gast said, rearing upward in her chair, "this is your fate if you don't."

Bena felt nauseated, not because she feared becoming a lame

woman whose body has been ravaged by childbirth and tumors feeding on her lungs but because she couldn't believe the extent to which she was being manipulated.

"And why do you need me?" she inquired.

"If someone sees you weak once, you're forever weak."

"No," Bena disagreed. "That's not true."

"You're young. It's a defining quality of youth to believe in unlikely evolutions of character."

Bena looked at her dust-clogged wristwatch. It hadn't told an honest hour in more than a month. "I have to be going."

"We desire the same outcome, you and I. Maybe not out of life, but in this predicament. We desire the same outcome."

"Which is what?"

"To expose a selective truth. You're curious, aren't you? I know you are. I was curious, too, once. Now I prefer to draw the shades. Not because I've learned a hard lesson by being curious, mind you. But because I've seen it all. There's nothing more for me to see. Except for one glorious sight."

Mrs. Gast lit another cigarette. She never seemed to smoke more than half of one before she stubbed it out and lit another, in a proudly wasteful manner.

"My maid's name was Hortense. An ugly name for an exquisite girl. Perhaps I took some pleasure in making her hang my underwear with silk gloves and collect my nail clippings, when she was deserving of a finer life. I made her put hair from my brush into a bag and write the date on a label. I made her point my shoes—all thirty pairs—each morning in the direction the wind was blowing. I knew that Horace found her lovely, which only made me seek to humiliate her more. Of course, at that age, eighteen, I had no doubt that shame and decency and fear kept people from behaving in ways I couldn't predict. I didn't believe I had anything to truly dread."

"But you learned otherwise," Bena said.

"I learned otherwise. But what I learned was more interesting than what you assume. I didn't learn that men are beasts, that they will chase down the girls they fancy and pull their legs open beneath them without a thought toward their wives."

"I didn't assume that."

"You did," Mrs. Gast said. "You did because you haven't learned the real lesson." She bent forward. "Have you ever seen your husband with another woman, Mrs. Jonssen? Have you ever witnessed how utterly pitiful and desperate a creature he is, his trousers bunched around his ankles and his buttocks bumping toward the ceiling like a white mole?"

Bena saw herself peeling back her husband's trousers to smell the woman on him.

"That's how I thought of it. I walked into the living room with a deer gun and I imagined I was looking at a white mole. A white mole that was stuck in a tree, the branches bouncing madly around him as he struggled to free himself. It was quite marvelous to think of it that way. It was so marvelous that I dropped the deer rifle and began to laugh. That is how my husband and my maid discovered me discovering them. They were naked and foolish and I was laughing." She laughed for Bena, as if to prove her story's veracity.

"Yet you still married him."

"I did," Mrs. Gast replied. "Because I had seen how absurd an act marriage is founded upon, how silly and unspecial. It didn't matter whom I married, as long as it was someone who entertained me."

"How could that possibly entertain you?"

"I'm entertained by acts of daring and stupidity, with which Horace is quick to oblige me. At first he only made love to women. Any woman, really. The occasional maid. Men's wives. Friends' wives. He would bring them to our living room while I read magazines upstairs on a divan and listened to them through the grate. But then he grew bored. He brought home his friends' daughters. He brought home whores."

Bena stared at her, disbelieving. "And you found humor in this."

Mrs. Gast exhaled a weak stream of smoke. "Lord, no, Mrs. Jonssen. Lord, no. Nothing else in the world had the power to devastate me more. But you come to depend on humility, after a while. It keeps you alive."

Bena wiped her forehead with her scarf, balled in her fist. The heat was making her dizzy, as was Leticia Gast's peculiar confession. It was a puzzle, a winding, somersaulting, betraying puzzle that revealed more peculiarities with every turn.

"But then I learned an interesting fact about myself. Interesting, because I was sixty-four and far past the age when one expects to discover new and intriguing truths about oneself. I learned there was a limit to the secrets I'd keep for another person, even if it was in the name of marriage. I learned that I could actually feel sorry for a meaningless little whore, like Maude Hewitt."

Bena perked up. "Why Maude Hewitt?"

"To believe yourself fatherless and yet to have your father watching you every day the way an owl watches a mouse. It was the most ideal form of paternity for Horace. He adores games, though he was never much of one for ball tossing."

Bena stared at her hostess dumbly. She remembered her suspicion that a sticky, penetrating substance existed between Maude and Horace Gast, like another body. The most sticky substance, as it turned out. "That's hideous," she said.

Mrs. Gast gazed at her pityingly. "Oh my dear. It is so much worse than that. You were at Reimer's party, Mrs. Jonssen. I saw your picture in the society pages."

"So?"

"Maude Hewitt is many things. But a liar she is not." Mrs. Gast looked at Bena most invasively, as if wondering how far down her mind and her understanding of the blacker things in life extended.

The long albino faces of lilies watched Bena impassively from the bureau as she stumbled to the window. She parted a drape and put her head against the glass, which evidently hadn't been opened for decades. In the distance she could see Pikes Peak; she could almost discern the trail beaten into its brown hide by Ute mothers as they climbed, arms outstretched and full with the children born without sight, without arms, their palates cleaving high and straight to the domes of their skulls.

Bena remembered how she and her father drove to the Canadian border after Jonas's funeral, how they were so grim and harmless-seeming that the border guard let them through, even though neither of them had any identification and both looked as though they'd been chased to this arbitrary line through the dirt between home and away.

They went to the nearest roadside restaurant, where the waitress gave her father bourbon after bourbon and the two of them ate steak, cleaning their big plates of all traces of blood with the fine butter rolls. And her father told her that he'd known, from the moment his son was born, that something was wrong with him.

Her father had seen this hesitancy to thrive in the animals he'd raised as a child on the family farm in Council Bluffs. He would nurse the goats and sheep in his arms with a bottle, he was the boy to whom people took their grudging newborn livestock, because he could work wonders. So when his son was born and living didn't come naturally, he made it his project, he fed him and coddled him and forced him into living.

The waitress appeared with a piece of banana pie and a candle. She thought it was Bena's birthday. "Make a wish," she said.

Bena gave the pie to her father, and told him to make a wish, but he sat there, and she sat there, and they both watched their wish melt away until the wax spread over the pie and made eating impossible.

"I have to go," Bena announced to Mrs. Gast.

She forged her way through the viscous air of Mrs. Gast's room and put her hand on the doorknob.

"You're not interested in helping me?" Mrs. Gast looked at her hungrily.

Bena's stomach contracted, from sickness and outrage, and yes, even from a small amount of pity for this birdy, dying woman. "I can't imagine there's a person on this earth capable of that." She opened the door just wide enough to fit through. As she was about to close it, she heard Mrs. Gast calling out to her.

"Yes?" she reentered the room.

Mrs. Gast looked contrite in her chair. Her hands trembled so severely that she couldn't light her cigarette.

Bena walked back to her and took the lighter from her cold hands. Mrs. Gast tilted her head as Bena produced a tall flame. Bena was at the door when she heard Mrs. Gast speak again.

"Don't worry, Mrs. Jonssen." She smiled. At first Bena thought she was going to apologize, but then she saw Mrs. Gast was sneering at her. "We are nothing alike, you and I. Nothing alike at all."

Bena took one last look at the ravaged woman, her cigarette dangling dangerously near her blankets, and shut the door.

SHE SMELLED AMMONIA in the hallway but otherwise detected no sign of Aurelita Trujillo. The useless decoration of the Gast mansion sprawled around her, room after room after room of dusted relics and shammed davenports, their rounded cushions unmarred by even the suggested depression of a human body.

Outside, the day had matured, the sky was high and white, the heat intense but dry. She stepped off the porch and looked up to Mrs. Gast's window. Nothing. No curtains moved, no single sign of life. *Thousands of rooms*, she heard in her head as she scanned the many blind, unlooked-through windows.

What was that from? *Thousands of rooms*. She recalled it as something Bonnie Parker had said to her. *Sort of like a rich widow in her mansion. Thousands of rooms to rattle around in, but no use to make of them.* Remembered now in the shadow of this empty mansion, it had the ring of a prophecy.

She hurried down the sidewalk. Behind her, she heard the sounds of someone following her. She turned to see Aurelita Trujillo's skinny form, appearing like a trick of sunlight behind her.

"I know where they are," Aurelita said when she reached Bena.

Bena regarded her skeptically, not at all sure why Aurelita would volunteer this information. "Where are they?"

Aurelita pointed a thumb south toward the Front Range. "Up Cuerna Verde way. But I don't imagine you'll find them anyplace people are bound to look."

"And where would that be?"

"They're in Gast's house." Aurelita said "Gast's" as if spitting out a grape seed.

Of course, Bena thought. The old Grissom house. "Why are you telling me?" she asked. Aurelita didn't seem to like her much.

"Like I said." Aurelita pulled the black patch off her face. "Never refused an opportunity, good or crummy. But I always make it worth my while." She grinned, exposing a row of straight, coppery teeth.

Aurelita walked back to the house with her blistered gait, her patch wrapped and bouncing around her wrist.

BENA REMEMBERED the way. Past the shacks turning their nearly blind faces to the Rockies, past the two-rut turn to the deserted home-steader's shack. She shifted the Ford into high gear and drove as fast as she could along the road that hugged the Front Range, because she'd be slowed by the twisting route west of Crow Junction. She drove with Little Ted on her lap instead of strapped in his bassinet. It was danger-ous, she knew, but she wanted him close. She had unbuttoned her blouse so that his head could rest on the bared, low swell of her stomach, still stretched and pouting from containing him.

She took the right turn off the Front Range Highway, and the road began to slope upward. She passed the feed store in the center of Crow Junction. The halfwit was outside, sunning himself in the no-color sun, his back propped against a gas pump. He had his rooty hand buried purposefully in his crotch, trying to bring himself some lonely pleasure against the fuming metal. She watched him in the rearview mirror, his jellied face soon obscured.

After Crow Junction, nothing looked familiar. She tried to remember Dr. Ashburne's instructions scribbled on the prescription slip. Dead tree. Gourd-shaped rock. Barn with rotted roof. The dead tree was easy to spot, she recalled the dead tree, its spine traced by a lightning strike, thin and wary as the seam on a woman's stocking. The rock also distinguished itself from the others in the passing landscape, upright and pot-bellied. The barn was the landmark they'd missed, having driven instead down La Punta Road.

Bena squinted through the trees to the right. The barn loomed up by the roadside. It sagged, massive and swaybacked on its haunches, like a cow giving birth.

She looked at the road that split off to the right past the barn, then at the left fork, what she thought was La Punta Road, though there were no signs. For all she knew, the old man had made the name up. Maybe "La Punta" was his idea of an inside joke, maybe it meant "Watch your step" in Spanish.

Bena turned the wheel. For a single, rash moment, she steered the car to the left. She wanted to see the sky, the air, the nothingness she'd mistaken for water. But just as quickly she lifted the ball of her foot off the gas pedal and the car glided to a stop, naturally losing enthusiasm for the adventure. She sat listening to the low chug of the idling motor and the rattle of the wind through the needles and leaves. Little Ted was asleep with a finger hooked in her navel as if attempting to pry himself back in through that tiny hole, back to a place where the only sound was that of blood through a heart, the only light the purplish illumination of skin and tendon and muscle.

She thought back to Harlan Baxter's buffalo, to the sensation she'd had when she'd stumbled across Red's account of their dramatic demise. Was it instinct, this impulse to hurl oneself off a cliff? Bena couldn't imagine what sort of instinct would command an entire herd of buffalo to destroy itself with one impetuous jump, unless their soft form of captivity didn't suit them. Maybe the constant petting by children in worn, ill-fitting clothes made their tea-colored coats thick with grief, maybe they felt unspeakably heavy and lusterless on their tiny mesa, trapped like a herd of unseemly princesses.

Whatever the cause, their act had the weight of an unthinking brain behind it. And that was the precise sort of irrational, bodily pressure that compelled Maude to heave her bundle into an animal grave, to be crushed against the skull-and-rib thatch of needful executions.

Bena rubbed where the rope had cut into her wrist the night of the dust storm. There was no corporeal memory of the cut now except new, smooth skin, lineless and immaculate.

She looked down La Punta Road, so common and unpromising, a road that would end in a weedy sandlot, an abandoned car, the blackened stone foundation of a burnt house. And yet there was an unanticipated vastness at the end of the ruts; there was sky and there was wind.

While Bena could envision the fall, and even feel the way her organs would be crushed against her heart and her arms pulled long, her body never struck ground. Instead, as her falling body neared it, the dry grass turned into choppy, reeling teeth of water. She recalled the story Reimer Lee Jackson's chauffeur had told her about his sister, and understood better how a trenchant fear of water might have prevented the girl from hurling herself out onto the cobblestones. She had probably looked down from the sweatshop window and seen not stones but the gray swells of waves, which would just as soon seal her up beneath their opaque surface as break her fall.

Bena wondered what the buffalo saw between their front hooves, splayed and vibrating in the wind as they cleared the blunt lip of the mesa. Was it water? Was it wave upon wave of colorless water?

SHE DROVE up the curving road, past the caretaker's house, moving at a casual pace to keep from calling attention to herself.

Most of the houses were empty because of the outbreak of rattle-snakes. Gerta's sure-shooting had brought to extinction only her lawn, the spray of bullets failing to put even the slightest dent in the rattle-snake population. Bena had heard people complaining at Reimer's party about the snakes at Cuerna Verde—baby rattlers in your gardening shoes, in your sugar jars, bleeding up through your porch boards when it rained.

She parked the car next to the tennis court, got out and tossed a blanket on the hood, then put Little Ted on it change him. The wind blew cold and pine-raggedy, and she hurried to pin the new diaper to keep him from catching a chill.

Bena took her tartan bag from the backseat and hefted it, heavy with diapers and bottles and talc, over her shoulder. With Little Ted in her arms, she followed the path over a footbridge, through a wooden turnstile meant to discourage horses—back when there were horses—from wandering into the residential area, across a narrow picnic meadow that mumbled with bees. Once in the woods, she was directly above the house, looking down on the roof. A tower, slightly detached from the house and made of round stones, thrust up toward her. She hadn't noticed the structure before. It looked like a water tower, or a place where ice was stored in winter.

She worked her way down the red-needled path to the house, watching for snakes. It had been more than a week since she'd seen

Red Grissom. Together those days seemed as long as the summer, a length of time over which nights have grown colder and the sky has taken on the atmospheric clarity of a new season. She was losing her nerve as she pushed through the scrub, not knowing whether her appearance would be welcome. He hadn't come looking for her, after all. Still, she reasoned, she was obliged to tell him what she'd learned from Leticia Gast. He should know. This lent a noble purpose to what might otherwise be perceived as a presumptuous invasion.

The back porch was empty save for a triangular stack of summer firewood wrapped neatly under a green canvas tarp. She eased open the screen. The door was unlocked. People didn't lock their doors at Cuerna Verde—a point of pride Gerta had made numerous times. Gerta viewed it as a mark of financial and social success if she could live in a place, far from the rioting masses of civilization and among her own small and trusted people, where locks were unnecessary. Myrna Voskamp used to dream aloud of going to the city, of going to a place where a life was precious enough, and coveted enough by others, to require protecting. People didn't lock their doors in Coeur du Lac, Myrna said, because no burglar would want to be burdened with the bland possessions of their humdrum lake-country lives. They couldn't get out from under it themselves. They left their doors wide open, hoping somebody would come and do them the mighty favor of carting all that gloom and excess away.

Bena walked through the kitchen into the living room. There were plenty of objects worth stealing in the Gast house, not that they weren't full of gloom and excess, too. Bena assumed that the house had been sold to the Gasts the way it was when Red was a boy, the Grissoms' leather chairs and crudely framed mountain oils and yellowed, wood-mounted stag horns occupying the same places by the hearth or hanging from the same nails they'd hung from for twenty years.

She stood at the bottom of the staircase. Dust covered the dining table; a sail of cobwebs sagged between the candlesticks.

Red wasn't here.

Her vision narrowed. The woods rushed up and collided around her. She was at the top of a mountain, lonely, cold, and anything resembling home was impossible to pull from the furthest down regions of her memory or imagination. She didn't belong in Pueblo with Ted Jonssen, she didn't belong in St. Paul with her father, she didn't belong at Cuerna Verde with Red Grissom, she didn't belong anywhere.

Bena sat on a sheet-draped davenport and unbuttoned her blouse for Little Ted to nurse; the rituals of motherhood, no matter how apparently futile these days, were soothing to her. It was the one place she belonged, at least for now.

She ruffled the porcupine hair on the baby's head. His hair was starting to grow, a rusty-gold color, and was prickly to the touch. His head was beginning to seem small to her in comparison to the rest of his body. Two days before, she'd laid him on the bed and stepped back to assess him. His shoulders had broadened, his arms lengthened, his entire body sprawling outward and trying to keep pace with his ravenous eating. But it was all dead weight. His head was as small as when he was born, Bena could swear it. How could she have neglected to wind a ribbon around his skull to ascertain that his head made its way down to the frayed tip of the ribbon? Or not. Or to see that his head didn't grow at all, to see that it grew smaller like a ball of string?

Somewhere in the house a clock struck seven.

Bena buttoned her blouse and put the baby over her shoulder. She patted his back as she walked to the kitchen. She needed some water. In a cabinet she found a glass, next to it a leather flask. She unscrewed the top of the flask and took a whiff. Gin. She wrinkled her nose. Homespun.

She took a cautionary sip, in case her nose had misled her and it was actually rattlesnake poison she was sampling. No. Gin all right. She took a bigger swig, liking the way it made the muscles in her arms and stomach sting hot and then loosen.

She reached for the faucet. The water ran silty and brown, but she drank it anyway, from a jelly glass that was still sweet and sticky around the rim.

She rinsed the jelly glass and reached to put it back in the cabinet. It bobbled at the edge of the shelf and fell to the floor, smashing on the slate tiles into pieces that scattered to the far corners of the kitchen.

Balancing Little Ted, she bent down to pick up the debris. She held the biggest shard in her palm. It was knife-shaped. She curled her fingers until the sharp edges pressed against her puckered flesh.

You're a nice girl. I want to give you the chance to be had all wrong.

She felt a sharp object against her neck. An arm spun her around.

Maude Hewitt, her hair wedged beneath a felt crusher, held a piece of glass in her hand. Her feet were bare, revealing toenails painted in three different colors.

Maude stared directly at Little Ted and flinched.

Bena tried to reconcile the nervous, buzzing woman in front of her with the priestly one holding her bundled sacrifice up for the moon's dim approval before hurling it into the gaping maw of the earth. There was no physical evidence of her crime, no way in which the act weighed on her mouth or crushed her body into a hunched, guilty shape.

Maude pulled Bena, still carrying Little Ted, by the arm alongside her. Bena allowed herself to be steered through the living room and up the staircase.

"I saw you," Bena said. They were heading down a dark hallway, past door after closed door.

Maude tightened her grip.

"I saw you at the rendering plant."

Maude stopped in front of the door at the end of the hall and turned Bena toward her. She held the piece of glass near her chest, level with Little Ted's face. Bena pushed a hand against Maude's wrist so that the glass was pointed away from the baby. Maude looked at the position of her hand and appeared suddenly horrified by her carelessness. She dropped the glass onto the floor and wiped her fingers on her shirt.

Bena nodded at the closed door. "Does he know?"

Maude pushed her lips close to Bena's ear. Her breath was sour, that of a malnourished person who has begun to feed on her own skin and muscles.

"Whatever he doesn't know you'll tell him, won't you?" Maude spoke in the low, throaty tones of someone on the verge of tears, or attempting a seduction.

Maude raised a finger and pushed a bitten nail against Bena's mouth.

"Don't answer," Maude said. "I'd rather not know." She turned the knob and flung the door open.

Red was sitting on a four-poster bed with his boots off, his lap obscured beneath the tent of a large, unfolded map.

He regarded Bena with a look that said he'd expected her; the fact she'd failed to disappoint him pleased and exhausted him at once. He ran a hand through his parched hair. He saw the baby in her arms. He'd forgotten that she was a mother, that the waters of her body had mixed with the waters from another man's body, that there was living, breathing proof of this.

"Found her taking nips off the gin," Maude said.

Red emerged from beneath the map and stood on the wideboard floor. Bena had never seen his feet bare. How mushroom-white they were, the toes long and thin, nothing at all what his gruff, muscular fingers had led her to expect.

"It is cocktail hour," he said.

Maude sat on the bed. She pulled her feet onto the spread and picked at a red toenail. "If only we had some salted nuts. We could have ourselves a proper little party."

"I suppose we could have a drink. Lord knows I need one." Red looked at Bena.

"Yes," she replied. "Me, too."

"I'll take a gin, neat, sweetheart," Maude called to her. "Toss an ice cube in if you stumble across one. Henry? Want to place your order?"

"I'll get my own drink, thanks."

Maude sat up straight. "If you two want to be alone, just say so, Henry. You don't need to make up excuses for me."

"I'm aware of that," he said without looking at her. He put on a pair of boots and touched Bena on the elbow. "I'll give you a tour of the bunker."

Before closing the door behind them, he turned. "Gin, neat, right?" Bena thought she heard Maude, low and gravelly, telling him to go to hell.

He led her around the house, delivering a dispassionate account of the times he'd jumped off beds, cracking a collarbone or chipping a tooth; locked himself in the hope chest and almost asphyxiated; hung a swing from the living room rafter. But there was none of the excitement he had conveyed when he showed her around Cuerna Verde the first time, when he'd told her about the clumsy love in the icehouse and the untimely impaling of a rich man's son on a saddle horn.

"This was my mother's watercolor studio," he said, standing at the base of the stairs to the stone tower. The stairs were reached directly through a door in the living room. He offered to take Little Ted from her so she could climb more freely.

"Shame about the baby," he said. There was a baiting, probing quality to his statement.

She froze. She thought he was talking about Little Ted.

"Stillborn," Red continued. "As if Maude hasn't had enough hard luck."

The stairs wound above them. Bena considered telling him the truth about Maude's baby, but decided against it. There were other, more important truths to impart.

"Your mother was a painter?" Bena asked.

She heard him laugh below her. It was a tepid laugh, but one the stone walls picked up and batted around.

"I'd think it would be more accurate to say she *fancied* herself a painter."

"Any specialties?" Bena hoped to keep him talking and relocate the part of him she thought of as belonging to her, the part that asked her to dance when there was no dancing and kissed her in a worn leather chair, the part of him that was buried now under a callused layer of exhaustion and irritation and some new form of disenchantment.

"The usual watercolor fare. Hummingbirds. Flowers."

Bena was winded by the climb. The room at the top was furnished with a rocking chair, a stool, an easel, and a rustic plain wood table. In the middle of the floor was an empty washbasin, presumably to catch rain from a hole in the roof. One round window faced east toward the prairie.

The walls were densely hung with framed watercolors of birds and flowers. They were hideous. Not just crudely executed, Bena thought, but malevolent. The birds looked like the false-scientific studies based on oral accounts of sailor-explorers who told of mermaids, creatures born of vitamin deficiencies and desire. Bena doubted that Mrs. Grissom had ever seen a hummingbird in her life: the sketches she'd produced of muscular, vividly colored birds bore a greater resemblance to lizards, reptile-skinned monsters whose swordlike beaks skewered supplicant renditions of tulips and daisies. Some of the birds had diamond rings circling the raw, pickled skin of their talons.

They stood side by side, considering the wall of pictures.

"What an unusual vision she had," Bena said diplomatically.

"I don't know why Gast hasn't burned these. Must suit his crooked sense of the world somehow."

"What was her name?" she asked.

Red looked at the floor, and for a moment she feared he'd forgotten her name, his own mother's name. He held Little Ted out for her to take, then put his hands in his pockets and walked around the room.

"Is that really why you came here?"

Bena was taken aback.

"Don't you find it tedious," he continued, "feigning interest in people's lives? In my life, specifically?"

"I don't believe I've ever feigned interest in your life."

He scowled and dropped onto the stool. " 'I don't believe.' Not terribly convincing, Bena."

He bent over his legs, elbows on his knees. A shaft of sunlight freed itself from a branch outside the tower and tilted in through the window. The wind sounded like rain cascading down the stone walls, pine needles rustling together like water in a hurry.

Bena walked to the washbasin, took off her sweater to cushion the interior, and tucked Little Ted into it. She approached Red, hunched over on the stool, and reached out a hand, watching it in the shifting, uneven sunlight, as it lowered over his head and her fingers caught in his mat of unwashed hair.

Red remained motionless as her fingers grazed his temple. She slid them along the smooth arc of his collarbone and paused lightly over the lump where the childhood break had knit itself. He grabbed her wrist. "You can't stop, can you?"

She tried to remain calm and reasonably perplexed at his outburst.

"You're here to find an ending to your story, isn't that right?"

"What story?" she said. "I don't have a story."

He struck her with the back of his hand. "Hell you don't. You and your innocent sniffing around in her business, pretending like you give a good goddamn about everyone but yourself."

Bena wanted to put a hand to her cheek, but no—she would let it burn unsoothed in that stone room, she would let the blood fill her cheek and blacken. She couldn't believe he'd hit her.

"That's not true," she said. She didn't sound convincing, even to herself.

Red rolled a cigarette and lit it. He threw the match over his shoulder, as if he didn't care whether they burned to death in this old tower. He went to the window and peered out, his arms spread wide, his hands flat on the stones.

Bena checked on the baby. Her face smarted in earnest. A heart beat in her cheek; the bone there had softened and turned to a heart.

She sat cross-legged on the floor with the baby in her lap. "Is what you said to me still valid?"

"About what?"

"About keeping what I find out to myself."

He glared at her.

"I'm not trying to insult you," she said. "I discovered something that you ought to know."

"You can save your breath. I'll read about it in the *Chieftain* tomorrow."

"I'm not going to write about it."

"I don't believe you."

She looked at his hard face, sun-worn and wind-raked and almost ugly now that he didn't let her in.

"It's Horace Gast," she said.

He didn't respond.

"Horace Gast is Maude's father."

His lips jumped. "Who was the father of the baby?" he asked.

She stared at him as Leticia Gast had stared at her.

Red nodded, agreeing with her even though she hadn't said anything.

"Right," he said, and walked calmly to the washbasin. He stared at it momentarily, then crouched over it as if he might be sick. He breathed three or four times, and stamped his boot heel repeatedly on the floor, gradually picking up speed.

Can you hear it? Yes, yes, I hear it.

Red threw the basin against the wall. It clattered and spun on the floor. He approached the nearest watercolor, lifted it off its hook. Then the next, then the next. He didn't throw the pictures as much as drop them, free them from their nails and let them yield to their own natural, destructive pull.

Bena cowered against the wall as Red worked his way around the tower toward her, breaking bird after bird, stepping on the fragments of glass and wood and paper with his boots. She sheltered the baby from the flying glass with her body.

She found his display curiously winsome, because he was a man to whom control was so dear. This was a part of him she'd never witnessed, and it made him human to her, fragile and uncareful in ways that weren't romanticized but weak and unattractive and real.

She put a hand on his arm, turning him slightly toward her. "Stop," she commanded.

He obeyed, heaving and red-faced and still. He put a cold hand over hers, and they stood there, holding on to him as though it took two people to quell his rage and keep his angry muscles quiet.

"I hit you," he said.

"You did," Bena confirmed. "You hit me."

He put his free hand to his head, pinching in at the temples with his thumb and forefinger.

"Is he all right?" Red asked, nodding at the baby.

"Just a bit scared." In fact, he'd slept through the entire tantrum. But it seemed that he should be scared, so she pretended it was true.

One framed watercolor remained—a hummingbird, a dandelion, a long, thin butterfly like a keyhole. "Jesus. I've always hated these." Red stepped over the rubble and lifted this last picture off the wall, then let it drop to the floor. He wiped his hands on his trousers. "High time for that drink. What do you say?"

She smiled. "I say that sounds good."

"About Maude," he began.

"It's your story," Bena replied. "You can do whatever you like with it."

They had reached the bottom of the stairs, when Red stopped short. Over his shoulder Bena could see Maude's felt crusher on the flagstones.

Red did a quick sweep of the first floor before bounding up the stairs. Bena heard the doors, bloated in their jambs, pop open, rub shut.

"She's gone," he said, reappearing in the living room.

They set off through the woods behind the house, Bena holding the baby. Red chose a path that led them up the hillside toward the corral. Betty lazed around the far edge. She came closer to the path when she saw Red appear through the brush. He was still carrying Maude's hat, as if on a polite errand, searching for the proper owner in order to return it. Betty smelled it and nibbled it with her loose lips.

Bena waited while he ran up the path to look inside the icehouse. He returned alone and looked toward the horizon. The sun was just above the flat summit of Table Mountain.

Red held her arm as they followed the ridge path toward his house. Bena could see a woman silhouetted against the dark and bright sky, her body pressed against the bars of his porch.

As Red rushed out to the porch, Bena wrapped Little Ted in one of Red's Indian blankets, to keep him from catching cold.

She heard Red's voice through the kitchen door. "The view's a little better from back here."

"I don't know, Henry. I can't imagine there's a better view than this."

Bena walked through the kitchen to the back door.

"Maybe when the sun goes down we can have those cocktails we were talking about," Red suggested. He was speaking to Maude as if to a child or a rabid dog.

Bena stepped onto the porch with Little Ted. Maude straddled the railing, the toes of one foot on the porch floor, the toes of the other dangling above a lurid and bottomless sky.

"Look who's here." Maude's words lacked their usual bite. "Did you bring your photographer, sweetheart? This could be your first front-page story. 'Silly whore thinks she can fly.'"

"What are you doing way out there?" Bena asked. Red had returned Maude's felt crusher. She'd pushed it low over her face so that only her mouth was visible.

"Having a look at the sunset. Henry finds it touching that a girl as thick as me could care about something so trite." She made a motion to Bena to join her. "Come take a look."

Bena glanced at Red.

"Come on now," Maude scolded. "You don't need his permission, do you?"

Bena walked against the wind and pressed a hand against the rail, bending to take a peek. She backed away from the edge, holding Little Ted at a careful distance.

"Pretty, yes?" Maude asked. She turned her attention to the baby. He seemed unaware, as usual, that it was cold, or loud, or bright. Maude lay a fidgety, raw finger against his cheek, and stroked it lightly.

"You're a lucky girl, Mrs. Jonssen," Maude said.

Bena didn't reply.

"Think I could hold him?" Maude asked.

Bena looked at Maude, her blotchy skin, her hair knotted below the shapeless felt hat. She had taken off her hunting shirt and tied the arms around the railing. The skin on her forearms, Bena noticed, wasn't dimpled with goose bumps as it should have been, but was warm and full of blood, pushing out against the cool air.

"He likes it if you hold him like this." Bena demonstrated, passing the baby into Maude's bowed arms. She held one arm in front of him, to protect him from the sky.

"He's sweet," Maude said. She jostled his hand with her finger until the hand fell open. "Do you feel like he's a person?"

Bena smiled. "What do you mean?"

"I mean, like a personality. Do you feel like you know he's going to be whip-smart, or rowdy, or a fine horseman, or a man who likes his girls and liquor, or a pathetic little pantywaist?"

The wind blew loud and low. It filled Bena's ears and worked its way down her throat, into her belly, with its reminder of the nothingness that awaited them all.

"I don't think much of anything. He's not right." She said it to the wind, the dropping-away sun, the dropping-away earth.

Maude put her face into his, pressed her lips to his forehead.

"He doesn't do anything," Bena said. "All he does is eat."

Maude pressed her nose against the baby's forehead. "Think he's hungry now?" She straightened and lifted her shirt, and Bena saw the handkerchiefs affixed there to soak up the milk that drained from her. She freed a nipple and presented it to Little Ted. He knocked against it with his nose a few times before taking it into his mouth.

Bena watched the two of them together and thought she might break into a million pieces—from despair, ecstasy, she hadn't the faintest idea. This was akin to finding your husband with another woman, and she imagined a younger, darker Leticia Gast with a deer rifle in her arms, trying to locate the humor in the spectacle of her husband nursing on another woman's breast.

Little Ted sucked readily for a few minutes; then his mouth dropped away and he fell asleep. Maude pressed her shirt down and lay his face against her sunburnt neck, patting him awkwardly between the shoulder blades. "It's nice to be made proper use of," she said. The breast she'd uncovered was weeping now, darkening her shirt.

"What do you say about that gin drink?" Red asked. His voice was high and too big for itself, the voice of a man who's seen more of the animal workings of humans than he could begin to process.

"A gin sounds lovely," Maude replied. She allowed Bena to help her off the railing and into the house. "Best way to start forgetting about this whole unpleasant business."

Maude grabbed a tasseled potholder in the kitchen and shook it over Little Ted's face. She pretended to be preoccupied as Red searched in his closet, but Bena knew better.

Maude stopped shaking the potholder and looked at Red. "You think you can forget about it?" she asked.

Red emerged from the closet and pushed his hair back from his face with two hands. His missing fingers lay against his forehead like a series of strange, raised welts. "No doubt it's best we try."

Maude looked as if she'd been punched. "I guess that would be best, wouldn't it?"

"Yes," he replied. He was pawing through his closet again. Bena could hear the click of the wooden hangers, the soft muffle of canvas and flannel. "That would be best." He turned around and looked at Bena, eager to change the subject. "Anybody need a sweater or a coat?"

"Yes," Bena said. "I suppose I do need a coat."

"Maude?" He looked into the closet, not at her.

Maude watched his laboring back, his falsely busy muscles. "No, thank you," she replied. "I'll just go fetch my shirt." She started for the porch, but stopped to hand Bena the baby before passing through the kitchen door. "It's cold out there for a baby," she said. "Right or not." She surrendered him to his proper mother.

Bena pulled out one of Red's bureau drawers and laid the baby atop a pile of neatly folded undershirts.

"Guess you ought to stay here tonight," Red suggested. "Wouldn't want you driving on those roads in the dark. Your husband be all right with that? We can use the phone at the caretaker's cottage."

Bena declined. Ted wouldn't be home from the conference until the next afternoon.

"You'll need something to sleep in." He handed her a pair of pajamas and a wool robe. "We've got some brisket for dinner. We've been living off the leftovers we steal from people's houses. No one's up here much now, because of the rattlesnakes."

The porch door slammed. They both looked up, expecting Maude, but there was no one. The door slammed again and again.

Red looked at her quizzically, and walked outside. Bena followed.

The porch was dark now, the sun having fallen below the horizon, only its pale wake lighting the rim of the sky and preventing it from being completely, thoroughly night.

It took only a moment to realize that the porch was empty, except for Maude's felt hat and hunting shirt, whose tails flapped in the wind, its arms tied tight to the railing.

Red picked up the hat. He looked inside for a long time, as though it might be deep enough to hide an entire woman.

He walked to the railing and hurled the empty hat into the growing black. It hung for an instant, buoyed as by the thickness of water. The wind caught it and whipped it high and away, and Bena watched it sail off into the night until there was nothing to see, there was nothing to do but to wait until the wake of the sun dropped below the flat back of the world.

10. SALT

Red walked with Bena toward the lodge to find the caretaker, Mick Thornton. Mick took the news without comment, nodding as if Mr. Grissom had asked for his kind assistance with a fussy chimney flue. The two men drove a truck to the bottom of the cliff with a large, canvas tarp used to keep the rain off the woodpile behind the lodge.

Bena watched them head into the darkness, then walked back to the Gasts' house to start a fire and feed Little Ted. Mick had given her a flashlight. The light came and went over the stone path, leaving them in near-darkness. She wasn't scared, even though the woods rustled and echoed. She wasn't scared in the woods, but inside the old Grissom house she was uneasy. There was a dip in the bed where Maude had lain less than two hours before, there was a pair of her worn sandals under the rocking chair, there was a hairbrush in the bathroom blooming with her long red hair. Bena walked around the two rooms Maude and Red had been inhabiting for the past week and opened windows. She found a fresh set of sheets and changed the bed. She collected Maude's belongings and put them neatly into a bureau drawer in another bedroom.

After she'd fed and changed the baby, she wrapped him in a blanket and walked back onto the path, carrying her whimsical light. It was safer outside, less full of ghosts. She walked up the path until she heard the sound of truck tires spinning on gravel and saw headlights through the cottonwoods. The lights illuminated a windowless log box. The icehouse.

Red and Mick weren't saying much: "Got it? Hold up." "Go on." "Watch your hand." It might have been a piano they were putting in the icehouse for safekeeping, not the body of a woman one of them knew.

Bena waited until she heard the icehouse door shut, and then hurried back to the house. She wanted to stoke the fire, she wanted to have the stolen food laid out and the gin cold by the time Red returned.

She put Little Ted to sleep in a linen drawer she'd pulled out of a bureau. She placed the drawer near the fire. Outside she heard Red's boots crunching across the dry lawn. From the sound of it, he could have been plundering through packed snow rather than high, dead grasses.

Bena assumed from his blunt, busy expression when he entered that he hadn't registered much of what awaited him at the base of the cliff. Maude was a dog with a broken neck, she was a fallen buffalo, she was a sack of feed to him because he could separate people from bodies, tragedy from bodies.

"Hungry?" She poured him a tumbler of clear gin.

Red dropped onto the faded davenport. Soon the tumbler listed, empty, in his lap. She took it and refilled it for him, placing his fingers around it.

"Good fire," he said. "Where'd you learn to build such a good fire?"

"In Minnesota," Bena said. "We used to camp on the lake islands."

He turned his head toward the hearth. Bena gazed at his riven cheeks; the weather had made him an old man. She figured this sort of knowing her didn't interest him any longer. She was dispirited to encounter obsession as a force with such a penchant for abandonment; she felt so bleak and hollow that she pulled herself over him and kissed him without touching any other part of his face.

At first he let himself be kissed by her, his neck tense against the davenport. She chewed his lips, not a kiss, really, but a search for a missing appetite.

He touched the burning spot where his hand had struck her cheek.

"Never hit a girl before," he said. He wasn't apologizing.

"Never been hit." Bena flinched. She wanted to know more of what it was like to be touched by him, but not in her hurting places.

She had to turn her head to the side, because his face was hard, his nose strong-willed and horsey. He tasted of gin at first, not at all how she'd expected him to taste from what she'd smelled of him. She pushed herself against his mouth to taste a more clandestine part of him, the cow blood and the weakness, the deep snow, the taste of a man who could cut off parts of his own fingers, who could wrap a woman he loved in a tarp and lay her out on an altar of ice cut from the pond he'd swum in as a boy.

The fire burned down and the mountain night seeped under the ill-fitting doors and overtook them on the davenport, driving them upstairs with Little Ted to generate their own warmth beneath the pile of moth-eaten duvets that blew feathers into the air, into their mouths and noses when they moved.

Red carried the baby in the drawer. He slept undisturbed atop a padding of stained napkins and tablecloths.

Bena stood on the icy floorboards at the foot of the bed as Red pulled the borrowed sweaters off her and unbuttoned her dress with his good fingers. She waited for the long-held weight of her wanting to spill and warm her as he stripped her bare.

But instead her nakedness was cold and unsettling. She had fantasized about this moment in awkward, stolen locales—in stairwells, in wheel ruts, against an alley's brick wall. Her desperation was such that discomfort and unease had never occurred to her.

And yet she was hugely uneasy. Her arms wrapped themselves around her torso, hands on opposite elbows. It wasn't guilt that made her want to cover herself. The promise she was breaking to her husband, God, the world seemed very much beside the point. It was doubt, or faithlessness. She and Red Grissom had chosen each other as ways to comfort themselves through an unpleasant stretch of living. It wasn't so much that they hungered for each other as that they hungered for a respite from their otherwise numb and painful days. They had only a finite use for each other, now that Maude was gone.

Red's nipples were oval-shaped and thrown to the far sides of his freckled chest. Bena was struck again by how unknown to each other she and Red were. She pushed the crown of her head into his chest, forcing him backward until they fell onto the bed in a cloud of feathers. He had an odd way of smoothing her hair as he swooped toward her, away, toward her, away, as if he feared he might be hurting her. It wasn't the kind of skin-forgetting, bone-forgetting stir of desire in which the slapping sweaty mess of love yields to something soothing and divine.

After a few awkward moments, he stopped. He lay his head against her shoulder. The skin of his mouth split and she could feel his teeth against her skin.

She expected him to cry. She wanted him to cry. She would feel closer to him if he cried than she had after he'd moved briefly inside her, because desire with him seemed a more remote intimacy than what might be achieved through the exchange of despairs. She put a hand between his shoulder blades and felt for the sobs working through the thick ribs across his back. She rubbed and rubbed, trying to coax the crying out of him. But he did nothing more mournful than breathe loudly once sleep overtook him.

Bena disentangled herself from the blankets to go to Little Ted. She pulled him out of the drawer and sat on the plank floor, rocking him while his tiny limbs quivered. Was he dreaming? What could he possibly be dreaming about, since he had seen so little in his life to puzzle together in unlikely ways while he slept?

Maybe he dreamed with his other senses, his dreams a patchwork of the few tastes and touches and sounds he'd experienced—wind, and the scratch of a wool blanket, and the thin taste of milk, broken from their true sources and reassigned so that the blanket made a windy sound when it scratched his arms, her milk a windy sound as it rushed warm into his small mouth.

Bena lifted Little Ted and lay his prickly head against her shoulder, still damp with a man's spit and sweat. She would have folded beneath the weight of her despairing if she hadn't been so tired.

Instead, she took the baby to bed with her. Red slept without moving, and she didn't sleep at all, but lay awake, her hands on the baby's chest, and watched as the day broke, gray and sunless on Red's wide back.

RED SUGGESTED they go to Mick Thornton's house for coffee. Mick apologized that his wife was not there to make them breakfast, then cooked up plates of loose eggs and wizened sausage. He didn't seem to find it unusual that Mrs. Theodore Jonssen was at Cuerna Verde without her husband, because he was the caretaker, a man hired for the care he took not to ask questions that were none of his business. Bena left her breakfast uneaten and went to nurse the baby in the living room; she could hear the men's forks scrape their plates and their coffee mugs hit the kitchen table with thick-bottomed thuds.

"Mick and I have some work to do," Red told her from the doorway.

"Of course," she said. "I should be starting home."

Red walked Bena to her car, and waited while she secured Little Ted in his bassinet. She shut the door and returned to where Red stood. He helped her into the car.

"What'll you do?" she asked him.

"Don't know."

She wanted to ask him about Mr. Gast. She wanted to ask him about what he planned to do with Maude's body, but it wasn't her business any longer. She figured he had some plan to bury her secretly under a tree she'd admired or on a hillside where the view of the sunset was unparalleled.

Red stared at the sky and at the strange gray clouds that boiled there.

This wasn't how she'd romanticized even the bleakest of good-byes. As a girl she'd been a fan of the tragic parting, because tragedy was the only scenario she could envision where the love was big and bone-crushing, not modest and parceled out for daily consumption. But this in no way resembled those fantasized departures, because people left at different times, she knew, in the same way that people loved differently, the surges of affection between two people rarely synchronized and coinciding.

Bena started the engine. "You coming back to Pueblo?" she asked.

"Not right away," he said. "Might take Betty on a camping trip."

Bena stared at the steering wheel. "You'll find me when you get back?"

He attempted a smile, and pushed his head through the window and kissed her. His lips were as cold as if he'd spent the night in the icehouse instead of next to her in bed.

"Have a safe drive," he said, patting the hood of the Ford.

She watched him pick his way through the cottonwood grove. At one point he stopped and put a hand against a tree as though an errant burst of crying had overtaken him. He bent over and removed his boot, shook it forcefully and looked inside. He pulled the boot back over his bare foot and continued walking, unhindered, away from her.

BENA PARKED across the street from 25 North Grand and sat with the engine idling. She remained in the car for half an hour, until it was almost one o'clock. She nursed Little Ted. She changed his diaper on the front seat, and then stared out the window, with nothing to do and nowhere to go. But the car grew hot and rank, so she gathered her things, and took the baby in her arms. She had her hand on the car's door handle when the front screen of the house opened, revealing two bodies.

Ted and Gerta. The large distance they maintained between each other was as condemning as if they had been holding hands.

Bena waited for the anger and the sense of wrongness to overtake her, as they had when she'd seen her husband touch the coat buttons of the woman in the jewelry store. But she felt neither angry nor wronged. She was curious. It was as though she were spying on herself, viewing, from a distance, the obvious way her marriage was a creaky, broken thing.

She slouched behind the steering wheel. She watched Gerta glance down the empty street and Ted try to lock the door with his temperamental key. He held a small glass aquarium under his arm, in which one of his sickly bluegills floated. He'd been taking his failing fish to the clinic on the slower days, poking them with needles and scraping bits of fungus from between their fins, in hopes he might discover they were suffering from a curable disease. An affair with Gerta, a barren woman, was a perfect project for an intrepid healer. He could push his believing self inside of her, douse her useless raisin parts with hopefulness.

Bena heard him swearing under his breath as he dropped the key and stooped to retrieve it, continuing his battle until the house snapped shut. He strode ahead of Gerta, not stopping to wait for her until they reached the gate at the end of the walkway. He held the gate open for her in rote gentlemanly fashion. Gerta searched his face, and Ted kept his head down, looking at his shoes. Despite her shock, Bena found herself pitying Gerta, and, even more unexpected, pitying her husband for the way his duplicitous life forced him to keep a careful distance from all the women with whom he attempted closeness.

Ted didn't notice that his own car was parked across the street, that his wife was in it, that his wife was watching him and his mistress beat a sullen retreat to lives the rest of the world supposed them to be leading on a Monday afternoon while their respective spouses were at work. No doubt an unwitting Clyde had dropped Ted at home after the morning lecture, just in time for Clyde's wife to meet him for a little tussle on Louise Sparks's brambly horsehair davenport while his wife was at the *Chieftain*.

Bena waited until they'd started down the hill and their separate bodies had disappeared by degrees below it. She hurried up the steps, eager to hide herself inside the house for fear her spying would be discovered.

And yet what was the discovery, and who the discoverer? Maybe she was just as terrified of being seen as he—not because either of them was concealing a stark, passionate triumph, but because they were both concealing another failure. Bena had envisioned herself freed with Red Grissom, her desires overrunning all concerns of comfort or propriety. Their union would prove she was capable of greater benevolence than she was with her husband. She and Ted had different appetites, which made them ungenerous with each other. He was as unhappy as she, and so went looking elsewhere for the bodies of women with whom his own body could easily and generously converse.

But she had been as wrong with Red as she had ever been with her husband, far more devastatingly wrong, given how lushly she'd envisioned the moment when the sweat-dusty layers of clothing were peeled off and nothing was left but their clean, clacking bones. Yet it hadn't happened that way. They'd retreated into their baggy flesh, into the furthest corners, where no one could reach them. She understood how much her hope for her marriage, her child, her life was tied up in her fantasies of a flawless intertwining of limbs with a man whose feet were strange to her. The impossibility of that easy joining made even the most clumsy forms of happiness seem impossible as well.

The smell of oranges and musk greeted her in the foyer. Gerta's scent, the scent of fear, excitement, remorse, loneliness. She knew the smell herself now. She smelled it on the dim insides of her own elbows, on the undersides of her wrists.

The house was dark and close. She couldn't be alone in here. She couldn't be here at all. Everywhere she looked she saw the body of her husband pushing itself into the body of a bad-skinned woman, she saw herself with a deer rifle at her side, she saw herself forcing out a loud, angry laugh that was more like vomiting than laughing. She dropped her bag and carried the baby upstairs to Florence's apartment.

Florence sported a wide smile, which meant she had news to tell or gossip to pass along. It faded when she saw Bena's bruised cheek and dirty dress, her eyes big and glassy with the crying she had yet to do.

When Bena eventually did cry, sitting at Florence's kitchen table and playing with a teaspoon, there was little water involved. Her sobs chafed her mouth. Her crying had the shape of a circle, Bena thought, listening to herself. She could see the shape of her sorrow, and it was a perfect, unbreakable circle.

Florence put a fleshy arm around her. She walked to a cupboard and made shushing noises from across the kitchen.

Florence put a plate of sugar cookies in front of her. Bena took a small bite. "See?" Florence smiled. "You're just tired. It's the mother's curse. I'll make you some tea and you'll see it's nothing but tiredness and nerves."

She set up cups on a metal tray with tiny, mismatched spoons. "You know," she continued, "my mother said she got so mad at us when we were wee babies, she wanted to stamp our heads in." Florence looked dreamily out the window. She turned and smiled at Bena. "And you wonder why I didn't want to have children myself."

"I thought you couldn't have children," Bena said, nibbling the edge of the cookie. Florence had used lard instead of butter, and the cookie was bland and greasy. Bena dropped it onto the table. She was tired of tolerating people's niceties and lies.

Florence glanced away. "That's right. I couldn't. I sure couldn't." She poured water into a teapot and carried the tray to the table. She was still wearing her bathrobe. A darkly veined calf popped through the robe's opening. "So," she said, "have you heard the latest?" She tossed her chin toward the center of town and beyond. "Over at the rendering plant."

Bena shook her head.

"They found a baby. A *dead* one."

As if you hadn't done your share, Bena thought, recalling what Ted had told her about Florence's supposed "miscarriages." If she squinted hard she could see a much younger Florence, not the misshapen and sun-spotty woman in her satin robe sitting across from her. Bena saw Florence on the edge of a dirty bathtub in God Knew Where, Texas, with her legs spread, her hand pushing up into the retracting folds of her body to scratch that itch of strange life bothering her insides. You might think she was pleasuring herself. Bena supposed it felt right enough to Florence to be outraged at the same type of acts she'd committed. Perhaps that was her way of forgiving herself.

Bena took a long drink of tea. It was achingly sweet. "Do they know whose it is?"

Florence lowered her voice. "Nobody's saying. But everybody knows."

Bena concentrated on the stains on one side of the table, on a hardened bead of raspberry jam, the telltale fossils of one woman eating alone.

"Mr. Gast has offered a reward to anyone who can produce the killer. 'During such a fragile time in history,'" Florence raised her voice—she was quoting Mr. Gast's own words—"'immorality of this nature cannot be tolerated. When women are killing their own children, we're tempting God to blight us from the earth.'"

Immorality. Nature. Bena laughed to herself.

She thought about Ted and Gerta emerging from her house. When had it begun? At Cuerna Verde? That night at the Mineral Palace? Maybe in his drunkenness, Clyde had left the play early and Ted had offered to escort Gerta home, and afterward had slid her bra straps over her thick, sunburnt shoulders and pushed his face between her breasts until the smoky clothing fell from them into two easy heaps.

But men don't marry the hungry ones, at least that's what she'd been told by her sorority sisters. She'd been told this in a variety of ways, back when she and her sisters knitted mittens when they felt too long untouched, and starved themselves, surviving on tea and toast and the thwarted advances of men they secretly wished would force them beyond their false primness with their sheer male weight and bulk. They retained their ascetic façades, undernourished bodies hidden beneath Persian lamb coats, because men don't marry the ones whose emptiness, whose wanting-to-be-fullnesses might exceed their own. Those were the girls relegated to lunch breaks and quick gropes and cocktails in a dark scatter. Those were the girls they tested their own boundlessness on and then abandoned when they understood they hadn't enough to give to a woman who dared to crave and yearn and ask. They would each go back to their silent wife, to their always happy, satisfied, silent wife, because she would make them feel brimming with appetites she had no taste for.

Bena looked at Florence, at her dopey, dreamy face. She thought of Leticia Gast rotting away in her hot room, she thought of the wind raking Maude's hair from her scalp as she followed the sun down, down below the horizon, she thought of her mother, a woman so lonely she gave up her life in order to return to a home inhabited not by people but by a pair of mute, mud-speckled ponies.

Florence picked up her teaspoon and turned it. The sunlight caught on the round back and reflected over Little Ted's face, making living shapes and water patterns on his forehead.

Bena put a hand out to touch Florence's knee. She wanted to

apologize for what she'd implied about her not wanting children. She wanted to admit to her that she'd seen her husband with his good friend's wife. She wanted to urge Florence to rid her jewelry box of the cheap trinkets she'd been given over the years, to toss out the chokers that had been bought with no particular woman in mind. She opened her mouth to speak, but could offer nothing but a choking noise that came nowhere near to making the words she'd hoped to make.

"Oh my Lord," Florence gasped.

She was staring at Bena's lap. Bena looked down and saw that the baby's face was blue. It was he who was making the choking noise, not she. His arms and legs stuck straight out from his body and shook as if his heart were being touched with a live wire. His eyes had rolled up into his head so that only the whites showed.

Bena didn't panic. She moved with a doctor's distant precision, reaching her fingers into Little Ted's mouth, pushing them as far down his throat as she dared, searching for the tongue that had fallen back in his throat and cut off his breathing. She probed in his hot mouth until she found his tongue, wormed her finger beneath it and flattened it back. The baby made a gasping noise like a pump sucking at a dry well. His chest filled and emptied, his face becoming gray, then white, then red. His body shook for a few more seconds and he sloped over her elbow, heavier now that he wasn't supporting any of his own weight. The black of his pupils dropped down from his head and he emitted a long, weak wail.

Bena walked around the kitchen rocking him, her body panicky and thrumming.

"Did his heart stop?" Florence didn't move from her chair, as if she no longer trusted herself with a baby so fragile and temperamental about the simplest acts, like breathing.

"He had a seizure." Bena put a hand on his wrist. She counted his weak and erratic pulse.

She recalled the baby's odd reaction to the flash of Mrs. Dubrowski's camera, before they'd driven toward Pikes Peak. His arms and legs had stiffened in the same fashion, then he'd fallen against Bena, dense and elastic.

She held him close and walked out to the car. She was full inside with all the lying she'd stomached from Clyde Ashburne, from her husband, who had said her baby was fine, fine, nothing but a persistent case of colic. Now she had proof. He was not fine. He was not fine in the least.

"CAN I HELP YOU?" A young receptionist, pretty, with the faintest ghost of a harelip, greeted Bena. "Glory Lang" said the sign on the desk next to her appointment book.

"I'm Dr. Jonssen's wife," Bena said. "We've spoken on the phone."

Glory smiled and her lip raised unevenly. "And of course, we already know this little fellow." She smiled at him, as if a smile were the simple cure for any infant's woes.

"May I go to his office?"

Glory's expression altered. "Your husband is still in Colorado Springs."

In fact, Bena wanted to inform her, he's not. "Has Clyde Ashburne returned? I'd prefer to speak to him."

"I'm afraid he hasn't. You could see Dr. Lily, if you like. He's new. He's taking over pediatrics today."

"I would like that. Yes."

Bena didn't move to the waiting room. She didn't want to read the *Chieftain*, she didn't want to examine the heroic images of men building railroads back when Pueblo was destined to be the pride of Colorado, back before the money and political influence shifted north to Denver, leaving the town with railroads and wide streets, parks and palaces, all the futile architecture of greatness. She stood in front of Glory, watching her trace the length of her scar with her index finger.

Glory grew uncomfortable. She rose from her desk and disappeared behind a fogged-glass door.

"Third room to the left," she said upon returning.

The clinic was quiet, the examining rooms open and empty. Bena walked down the short hallway to the third room on the left and sat in a wooden chair. The room was clean, and every surface she touched was cold. This was more like a morgue than a clinic, a space where death was the foregone conclusion. She pushed the blankets away from Little Ted's face. He'd slept as though in a coma the entire way to the clinic, waking intermittently to emit weak pained noises. His breath was shallow but his heartbeat had improved, strong and predictable even as the rest of him remained purposeless.

"Mrs. Jonssen?"

A dark-haired man thrust his head through the doorway. He wore black glasses that obscured half his face. She remembered him from Reimer's party. She'd seen him dabbing disinfectant on the foot of the young Mexican baritone.

"Dr. Lily," he said, extending a wide, short hand. Bena shook it. It was warm and dry.

He looked to be about forty, his face plain until you searched beneath the glasses and discovered the full, attentive features that every bit of him lived inside. He had a lazy, thick mouth and a drawly manner of speaking.

"Clyde's our usual pediatrician," Bena explained, "but I was hoping you might be able to look at him."

"Anything in particular worrying you?"

Bena started to tell him about the seizure, but then stopped. "Nothing in particular, no."

Dr. Lily lifted the baby out of her arms and placed him on the examination table. He listened to his heart with his stethoscope, pulled his eyelids up with the tip of his thumb. Little Ted shifted but didn't wake.

"How old is he?"

"Nineteen and a half weeks."

Dr. Lily tapped the baby's knees with a tiny hammer. Little Ted's bloated, turned-out feet didn't respond. The doctor removed a pencil from his shirt pocket and made notations on a clipboard. Bena listened to the endless scratching.

The doctor looked up. "Did you experience any difficulties during your pregnancy, Mrs. Jonssen, that you can recall? Fevers, for example?"

"I was terribly sick. I didn't eat much the first few months."

Neither of these confessions interested him. Dr. Lily massaged the length of Little Ted's arms and legs, kneading his limbs deeply as if feeling for a broken bone.

"How about the birth? Any complications?"

Bena thought back. It was so bleary and painful a memory, she couldn't remember much of anything in focus. "Not that I recall," Bena said.

Dr. Lily put a hand around the baby's skull.

"He was born headfirst?"

"Yes," Bena said. "He was breech, but the doctor turned him. The doctor said he was fine. Dr. Ashburne examined him a few weeks ago and said he was fine."

Bena wrapped her arms around herself. The antiseptic, mortuary cold of the room was pushing under her clothes, her skin.

Dr. Lily placed two pillows around the baby to prevent him from rolling off the table. He bent in front of Bena with a cotton ball and a bottle of rubbing alcohol. He said, "Turn this way," and dabbed the wet cotton along her cheekbone. She remembered that she had a bruise on her cheek, that she was wearing a filthy dress, that she hadn't bathed in days.

"He had a seizure." She forced herself to say it.

Dr. Lily sat in a chair opposite Bena. He pulled off his big glasses and rubbed the red indentations on the sides of his nose.

"Clyde Ashburne is a fine physician, Mrs. Jonssen. I would hate to override any decisions he's made with respect to your son and yourself."

"But he was wrong," Bena said.

"I don't know that Dr. Ashburne was wrong."

He confused her. "So my son *is* fine."

Dr. Lily reddened. "No, Mrs. Jonssen. Not Dr. Ashburne, not any doctor I know would say your son is fine."

Bena turned to the side, fearing she might be sick. When she opened her eyes she saw a kidney-shaped bedpan in front of her, and she retched into it, pathetic surges of greenish bile.

The doctor handed her a glass of water.

"What does that mean?" Bena asked hoarsely.

Dr. Lily walked over to the baby and put a hand on his head. He read the notches in his skull with his fingers. "It means he was deprived of oxygen at birth. It means he'll have little to no use of his legs and arms. He'll never walk. He'll never speak. I suspect he's blind to all but bright light, though his hearing appears to be functioning properly. He'll continue to be plagued by seizures. They'll become more frequent and severe as he gets older. Of course, it's unusual for infants so damaged to live to their first birthday."

Bena stared at the floor. The tiles were cracked, but the grout was spotless.

"Do they hurt him?" she asked. "The seizures?"

"It's hard to know for certain. I don't imagine he finds them pleasant."

Bena's stomach clenched again. She pressed the back of her wrist against her clammy mouth.

"Why didn't Clyde tell me?"

"As I said, it's not my place to judge. Many physicians feel it's best to let the mother remain hopeful and happy for as long as possible."

"Such as my husband," Bena said. "He wanted me to remain hopeful."

Dr. Lily picked up his clipboard. "A doctor's never more blinded by hope himself than when the patient's a member of his own family. Don't blame your husband, Mrs. Jonssen. He didn't do anything but wish, against all reason, for the best."

He suggested she move the baby's crib into her bedroom and tie a string from his wrist to a bell, so that she'd be woken up if he had a seizure in the middle of the night. He wrote this and various other instructions on a series of prescription pad pages, carefully numbering them on the bottom.

When she felt well enough to walk, Dr. Lily escorted her with Little Ted into the waiting room. He put his arm around her shoulder and helped her past the reception desk, smiling at Glory Lang and promising to bring her back a cream cruller from the doughnut shop. Bena held the baby's sleeping body as close to her as possible. His weight was the only force preventing her from disintegrating into a pale heap on the floor tiles. Her ability to hold him and pull him through the world might be the only form of living he would ever know, and she resolved to do it well.

She stood with the doctor on the clinic steps, and the wind blew hot and rough between them. Bena felt she ought to thank him, but then she thought better of being polite when she really wanted to throw herself under the shade of the nearest tree and sleep and sleep. Little Ted could sleep with her, because in sleep he was a normal baby, in sleep he was as full of promise as anyone.

"Where are you from, Doctor?" Bena asked. She pushed a lock of dirty hair behind her ear as though preparing herself to listen. She wanted him to stay with her, she didn't want to be alone.

"Texas," he replied. "Little town called Shiloh."

Shiloh. Shy Low. A town of short, timid people with loose, drawly mouths. She saw them on cowback waving a glum good-bye to their Dr. Lily as he crossed the town limits with his crocodile doctor's bag and his broad-rimmed hay-skimmer, off to make something bigger and bolder of his nearsighted self.

"You ever think of going back?"

She watched him think about going back. His glasses pulsed on his nose when his heart beat.

"I know I'm not staying here, if that's what you're asking."

"I'm not wondering if you're ambitious, Doctor. I wonder if you're myopically sentimental. I wonder if you're foolish enough to want something back that you never liked much to begin with."

Dr. Lily stared down Union Avenue. He was thinking of that cream cruller, Bena figured, he was dreaming of feeding it to the lovely Glory, pushing it playfully into her mouth so that her scar would be hidden beneath a thick layer of pastry filling. "Who's to say I never liked it much?"

"You're answering me with another question?"

His glasses jumped on his nose. Thump. Thump. "I heard you were a funny woman."

Bena started down the steps, jerky and uncertain. "Good-bye, Dr. Lily. I'll never forget that you didn't answer my question."

"I'll never forget that I didn't know how to answer it."

She was struck by his honesty. It almost made her weep.

"It's not about knowing how to answer," Bena called over her shoulder. "It's simply about knowing the answer."

This seemed a silly but crucial distinction. Yet the more she repeated the words to herself, the more crucial and less silly they seemed. Bena thought about the distinction as she propped the baby in her lap and started the car, loneliness overtaking her like another swift push of nausea. She repeated her own words until they mutated into believable nonsense. It's not about the answer, it's about answering with knowing. Not the knowing, but the knowing answer. The answer of knowing is it. It is the knowing answer.

· · ·

BENA CONSIDERED taking Little Ted to the church on South Gunnicker, because she needed to be in a place where she'd feel protected
by forces larger and more responsible than herself. But the church was
a forlorn structure with a stunted spire and meek, godless windows.
She decided to go to the Mineral Palace instead, with its vast and empty
and permissive interior. She could sit on the fatherly lap of King Coal,
she could cry and beg aloud to nobody, she could put her hand up the
Silver Queen's robe and root around for luck or money.

As she drove up North Grand, Bena looked out at the hazy emptiness of the streets, sidewalks, lawns, porches. The cars were pitted
from the sandstorms, the flower beds and window boxes covered with
layers of dust, the shutters of the houses clamped against the sun.

She parked the car near the fountain. A pair of great, dark clouds
billowed up behind the Mineral Palace, making it appear to be quietly
on fire. Bena walked with Little Ted toward the front door. The hole
in the northeast wall had been sealed. A splashing of white plaster
glowed separately from the rest of the gray, mildewed wall.

She felt the same scared excitement she'd felt those mornings when
she and her brother rolled the *Ingrid Duse* down the rusty rails until her
hull touched water. Bena was in charge of stowing the sandwiches and
securing the centerboard while Jonas rigged the boat. He would clap
at her while she closed the boathouse doors, clap at her to hurry because
whatever it was they were looking for was receding farther and farther
from them as she fumbled with the padlock.

Bena passed the front pillars to the copper door. She could see her
reflection in the clear, reddish metal, and was somewhat pleased to find
herself unrecognizable—striking in a dark, abandoned way that her
cupcake blond looks had rarely before achieved. Her face was sunken,
her unwashed hair flat against her skull, her skin—except for the bruise,
sprawling and shadowy across her left cheek—whitewhite as if she'd
suffered an extreme loss of blood.

Inside, she expected to find men with paint, she expected to find Reimer with her elephant tusk banging about on the floor, issuing instructions to workmen as they threw the wrinkled piles of chorus-girl magazines into bags without even so much as a longing glance, as they pried dead mice from sprung traps, as they scrubbed the filth of human living from the corners. But the Palace was uninhabited. Not even the wind lived inside now that the wall had been plastered. The entire building was suffocating, losing consciousness as its air supply was depleted and its brain hardened to marble and started to die. With no wind to sweep it clean, the stench of a dying place was oppressive.

Bena could hear the cheerful tinkling of water. She could see where improvement had been initiated—the trash coerced into four large piles against the west wall, a few cans of paint stacked high and bright and waiting to be opened, a collection of unscrewed copper plaques in a bucket, expecting a polish.

But the water, the water. She could hear the water behind her. She turned around and saw that the nymph with the bolted ankles had been replaced by the statue of a kneeling woman who glowed as white as a shapely pile of table salt. Her face was turned as if lost in thought over a mole she'd just discovered above her right buttock. The light shone from the dome directly over her head, and she caught it in her upturned palm, a deceptively lazy one that might shut at any instant, trapping whatever was foolish enough to alight on the blithely offered fat of her hand. The water flowed from a rusted pipe between the salt woman's feet. The basin had been scrubbed of its green penny fossils. The water, ten inches deep over the white tiles, was a lovely pale blue.

Bena wandered back toward the stage. She looked at the new curtains, the new gold cords cinching them back.

Then she saw the stains. The pedestal on which the Silver Queen's Viking-prowed throne had rested left a pristine oval inside a splash of rust on the marble floor—evidence that she wasn't, as touted, made of silver at all, but of some cheap alloy that browned and leaked.

Bena looked around for the familiar shapes of the king and queen, or of their successors. The palace was like a church without a crucifix, nothing and no one reigning above the still depravity that collected under the roofs of public spaces.

She proceeded to a back hallway that smelled of bleach; it must have served as a janitor's storage at one time, brimming with buckets and mops. The buckets had left round stains on the floor. Farther down the hall she found a set of metal double doors that had warped so badly they no longer fit in their frames. They ground on their hinges as she pulled them open.

It was impossible to make out more than the jagged silhouettes on the floor. Bena's eyes adjusted. Arms and throats and hard drapery were piled on the floor, along with a silver-dollar staff, the curved prow of a boat.

The room had a dirt floor. One wall featured the door to a defunct incinerator. A band of high-up windows let in a stripe of muted light. There was a lingering smell of garbage—crumpled paper cups, chocolate and taffy wrappers. A torn admission ticket like the one she'd seen in Reimer's registry book had been ground into the dirt.

". . . neral Pala . . . come to the world's fin . . ."

She put the scrap in her pocket. In the corner, she noticed the water nymph. Her feet had been shorn off at the ankles. She was lying facedown, her body still poised as for a heavenward leap. Now, however, she appeared to be digging at the earth with the cupped hands that used to hold a silver ball. She was digging, digging, digging to China, she was trying to escape the fate of the monarchs who lay in a dismembered heap beside her.

The assassins had been methodical in their approach at first, disassembling the king and queen as they had been assembled, respecting the welder's seams. Then they'd become impatient, and taken spike drivers to break the thrones into hand-sized chunks. They'd abandoned their weapons in the corner, propped them against the wall, innocent as brooms.

But what about the heads? Bena wondered. Where were their heads? They were here, unless of course the assassins had taken them as proof of their bounty, tied from ropes by the tips of the crowns, so they swung and knocked together like bells.

Bena began to pull pieces off the pile with her one free hand. Soon she was perspiring, a combination of the heat and the airlessness. She heard a fly against the windows like a small mallet. After a few minutes she felt the need to rest. She sat on the floor. Out of habit, she unbuttoned her shirt and offered her breast to Little Ted. He was still asleep, but she prodded him awake with her finger, pushing the tip between his lips until his tongue hollowed into a spoon and he began to suck. The two of them sat there, listening to the bumping of the fly.

It was all Mary's doing, Bena thought. Mary was the one who had doomed her with the predictions she had only hinted at. Bena looked at her hand, filthy from sorting through the lonely remnants of king and queen.

All this stuff about hands, as if the head didn't matter, as if the head weren't enough to save a person from herself. She inched close to the rubble, and again pulled off piece after piece and tossed it behind her. She exhaled audibly. *There. There.*

She reached and tossed, reached and tossed, without looking at what she was reaching for. It wasn't until the blood began landing with a pat-pat-pat at her feet that she realized she'd hurt herself.

She could see the clumsily cut tendons of her hand like the bodies of earthworms sliced in half by a gardening spade. She could see bones, too, a trellis of bones in the far back of her hand, all but lost in the flood of red. She looked into the rubble and saw her blood smearing the broken wing of the glass eagle that had once guarded the marble canopy over the queen's head. The hard feathers glinted in the gray light.

She tried but failed to move her fingers. She put her arm over her head to discourage the bleeding, and took a few cramped breaths. She was going to lose consciousness. Then the lightness left her. Her body was any body, not her own, necessarily, not a body to whose pain she was accountable. It was a broken, leaking, spoiled object, and she was simply the person to withstand it and mend it.

With the baby in her lap, she used her good hand to tear the hem off her dress. She wound the fabric around her injured hand, one, two, three wraps, just enough cloth to keep ahead of the blood that moved unstanched through the cotton. She ripped a second piece of hem, and a third, and wound them until her new deformity was obscured beneath a numb mitten.

She struggled to her feet, holding Little Ted with her good hand. She left the legs, arms, torsos scattered across the floor. Who knew what would happen to the remains? Perhaps the Christian club women would order them to be burned in the incinerator. The cheap alloyed bodies would toss black smoke into the sky like a flock of crows.

She walked down the long hallway, amid the rusted imprints of bucket bottoms and the smudge of missing mops on the wall, back into the grand room of the Palace. She walked between the real columns and the columns of distracted, high-up light. The room was sweet with the overripe-apple scent of human waste. She put her wounded hand to her forehead. Blood ran down her arm, alarming and bright, coagulating into sticky beads at the tip of her elbow.

Bena moved toward the sound of the water. She knelt by the salt woman's pool, and rested Little Ted on her knees as she carefully lowered her hand into the water. The blood bloomed out as she unwound the bandage. She held her palm down so that she wouldn't have to look inside herself. Her fingernails were gray. The water stung.

Bena fit her ribs against the marble lip of the fountain. She closed her eyes and imagined lifting her hand from the green water to find her wound healed. There would be no scar from the cut, and all the other lines on her palm would have disappeared as well, her bad fate eradicated by the burning, mineral water.

In her lap, Little Ted began to shake. Bena looked down. He was clenched and quivering, his pupils were gone. His shaking was so extreme that she had to clamp him down with her arm to keep him from whipping onto the floor.

Stop, she begged him, please, please stop. She saw how much the jerking hurt him, his little legs and arms full of lightning.

stopstopstopstoppleasestop

He started to choke. He was choking on his own tongue again; it had slipped back in his mouth and blocked his air passage. Bena put a hand to his lips and tried to wiggle a finger inside. She pushed between his gums, and drew blood with a fingernail trying to part them.

stopstopstop

As if listening to her own crazed ranting, she stopped. She stared into his blue, constricted face. What was the point in saving a creature so afflicted?

"What's the point?" she said aloud. She imagined a morning, a month from now, two months, three, when she would look into his crib and find he had died during the night because she hadn't heard the telltale bell tinkling in her sleep as lightning shook him. She could sense the dread of every morning until, one morning, she would wish that he'd be dead so that she could stop this hideous waiting.

And that would be the most terrible morning. More terrible than the morning he died would be the morning she woke up wishing he were dead.

She looked into his purpling face and took a breath. If he was going to die, she wanted to know how it sneaked up on him, by accompanying him partway. She turned her lips under and bit down with her teeth. Her lungs burned with old air and old crying, both expanding in death and needing release.

She couldn't do it. Bena let out the air and, without pausing to breathe anew, pushed her finger past the ridge of Little Ted's teeth, which had yet to break the surface of his gums. She hooked his fallen tongue and pulled it forward. She could hear her noises echoing through the Palace. She sounded like an animal. She and Jonas had once come upon a small bird with two broken wings, toppled by the side of the road. He told her that if she was truly brave she would stamp in its head, because that was the brave thing to do. She'd stamped on it but hadn't killed it. The bird shrieked, and shambled away from her. Bena ran into the woods and Jonas had to kill it with his bigger boots. One brave step was all it took to smear its skull into a wet paste.

The baby breathed. He breathed, and moments later the shaking ceased, as he was abandoned by the storm of his seizure. It left him as limp and beached and lifeless as one of Ted's fish. His eyes floated downward with the purposelessness of leaves; he appeared dumbstruck as his poor, jostled brain regained its equilibrium.

Bena lifted her child and started walking, she didn't know where, holding her injured hand over her head.

She paused in front of the smooth new glass of a display case and caught a glimpse of herself and her son. Their faces hovered over the velvet pillow, its dimpled middle waiting to nestle a raw ruby or a foggy peninsula of jade. But there were no minerals, there were no jewels. Instead, their heads were on display, two skulls. Hers was white, the blood having escaped by the hole in her hand, while his was marked by a stripe of blood, a terrible blessing from her wound.

Bena put a finger in her mouth and wet it. She rubbed his forehead until the false scab loosened. The blood was in his hair. Dry, the blood looked like black soil in which anything could grow. But of course nothing could grow there. His was the least fertile ground, less fertile even than the desert that surrounded Pueblo, its stark, splintered fences like the blessedly fading outlines of misguided ideas.

She thought she would at least reach the door, perhaps ponder the bleak sky from the threshold and consider the weak temptations of the stultifying afternoon. She'd at least waver on the line between two worlds, and feel weightless as they pulled at her with equal gravity.

Just as she reached the edge of the stage, she turned around. She walked back over the rusty rings of royalty, and stood inside the bare circle left by the Silver Queen's throne. She looked at the glass dome overhead: maybe, if she looked high enough and hard enough, she could find a reason not to do what she knew she had to do. She'd see a sign. A bolt of lightning. Rain. A hat. She was willing to give herself one chance, but she was lying to herself, trying to find responsibility for her actions in the whims of the world one final time. The truth was, she wasn't looking. Not an earthquake, not a disembodied, sky-sized voice could convince her against it.

But looking up made her dizzy. She saw the design she'd drawn on the floor, an irregular trail over the tiles. It was a map of her decision, with a puddle, like the big dot of a city or some other dense, meaningful destination, marking the spot where she'd made up her mind.

Bena walked to the fountain, her steps queasy. Not because she didn't dare to. She dared to. She dared to, without any stupid charm given to her by a dead criminal who'd never done anything truly daring in her short, wasted life; she dared to because it was right, righter than standing by and watching as her son yanked a little bell to alert her to his suffering.

She held the baby to her chest and put his head against her neck. His breathing was weak, he was as windless as the day. She let him fit against her, his body puzzled against hers, and she knew he'd given up his own shape, she knew he'd had enough.

Bena kissed his sleeping head. She kissed his eyes, one, two, his nose, the lobes of both his ears. She kissed his palms, his knees, the bottoms of his feet. She put her mouth against his and took one long breath from him.

In her mind she was holding the hand of an older boy, he was maybe six or so. They were standing on the edge of a dock, laughing. They'd count to three, over and over, because one of them would balk at the last second, pull a hand free and run from the edge, howling, hands around their cold middle, until they promised each other that this time they would jump.

One. Two.

Three.

Despite a lifetime of hesitation, the water was warm. She let him rest on the tile floor of the pool and rubbed his body down. She never let her eyes stray from his face, even though his eyes remained closed as he moved from one unconscious state to another. He didn't struggle. He accepted the water as he accepted everything, without criticism or question. His mouth worked as if trying to make sense of this milk around him everywhere, and then it came to rest. Bena placed one hand on his chest while the other, her broken one, stroked his lovely head. Her blood curled into the water to mark her movements.

She put a finger in his mouth. He didn't suck it. His tongue was soft and unhungry. He had disappeared without a trace.

As she stared into the placid water, she recalled with eerie clarity that day on the *Ingrid Duse*, the water high and black and the sails snapping, the boom swinging through the air, threatening to knock their heads clear off their shoulders. They never believed that she would capsize, the *Ingrid Duse*, but then in an instant they were underwater.

It was white under there. Black was not the color of death and fear and drowning, white was. She could see her brother's dark spinning arms, felt the inadvertent kick in her shin as he struggled his way back to the surface.

The two of them popped up, blowing water from their mouths.

They scrabbled at the slippery underside of the boat. Jonas was yelling to her, but she couldn't hear him above the screech of the wind. Water washed into his open mouth. A wave caught their upside-down boat and threw it toward Jonas. The gunwales hit him in the face, knocking out his front teeth.

This made him furious. Pain made him furious, she knew, because he felt singled out. He howled into the oncoming wind. He punched his fist against the hull of the *Ingrid Duse*.

Bena pointed to the centerboard. If they could pull themselves up to the centerboard, both of them on the same side, they could right the boat. Jonas swam around to her side and they lunged for the centerboard. They tried several times and then lay low, their arms limp and exhausted, clinging to the gunwales. They were resting this way when the centerboard sank into the hull.

Jonas stared at her, disbelieving. You didn't secure the centerboard.

Bena was going numb in her hands and feet. The water of Lake Susquetannah was never warm, not even in August, and not when the coldest parts were stirred up from the bottom, as they were during the storm.

I don't remember, she said. Or perhaps she didn't reply, knowing that nothing she said would convince him otherwise.

She thought he started to cry then, but who could tell with all that water? She remembered being astonished, because he'd never seemed to value his life much. He'd always lived stupidly and irreverently, tempting many larger forces time and time again—horses, heights, weather.

The *Ingrid Duse* began to founder on the tips of her gunwales. The domed horizon of her hull sank lower and lower in the white waves. Bena never knew whether her brother was aware of this sinking, whether he tried to throw her off the side of the boat because he knew that they both would die unless one of them did. He grabbed her numb fingers and bent them backward until she released her grip. He hefted all his weight on her shoulder and, pushing himself up by the sinking gunwale, fell on top of her. Bena sank under him, her shoulder wrenching in its socket.

When she bobbed to the surface, he was waiting for her. He pushed her by the top of her head, his fingers knotted and pulling on her wet hair. He held her under, and she watched his legs tread and kick and whip the lake to a greater froth, and her own diminishing air bubbles float past her like translucent fish.

With her free hand, she reached up and twisted his fingers backward until he let her head go; then she found his thumb with her mouth and bit hard until she tasted his blood mixed with the icy water. She fought with the fury of a sibling fighting for a toy, for the bigger piece of meat, for a storybook, for a life, because it was all about winning, no matter what the prize. She slapped and kicked, she thrashed the water until she had blinded herself. Purely by chance, it seemed, she found her hand on his throat. She left it there for a moment, resting her thumbs in the sharp, panicked hollows above his collarbone. She squeezed her fingers closed. Let go, she said to him.

And he did. He let go, falling back from the hull as if falling off a ladder. She stared after him. For the first time, that look of exhaustion was unmistakable to her—she'd seen it all her life but never, until now, known what a cowardly soul it disguised. She watched him drift between the waves, no longer interested in winning. It amazed her that he would give up so easily. But he did give up, and in seconds he was too far away ever to swim back against the waves and the wind; no one was that strong.

Bena clung to the gunwales. The *Ingrid Duse* continued to sink and then leveled off. Bena looked and looked at the place where her brother had disappeared, but then even the hole he had left sank in on itself, and the wind went away, and the lake turned bland and forgetful.

With her one good hand, Bena lifted the baby from the water. She put her lips to his and returned the air she'd been holding for him. She wrapped him in his blanket, careful not to stain his body with her weeping hand. She made dry, heaving noises, just two or three. She held Little Ted to her chest and listened to the weak water of the fountain.

BENA REACHED the front steps of 25 North Grand and had to pause, half bent, her vision buzzing with silver dust. She adjusted the baby in her arms, he was wet and heavy, and slipping down under her elbow. The steps creaked and her dress was heavy with sweat, heavy with water, heavy with blood. There was blood on the car upholstery, on the metal door handle. There was blood following her up the flagged path. She couldn't believe how much blood she had in her that was simply excess, not the stuff of life at all.

The hallway was dark, the orange-and-musk scent dissipated.

What a dispirited house, she thought to herself. She hated the hard horsehair cushions and the sad widow's knickknacks, she hated how the place was starkly purged of its past inhabitants and yet lonely in that it persistently recalled them—Mr. Sparks's *Collier's* magazines, the meaningless pencilings of the children's heights on the back of the pantry door, the blank faces of sweet porcelain shepherdesses without their flocks. She'd accepted the way the Sparkses' home had made her sorrowful, the strange furniture and plates and silverware weighing on her every morning with their foreign smells and textures, their chips and stains the proof of other people's mistakes and clumsiness.

She dropped onto the hard armchair. Her blood soaked into the sun-leached upholstery, mingling with the flower pattern and then blotting it out as the stain grew, ticking voraciously through the fabric grain, sinking between the ancient strands of horsehair.

Bena held Little Ted in her good arm and rocked him. Anyone would think she was crazy, she reflected. Even she would think she was crazy, if she saw herself doing what she was doing. She removed the bloodied blanket from his face. It was pale and mottled, his blue fingers still curled in the shape of her finger.

What struck her then was not guilt or horror at what she'd done, but a gut-yawning loneliness. She missed Little Ted in a way she'd missed no other creature. She held him to her and she missed him, missed him, missed him until he went missing.

She noticed there was a shoe in the middle of the living room. An oxblood loafer. The shoe belonged to Ted, one half of the pair he usually wore to work. She glanced at the wall clock. Four. Far too early for him to be home, if, that is, he'd ever made it to the clinic.

She stood woozily and looked behind the chair. Another shoe. This one upright, and trailed by two squiggled black socks. His jacket was bunched by the entrance to the kitchen, his tie draped over the kitchen table, his shirt on the floor near the sink. His white undershirt hung on the porch door.

She opened the screen and let it clap behind her. She was the mother with the pie smell on her forearms, the baby hooked on her pelvic bone.

Where you digging to, honey? she called out to her husband, her bare-chested, barefoot husband with the Christian-killer in his big hand. *Where you digging to, China?*

Ted didn't look up. He was on his knees, bent over. She could see every rounded bone of his spine.

He tried to block her view, but she saw the garnet glint of hair between his fingers as he healed her or made love to Gerta's barren body. Bena tiptoed across the lawn. She wanted to catch him in the act—not just coming out of the house with another woman but touching this woman in a way that would leave no question. She wanted to take all her rage and loneliness and throw it at him like an armful of wet, bloodied sheets.

Heal us, she wanted to yell at him. What here is not in need of healing?

He turned around just as she reached him. She saw that it wasn't a woman's hair he held between his fingers but the panting bodies of his fish. He had scooped them out of the pond with a net and laid them out on the edge as if drying them in the sun. One fish was already dead, its eye milky, while another pulled at the air with its flashy gills. The fish looked like a heart to her, a heart without a body to support, struggling to find some usefulness in the open air.

Bena knelt on the ground and bent her head over the pond, fearing she was going to be sick. Blessedly, she couldn't see her reflection. She couldn't see her reflection because the pond was disturbed by tiny drops of water.

It was raining.

She turned her head to the sky, but sensed only the scalding wind on her skin. It was time to lie down; she'd walked miles to reach this place. She placed the baby beside the fish with the quiet lungs. She lay next to him and looked up at her husband.

Ted stared at her, horrified. By what? she wondered. By the blood? By the lifeless baby near her arm? His body was cold now. She was cored and bloodied as if she'd given birth again, to a stillborn.

She shut her eyes. Ted wrenched the baby from her and she heard him weeping, ragged and bestial, with long silent pauses that made her think, wrongly, many times, that he'd finished. She'd never heard her husband cry before, and it was unattractive, frightening, not anything she recognized as human sorrow. He knew, she thought to herself. He's known for a long time. This recognition made her pity him. She understood her husband then, not as a staunch man of science to whom superstition was a foolish and misleading sorcery, but as a man who was watching his faith in the magic of his own convictions perish at that instant—his vacant, ineffectual beliefs that creatures flourished simply because he'd decided they should.

She felt his shadow over her. Bena looked up at him and the fluids drained from her. Even her milk rushed to flee her sinking self, wetting the fabric of her dress.

She thought he might strike her; or maybe she merely wished he would strike her, for she wanted to be alone. But then his face, red and crunched and unrecognizable, was pushed into her face, so close that she could see every shred of remorse and secrecy and impotence. He knew her and she knew him, and it was not a pretty knowing. She'd never felt uglier, or more at home.

Bena reached into her pocket and handed her husband the torn ticket stub she'd picked up from the dirt floor of the incinerator room at the Mineral Palace.

". . . come to the world's fin . . ."

It was an invitation.

Ted put a hand on her shoulder and lowered his half-naked body until he'd curved his spine around hers. They lay that way for what seemed like hours, through the blowing of the whistle at the iron-works, and the chimes of the church clock on South Gunnicker at sundown, and the stifling, final onset of night.